*I*n this little attempt at picturing the after-adventures of some of Jane Austen's characters I have made use of the references to them which she herself made, and which are recorded in Mr. Austen-Leigh's "Memoir."

More grateful acknowledgments than I can ever express are due to my friend Edith Barran, without whom this book could not have been written.

The difficulties, as well as the presumption, of such an undertaking, are alike evident; but the fascination of the subject must be our apology to those who, like ourselves, "owe to Jane Austen of the happiest hours of their lives."

S.G.B.

OLD FRIENDS *and* NEW FANCIES

AN IMAGINARY SEQUEL TO THE NOVELS OF JANE AUSTEN

SYBIL G. BRINTON

SOURCEBOOKS LANDMARK™
AN IMPRINT OF SOURCEBOOKS, INC.®
NAPERVILLE, ILLINOIS

Published by Sourcebooks, Inc.
P.O. Box 4410, Naperville, Illinois 60567-4410
(630) 961-3900
FAX: (630) 961-2168
www.sourcebooks.com

This is a reprint of the first edition, written in 1913 and originally published in 1914 by Holden & Hardingham, London.

Library of Congress Cataloging-in-Publication Data

Brinton, Sybil G.
  Old friends and new fancies : an imaginary sequel to the novels of Jane Austen / Sybil G. Brinton.
    p. cm.
  ISBN 978-1-4022-0888-1 (trade pbk.)
    1.   England--Social life and customs--18th century--Fiction.   I.   Austen, Jane, 1775–1817. II. Title.

PR6003.R384O43 2007
823'.914--dc22

                                2007014573

ISBN-13: 978-1-4022-0888-1
ISBN-10:1-4022-0888-X

Printed and bound in the United States of America
VP 10 9 8 7 6 5 4 3 2 1

The following characters are introduced into the story.

FROM PRIDE AND PREJUDICE.
Elizabeth Bennet
(now Mrs. Darcy)
Jane Bennet
(now Mrs. Bingley)
Mr. Darcy
Mr. Bingley
Miss Bingley
Mr. and Mrs. Hurst
Kitty Bennet
Mr. Bennet
Georgiana Darcy
Lady Catherine de Bourgh
Miss de Bourgh
Colonel Fitzwilliam
Mrs. Gardiner
Mrs. Annesley

FROM MANSFIELD PARK.
William Price
Mary Crawford
Henry Crawford
Mrs. Grant
Mr. Yates
Mrs. Yates
Tom Bertram

FROM NORTHANGER ABBEY.
James Morland
Eleanor Tilney
(now Lady Portinscale)
General Tilney
Captain Tilney
Isabella Thorpe

FROM SENSE AND SENSIBILITY.
Elinor Dashwood
(now Mrs. Edward Ferrars)
Edward Ferrars
Robert Ferrars
Mrs. Jennings
Lucy Steele
(now Mrs. Robert Ferrars)
Anne Steele
Mr. Palmer

FROM PERSUASION.
Captain Wentworth
Anne Elliot
(now Mrs. Wentworth)
Sir Walter Elliot
Miss Elliot

FROM EMMA.
Emma Woodhouse
(now Mrs. Knightley)
Mr. Knightley

Chapter 1

THERE IS ONE CHARACTERISTIC which may be safely said
to belong to nearly all happily-married couples—that of desiring
to see equally happy marriages among their young friends; and in
some cases, where their wishes are strong and circumstances
seem favourable to the exertion of their own efforts, they may
even embark upon the perilous but delightful course of helping
those persons whose minds are as yet not made up, to form a
decision respecting this important crisis in life, and this done, to
assist in clearing the way in order that this decision may forthwith be acted upon.

Some good intentions of this kind, arising out of a very sincere affection for both the persons concerned, and a real anxiety
about the future of the younger and dearer of the two, had actuated Elizabeth and Mr. Darcy in promoting an engagement
between Georgiana Darcy and Colonel Fitzwilliam. Georgiana was
then twenty, and had lived entirely with her brother during the
three and a half years of his married life. Reserved, shy, without

self-reliance, and slow to form new attachments, she had been accustomed to look upon the Colonel as, after her brother, her eldest and best friend, a feeling which the disparity of their ages served to strengthen. She had therefore accepted the fact of their new relations with a kind of timid pleasure, only imploring Elizabeth that nothing need be said about marriage for some time to come.

"Elizabeth, when I am married, shall I have to go and stay at Rosings without you?" she had asked; and on being assured that such might be the terrible consequences of matrimony, she had manifested a strong inclination not to look beyond the present, but to enjoy for some time longer the love and protection she had always met with as an inmate of her brother's house.

Lady Catherine de Bourgh had thought it necessary to go through the form of expressing displeasure at the whole proceeding, in consequence of Darcy's omission to ask her advice in the disposal of his sister's hand, but in reality she so thoroughly approved of the match between her nephew and niece that she forgot her chagrin, and talked everywhere of her satisfaction in at last seeing a prospect of a member of the Darcy family being united to one who was in every respect worthy of the position.

Mr. and Mrs. Darcy were seated in the library at Pemberley one April morning when the engagement was about six months old. Their two children, a handsome boy of two, and a baby girl of a few months, had just been taken upstairs after the merry games with their parents to which this hour was usually devoted, and Elizabeth was arranging with her husband the plans for the day.

"What has become of Georgiana and Fitzwilliam?" inquired Darcy. "I understand they were going to ride together; but they both said they would prefer to put it off till twelve o'clock, when I could go with them."

"They have been walking on the terrace, but Georgiana has gone in now," replied Elizabeth, glancing out of the window. She returned to her husband's side, and, sitting down, began to speak with great earnestness. "Do you think that they are really happy in their engagement? I have been watching them closely for some days, and I am convinced that Georgiana, at all events, is not."

Mr. Darcy's manner expressed surprise and incredulity. "What fancy is this you have taken into your head, Elizabeth? No, certainly no such idea had ever crossed my own mind. You must be mistaken."

"I do not think so," said Elizabeth. "Their relation to one another has not, since he has been staying here this time, its former ease and naturalness, and I have noticed other indications as well, which make me think that freedom would bring them mutual relief."

"I am sorry for what you say, Elizabeth," said Darcy gravely; "but it is possible you lay too much stress on what may be merely a passing mood. When we first consented to the engagement I thought them to be excellently suited to each other, and so far I have not seen anything to modify that opinion. What has Georgiana been saying to you?"

"She has said nothing, but knowing her so well, I can see she is not happy. She is nervous, restless, unlike herself; she tries to escape being alone with Robert; she avoids with a painful embarrassment any reference to her future plans; nay, you must have noticed incidents like that of yesterday, when she almost cried and begged to be excused from going with us to Bath next week."

"That is mere foolishness; there is no shadow of reason why she should be more afraid of her Aunt Catherine now than she ever was."

"There is more reason, if she dreads to hear her marriage talked of as rapidly approaching, and herself and Robert referred to as a most fortunate and admirably-assorted pair—you know how your aunt harangues them on all occasions."

Darcy smiled slightly, then rose and began to pace the room. "If your conjectures are correct, Elizabeth, and Georgiana is unhappy in the prospect of this marriage, of course it cannot go on; but I shall be deeply grieved for all reasons, and I hardly know how to ask Fitzwilliam to release her. Excellent fellow though he is, he might well resent being thrown over after half a year for what seems like a girlish caprice."

"I do not believe that in any case he would resent it," replied Elizabeth. "There would be regret on both sides—regret that they had not been able to make each other happy; but I more than suspect that if we could ascertain his feelings, we should find them to coincide with Georgiana's. In six months, you know, they have had time to reflect and to realize what the engagement means to both of them."

"You assume a good deal, Elizabeth. I cannot believe that it is so uncongenial to Fitzwilliam."

"That is because he is too good, too honourable to show it; and yet I am sensible that it is so—that his regard for Georgiana is that of a friend, a brother, nothing more. I suppose you cannot remember the time when we were engaged, Darcy, and Bingley and Jane also?" she added, looking archly at her husband.

"My dear, I recollect it all with the deepest satisfaction; but, you know, everyone does not display their feelings in the same way. Fitzwilliam is an older man than I am, and was never prone to raptures, and Georgiana has not the liveliness of mind of my Elizabeth."

"I know they are not likely to be run away with by their feelings, as Mr. Collins would say," replied Elizabeth, smiling; "but even taking Fitzwilliam's age and Georgiana's gravity into consideration, this is not at all the same thing. I am convinced that they do not find that complete joy in their engagement that people should, and that these two might if they were each engaged to the right person."

"Do you mean that Georgiana has seen someone whom she might prefer?" asked Darcy sharply.

Elizabeth gave a decided negative to this, and her husband remained for some minutes wrapped in thought. At length he roused himself, and said: "You had better speak to Georgiana on the subject, Elizabeth, and if it is as you suppose, we will talk it over with Fitzwilliam together. For my sister to dissolve her engagement is a serious step, and must be well considered."

His wife agreed, and added: "Pray, dear Darcy, if it should come to an end, do not show any resentment in your manner towards Georgiana. She cannot help not caring enough for Fitzwilliam, and it will be painful enough for her to break with him and to know that she has disappointed you."

"I will try not to do so, Elizabeth; but you know how much I desire a safe and honourable settlement in life for Georgiana, such as this marriage would have been."

"We both wished it so much that I am afraid we were led into mistaking the real nature of their attachment," said his wife. "At any rate, since we assisted in bringing the affair about, we must share the responsibility of ending it—a fact which your aunt is not likely to allow us to forget, is she, Darcy?"

"True," returned Darcy. "It is regrettable that the engagement was so generally made known. However, Georgiana may stay away from Bath if she prefers."

It was a relief to Elizabeth to have fairly talked her husband into accepting the possibility of such an unwelcome turn of affairs, for events proved her misgivings to have been well founded. She had truly gauged the feelings of Georgiana and Fitzwilliam with regard to each other and to their engagement. Georgiana confessed, with deep distress and confusion, that she knew it was very ungrateful and naughty, but—she did not seem to be able to care for her cousin in that way, and would have said so before, but that she was afraid her brother and her aunt would be angry. Fitzwilliam admitted that he had long feared his inability to make his cousin happy, but showed how very great was his dread of causing her, by his defection, to be wounded, reproached, or unkindly talked about. Elizabeth had a difficult task to smooth away all obstacles and to bring comfort to the minds of two very troubled and scrupulous people, besides her other duty of persuading her husband that the separation was the right thing, and of shielding Georgiana from all disagreeables; but in a few days everything had been accomplished except what time alone could do.

Darcy could not altogether conceal his regret and disappointment at this termination of his hopes, and Georgiana was miserable in the consciousness that he blamed her for not having known her mind at the beginning of the engagement. Had she really cared for Fitzwilliam, he was convinced that it must have gone on to a happy conclusion; and naturally his cousin could hardly be the one to uphold a different opinion.

Fitzwilliam could only assert and reassert that Georgiana was undeserving of the slightest reproach, and endeavour to divert his cousin's attention to himself.

It was arranged that he should accompany the Darcys as usual to Bath, where they were to meet Lady Catherine, and meanwhile Georgiana accepted an invitation from Jane and Mr. Bingley, which on a hint from Elizabeth was warmly extended to her, to go and stay with them at the same time at their house on the other side of Derbyshire.

Chapter 2

LADY CATHERINE DE BOURGH, with her daughter and Mrs. Jenkinson, had been established in her favourite lodgings in Pulteney Street since the middle of March. It had been her custom of late years to spend six or seven weeks in Bath every spring. She had considered it to be good for her daughter's health; she also considered that her own constitution and spirits benefited greatly by this yearly change of social environment. The Rosings' card-parties lacked variety. Mr. and Mrs. Collins remained admirable listeners, but their conversation, like their civilities, occasionally wore a little thin. Lady Catherine, would she but have admitted it, thought that Mr. Collins was too much interested in his own asparagus-beds and too little in her peachhouses; and the ailments of the children kept Mrs. Collins at home on several evenings when it would have been convenient to the hostess at Rosings to make up a quadrille-table. Obviously the most suitable spot in which Lady Catherine and her daughter could have sought change of air would have been the residence of her nephew; but Darcy and Elizabeth had very early in their married life made it clear that they did not intend their house to be turned into a hydropathic establishment for their ailing relatives, and that they would entertain their visitors at such times and for as long as they chose; consequently Lady Catherine had been reduced to the expedient of going to Bath in the season, and to Pemberley when she was asked. She, however, reserved to herself the right of insisting that her relatives should visit her at Bath, and Darcy, who wished to give no occasion of offence to his mother's only sister, was in the habit of taking his wife and sister down there every spring for a short stay at one of the hotels, thus forming among themselves a pleasant and independent little party, which was usually joined by Colonel Fitzwilliam. This year Lady Catherine, having been there for some weeks previously, had been collecting round her a circle of acquaintances, some more and some less likely to be congenial to the relatives whose visit was pending.

"Elizabeth," said Mr. Darcy to his wife, as they stood together in Lady Catherine's drawing-room at a large reception which she was giving in their honour, two days after their arrival, "I think I see General Tilney over there; and, unless my memory is failing me, surely this is his daughter coming towards us, whom we made friends with last year."

"Why, so it is; what a delightful surprise!" exclaimed Elizabeth. "Dear Lady Portinscale, how glad I am to see you again! Do not say you have forgotten me, or I shall find it hard to forgive you!"

"No, indeed, Mrs. Darcy, I was coming to introduce myself, in fear that you might have forgotten me. How do you do, Mr.

Darcy? Lady Catherine told me that she was expecting the whole party from Pemberley this week."

"Yes, we have come to put in our period of attendance, as you see," said Elizabeth, "but I never dreamed of anything so pleasant as meeting you again, after what you said last year."

"The truth is that my father has not been at all well, and as he felt himself obliged to come here for a short time, he begged us to join him for two or three weeks."

"Your husband is here this evening?"

"Yes, he is in the next room; I see him talking to Colonel Fitzwilliam."

"And are your brother and his pretty wife in Bath this spring? I remember her so well."

"No, they are at home; but we have a brother of hers staying with us—James Morland. He has a curacy in a very unhealthy part of the Thames Valley, and he has been extremely ill with a low fever, so we have brought him here for a fortnight in the hope that it will do him good."

"How very kind of you to take care of him! He is fortunate to have such friends."

"Oh, no, it is a very small thing; and he is such an excellent young fellow—sensible and agreeable, and so hard-working! My husband has the highest opinion of him; and were he less amiable, it would be a pleasure to be of service to anyone connected with Catherine."

"You oblige me to repeat that anyone who has you for his or her advocate is indeed fortunate, Lady Portinscale," answered Elizabeth, smiling; "but now that you know your character, pray perform the same kind office for some of the people here. They are nearly all strangers to me, and if my husband were not listening, I should say that I wonder how my aunt manages to pick them up."

"Lady Portinscale will soon gauge your character, Elizabeth, if you make such terribly outspoken comments," said Darcy, smiling. "You must not mind her, Lady Portinscale; my aunt's presence has a demoralizing effect upon my wife. It is a very sad thing, but I have often remarked it."

"Not her presence in the ordinary way," said Elizabeth; "but to-day we have been through such a stormy scene together, that I may be excused for feeling that my aunt and I must go diametrically opposite ways for the rest of our lives."

"Really?" said Eleanor Portinscale, with the faintest suspicion of laughter in her eyes. "Poor Lady Catherine! I recollect last year that you and your sister-in-law were continually brewing some kind of rebellious mischief against her."

"That is just the cause of the trouble now," responded Elizabeth. "My sister-in-law became engaged to Colonel Fitzwilliam last November; but I saw that they were both so extremely unhappy in their engagement that I was instrumental in breaking it off, and this happened only last week; so that is why Robert Fitzwilliam is looking ten years younger, Georgiana is sheltering safely at home, and Lady Catherine is furiously angry with everyone all round, especially with me."

"I am sorry," said Lady Portinscale with gentle sympathy. "These things cannot be done without regrets and heartburnings. I hope it will mean real happiness for them both in the end."

"One has to take that part of it on trust," was Elizabeth's answer; "in the meantime it has upset my husband dreadfully, and I am afraid he will never be quite reconciled to it until he sees Georgiana happily married to somebody who has at present not appeared on the scene."

"I suppose she felt altogether disinclined for coming with you to Bath, else she might have met friends here who would have distracted her thoughts."

"Yes; but, of course, she would not come, and I could hardly persuade her even to accept an invitation to go and stay with my sister Jane for part of the time that we shall be away. We left her in such terribly low spirits that it is really some consolation to see Colonel Fitzwilliam looking as if a weight had been taken off his mind. It would be a sad pity that we should all have got into hot water with Lady Catherine and nobody be a penny the better for it."

Lady Portinscale smiled. "He is a very handsome man, and extraordinarily young-looking; he is nearly forty, is he not?"

"Yes, one would not suspect him of it. There is Captain Wentworth talking to him now; they seem to come here every year. Mrs. Wentworth and Georgiana became rather friendly, and they correspond. But those relatives of hers are impossible! Why, what is going on? Lady Catherine seems to be carrying off Colonel Fitzwilliam; poor man, he was in such a congenial group! Whom can she be introducing him to? They are people I never saw before."

"I do not know them myself, but I have several times seen them with Lady Catherine," replied Lady Portinscale. "They are called Ferrars; at least, one of them is Mrs. Ferrars, I am not sure which."

The persons who had attracted Elizabeth's attention were three in number; the two ladies somewhat resembled one another, being rather thin, small in stature, and very elaborately dressed in the height of the fashion. One of them might have been considered pretty, but for her sharp, almost shrewish features, restless eyes, and the discontented, irritable lines which had formed themselves in her face. The other had these characteristics in a more marked degree, together with a general air of much less refinement and sense. It was not to be expected that Lucy and Anne Steele would have altered very greatly for the better since the empty-headed and overdressed fop who now accompanied them had exalted Lucy to the honour of becoming Mrs. Robert Ferrars. After four years of family quarrels with Mrs. Ferrars and Mrs. John Dashwood, of spending more than her husband's income, of scheming to obtain Anne a husband, of striving to push herself into fashionable society and to hold her own there; she found her only happiness in visits to gay watering-places, where she could pick up new acquaintances, and in their company forget for a time the incessant worries and vexations of her home-life. Anne spent the greater part of the year with her sister and brother-in-law, occasionally diversifying her programme by a visit from Mrs. Jennings, or to Elinor and Edward Ferrars, when out of kindness to Lucy they would consent to receive her for a time; but these visits of Anne's to the rectory at Delaford were a trial to all concerned; and since, on the death of Colonel Brandon, Edward had effected an exchange of livings with a clergyman in Derbyshire, Elinor ventured to hope that Anne would no longer find it a convenience to stay with persons who resided in such an out-of-the-way part of the country. For the present, both Lucy and Anne were quite satisfied with their surroundings. They had had the good fortune to become known to Lady Catherine de Bourgh, and by the exercise of all the tact, flattery and obliging manners at their command, had rendered themselves indispensable at whatever entertainments she gave, large or small, and were being treated by her with such marked graciousness as to rouse their hopes of receiving an invitation to Rosings, a mansion of the glories of which they had heard much, as had all Lady Catherine's friends. The introduction, on this evening, to such a handsome, soldierly and aristocratic-looking man as Colonel Fitzwilliam was a piece of good luck which exceeded Anne's wildest dreams; and although, as soon as the proper civilities had been exchanged, he seized the first opportunity of returning to his men friends, Anne lost no time in confiding to Lucy her extreme satisfaction at the addition of such a very smart beau to Lady Catherine's party.

"Don't be a fool, Nancy," was Lucy's answer, in somewhat discouraging tones; "what's the good of expecting a man like that to look at you? And, besides, isn't he engaged to Mr. Darcy's sister?"

"No," Anne answered eagerly, "the engagement's broke off. Miss de Bourgh told me so to-day. And fancy Lady Catherine introducing him to us at once! She must want us to be all friends together, mustn't she?"

"Well, it's likely you'll go and spoil it in some way; you never caught the doctor, for all his attention," Lucy responded with true sisterly candour, "and I expect we'll find we don't see much of Colonel Fitzwilliam. He's staying at the hotel with the Darcys, and from the look of Mrs. Darcy I don't know as she'll want to do just what Lady Catherine tells her, all day long."

"I shall go and sit by Miss de Bourgh," said Nancy, after a moment's contemplation of this dismal prospect, "and perhaps Lady Catherine will introduce me to the Darcys. You'd better come too, Lucy. We can't get along without knowing them now."

Lucy consented, after some demur; and in the course of the evening their hopes of an introduction were realized, and their self-importance greatly increased; for Mrs. Darcy, curious to ascertain what kind of hangers-on had found places in her aunt's *cortège* this year, had conversed for a short time with them both; and with the prudence and consideration which was characteristic of her, had refrained from expressing to her husband the full extent of the unfavourable impression which they created.

"I do not much care for those new friends of my aunt's," Darcy remarked to his wife when they reached home.

"Why, my dear, you were not even introduced to them," exclaimed Elizabeth. "Robert, I noticed, did not escape, but you did. Besides, they are related to the Ferrars at home; there is no getting away from that."

"I gathered that they were, but I can hardly believe it. That man brother to Edward Ferrars! I heard him trying to argue with Robert about Nelson's tactics at the battle of the Nile, and it was enough for me. I have heard far sounder sense talked at a tenants' dinner—at the end of one, too."

Fitzwilliam and Elizabeth laughed. "His views upon life in general appeared to suffer somewhat from lack of breadth," said the former, "and I can imagine it would be possible to find him a tedious companion. As for the ladies of the party, I did not have much conversation with them."

"I think the look of them rather frightened Robert," said Elizabeth; "but, on the whole, they are tolerably unobjectionable. After all, one can't always pick and choose at a place like Bath, and, anyhow, we must be civil to Aunt Catherine's friends—it is not for very long. I am really going to practise what I preach, so you need not look at me like that, Mr. Darcy."

The following evening the whole party met again at a concert in aid of a charity, which had been patronized by Lady Catherine to the extent of several pounds' worth of tickets. The morning had been spent by the Darcys and Fitzwilliam in their own occupations; but they had been obliged to dine with their aunt, and to meet at dinner the Robert Ferrars, with Miss Anne Steele. General Tilney, Lady Portinscale's father, and his son Frederick made up the requisite number of gentlemen, and Elizabeth found much to divert her in watching, during dinner, the manœuvres of Miss Steele, who, seated between the two bachelors, was fully occupied in efforts to make herself equally and incessantly agreeable to both of them; the dire failure of which might have aroused some compassion had she not been so completely self-satisfied and confident. Captain Tilney certainly kept up the conversation in the style that was expected of him as long as he could, and then turned to Miss de Bourgh and devoted himself to her, having been informed by his father that she was a considerable heiress, and his attentions to her must be regulated accordingly. Colonel Fitzwilliam, for his part, found three-cornered discussion carried on with great animation between himself, his aunt, and General Tilney, who sat opposite, on the military genius of the French generals, considerably more interesting than Miss Steele's observation on the Bath assemblies and her openly-expressed predilection in favour of officers as partners. Elizabeth and her husband were no better off in their respective companions. The inanities of Robert Ferrars, and the pretensions of his wife, were calculated to put a severe strain on the good intentions of Lady Catherine's niece and nephew towards her guests.

"How elegantly Lady Catherine's dinner-parties are always carried out!" remarked Lucy to Mr. Darcy, in a kind of loud aside, as they unfolded their napkins. "She seems to be one of those fortunate persons who always manage to have everything about them as *recherché* as it is at home, wherever they may be staying. Don't you think so, Mr. Darcy? No one else could have made this apartment what it is, but with Lady Catherine's delightful appointments you could, I daresay, easily imagine yourself to be in one of the smaller dining parlours at Rosings, could you not?"

Mr. Darcy was rather taken aback by this speech, and hastily making a mental review of his aunt's usual visitors, failed entirely to connect Mrs. Robert Ferrars with the dining parlour, or any other room at Rosings; so his reply was not very satisfactory to his questioner.

"It seems a pleasant and convenient room. My aunt, I believe, generally takes these lodgings; and when she settles down in a place for a few weeks, naturally likes to make it comfortable."

"Oh, but I think it is a special gift of dear Lady Catherine's," exclaimed Lucy. "You cannot deny it, Mr. Darcy, knowing Rosings as you do. Now at our lodgings—well, I daresay the rooms are very little smaller than this—but try as I will, I cannot give them a home-like air, though I assure you I brought two large packing-cases of dainty trifles from our country house."

"Indeed!" said Darcy.

"Yes, but the lavish refinement, combined with substantial comfort, of Lady Catherine's surroundings always appeals to me so strongly when I come here. I am sure you understand what I mean, Mr. Darcy, with a home like Pemberley as a standard to judge other people's houses by."

"I had not regarded Bath lodgings from that point of view," said Mr. Darcy. "Are you making a long stay here, may I ask?"

"Yes, we hope to remain for some weeks. I always enjoy Bath so much at this time of year; and so does Mr. Ferrars. I consider it infinitely preferable to the autumn season, do not you, Mr. Darcy? All the best people seem to come now, and one is not likely to meet anyone whose acquaintance one would not wish to continue afterwards."

Mr. Darcy took advantage of this pause, during which his companion helped herself to fish, to consider what reply he should truthfully make to such a sentiment; but before Mrs. Ferrars could insist upon his agreeing with her, he was called upon by his aunt from the end of the table to support her in a flat contradiction of General Tilney, who was undoubtedly getting the best of a somewhat heated argument. Elizabeth was not more fortunate in her companion. The wearisome descriptions of this or that friend's house, habits, achievements, which were all that Robert Ferrars could contribute to the conversation, were almost more than could be endured with patience throughout a long dinner, even by one who could derive quiet amusement from almost any kind of harmless absurdity; and it was with a sigh of relief that Elizabeth heard her aunt's peremptory command that everyone should go and put on their coats and cloaks, for she would not have her party arrive late for the beginning of the concert.

The ladies were distributed among various coaches, while the gentlemen walked on. Elizabeth found that her companions were to be her cousin and Miss Anne Steele; and during the drive she had leisure to remark, with great astonishment, the evident intimacy which existed between the young women. Anne tried to draw her into their discussions; but finding Mrs. Darcy resolutely silent, she turned to Miss de Bourgh, and began to rally her on the becomingness of the gown which the latter was wearing, accompanying her remarks with many giggles, mysterious whispers and covert references to "favourite colour" and "smart uniforms" which made Elizabeth wonder that her cousin could tolerate such treatment for an instant. But poor Anne de Bourgh's nature, only half developed by reason of her ill-health and her mother's forcefulness of character, had yielded entirely to the dominating influence exercised over her by a person nearer her own age, and one who made an effort to understand and play upon her weakness. Elizabeth soon began to perceive the secret of the intimacy—Miss Steele, in her anxiety to recommend herself to the de Bourgh family, had discovered that by enlivening and flattering the daughter she might best become a person of value to the mother. Anne Steele's last words before the carriage stopped were intended to be inaudible to Elizabeth, and put the final touch to her disgust and dislike.

"Me and Lucy will be *so* miserable if you give us up now these grand cousins of yours are come down, Miss Anne!"

Miss de Bourgh made what was for her a vehement motion of dissent, and when they had entered the room, Elizabeth, having piloted her charges to Lady Catherine's side, found a seat for herself as far as possible from anyone connected with the Steele family. Her husband joined her just before the concert began, and in the double pleasure of listening to the music and feeling his proximity, she forgot the previous vexations of the evening.

"Well, how have you been getting on?" inquired a voice behind her, in the first pause.

"Why, Fitzwilliam!" exclaimed Darcy, glancing round, "what business have you up at this end? You ought to be squiring the young ladies down there by my aunt."

"Poor Robert!" said Elizabeth. "He is only off duty for half an hour."

"That is it," replied Colonel Fitzwilliam. "I was exhausted, and seeing this empty chair, I forthwith occupied it. Besides, I want to hear the harp solo in peace and quiet. I have not heard the harp played for years, and I am exceedingly fond of it."

"That is the next one, I see. Hush, now! I know this man is going to sing out of tune. He looks like it."

"We ought to have some compensation for listening to that," murmured Darcy, when the song was done. "I believe Mr. Collins would have given us a better performance."

"He certainly is rather like Mr. Collins," remarked Elizabeth reflectively. "Here comes the harp—and what a lovely girl! Is her name on the programme? Yes, Miss Crawford."

Mary Crawford, who since Dr. Grant's death had entirely lived with her sister, Mrs. Grant, at Bath, had lost none of the beauty and charm which had captivated the heart of Edmund Bertram: indeed, the four years which had elapsed since then had given her form and air more regal elegance. The knowledge of sorrow, and regret that she had so much to injure her own chances of happiness, had softened her nature, and now, more gentle, womanly and sympathetic, she was in many ways a different creature from the brilliant Miss Crawford of former days. Mrs. Grant, while loving her devotedly and rejoicing in her companionship, still grieved in secret that no suitor worthy of her dear Mary should ever have succeeded Edmund Bertram, and that no second attachment should have taken place of one which, though renounced without bitterness, had nevertheless left a deep mark upon her sister's character. In Bath their lives were full of interest, and they made many friends; but Mary always laughed at her sister's plans for her marrying, and returned the same kind of answer. "I expect so much, you know, and the chosen he must expect so little, that I doubt whether we should ever come to terms."

Her sister would protest against this, knowing well the real worth of the disposition which Mary hid under a careless and sometimes cold manner; but she also knew that Mary would be more difficult to satisfy, both as regards her own qualities and those of her possible husband, in consequence of the better taste she had acquired at Mansfield. This evening, Miss Crawford, who had consented to perform solely on account of the charitable object of the concert, was out of humour with herself and all the world. Her sister being unwell, she had been obliged to accept an escort to the concert, the company of Sir Walter and Miss Elliot, whom, as residents in Bath, she had known since the time of her sister's settling there. Miss Crawford's beauty of face and figure were exactly what would recommend Sir Walter; and while condemning her sister as dull and unfashionable, nothing delighted him more than to be seen in public as squire of the charming and elegant Miss Crawford. Six months' acquaintance had caused her, on her side, thoroughly to weary of him, and on the few occasions when she could not avoid a meeting she endeavoured to converse with his eldest daughter, whom she found only a degree less tiresome and empty-headed. To-night, however, there was no help for it. With them she had come, with them she must remain, unluckily placed at a distance from any of her other Bath friends, her enjoyment of the music spoiled by her companions' irrelevant chatter, her only pleasure to acquit herself creditably in the piece she had chosen to play. This, at all events, was in her power, she felt, as she ascended the platform and shook off sensations of listlessness and ennui; and she succeeded so well that the audience were roused to a display of their delight and enthusiasm, and she had to return twice to acknowledge their plaudits. Next moment she perceived, or thought she perceived, that owing to an increased crowd in the lower part of the room she could not easily get back to her seat without making a little disturbance; so she slipped into a chair in the front row, which was allotted to the performers, thankful even for a short respite.

When the interval came, she remained where she was, and, a few minutes later, seeing the gentleman who had been the chief promoter of the concert trying to attract her attention, she rose unwillingly, supposing that Sir Walter Elliot had come to claim her. What was her surprise to hear Mr. Durand say: "Lady Catherine de Bourgh particularly wishes to know you. May I present you to her?"

Mary felt that she had not had much choice in the matter, but she found herself curtseying to a tall and formidable-looking elderly lady, dressed in rich brocades, who surveyed her as if from a great height, and said: "Allow me to tell you, Miss Crawford, how much pleased I was with your late performance on the harp. I have heard every harp player of note in Europe during the last forty years, and I may say I consider you quite equal to those of the second rank. Though not a performer myself, I am quite acquitted with the difficulties of the instrument."

Mary hardly knew whether to be more vexed or amused at this extraordinary address, and might have been inclined towards the former, had not Mrs. Darcy, who had seen the beginning of the incident, and hastened forward lest her aunt's insolent patronage should offend, interposed with a kindly: "We have all been enjoying your piece so much. It must be delightful to be able to play like that. My aunt is such a lover of music that she cannot hide her enthusiasm."

"And why should I hide it, may I ask?" demanded Lady Catherine. "My judgment has often been of great service to young amateurs, among whom you might include yourself, Elizabeth"

"Yes, I know," replied Elizabeth, good-humouredly. "But Miss Crawford cannot be classed with the average amateur. May I introduce myself, as Mr. Durand has gone away? I am Mrs. Darcy. I saw you sitting with the Elliots, so perhaps you know a great friend of mine, Mrs. Wentworth."

Miss Crawford was about to enter gladly into the subject of Mrs. Wentworth, when Lady Catherine interposed, and in a few minutes, before Mary had quite realized what was happening, she found herself giving the assurance that Mrs. Grant would be delighted to receive a visit from Lady Catherine and Mrs. Darcy, and that she herself would be present at Lady Catherine's reception in Pulteney Street in a fortnight's time. She hardly knew how it had all come about, and she found herself wondering, as she was led back to her seat by Sir Walter Elliot, whether it was Lady Catherine's domineering manner, or Mrs. Darcy's kind looks, that she had yielded to so easily. The Elliots were eager with their questions. What? she did not know that that was Lady Catherine de Bourgh? Everyone knew Lady Catherine, she came to Bath every year—a very well-preserved old lady, must be quite sixty and does not look more than forty-eight—people of property—large estate in Kent—"an acquaintance quite worth following up, my dear Miss Crawford; of course *we*, with our already large circle of friends, could not attempt to include persons who only come here for a short time; otherwise we should have been very happy to have visited Lady Catherine."

Chapter 3

THE DARCYS FOUND PLENTY to enjoy during their stay in
Bath, as after dutifully allotting part of the day to a call on Lady
Catherine, or to joining her at the Lower Rooms, they were free
to make their own engagements, and passed a good deal of their
time with Lord and Lady Portinscale, Mr. Morland and the
Wentworths, Colonel Fitzwilliam invariably forming one of the
party. James Morland, the Portinscales' youngest guest, had
favourably impressed them from the first, being a young man of
sense, education and good address. The experience he had gained
from his somewhat unfortunate friendship with the Thorpe family, followed by his closer acquaintance with the Tilneys, had
been an incalculable benefit to him in helping to form his character and in teaching him what are the qualities in a friend which
win sincere love and respect. Hard work, resolution and regret for
his own follies, and the encouragement and kindness he had
received from his relations, had combined to put Isabella Thorpe
out of his head, and to recuperate a heart he had thought blighted

over for ever. He had within the last few weeks been obliged to resign the curacy he had held since his ordination, on account of the ill effects of the air of the valley on his health; and was now earnestly hoping to grow strong enough to resume work in some other part of the country, as he had, of course, resolved upon remaining a bachelor all his life, and making his church and parish suffice in place of domestic joys. His somewhat diffident manner in the society of men so much older than himself as Mr. Darcy and Captain Wentworth did him no disservice with them; and before they had known the particulars of his history for many days, Mr. Darcy was meditating upon the possibility of giving him material assistance in his career.

In the meantime, Elizabeth, independently of Lady Catherine, had exchanged calls with Mrs. Grant, whom she found anxious to be friendly, more anxious, indeed, than Mary, who, while appreciating Mrs. Darcy's kindness and charm, greatly disliked the patronizing manners of the mistress of Rosings Park. A few days after the concert the sisters spent a morning in Mrs. Darcy's sitting-room. Elizabeth had never neglected her study of the pianoforte or of singing, and as Mary, at the earnest request of her hostess, had brought her harp, the pleasure of the whole party, sometimes in conversation, sometimes in music, was ensured.

"Colonel Fitzwilliam is very fond of music, is he not?" Mrs. Grant said to Mrs. Darcy, glancing across the room to where the Colonel and her sister were engaged in animated discussion of the latest importations from German composers. "He really does like it, does not praise it out of mere politeness?"

"My dear Mrs. Grant! He is the most enthusiastic amateur I know. I often tell my husband that he would never had fallen in love with me if Colonel Fitzwilliam and I not struck up a friendship over music, which made him think there was more in me than he had perceived before. He himself is not such a good judge of it, but my cousin was greatly struck with your sister's playing the other night, and it really is appreciation from him."

"I am so glad: it will be a pleasure to Mary to meet him. Excuse my asking—I cannot quite understand—does he live with you or with your aunt?"

"With neither; he is our guest when we are in Bath, and he stays a great deal with us in the country; but he has rooms in London, and, I think, honestly prefers town as a residence, but that he is so fond of my husband and all his belongings."

There was a pause, and then Elizabeth added, a sudden thought having flashed through her mind: "He is an excellent man; it is impossible for us to think more highly of anyone than we do of him; but he labours under what he considers to be an insuperable disadvantage—he is a younger son, and therefore not much blessed with this world's goods."

She had hardly finished speaking when the door opened to admit two ladies, whom she recognized as her aunt's latest protégées.

"Dear me!" exclaimed Anne Steele, before she was fairly in the room; "quite a cosy little musical party, I declare! Lord! what a pity we have interrupted the music? We wouldn't have if we'd have known! And here we've run all the way upstairs—"

Lucy managed to silence her sister, and began a kind of tour of the room, making formal greetings to everyone she knew, and pausing in so pointed a way before Mrs. Grant and Mary, that Elizabeth, with great reluctance, was obliged to introduce Mrs. Robert Ferrars and Miss Steele. This accomplished, Lucy's errand was allowed to be divulged.

"We are driving out with Lady Catherine in the barouche landau, and she called here in passing, to say if Colonel Fitzwilliam was in she would like him to come too and make a fourth," she explained, with assistance from Anne. "We are not going far," she added for the benefit of the company in general; "only to Monkton Combe and back before dinner. Poor Miss de Bourgh is so very unwell to-day she did not feel inclined to drive out; and my sister and I just happened to be calling in Pulteney Street as Lady Catherine was starting out, so she was so very kind as to bring us along."

"It is fortunate," said Elizabeth smilingly, "that my aunt was able to secure your companionship; for, as I have visitors, I am not sure that I could spare my cousin this morning." She glanced at Fitzwilliam, who was impatiently waiting for an opportunity to answer. "No, certainly not. I am much obliged, but I am not able to come to-day."

Miss Steele's manner suffered from a diminution of sprightliness, even while she urged on the Colonel the necessity of taking advantage of the fine weather; but Darcy quietly interposed with: "Is my aunt's carriage at the door?" Lucy was obliged to admit that it was.

"Shall we go and make your excuses then, Fitzwilliam," he continued, "if our guests will kindly excuse us for a moment? Will you give Mrs. Ferrars your arm? Mrs. Ferrars, I greatly regret not being able to detain you, but I know it would not be kind, as my aunt has such a dislike to be kept waiting, especially in the open street."

The result of this was, that without quite knowing how it happened, Lucy and her sister found themselves in the hall again almost as soon as the waiter showed them up; were in the carriage, and driving away, the apologies of the gentlemen having been graciously accepted, and Mr. Darcy was saying to his friend as they returned: "The only way with these people is firmness; you are much too gentle."

"I don't feel particularly gentle after that interruption," replied the other, "though you got me out of it very well. My aunt seems to have a special grudge against me this time. I suppose she is working off her irritation; well, rather on me than on your sister."

"I do not believe it is that," answered Darcy; "she is, and always was, a tool in the hands of unscrupulous flatterers. If it were worthwhile, Elizabeth and I would rush to the rescue; but there is sure to be a tremendous explosion before long; they will all quarrel violently, she will come and tell us that they are ungrateful vipers, or something like that, and next year it will begin all over again with someone else."

"Well!" cried Elizabeth, as they opened the door, "did Aunt Catherine mind?"

"No, he has got off with a whole skin this time," replied her husband, "or rather, not quite a whole one, for he has had to pledge himself to join the expedition to Clifton to-morrow instead."

"I had forgotten that expedition to Clifton," Elizabeth exclaimed in dismay; "I wish it would rain! But if it did, we should only have to go another day. Mr. Morland, have you been to Clifton? Oh, do say it will be quite new to you! You can't? Is there no one who has never been there? My aunt makes up a party every year, for her newest friends, and we always do the same things and make the same remarks."

Elizabeth's forecast created much amusement, and Miss Crawford said: "Everything I hear beforehand of Lady Catherine is very alarming to a stranger like myself. I shall have to have caught a bad cold before her reception next week, for I shall not have the courage to appear and play."

"Oh, no, Miss Crawford, you must appear," said Darcy. "We are all too bad, with our jokes about her, for really she means to be very kind. But we have got into shocking ways since my wife married into the family."

"On the contrary, I think I have educated you all admirably."

"You are a privileged person, you see," said Colonel Fitzwilliam. "Miss Crawford, will you do us the kindness of playing again? I want to reap the advantage of the present moment, as the reception is a long way off."

The lady acceded with willingness, and at the conclusion of her piece Colonel Fitzwilliam sat down near her and found himself soon conversing with more ease and enjoyment than he had done for many months. Their talk was only of the most ordinary subjects; but the Colonel's simplicity and culture appealed to the best that was in Mary, and he found in her a ready sympathy, felt rather than expressed. His views of London life—so pleasant, so stimulating for the greater part of the year, but the country was better for a permanent home—exactly coincided with Mary's; and almost to her surprise, she heard herself vehemently asserting that town might be the place to make friends, but the country was the place to enjoy them. "You are a lover of country sports?" questioned the Colonel; "of riding and driving?" Mary answered enthusiastically, though repressing a sigh at the recollection of her first riding lessons. Did she ride at Bath? He could recommend her some good livery stables. His cousin, Mrs. Darcy, did not care for it, else some agreeable plans might have been made.

Meantime, the conversation was quite as animated in the other group. James Morland was asking if the ladies were those whom General Tilney and his son had lately met at dinner in Pulteney Street.

"Yes, you are right," replied Elizabeth. "Did you hear of that dinner-party?"

"Lady Portinscale told me. I should not otherwise have known, for I don't see mush of the General and Captain Tilney," James Morland answered with a smile.

"I thought Eleanor told me all was forgiven?"

"Catherine is, but her relations do not pass the censor. Still, it does not matter in the least, so long as he is kind to her, and I think I may say he is."

"I suppose he is often at the Portinscales'?" observed Elizabeth.

"Fairly often, but Lord Portinscale contrives that he does not stay too long; he thinks it worries Eleanor, and, as you know, she is anxious to take care of herself and go in thoroughly for the cure."

"Dear Eleanor! I am so devoted to her."

"Yes, indeed, one would be; she is the kindest friend anyone could possibly have. Do you know, Mrs. Darcy, they insist on my having a sitting-room to myself, where I can read undisturbed, or I can spend my time with them, just as I like."

"That is a nice arrangement; and you are better for coming to Bath?"

"Yes, a great deal better. I should be able to get to work in a very short time now, if only" (rather mournfully), "some work could be found."

"I am sure it can, if you are patient," said Elizabeth kindly. "The very thing one wants often drops upon one unexpectedly.

Do you know our part of the world at all? You must come and pay us a visit some time; the Derbyshire air is splendidly bracing, and would benefit you."

Morland said all that was proper, and Elizabeth, who had been trying unsuccessfully to catch her husband's eye, continued: "We are fortunate in our Rector at home, and even more fortunate in his wife; they have just come to Pemberley, and oddly enough, they are related to these very people of whom we have been talking, but as different from them as possible."

"Indeed! the Ferrars, or Steele—I have not made them out yet—"

'Mr. Edward Ferrars, our Rector, is a brother of Mr. Robert Ferrars, husband of the lady in blue. It is rather difficult to keep Mrs. Robert Ferrars off the subject when she is with us, as she seems to think it establishes a sort of connection, although they don't visit their relations."

"Perhaps they will do so now," said Morland, with a slight smile. "It is your own parish that you mentioned?"

"Yes, it is a fair-sized village that has grown up round the house, or, rather, round a much older house that formerly stood on the site, It is such beautiful country, Mr. Morland! You really must see it."

Mrs. Grant came towards Elizabeth to take leave, and they stood chatting together while Colonel Fitzwilliam and Miss Crawford rose and joined them.

"To-morrow, then, at eleven o'clock, you are sure suits you?" the gentleman was saying. "Mrs. Grant, your sister has been so kind as to say that, with your permission, I may be her escort on a ride, if a horse can be found that suits her."

"Riding? She will enjoy that," said Mrs. Grant, with momentary surprise. "She has not ridden for a long time. We have never tried to get her a horse in Bath."

It seemed that the whole thing had been thought out—all difficulties could be got over, Colonel Fitzwilliam assured her, if she would trust her sister to him for an hour or two; and Mary having expressed a proper amount of amiability and approbation, the arrangement was confirmed.

"But what about your engagement—the day at Clifton?" Mrs. Grant unluckily remembered, in the midst of the adieux. Colonel Fitzwilliam looked as if he were determined to forget the existence of such a place; Mr. Darcy reproached himself for having furthered the scheme; and Miss Crawford immediately said: "Oh, pray do not give that up on my account. We can ride another day, if we care about it."

"Not at all, Miss Crawford. Excuse me, but I should not think of giving up our plan. It is not at all necessary for me to go to Clifton."

"It would not be fair to make you break a prior engagement. No, let us put it off from to-morrow," was the lady's response.

Elizabeth interposed with, "If you and Miss Crawford went out a little earlier, you could still be at Clifton in time for dinner, Robert, which would quite satisfy my aunt."

Darcy joined his advice to his wife's; and as a matter can generally be easily arranged by a number of people who are all in favour of it, the ride was fixed for ten o'clock, and the ladies took their departure among many promises of meeting again. James Morland shortly afterwards left, Colonel Fitzwilliam accompanying him as far as his road lay in the direction of the livery stables;

and Elizabeth sat down to write letters, but she had not got very far before a new idea struck her which must immediately be acted upon. "Darcy," she exclaimed, rising and going to her husband, who was occupied with the newspaper, "can you listen to me? I want to help Mr. Morland in some way. I was thinking about it this morning while I was talking to him. He ought to have work to do, and he is such a good young fellow. Could you not make him Mr. Ferrars's curate, or something?"

Darcy smiled at his wife's earnestness. "You will be surprised to hear, my dear, that I had already thought of helping him."

"You had? How good of you. You can do it better than anyone else. He will be an object worthy of your interest."

"But though I had considered the question of the curacy, I had dismissed it as unsatisfactory. Mr. Ferrars does not want a curate, and Mr. Morland does want a living. I do not know if I told you that I heard before I went away that the old Rector of Kympton was likely to resign. If so, I shall have a living to present."

"And did you think of Mr. Morland? How delightful that would be. The very thing for him."

"We must not say anything about it at present, for I cannot hurry the old man out; but I expect to hear in the course of a month."

"I am sure you can bring it about successfully. How well everything is going to-day! Some dreadful catastrophe is sure to happen soon."

"What else has gone well?"

"Why, Robert's getting on so excellently with Miss Crawford. She is such a thoroughly nice woman, and it is certain to do Robert good."

"I would not think too much about that, Lizzy. Robert gets on well with all nice women, and as to Miss Crawford, I should say she is accustomed to receiving a considerable amount of admiration."

"Nonsense! You shall not spoil my pleasure in it. Why should they not be friends and nothing more? I took care to do him a good turn too; I told Mrs. Grant the thing I could about him, namely, that he is not well off. I knew he would tell them himself, and make the most of it, in that disparaging way he has, as if it were a great blot on his character, or some serious personal defect. He has become so diffident the last few months that I have no patience with him! He does not value himself properly, and causes people to undervalue him."

"One cannot say that diffidence is a fault of Miss Crawford's other admirer, Sir Walter Elliot."

"No, the tiresome, dressed-up doll! She is so sensible, that I cannot understand her having those people for her friends."

"Perhaps she has no choice. Possibly the acquaintance was of their seeking; she may have made a mistake. Who knows? Even the wisest of us may sometimes be mistaken in our estimates of one another, may we not, Elizabeth?"

Chapter 4

THE RIDE DULY TOOK place on the following morning, and the circumstances caused Elizabeth much secret pleasure. Her husband hesitated to attach any importance to the friendship thus inaugurated, and did not care to consider the possibilities arising out of it, for the engagement between his sister and his cousin had been a scheme very near his heart, and when it failed he was so much disappointed that he could not give up the idea of Fitzwilliam's being disappointed too. It was difficult for him to imagine that a man who had lost Georgiana could console himself with another woman, however talented and charming. It therefore followed that Elizabeth was compelled to keep her satisfaction to herself, and being very anxious that nothing should be said to dispel it, she refrained from giving any account of her cousin when the carriages assembled before her aunt's door at eleven o'clock. With a warning glance at her husband, she replied to Lady Catherine's peremptory inquiries that Robert had an engagement that morning, but he would join them at dinner, coming over on horseback.

"An engagement!" repeated Lady Catherine haughtily. "I was not aware that any engagement could have a prior claim, when my party has been made up for some days. It is very annoying. The result is that you have an empty seat in your carriage; if we had known, Captain Tilney's gig would not have been wanted."

"Perhaps Captain Tilney would not mind giving poor little me a seat in his gig," suggested Miss Steele, who, since she saw that the honour of sharing a back seat with Colonel Fitzwilliam was denied her, had been revolving the next most advantageous plan in her mind. Captain Tilney, who was already in his gig, hoping that his destined companion had not yet appeared, looked round for a way of escape: but from Lady Catherine's generalship there was none, and she said, after a moment's consideration: "Very well, I suppose that must do. I had intended—but when people are so extremely ungrateful—I sent a note round last night to Mrs. Grant and Miss Crawford, Elizabeth, asking them to join us. They actually declined. It is not often that I go out of my way to take notice of strangers—"

"My dear aunt," interrupted Darcy, "had we not better start? We are collecting a crowd in the street. Miss Steele, may I help you into the gig? I suppose your sister and her husband will go with my aunt and Miss de Bourgh. Take care of the wheel. Tilney, your horse looks as if he were going to leave us all behind. Now, Mrs. Ferrars. It is a good thing we have a spare seat, you know, madam. Mr. Morland can take care of the baskets and the wraps. If you like, we can make different arrangement in coming home."

The carriages drove off, and Elizabeth, in the highest spirits, congratulated her husband on his disposal of the Steele faction.

The party, however, was not destined to be so successfully divided for the whole day, and while they were all strolling about at Clifton, in the hour preceding diner, Elizabeth was taken possession of by her aunt, to listen to some severe strictures upon her management of the family affairs.

"I blame you exceedingly, Elizabeth, for not using your influence with Fitzwilliam. He ought to go about with the rest of us in an ordinary way, not wander off by himself, heaven knows where. *That* is not the way to teach him to forget that affair, which so unfortunately miscarried under your guidance."

"But, Aunt, we cannot control his movements as if he were a child. He naturally goes where he likes and makes his own friends."

"His own friends, yes, indeed! Desirable friends they must be, to cause him to break an engagement with his nearest relations. I think it is quite time that he were taken in hand by someone who cares as much for his welfare as I do. Even at his age a man cannot be trusted to know what is best for himself. I always thought no good would come of it when you and Darcy took so much pains to throw him and Georgiana together. Your own family's matrimonial affairs have always been conducted in such extraordinary lines—"

"We will leave my family out of the discussion, please, Aunt Catherine. I do assure you that the breaking of Georgiana's engagement was for the best in every way."

"Of course, I know you feel bound to defend your handiwork, and I am only too glad to think that my dear nephew has not suffered more than he has from the effects. perhaps next time you will agree that he should be guided by the advice of those older and wiser than himself."

"Certainly, Aunt Catherine," returned Elizabeth, who only endured these remarks by making allowance for her aunt's disappointment. "Or perhaps it might be better to let him choose a wife, if he wants one, entirely by himself."

"I should prefer that he should choose one of whom I could approve, and that I could be sure, next time an engagement is made, that it is not likely to be broken," returned Lady Catherine. "When I was a young girl a betrothal was regarded as a very serious thing, one not lightly to be cast aside because of a fancied change of feeling."

Elizabeth had begun to wonder how much longer she could bear this conversation, when the opportune arrival of Colonel Fitzwilliam caused his aunt's attention to be concentrated upon him to the exclusion of everyone else; and Elizabeth was pleased to observe his contented air and cheerful manner while he laughingly parried his aunt's cross-examination, and even submitted to the advances of Miss Steele, who, delighted to find him more approachable than usual, continued to address all her remarks to him while they visited the Pump Room and strolled down towards the river. Elizabeth found herself obliged to pair off with Mrs. Ferrars, but Lucy, who possessed a considerably larger share of adroitness than her sister, perceived at once that the different methods were necessary to recommend herself to Mrs. Darcy than to Lady Catherine, and had for some days been endeavouring to show herself equal to the standard of elegance required by a young lady. On this occasion she began by expressing warm enjoyment of the concert a few nights before.

"Yes," said Elizabeth, "it was a good concert, very much above the average of those things, I thought."

"Oh, it was charming! I do not know when I have been more delighted! That exquisite Italian song! The air of it runs in my memory still."

"You must have a good memory, for those florid operatic songs are the most difficult things to remember."

"Ah, dear Mrs. Darcy, I fear you undervalue your powers. We all know what an accomplished musician and critic you are." Elizabeth disclaimed; but Mrs. Ferrars continued perseveringly: "You prefer instrumental music, perhaps? It is no doubt a sign of a more cultivated taste."

Elizabeth was somewhat amused. "I do prefer instrumental music, but only because it is the kind I understand best."

"Then of course you appreciated the playing of that young lady, Miss Crawford. I suppose it was very wonderful. Lady Catherine was much struck by it."

"I do not know that it was wonderful, but Miss Crawford has a great gift, and plays with all the feeling and charm one would expect of her."

"You know her well, do you not?" asked Lucy.

"Not very well, but I do hope to know her better."

Lucy meditated upon this: it was not very agreeable news to her; if Mrs. Darcy saw much of Miss Crawford, it would mean that Colonel Fitzwilliam would see a good deal of her, too. Lucy felt that after poor Anne's many failures, success did not look more probable here; and the result of her reflections was the question: "Is Miss Crawford as rich as they say?"

"I do not know what Miss Crawford's fortune is," replied Elizabeth in cold surprise. "She and her sister appear comfortably off."

"Oh, I only meant—" began Lucy, confused. "She is said to be such a great heiress, that I often wonder why she has never married." Then, as her companion did not speak, she added: "They say that perhaps she will be the next Lady Elliot, and that would be most suitable, would it not? *his* title and *her* fortune."

"I should not think such a match was very probable, but I scarcely know Sir Walter Elliot," replied Elizabeth.

Lucy could not help pursuing the subject. "Do you think Miss Crawford very pretty?" she inquired?

"She is very graceful and sweet looking; and her face has a great deal of animation, which is always so attractive," answered Elizabeth.

"Her complexion has rather last its bloom, though, and she is so unbecomingly thin," Lucy ventured to say.

"I have not remarked it," returned Elizabeth, vexed with herself for having drifted into anything like an intimated conversation with Mrs. Ferrars. "Shall we join Lady Catherine? She is evidently wanting to collect the party. It must be nearly time to start for home."

Lucy saw that she had made a mistake, and covered it as well as she could by saying: "Oh, but I think Miss Crawford charming, I assure you, and so talented. I wish we could have heard the harp when we were calling on you yesterday morning."

"You will have another opportunity of doing so at my aunt's reception next week," said her companion.

Mrs. Darcy had been quite conscious of the undercurrent in Mrs. Ferrars's mind during this conversation, for she had perceived the aspirations of Miss Steele, supported as she was by her sister, towards Colonel Fitzwilliam; and Elizabeth felt the extreme importance of preventing any hint from being dropped which might open her cousin's eyes to the situation, or even to the fact that anyone thought there was a situation. A word of raillery from Miss Steele, or of archness from Mrs. Ferrars, would be enough to drive him from Bath in disgust; he would resent nothing more deeply than the imputation of his paying court to an heiress, and persons of the Steele kind, Elizabeth knew, would be able to make remarks of a character most difficult for him to bear. The friendship between himself and Miss Crawford was at that time in the stage when a very small incident might affect it one way or the other; and Elizabeth felt miserably uncomfortable until she found herself safely at home again, and their little party of three collected round the fireside in their lodgings, Mr. Morland having been dropped at his rooms.

"Well, Robert, I did not have the chance to ask you," she began, trying to speak unconcernedly; "did you enjoy your ride this morning, and where did you go?"

"I enjoyed it very much, thank you," replied the Colonel, "though we did not go far, only about three miles on the Wells road."

"That was a pity," said Darcy; "you ought to have had a good gallop on the downs."

"I wished to do so," said the Colonel, "but I fancied Miss Crawford was a little disinclined for it. She seemed so much afraid I should be late in arriving at Clifton and always talking of turning back."

"You must go farther another time," said Elizabeth.

"Yes, I hope so indeed," responded her cousin; "it is perfect weather for riding, and Miss Crawford is a horsewoman such as one seldom sees."

"Talking of horses, either Tilney is not much of a driver, or else he took pleasure in frightening that Miss Steele to-day," remarked Darcy. "You did not see, did you, Robert? No, it was on the way up there. He let his horse gallop down the long hill—I thought the gig would have been upset—and the silly girl actually caught hold of one rein."

"I thought Miss Steele seemed very unwilling to drive back with him," said Fitzwilliam with a smile. "By the way, have you noticed what a wonderful girl she is for asking questions? She almost equals my aunt."

Elizabeth felt her fears returning, and inquired: "Did she manage to find questions to ask *you*, Robert?"

"I should think she did. She was trying to extract from me why I had not arrived earlier and what I had been doing. I had to admit that I had been riding, and in some way of her own she dragged Miss Crawford's name in too. I simply pretended not to hear, and began talking vigorously about something else. How in the world it can matter to her whether I was riding with Miss Crawford, or Miss Anybody, I fail to understand."

"She is an inquisitive little minx, and I cannot bear her," Elizabeth exclaimed emphatically. "Fitzwilliam, do let us go home. I don't like Bath this year, or the people in it. We can ask the nice ones, like Miss Crawford and Mr. Morland, to stay with us at Pemberley."

"I am quite willing to return, my dear," replied Darcy; "but it would not do to leave before my aunt's reception, or to admit ourselves driven away by a Miss Steele."

"Of course we will stay over the sixteenth, but we will go after that; it only means a week or two less than our ordinary visit. The Wentworths are leaving and Eleanor Portinscale is too unwell for me to see anything of her, and Aunt Catherine has her extraordinary friends to amuse her; there is really nothing to keep us. You will come too, will you not, Robert?"

To this the Colonel made no reply, and Elizabeth interpreted his silence as her wishes dictated.

The next few days passed without any special event to mark them. Elizabeth wished more and more to leave Bath, and to be able to persuade Colonel Fitzwilliam to come too; for she felt an uneasiness that would not be stifled as to the outcome of the various friendships that had been inaugurated that year. In particular, she suspected the Steele and Ferrars faction of making some mischief with her aunt; they were incessantly with her, and it seemed to Elizabeth that Lady Catherine was becoming what, with all her faults of overbearing pride, haughtiness and love of flattery, she had never been before, namely, suspicious of evil motives and thoughts in those around her. When her nephew and niece were with her she would question them, and hardly accept their explanation of their occupations at other times; she blamed everybody for what they were doing, Mr. Morland for accepting the hospitality of the Portinscales, Lady Portinscale for not entertaining, Captain Tilney for not marrying, Anne Steele for wishing to do so, Colonel Fitzwilliam for coming to Bath, and Georgiana for staying away. Mrs. Grant and Miss Crawford were criticized for being in such an expensive place; but on the whole, Lady Catherine said but little about them in a general way, which Elizabeth regarded as a bad sign, for she was sure, that as friends of *her* choice, Lady Catherine must have a great deal to say in private in their disfavour.

As to James Morland, Elizabeth felt there was everything to be said in defence of his present situation; but she was so anxious for it to be known that he was on the way to obtaining work, that she wanted to be at home, in order to set the necessary arrangements in motion; though her husband laughed at the idea of the vicar's resigning any sooner, because the patron happened to be at Pemberley instead of at Bath.

It was, however, in regard to the progressing friendship between Mary Crawford and Colonel Fitzwilliam that Elizabeth felt most troubled, and as long as she remained in Bath, most helpless. Mary and Mrs. Grant would not come and see her more often than she visited them; and although there were numberless opportunities of meeting at the Rooms, the gardens, the theatre, and other public places, on these occasions there always seemed to be something to interfere with the enjoyment of their little party. Either Lady Catherine was there, with the Steeles, who could be depended on to break up any rational conversation or other amusement, or, worse still, Sir Walter and Miss Elliot would appear on the scene, and assuming the privileges of an older acquaintance, would take possession of Mary and draw her away from her newer friends with many protests of "having been *quite* deserted—of having so much to say to our dear Miss Crawford, whom we have missed so terribly lately." They had, of course, a slight previous acquaintance with the Darcys, whom they had intended to become intimate with at one time, as people of fashion; but to Miss Elliot's intense chagrin, Mrs. Darcy had been quite unresponsive to her, and had instead formed a friendship with her younger sister, Mrs. Wentworth. Although the Wentworths and the Darcys were frequently together,

Elizabeth could not well confide her difficulties to Anne, when it was so evident that Sir Walter Elliot was another admirer of Miss Crawford, and not at all evident in which direction the lady's choice would lie! It was hard to believe that she could find true pleasure in the company of Sir Walter, with his tedious inanities, or of Miss Elliot, with her artificiality and pride, and yet at times she seemed to greet them almost with a heartiness, and be glad to join them, even though she might have been a moment before in conversation with the Darcy party and showing them her real self in a charming and spontaneous gaiety. But those who watched closely might have noticed that these times coincided with the appearance of Lady Catherine, who, on seeing her nephew Colonel Fitzwilliam, usually endeavoured to detach him from the group he was in and to join him to her own. He, on his part, was always most unwilling to relinquish the society of Miss Crawford, but she gave him no chance to do otherwise, gliding away with a pleasant word of farewell before Lady Catherine's insistent "I want you, Fitzwilliam, if you can spare me a *few* moments," made itself heard. He had no key to her behaviour; sometimes it seemed to him as if she really liked him, and as if he might venture to hope he could make her like him more; and then, again, Sir Walter Elliot was so frequently at her elbow, with the compliments and gallantries which seemed to be his native language, and were so foreign, Colonel Fitzwilliam thought, to himself, that, naturally diffident, distrusting his powers to charm and attract, he often felt as if it were hopeless even to think of becoming a suitor; while at the same time his deepening love for Mary compelled him to persevere.

Elizabeth perceived some part of all this, and longed to help; but there was something about Mary's reserve that made it impossible to win her confidence, or to do anything more for Colonel Fitzwilliam than his own powers were able to do for him. Mary never gave him what could be construed into the smallest encouragement; it was only by observing that with him she seemed to be able to talk more naturally, to express her real opinions more frankly, that Elizabeth could surmise his interest in her to be in the slightest degree reciprocated. Had it not been for the very strong liking Elizabeth had formed for her new friend, she would have been disposed to think that her cousin's happiness would best be furthered by separating him from a pleasure that might become such great pain. But after a conversation with him, in which he briefly admitted his growing attachment and the existence of his hopes, she could not advise him to give up the quest, and could only assure him of her sympathy and belief in Mary's being a prize worth winning. He confessed that he felt it was doing a wrong to Georgiana to indulge in such thoughts so short a time after leaving her, and reproached himself with his presumption in thinking that so brilliant and admired creature as Mary could have any warmth of feeling for "a battered old soldier like this," as he styled himself. Elizabeth tried to reason him out of these scruples, and to give him all the good counsel that her knowledge of his character suggested. She found that he did not believe he had at present the remotest chance of being accepted; he only hoped, while they remained in Bath, to win his way in Miss Crawford's esteem, and to be assured that she had no preference for any other man.

Chapter 5

ELIZABETH WAS ANXIOUS TO see as much of Miss Crawford as possible before their departure from Bath, which was now fixed for the 17th of April, the day after Lady Catherine's reception. She accordingly made an excuse to walk down to Mrs. Grant's house on the day before with the piece of music, which it had occurred to her might be arranged with a setting for the harp; and she found Miss Crawford in and alone. Mary was wearing her bonnet and cloak and was wrapping up a parcel when Mrs. Darcy was announced; and the latter exclaimed that she would not stay, as Mary was just going out.

"No, no, I am not—it does not matter—I was only going to take this parcel to Miss Elliot's—pray sit down, Mrs. Darcy—I can send it by the boy"; and recalling the servant, Miss Crawford handed him the package with directions to take it to Camden Place. Then returning, she threw off her cloak and said: "It really does not signify in the least; it is only a fan Miss Elliot lent me a few evenings ago—as an excuse, she said, for seeing me again when I brought it back." This was spoken with a slight blush, but on Elizabeth's repeating her regrets she exclaimed: "Oh, but I would much rather stay and talk to you. I so seldom see you alone; one seldom does see anyone alone in Bath, I think. What have you bought? Some music? How delightful! You will play it to me now."

Elizabeth explained her scheme, and Miss Crawford examined the piece with great interest, and presently declared she thought it would make an admirable duet. As she walked across the room to the harp, Elizabeth remarked: "If you like it, we might play it to-morrow night at my aunt's reception."

Miss Crawford appeared to be busily tuning the strings of her harp, and it was after a moment's pause that she replied: "I do not think we shall be at Lady Catherine's reception."

"Not be there!" repeated Elizabeth, concealing her dismay as best she could. "I am very sorry for that; we shall all be sorry not to see you there."

"Thank you," returned Miss Crawford, and seemed unwilling to say more. Elizabeth, however, could not bear to leave the subject at that point, and after a few moments suggested that if Mrs. Grant did not feel equal to going, she herself would be delighted to call for Miss Crawford and take her to Pulteney Street.

"You are very kind, Mrs. Darcy, but it is not that," said Miss Crawford, at length turning round and showing a countenance expressive of some embarrassment. "The truth is," she continued, "and I know I can speak it to a friend like yourself, that I don't think Lady Catherine really wants such very small rush-lights as ourselves in her firmament of glittering stars. She cannot be said to know us; she has not called here since I was introduced to her at that concert, and only sent us a note late one evening asking us to come next day to Clifton. I do not in the least mind being invited only on account of my music, but, as Frances and I always agree, since I am not paid in money, I must be in manners. Oh! I beg your pardon—" she stopped short, colouring and biting her lip—"I should not have said that. Lady Catherine has, of course, a perfect right to do as she likes. I daresay she has long forgotten having given me an invitation."

"My dear Miss Crawford," exclaimed Elizabeth, whose colour had also risen, "say no more; you quite put us all to shame. Was there ever such an ill-mannered family? Of course, I thought that my aunt had sent you and your sister an invitation in due form. You must let me take all the blame to myself, for having omitted to remind her; we had talked, we had assumed all this time that you would be at the reception, which must account for my unpardonable forgetfulness of what should have been an early and most pleasurable duty."

Miss Crawford tried to laugh the matter off by saying that it was in no respect Mrs. Darcy's fault, and that the whole thing was too trifling to deserve a moment's consideration; besides, she added, Mrs. Darcy had presented her sister to Lady Catherine on one occasion, and could not have done more; that she was sure she and Mrs. Grant would not be missed at such a large party, and that she hoped to have other opportunities of meeting Mr. and Mrs. Darcy.

"It is because I fear there will be so few more in Bath, owing to our departure for home, that I am so particularly sorry to lose this one, and also for the cause of it," returned Elizabeth. "I can quite enter into your feelings, Miss Crawford, but will you do a very kind and generous thing, and show that you have forgiven me by availing yourself of my aunt's invitation if she tenders it in a manner you can accept?"

Miss Crawford could not be persuaded to give a definite assent to this proposal; she tried to treat the matter of her going to the party or staying away as no consequence, and laughingly protested that she would send the harp alone, which would answer all purposes as far as Lady Catherine was concerned. The utmost she could be induced to say was: "I should be very glad to give *you* the pleasure"; and with this Elizabeth was obliged to be content. Nevertheless, Elizabeth was so extremely desirous of securing Miss Crawford's presence, partly in the hope that Lady Catherine might be more kindly disposed to her on a closer acquaintance, and partly in order that Colonel Fitzwilliam might be enabled to enjoy her company without fear of interruption from the Elliots, that on leaving Mrs. Grant's house she hastened at once to Pulteney Street, trusting to find Lady Catherine alone and disposed to listen to her errand. In both these objects she was successful; for though the inevitable Miss Steele was in the house, she was upstairs with Miss de Bourgh, and Lady Catherine having just had a disappointment in hearing that some old friends found themselves obliged to quit Bath before her reception, was in a mood to demand Elizabeth's sympathy and to discuss matters connected with entertainment.

"It really is exceedingly trying," she said. "I am not prepared for these annoyances. At my age my friends should take care to spare me them. I am convinced that Lady Alicia Markham's son is not so ill but that he could have done without his mother for another two days."

Elizabeth condoled warmly, and listened to a description of the arrangements for the evening, in which, it appeared, Mrs. Ferrars's help had been invaluable; and when Lady Catherine named the musicians she expected, Elizabeth took advantage of the opening thus afforded her, by suggesting that a more formal invitation should be sent to Miss Crawford, to ensure her presence.

Lady Catherine stared, and in a tone of offended surprise reminded her of the first meeting with Miss Crawford. "You were present, I recollect, Elizabeth, when she was introduced to me, and I gave her the opportunity of bringing her instrument on this occasion."

"Yes, I remember its being mentioned," said Elizabeth, "but I hardly think she took it as an invitation. I fancied you meant to follow it up by calling on her and her sister."

"I may have had some thoughts of doing so," returned Lady Catherine haughtily; "but in the end I decided that I did not choose it; I cannot take up with all the new young ladies who come to Bath, and least of all those who are talked of as much as she is. She is the greatest flirt imaginable: that foolish old beau, Sir Walter Elliot, and half the men of Bath are running after her."

"No, indeed, dear madam; you have been misinformed, and I must defend her," said Elizabeth with more earnestness. "She is not in the least a flirt, and though men may run after her, they receive no encouragement to do so. But if you do not like her, there is no more to be said. Now, whom could you get in her place? I do not know any other lady, but there is a man at the theatre who is said to play the harp tolerably well."

Lady Catherine was silent for a moment with anger; then she broke out, as Elizabeth had expected: "There is no one I can get in her place. The impudent girl! She should be glad to come to a house like this. Probably she is intending to come all the time, if the truth were known; how can you tell she is not?"

"Only that when I last saw her she distinctly said that she and her sister had no reason to think themselves expected."

"No reason! when with my own mouth I said, 'I should like you to come and play at my house on the sixteenth.' Nothing could be clearer. As to her sister, if that is the very ordinary-looking person whom I believe you presented to me one morning, no, I do not recollect saying anything to her; but it is not she who plays the harp."

"She is a very agreeable and cultured woman, widow of a Canon of Westminster, and Miss Crawford goes nowhere without her."

"Well, it is all extremely annoying, and I do not know when I have been so upset. You should have told her, Elizabeth, told her plainly that she was to come. Really, the airs these people give themselves! Here is a card; I will write their names and send it round this afternoon, and I hope after that we shall have no more nonsense."

This by no means satisfied Elizabeth, and the next ten minutes were spent by her in using every means of persuasion she could think of to induce her aunt to repair all previous omissions by going to visit Mrs. Grant and conveying her invitation in person. Lady Catherine at first resisted the proposal indignantly, and would have continued to do so but for her knowledge that Miss Crawford's music was to have been an attractive part of the evening's entertainment, and an uncomfortable recollection of having told many of her friends that they would hear a person scarcely known, in whom she had discovered some remarkable talent.

This she did not betray to her niece, and when the latter left the house it was without having secured a definite promise, but

Elizabeth felt she had said as much as she safely could, and she walked home, pondering on what had passed, and wondering uneasily whether what she had done had been a real kindness to Mary. This question was also raised by her husband, to whom she had related the affair on her return. He shook his head over it, and gave it as his opinion that as his aunt had been rude to Miss Crawford, and the latter was fully conscious of it, they would not meet in a spirit conducive to future good feeling.

"But it would have been worse," said Elizabeth, "if Aunt Catherine had counted on Miss Crawford's coming and she had not appeared. There would have been no healing the breach then."

"Would it have greatly signified if there had been a breach?" inquired Darcy. "But never mind, my dear, you have done your best, and it will be interesting to see the result of Aunt Catherine's efforts at conciliation—the first time she has ever appeared in such a rôle, I should think."

Strangely enough, Lady Catherine's efforts were successful enough, although no one ever knew precisely how she accomplished it. But it was partly accounted for by the fact that she saw Mrs. Grant alone, Miss Crawford being out. She had taken only her daughter with her, not choosing that Miss Steele should be a witness of an interview which was undoubtedly galling to her pride; and Mrs. Grant, realizing but a small part of the great lady's insolence towards her sister, and the nature of Mary's resentment of it, only perceived that Lady Catherine was anxious to have them at the party, and was willing to acknowledge any remissness in her manner of issuing the invitation. Lady Catherine was so relieved at not having to apologize directly to the object of her dislike, that she became, in the course of the interview, more and more condescendingly gracious to Mrs. Grant, whom she found, as she afterwards remarked to her daughter, an amiable, unpretentious person; and actually admitted that she ought to have called sooner, but the pressure of engagements in Bath at this period of the season was so great. The call was strictly limited to a quarter of an hour, and Mrs. Grant described it all to Mary when she came in with much spirit and humour.

Mary, on hearing that her sister had actually accepted, was inclined to be defiant, and to declare that she would have a headache and not go; of course it was kind Mrs. Darcy's doing, but she did not care to accept favours thrown at her at the eleventh hour like this, by ill-tempered old ladies who only wanted to make use of her. Mrs. Grant, whose pride in, and love of, her sister were unbounded, and who delighted in seeing her shine by means of her beauty and talents, had great difficulty in persuading her; in fact, when they met the Darcy party at the Lower Rooms the following morning, Mary still declared that her coming was so doubtful that it was not worth while to give Mrs. Darcy the trouble of learning the duet.

Elizabeth, however, felt fairly confident of seeing her there, and Colonel Fitzwilliam confirmed this by telling Elizabeth with a cheerful glance that "she had not actually said she would not go." Their hopes were realized by the arrival of the two sisters, Mary looking lovely and sparkling in white with a few fine jewels, the gifts of her devoted brother. Elizabeth, who had arrived some time earlier, happened to be near her aunt, and so was able to satisfy herself that their reception by their hostess was properly courteous, if not cordial. Lady Catherine even took the trouble to mention the name of her daughter, who stood close by, and Miss de Bourgh actually exerted herself so far as to make two separate curtsies, though the remark that it was a cold evening was taken out of her mouth by Anne Steele, who was standing next to her, and evidently considered herself included in the introduction.

Elizabeth saw with delight that Colonel Fitzwilliam was impatiently awaiting his turn after these formalities should be over, and that he immediately placed himself by Miss Crawford's side. They seemed to have much to say to one another; and Elizabeth, after greeting the two ladies, and giving Mary an expressive glance of gratitude which conveyed much more than her quiet remark: "It was kind of you to come," began to converse with Mrs. Grant until music should be demanded of Mary.

Elizabeth was very well amused in watching the arrival of the guests, and in noticing which of them were under the special patronage of the Robert Ferrars, who appeared to have brought into Lady Catherine's circle a number of individuals of about the same standing in the world of fashion as themselves. Robert Ferrars was in his element, as though he found entertaining in another person's house a much more satisfactory matter than when the trouble and expense had to be incurred by himself, besides having the advantage of being able to introduce his friends to an earl's daughter as their hostess. When all who were expected had arrived, he, in company with a showy-looking young man, dressed in the extreme of fashion, began strolling about the rooms in search of someone upon whom they could make an impression. Elizabeth thought that she and her husband might at least have escaped Mr. Ferrars's civilities; and great was her surprise when the young men paused before her, and Mr. Ferrars begged leave to introduce his friend Mr. Yates, who had newly come from London. Mr. and Mrs. Darcy, he thought, might be interested to meet Mr. Yates, in view of their intended journey, as Mr. Yates would be able to give them all information as to the state of the roads.

Mrs. Darcy had scarcely made her curtsey and was about to frame some suitable reply, when the glance of the new-comer happened to fall on Mrs. Grant, who was seated on a low chair close by. He immediately pronounced her name in tones of questioning surprise, and when she looked up, exclaimed: "Yes, I was sure it was. Upon my word, madam, I take some credit to myself, considering the length of time it is since we met. I hope I am so fortunate as to recall myself to your remembrance?"

"You are very good, sir," replied Mrs. Grant, with a perceptible effort. Her countenance expressed no great pleasure at the encounter. "Of course, I recall you perfectly. Mrs. Yates, I trust, is quite well."

"Very well, I thank you, madam; and I hope the same may be said of your fair sister, Miss Crawford—but perhaps she is no longer Miss Crawford?"

"Don't be under any alarm, Yates," struck in Robert Ferrars; "she is still Miss Crawford, and you can judge for yourself how well she is, for you will see and hear her to-night."

This speech was so offensive to Mrs. Grant that she cut short Mr. Yates's compliments, and remarking, "Yes, I am glad to say my sister is still with me," rose and prepared to move away. Elizabeth immediately suggested that they should go in search of some tea, and the dismayed Mr. Yates saw Mrs. Darcy departing before he had uttered a single word about London, or about the distinguished people he had dined with the night before last.

"Well, I'm very sorry, Ferrars," he replied to his friend's reproaches; "I'm sure I didn't want to talk to Mrs. Grant at all, but seeing her was the greatest surprise; I never dreamt of meeting her here, and, of course, I had to speak a civil word, or she would have thought it so strange."

"My dear fellow," retorted Ferrars, "what on earth did that matter? I should have thought you would understand that Mrs. Darcy is the person to make yourself agreeable to here, not Mrs. Grant, who is only a clergyman's widow. I suppose, as you knew her before, that she lived down at that precious dull place in the country, where you took your wife from."

"Yes, she did," answered Mr. Yates; "but there's a good deal more in it than that—not through her. Do you mean to say that sister of hers is really here, going about in Bath?"

"Of course she goes about; why shouldn't she?" demanded Ferrars. "Is there anything against it? The women are all down on her, I know—you should hear my wife and sister—but only because she's such a devilish pretty girl and proud; she won't have any friends but the Darcys."

"But do you actually not know? Have you never heard all about her and her brother? Between the two of them they managed to lead my wife's family a pretty dance. Neither of them can ever show their face faces in Mansfield again, so it was a lucky thing the Grants moved when they did. To think of meeting Miss Crawford again! I shall tell her that Edmund Bertram is uncommonly well and prosperous, and Tom Bertram isn't married yet; and you see how she looks when I do it."

This amiable intention was frustrated, as Elizabeth, who could readily see that Mrs. Grant was disturbed by what had happened, did not need even the hint dropped by her that she hoped Mary would not meet Mr. Yates, as he was connected with the Bertrams, and all that part of her life that it was painful to her to remember, in order to make her strive in every way to protect Mary from any disagreeableness. They went to the tearoom, whither Colonel Fitzwilliam and Mary had, fortunately, preceded them some time before Mr. Yates's appearance. They were there joined by Darcy, and all five formed a happily conversing group. Mrs. Grant whispered a word to her sister, whose countenance changed for a moment; but she shook off the cloud and gave herself up to the delight of the present. Once Elizabeth received a message from her aunt requesting her to "make Miss Crawford play now," and she escorted her friend back to the music-room and did not leave her after the performance until she saw Colonel Fitzwilliam safely stationed beside her. No command to play a second time followed, rather to Elizabeth's surprise, but having a number of friends to take leave of, she could not give it much thought before her own departure, which her husband had insisted should be an early one, in view of the journey on the following day.

Mr. Yates did not, in fact, come near any of this little party during the rest of the evening, but might have been observed conversing earnestly in a quiet part of the room with Lucy Ferrars and her sister, who, judging by their rapt attention and animated countenances, found what Mr. Yates had to say deeply interesting; so much so, in fact, that when his narration was finished the two young women, having faithfully promised to repeat no word of what he had told them, took the first opportunity of slipping away unostentatiously in the direction of their hostess; and having drawn her aside, with a hint of having something very important to communicate, poured into her ears that whole story just heard, a story which, as may be imagined, lost nothing in their version of it. Lady Catherine was so exceedingly angry that her instantly expressed desire was to have both Mr. Yates and Miss Crawford—the latter being, of course, the heroine of his tale—brought before her, with some confused idea in her mind of proving to the world at large that her dislike of Mary Crawford had all the time been well founded; but Lucy's extreme terror of the consequences of this act and her part in it, while Mr. and Mrs. Darcy were there to protect their friend, caused her to implore Lady Catherine to suspend pronouncing judgment till the following day. There would still be plenty of opportunities of meeting Miss Crawford, Lucy assured her patroness. Lady Catherine would make no promises. Only the necessity of attending to her other guests, she replied, delayed her from informing Miss Crawford of her strong disapproval. She would not appear to condone such conduct as Miss Crawford's had been one moment longer than she could help. Lucy and her sister thought it safest to mingle inconspicuously with the crowd until the storm should break over some other heads.

Meantime, Elizabeth and her husband had made their farewells to most of their friends, and were exchanging a few last words with Mrs. Grant and Mary. The latter looked unusually lovely, and an expression of quiet happiness illumined her countenance. Colonel Fitzwilliam did not allow himself yet to adopt the easy manner of an intimate friend, but the earnestness of his glance towards Mary, the eagerness with which he obeyed her slightest request, betrayed the state of his feelings, and his air and manner were those of a man whose thoughts are wholly pleasant.

"I am so sorry that this is really good-bye," Elizabeth was saying, "but I am consoled by thinking it is only for a little while. You will keep your promise and come to us this summer, will you not?" Mary Crawford and her sister repeated a cordial acceptance, and the former added: "You must tell us exactly how to come, Mrs. Darcy, you must explain all the intricacies of travelling between Brighton and Derbyshire, or we shall undoubtedly be lost on the road."

"Brighton! Shall you come from there?" and it was explained that the ladies generally spent the months of June and July at some seaside place, and Brighton had been thought of for this year. "Or we may be in London with my brother," continued Mary, "but wherever we are, if you remember to ask us, we shall come."

The usual protestations of the impossibility of forgetting followed, and very warm handshakes were exchanged; then Elizabeth, turning to her cousin, said: "Are you coming home now, Robert? It will be most unfriendly of you not to, for how else shall we see you again, since you positively decline to go with us to-morrow?"

Colonel Fitzwilliam hesitated, and said he had not thought of going home just yet; but Mary interrupted him by saying: "Pray don't let us keep you, Colonel Fitzwilliam. I am sure our coach will be there now, if you would kindly inquire. Colonel Fitzwilliam was so kind as to wish to put us into our coach," she added to Elizabeth, "but it would not be worth while, just for that, to prevent him from driving home with you and Mr. Darcy."

"I will go and see, certainly," said the Colonel, moving off;

"but don't wait for me, Elizabeth. I would just as soon walk back, and I will see you and Darcy at breakfast."

Darcy drew his wife's arm within his, and they made their way to Lady Catherine, who was sitting very upright in an armchair and wearing her most stern and forbidding expression. To Elizabeth's civilly-worded thanks for all the kindness and pleasure which their aunt had bestowed on her relatives during their stay, she made no reply; but when Elizabeth referred to their departure on the morrow, she started, placed her hand coldly within her niece's for a moment, and said: "Yes, you are going, I recollect. You did not consult me in the matter, but still, perhaps this year it is as well you are not staying longer."

Elizabeth was too well accustomed to her aunt's insolent speeches to seek to account for them, and turned away; while Darcy, remarking, "Yes, we have stayed as long as we care to for this year," also shook hands with his aunt, cutting her rather short in the midst of a statement that she could send no message to Georgiana, and without further delay escorted his wife downstairs.

Mary Crawford watched them from the room, and then said to Mrs. Grant: "Let us go and say good-night also, Frances. We may as well be ready—and there will be the harp to be carried down."

"Very well, my dear," returned her sister. "We shall have to take our turn, for everyone else seems to be preparing to leave at once."

They approached Lady Catherine, and when after a few minutes they reached her side, to their surprise she addressed them in a more stiff and stately manner than usual. "Ah! Miss Crawford! I was awaiting you. Will you kindly come this way?" And she preceded them towards a small library, where cardtables had been placed, but which was now deserted.

Mary was not the least apprehensive of harm, and even whispered mischievously to her sister: "Perhaps she is going to present me with a fee!" so that her astonishment was unbounded when Lady Catherine, having closed the door, turned to her and exclaimed in a voice shrill with anger, which she did not attempt to control: "As this is probably the last time we shall meet, Miss Crawford, you will allow me to inform you that I have been entirely under a misapprehension in inviting you to my house, and that I very much regret having done so." The two sisters gazed at her, both silent from surprise, and Lady Catherine made haste to continue: "I see you are on the point of asking me what reason I have for coming to this conclusion. I do not care to enter into particulars; it must be sufficient for you that facts have come to my knowledge—facts which, if you search your memory, will no doubt—"

Mary had by now found words, and she broke into Lady Catherine's speech in a voice that distress and wounded dignity caused to tremble: "I was not on the point of asking you why you propose to forbid me your house. In that matter my decision had anticipated your wishes. But I have a right to ask the meaning of this insult; even your ladyship will hardly refuse to inform me of what and by whom I am accused."

Lady Catherine drew herself up still further, and said: "I repeat that I do not care to enter into particulars. I have no wish to say anything that may be injurious to you in your future life. The facts which have come to my knowledge are facts which you must be well aware are damaging to yourself and any member of your family—only in a lesser degree to you, Mrs. Grant. I shall repeat them to no one. I only wish you to understand our acquaintance is henceforth at an end."

Mary scarcely heard the last words; she had turned to her sister, who seemed quite overwhelmed and could only say, almost indistinguishably: "That dreadful Mr. Yates! I feared—I feared—"

"Frances, dear Frances, do not give way, I implore you. Do not let her make you unhappy. What does it matter about Mr. Yates? The truth cannot harm either of us." Then, confronting Lady Catherine once more, with head proudly thrown back, she demanded: "Now, madam, in justice to my sister, if not to me, will you kindly state what Mr. Yates has told you?"

Lady Catherine, who had expected a shamefaced attitude, was unprepared for this counter-attack, and replied after some hesitation: "It is evident that you know Mr. Yates has something to tell."

"Certainly, we know exactly what Mr. Yates knows," retorted Mary with spirit, "but what he may have told your ladyship is quite another matter. Will you tell us, or are you disposed to wait for the presence of Mr. and Mrs. Darcy? A message from us would cause them to postpone their journey to-morrow."

The taunt was a well-judged one; Lady Catherine felt its truth, and anxious not to involve herself more deeply, she exclaimed: "Mr. Yates has not spoken on the subject to me; it is sufficient for me that he has told others, upon whom I can rely, the whole story of your brother's disgraced connection with that married woman, with whose dishonoured name I will not sully my lips—is that the true, or is it not? You say the truth can do you no harm."

"The fact is true," replied Mary, who had grown very white.

"Oh, Mary, Mary!" exclaimed Mrs. Grant, "let us come away now that we know the worst."

"No," answered Mary, who was retaining her calmness by a great effort, "we will not deprive Lady Catherine of the pleasure of telling all she has heard."

"And you express no contrition, you shameless, you bad-hearted girl?" broke out Lady Catherine, giving rein to her anger. "You think it can do you no harm to have all known of that shocking affair, which alone should make you shun the society of respectable persons, but beyond and above all that, there are your own intrigues with the two brothers of that wretched woman, one of whom you enticed away from the girl to whom he was attached, and your own flirtations here, which I will not enter into, but which I have watched taking place under my very eyes—"

"That will do, I think," said Mary, raising her hand. "You can have nothing further to say. You have insulted us in every possible manner. I only hope, Lady Catherine, that by this outrage you will consider yourself to have taken ample revenge."

"How dare you speak so to my poor sister?" demanded Mrs. Grant, wrath at last overmastering her distress. "If you only knew the real truth of the matter—if you only knew who had suffered and who was to be blamed!—God forgive you your wicked thoughts and your poisonous tongue!"

"Hush, hush, Frances!" interposed Mary, drawing her sister away. "Do not try to convince her. She is not worth it," and the two sisters left the room and walked with fairly firm steps downstairs, where they procured their cloaks, and Mrs. Grant was able, by drawing down her hood, to conceal the traces of her emotion. Mary directed a servant to bring her instrument downstairs, and they awaited it within the cloak-room. A few minutes later the servant knocked at the door, asking for Miss Crawford, and both ladies hastened forward, expecting the announcement of their coach, but Mary drew back on encountering the pale and anxious gaze of Colonel Fitzwilliam, and hearing his eager words: "I feared I had missed you—that you had gone—I searched for you through the rooms—and then I heard you were with my aunt. Is anything the matter, dear Miss Crawford? I fear there something."

"It is of no consequence, thank you, Colonel Fitzwilliam," she replied, speaking with cold pride. "You are come a little too late to be of any assistance. I see the footman has brought my harp, so if you will kindly allow us to leave the house, that is the most you can do."

"I implore you not to speak so, dearest Miss Crawford," he exclaimed, though keeping his voice low on account of the persons standing round. "Is there nothing I can do, nothing I can put right? I could, I am sure, if only I knew what had happened."

Lady Catherine can best inform you of that," returned Mary in icy tones. "May I again request that you will ask for our carriage?"

"One moment only, and I will not detain you," he said hurriedly. "May I call on you to-morrow, at an early hour? Pray give me permission."

"I shall not be at home to-morrow," answered Mary, and swept proudly past him towards the front door, where a footman had just announced: "Mrs. Grant's carriage stops the way."

"Mrs. Grant!" exclaimed Colonel Fitzwilliam, placing himself beside that lady as she followed her sister, "you will allow me to come and see you? I will not torment your sister, but—you will not close your door on me without at least explaining the reason for this dreadful change?"

"Oh, Colonel Fitzwilliam!" exclaimed Mrs. Grant, with difficulty controlling her agitation, "if you knew all, you would not expect me to receive you; but I cannot altogether refuse, only I must have time to reflect, to consider—and my sister must be my first care."

He could only bow and acquiesce; and he assisted her into the carriage, which immediately rolled away.

Chapter 6

MR. AND MRS. DARCY were dismayed at the haggard aspect of their cousin when he joined them at breakfast the next morning. He looked like a man who had not slept, and whose wakefulness had some distressing cause. To their inquiries he replied by giving as brief and quiet an account as he could of the incident of the preceding evening. Elizabeth exclaimed with consternation when he described Miss Crawford's manner to him at the door, but refrained from making any comment until he had related how he had gone in search of his aunt, to obtain, if possible, an explanation from her. He had had to wait some time, until all but one or two of the guests had gone and he could be alone with her, but she had been most difficult to talk to on the subject; when reproached with her treatment of Miss Crawford and Mrs. Grant, she had admitted that perhaps she did speak rather severely to Miss Crawford, but the latter's attitude had annoyed her; that everything she had said was fully justified, and she was perfectly convinced that Miss Crawford was a most undesirable person, and one she should never have had in her house.

"Good heavens! can such things be said without impunity?" exclaimed Elizabeth. "What did you say, Robert?"

Colonel Fitzwilliam replied that he hoped he had controlled his temper, but it had been no easy matter. His aunt would not even substitute her charges, and only referred to the shocking conduct of Miss Crawford and her brother towards a family called Bertram, adding that though this information had only just come to her ears, she believed that in London it was common property. Needless to say, her nephew's assurances that whatever the brother might have done Miss Crawford herself was absolutely innocent of any wrongdoing whatever, had not the slightest effect. Neither was she able to perceive that upon no basis but a shred of vulgar gossip she had done a vile thing in attacking and defaming two guests under her own roof.

"That made her more enraged than ever," continued Colonel Fitzwilliam; "she said it was not vulgar gossip, but a well-founded fact; and though she evidently was under a promise not to reveal the source of her knowledge, the word Ferrars slipped out once, so I was assured of what in fact I had guessed before, namely, to whom we owe this whole abominable affair."

"It is most deplorable," said Darcy gravely. "We can never regret it enough. I am sorry for you, Fitzwilliam, and still more sorry for Mrs. Grant and her sister, but I do not see that there is anything to be done, beyond apologies from all who are in any way connected with my aunt. It must be talked of as little as possible, for Miss Crawford's sake. The Ferrars will do their mischievous part; and it must be the duty of her friends to take it for granted and ignore it; there is a modicum of truth in the story, I suppose?"

"I do not know, or wish to know, anything about it," began Fitzwilliam, but Elizabeth interposed eagerly: "I can tell you all there is to know. I heard the story, if you can call it so, from Anne Wentworth only the other day: but I did not mention it again, for there is no use in reviving these things. It is true that Miss Crawford's brother ran away with Mrs. Rushworth, who had been Miss Bertram. He had treated her very badly before her marriage, gaining her affections and then showing her he did not intend to marry her. Mary Crawford had been on terms of friendship with the whole family, and one of the brothers, a young Bertram, had paid her attention. Naturally, the scandal of the divorce separated the two families; and I suppose ill-natured people can find some reason why Mary should be blamed for it, but I know of none."

"How came Mrs. Wentworth to be acquainted with these events?" asked Darcy. Colonel Fitzwilliam seemed to pay little heed; he rose from the table, leaving his untasted breakfast.

"Because they have a great friend, a naval officer, young Lieutenant Price, who is also connected with the Bertrams; his sister married one of the sons. In fact, she was adopted by the family as a child, and would naturally know all its affairs. I suppose the Ferrars got their information from that Mr. Yates who was there last night; I do not know anything about him, but I will ask Anne Wentworth."

"You know my advice, which is, as little said as possible," was Darcy's reply; and he crossed to the window, to lay his hand on his cousin's shoulder, and say warmly: "Do not take it too much to heart, my dear fellow. On reflection, Miss Crawford, when she is a little less upset, will see that you are not to blame, and Mrs. Grant, who is evidently a sensible woman, will take the right line when she has had time to think things over."

"I hope so," returned Colonel Fitzwilliam; but very little hope was expressed in his voice or bearing.

"I wish we could stay another day or two, to do some good in this miserable business," exclaimed Elizabeth. "We might even now put off starting."

"No, Elizabeth, we could hardly do that, and it would not be advisable," said Darcy, with decision. "None of us could make my aunt's peace with these ladies; and if we have to make our own, as well as Robert his, we can do it better by letter. By the way, Robert, how do you stand with my aunt?"

"We parted in anger, I fear," replied Fitzwilliam; "it was inevitable, after the argument we had had. It is immaterial to me; she knows now that I am an advocate for Miss Crawford, and she will consequently not expect to see me again."

"In spite of what you say, Darcy, I do think we might do some good," Elizabeth interrupted. "Let us countermand the carriage. We can easily tell the landlord we wish to keep these rooms till Monday."

Fitzwilliam begged his cousins not to put themselves to such an inconvenience on his account; and Darcy being also unwilling to change his plans at the moment when the carriages were driving to the door Elizabeth was obliged to give up the idea, which she did with greater reluctance through feeling that had she not persuaded Miss Crawford to go to Lady Catherine's reception, this disaster would not have occurred. Revolving in her mind plans for the future, when all the parties concerned should be removed from the influences at work in Bath, she continued her preparations for departure; and when all was ready, and the luggage placed on the vehicles, she walked downstairs with Colonel Fitzwilliam, speaking words of consolation and encouragement to him, promising to write to Miss Crawford from their first stopping-place, and urging him to wait patiently and not be deterred by Mary's being reluctant to see him again for some time after her very painful experience. He promised not to give up hope, but feared that this might cause him to lose the ground he had gained.

"You are very good, Elizabeth," he said, as they shook hands. "Whatever happiness comes out of this I shall owe to you. But it is beyond what I can expect. There never was much reason why she should look at me, and now, if she connects me with this wretched affair, there is less than ever."

Elizabeth once more earnestly begged him to take a more cheerful view, and immediately afterwards she and Darcy started their long journey northwards; and their cousin, having exchanged a few words with James Morland, who had walked round to the hotel a few moments earlier to take leave of his friends, returned to his own rooms and to the thought of Mary Crawford, which, indeed, was never absent from him. His eagerness to be with her once more was only exceeded by his desire to protect her fair name against the danger which threatened it; and in spite of Darcy's advice he came to the conclusion, after long thought, that he was justified in going first to the Ferrars's and then, if necessary, to Mr. Yates, to demand that whoever was responsible for the calumny should retract it. He did not wish to pose as Mary's champion until she had given him the right to take a warmer interest in her than he might yet assert; but as he could not in any case have failed to be aware of the insult last night, and as he was at the same time Miss Crawford's friend and Lady Catherine's nephew, he felt that he could do no less than endeavour to right the wrong himself, having been unsuccessful in an appeal to his aunt, which seemed the most direct.

He accordingly repaired at once to the Ferrars's lodgings, the address of which had been given to him by Anne Steele on one of the many occasions on which she had begged him to call there—a request hitherto ignored; and as soon as he was shown into the room he perceived that his two errands would be accomplished in one, as Mr. Yates was sitting with the Ferrars and Miss Steele. Fitzwilliam would neither shake hands nor take the offered seat, and addressing himself to Ferrars and Mr. Yates, he requested, in a tone as calm and deliberate as he could make it, that they would immediately and unreservedly withdraw all the accusations they had brought against Miss Crawford, and would furthermore go to Lady Catherine and make to her the same complete denial of their previous statements. He was careful to utter Miss Crawford's name as seldom as possible, and refrained from demanding an apology to be made to her personally, as he felt the greatest delicacy about appearing to act on her behalf, and could judge also that it was not the unkind talk, but the insult from her hostess, that had given her such deep offence. He found his present task an easier one than he had expected; and had his heart been lighter, he could have derived amusement from witnessing the kind of turmoil which his words immediately created amongst his hearers. Neither Robert Ferrars nor Mr. Yates was of a quarrelsome disposition; they were alike in living only for trifles, and in being of an idle, careless, gossiping nature, tolerably good-humoured when it did not interfere with their pleasure or comfort. At that moment the matter of greatest importance to them was to set themselves right with this extremely distinguished gentleman, who came to them with an air of such authority; and they hastened with the utmost zeal to assure and protest, to deny, regret or explain away whatever might have happened to annoy any friend of his.

Robert Ferrars, who, beyond listening eagerly to the story, had had nothing to do with the affair, was not long in discovering that his wife and her sister were really responsible for the mischief; and both he and Mr. Yates bitterly reproached the ladies for having broken their promise and carried Mr. Yates's information to Lady Catherine. Anne Steele's composure was not proof against this attack, especially in the presence of her admired Colonel Fitzwilliam, and she found a burst of tears the most convenient resource, but Lucy defended herself with spirit, and declared that she had only told Lady Catherine what it was right for her to know, as certainly her ladyship would not wish to receive Miss Crawford if half of what Mr. Yates had said was true. This produced a renewed flood of eloquence from Mr. Yates, who denied in the handsomest manner having said anything to Miss Crawford's disadvantage, and wound up by boldly asserting that she was a lady for whom he had the greatest respect; that she could not help the faults of her brother, and that as for Edmund Bertram, everyone considered that it was *he* who had treated her badly, "hanging round her always and never making her an offer—we none of us knew what he could be at."

Colonel Fitzwilliam intimated that he did not wish to know any of these particulars; that he was come simply because he had learnt that Lady Catherine, in consequence of what she had heard, had been led to treat her guests with great injustice—injustice was the strongest word he would allow himself to use—and that, for everyone's sake, it was highly necessary for her mind to be disabused of all false impressions. Mr. Yates, when it was made clear to him, professed himself perfectly ready to go to Lady Catherine and give her what he termed the true facts, and he heartily supported Colonel Fitzwilliam in the latter's request that Mr. Ferrars should accompany him. Mr. Ferrars looked from his friend to his wife, extremely ruffled and uncomfortable; Lucy was reduced to such a state of anger that she could scarcely speak; but Mr. Yates speedily recovered his usual state of easy *insouciance* and volubility, and was the only one of the party able to walk with Colonel Fitzwilliam to the door and usher him out with many bows and smiles and promises to wait on him in the course of a day or two to tell him the result of his forthcoming interview. Mr. Yates was not a man who could long be disconcerted by anything; and he probably looked forward to his scene with Lady Catherine as one in which he could play a leading part.

Colonel Fitzwilliam walked away, smiling for a moment at the thought of the storm of mutual recrimination that was going on in the room he had just left; he feared that what he had achieved would be of little use, for his aunt would be much more desirous of believing the first version than the second. Everything depended now upon the effect of his own influence upon Mary and her sister—upon whether he could succeed in atoning to them to any extent for what they had suffered. He greatly distrusted his own powers, and walked to their house in the deepest dejection of spirits.

The servant said the ladies were at home, and he waited for some time in the drawing-room. Mrs. Grant's countenance, when at last she appeared, was not such as to reassure him. She did not ask him to sit down, and remained herself standing at a little distance while she explained, briefly and formally, that her sister was not at all well, and was unable to receive visitors. Colonel Fitzwilliam's heart sank at this confirmation of his worst fears. He hastened to reply that he knew he could not have expected her to be willing to see any member of his family after what had happened the night before, but that he brought the sincerest, most heartfelt apologies on his own behalf and that of his cousins. He was only too sensible that nothing he could say could obliterate the memory of the treatment to which Mrs. Grant and her sister had been subjected, but he had been endeavouring to right the wrong, and hoped that "when Lady Catherine should be brought to acknowledge—"

Mrs. Grant here interrupted him. "Colonel Fitzwilliam, I must tell you plainly that it is not of the slightest use to mention that lady's name to my sister or myself. I know you mean very kindly, but the harm is done now, and nothing Lady Catherine can do or say can repair it. I do not wish to go into the whole matter, it is too unspeakably painful; but if you had been aware of the language she used towards us, you would see that it is not a thing which can ever be forgotten—I had almost said forgiven."

Colonel Fitzwilliam admitted it fully. He told her who were the real authors of the calumny, as far as regarded Lady Catherine, and he could guess how she had been incited to anger, and how she must have spoken, even though he had not been present, and he repeated that Lady Catherine would be enlightened, and would regret as much as anyone having spoken so hastily; but none of this had any effect on Mrs. Grant. She gradually realized Colonel Fitzwilliam's anxiety to spare her and her sister pain, and thanked him for what he had endeavoured to do; but concluded by saying that she sympathized with her sister in feeling that all intercourse between the two families had better cease.

Colonel Fitzwilliam's dismay was extreme. He felt himself dismissed, but rallied his energies enough to ask: "But you do not identify us, Mrs. Grant, my cousins and myself, with everything that my aunt does? Surely you must know Mrs. Darcy, at least, better than to include her in such a condemnation?"

Mrs. Grant appeared confused. "Mrs. Darcy has been very kind," she said hesitatingly. "I have appreciated it."

There seemed a "but" behind this, and Colonel Fitzwilliam gently pressed for further reasons, when the lady at last said: "The truth is, Colonel Fitzwilliam, if you will have it, my sister feels—and I, though not going the whole way with her, do understand her point of view—feels at present too bitterly about it to be able to judge impartially. She thinks that she should not have allowed Mrs. Darcy to over persuade her—that she did wrongly to go to Lady Catherine's on what was practically Mrs. Darcy's invitation."

"Good God!" broke from Fitzwilliam; "but she does not consider my cousin in any way to blame for this behaviour of my aunt's?"

"No, certainly not," returned Mrs. Grant; "she blames herself, as I have said; but she regrets also that Mrs. Darcy took so many pains to induce Lady Catherine to induce to show us any civility. Lady Catherine disliked us, and when the opportunity of showing her real feelings arrived, she was glad to take full advantage of it."

"Mrs. Grant, believe me, it is not as you think," said Fitzwilliam earnestly. "My aunt is just now entirely in the hands of some evil-natured and unscrupulous persons, who can make her act in any way they chose."

"It may be so; I try to think so; but it does not excuse her conduct," returned Mrs. Grant.

Fitzwilliam took two or three turns about the room, wrapped in thought. At length he approached Mrs. Grant, and in tones which scarcely concealed his emotion, said: "Forgive me, but I cannot take what you say as final. It is, of course, for you and your sister to decide, but I cannot think that you mean to cast us off, myself and my cousins, on account of this thing which has happened, a thing which you know we deplore as much as we condemn. May I not hope to be allowed to call upon your sister, if only for a few minutes? not to-day, I know, but to-morrow, or the next day? Mrs. Grant, I have no right to say anything; but I think you can guess what it means to me."

Mrs. Grant's countenance softened, and she spoke more kindly than she had done during the interview. "I will not pretend to misunderstand you, Colonel Fitzwilliam; but, frankly, my sister would not see you just now, and it would do no good to anyone if you did see her. Her feelings have been deeply wounded—more deeply, probably, than you have any idea of. It would be far better for you not to think of it any more. You are shortly quitting Bath; we, too, shall be leaving for the summer; and at some future time we may, possibly, meet again, and be able then to gather up the threads of our friendship."

Fitzwilliam had turned very pale; for though partly prepared for the blow, he had hoped for some mitigating circumstances, and Mrs. Grant's words conveyed to him at that moment nothing but a counsel of despair. He could not immediately reply, but mastering himself with an effort, he said, steadily: "I only care for your sister's happiness, and whatever she wishes shall be done"; then bowed and quickly left the room.

Mrs. Grant, left alone, reflected with an aching heart upon the scene that had just closed. Resentful though she felt both on Mary's account and her own, yet she had been a very unwilling bearer of the message which she had delivered to her visitor. She had liked him, she liked him still; she had observed with keen pleasure the growing mutual attraction between himself and Mary, for she considered him *almost* worthy of that beloved sister. The event of the night before had not shaken that belief; whoever was to blame for it, she knew it was not Lady Catherine's nephew; and when she had partly recovered from her agitation she had tried to persuade Mary to do him equal justice, knowing well that he would not let the matter rest and that they would hear from him again. But Mary had been unpersuadable. The shock had been very great, not only from the incredible insult, but from the sight of the buried past, risen up again to be an undying reproach to her. All that she most bitterly regretted, of her own acts and of other persons', all that she most wished to forget, had been revived in her mind, exactly at a time when she had allowed herself to think that a new prospect of happiness might be opening up before her, in the midst of a set of people and circumstances with which the past should be wholly unconnected. But now the painful memories had intruded into the present, and, thrust upon her in a peculiarly galling manner, threatened to mar and taint the new life. Mary's mind was in a state of too great distress and tumult for her to see that their power of doing so lay in her own hands, that she only could let herself fall back into that wretched, listless, discontented condition from which she had so lately emerged; she only knew that the old influences had returned, and she was bitterly angry at the knowledge. In response to her sister's pleading she replied that she was determined not to see any of them again, they were all alike, proud and hard-hearted; they patronized her, they made her do things she did not want to do, and she wished she had never met one of them. Mrs. Grant ventured to speak a word on Colonel Fitzwilliam's behalf, but Mary, sore at heart and suffering the more for knowing she was unjust, replied that Colonel Fitzwilliam meant well, but really he ought to keep his most terrible old aunt in better order. She would not confess even to herself, far less to her sister, how much she had learned to care for the man whom she was now sending away—through wounded pride, perversity, anger . . . she could hardly have told for what reason.

Mrs. Grant could only endeavour to soothe and sympathize. She saw it was better not to continue the discussion of the subject, and looked forward to the lapse of time, and a change of scene and companionship, to restore to Mary some measure of comfort and serenity.

Of these blessings Colonel Fitzwilliam was in even greater need. He walked back to the hotel in an agony of mind such as he had never before in his life experienced. To the pain of his disappointment was added hopelessness, for he felt that the cause of his repulse lay beyond his power to remove. She was too deeply offended to see him, or to hear what he had to say, and as she would not do these things he thought she could not possibly care for him. And now, completely cut off from her, he had no chance of ever winning his way. His anger against his aunt remained unabated; but even were she persuaded to make all the reparation in her power, he had been told that it would be unavailing; there was nothing more that anyone could do.

He called his servant, and gave him directions for leaving Bath early on the following day, then made a pretence of dining, and threw himself into his chair for an evening of sad and solitary reflection. It was nearly half-past nine when a card was brought up to him, and it was with a start of surprise that he recollected he had been promised a visit from Mr. Yates.

That gentleman, well-bred, easy and talkative as usual, was shown into his room a few moments later. Colonel Fitzwilliam had never been more ill-disposed to receive a guest, but this one must be listened to, and it was a relief when he passed from his compliments and observations on the weather to the business at hand, which he introduced with an air of nonchalance, as if he had only just remembered what he had come to say.

"By the way, Colonel," he began, "I was calling on Lady Catherine this afternoon, and I took the opportunity of mentioning to her that subject which we were discussing this morning."

"Did you indeed?" returned Colonel Fitzwilliam. "And I hope you were able to convince her."

"Why, as to that," proceeded Mr. Yates, settling himself more comfortably in his chair, "I hardly know; I have seldom found a lady so hard to convince. But wishing to oblige you, my dear sir, I did my best; in all honesty, I did my best. I explained, as I told you I should, that she had been quite misled. Miss Crawford was not at all the sort of person she assumed her to be, and that was very nearly the end of our conversation; for I give you my word, Colonel, with all respect to her ladyship, that she became quite violent; declared that she did not want to hear the young lady's name or another word about her, that she was tired to death of the whole affair."

"It is probable she would not like to find she had made a mistake," said Fitzwilliam, as Mr. Yates paused, evidently expecting some comment.

"Well, no; I suppose that was what caused the sting; for it seemed as though she did not want to have to think well of Miss

Crawford, which could not be so really, you know. I told her what I had said, I mean, what I had intended to convey to the Ferrars, that I was surprised no one knew the story about her brother, and added that I could not imagine how anyone could twist and turn my remarks—merely general ones, made in no ill-natured spirit—to Miss Crawford's disadvantage. That set her off cross-questioning me, as to what there was at the back of it all, till I hardly knew where I was; and I finally had to point out to her that owing to my connection with the family I could not enter into the details of its affairs."

He paused again, and Fitzwilliam forced himself to say: "I am obliged to you for doing what you could, though I feared it might not be of much avail."

"True enough, I thought it was not going to be, but just at the end, her ladyship said, evidently with much resentment: 'There must be something in all this, though you deny it. Why should Mrs. Ferrars and Miss Steele concoct a story to tell me? Why should it be in their interest to vilify Miss Crawford? There was no reason why they should make the worst of what they had heard.' So, of course, in reply to that, I simply told her the truth: 'My dear Lady Catherine,' I said, 'you ask why; the reason is, as everyone knows, that Mrs. Ferrars was anxious to secure Colonel Fitzwilliam for her sister, and both the ladies were very much disappointed when he paid attention to Miss Crawford instead.' Why, Colonel, you are looking quite annoyed; don't trouble to protest, my dear sir; between friends, you know, it is not necessary."

"I wish you would confine yourself to talking of things you know something about, Mr. Yates," broke out the Colonel in extreme vexation; "this is not one of them."

"Nonsense, my good sir; not know anything about it! I could not fail to see what was before my very eyes. Before ever we started for your aunt's reception last night, Mrs. Ferrars and her sister were talking of you in a manner as to make me expect that it would be you who would be in attendance on Miss Steele all the evening—or at all events, that that was what she hoped for. Of course, I said not a word, but I could see that things turned out very differently. And if that were not enough, Ferrars himself told me all about it during the evening, of Miss Steele's fancy, and what they had planned, and so on. Really, I can hardly suppose that being as they are, such friends of Lady Catherine's, she should not have had some idea of it."

Fitzwilliam had not thought that anything was needed to complete his disgust and annoyance where the whole Ferrars party was concerned; but his tale of gossip and vulgar intrigue had that effect, and he was conscious of a strong desire to get rid of his visitor and hear no more of the whole nauseous affair. He rose, and again thanked Mr. Yates coldly for the trouble he had taken, and that gentleman, too courteous not to take the hint, rose also, though with evident unwillingness to end the conversation, and, drawing near the fire, stretched out a foot towards the blaze, and continued: "But I must not leave you with the impression that Lady Catherine was *not* convinced. On the contrary, I am inclined to think she eventually was, for her manner quite changed after what I had told her; she seemed first astonished at it, and showed considerable incredulity and indignation, asking how anyone dared to think or say such a thing, though, as I explained to her, sorry though I was to have given her any unpleasing intelligence, the idea did not emanate from me.

Upon that, she became calmer and seemed to be reflecting, then thanked me and asked to be excused, requesting me, if I was going back to the lodgings, to send Mrs. Ferrars and Miss Steele to her at once. I was not particularly anxious to be her messenger, and I fancy she saw this, for she called me back and said that it did not signify, she would write to them instead."

"I have gathered," said Fitzwilliam, "that Mr. Ferrars did not accompany you on this occasion."

"Oh, Lord, no! I should have mentioned that at first, but it escaped me. No, I could not persuade him to come. I fancy he had private information that his wife did not wish it."

"It was a pity, as he might have confirmed your statements, and afforded further proof to Lady Catherine," observed Colonel Fitzwilliam.

"He might have said something, no doubt, but I hardly think he would have succeeded if I had failed," was Mr. Yates's complacent reply. "My dear sir, I think you may sleep easily. If Lady Catherine is not persuaded of her error now, she never will be. At this moment she is very probably explaining to the Ferrars how unfortunately they have caused her to be mistaken."

Colonel Fitzwilliam felt tolerably certain that his aunt was doing nothing of the kind, and that the interview pictured by Mr. Yates was turning upon a different subject from Miss Crawford's rehabilitation. But even if Mr. Yates's explanation had caused the Ferrars to fall into disfavour, it would not mean that the harm they had done the day before would be wiped out; Lady Catherine would not be more inclined to forgive Miss Crawford because her own friends had made her angry. And angry Fitzwilliam guessed that she must be at the machinations which Mr. Yates had casually disclosed. It was always particularly offensive to her, and her nephew could conjecture that even the tact and ready wit of Mrs. Ferrars would not be able to avert the torrent of her displeasure. It was but poor comfort to him to feel assured that she would disapprove of Miss Steele as a possible wife for him, quite as much as Miss Crawford; and the very idea that such an alternative could have been thought of was so repugnant to him that he was glad to dismiss it from his mind. These people had done their worst, and whatever happened now, they could not injure Miss Crawford any more, or blight his own prospects more completely.

Mr. Yates having, as he considered, disposed of the subject in hand, proceeded to others, but Colonel Fitzwilliam contrived to cut him short, and to hasten his guest's departure, by indicating his wish to make preparations for his early start the following morning. Mr. Yates was desolated to hear that the Colonel would actually have left Bath by eight o'clock. He himself proposed leaving on the morrow; he had come intending to stay with the Ferrars for a week, but really everything was so infernally upset, owning to this tiresome affair—he declared Mrs. Ferrars had as good as called him a liar!—and that he was inclined to shorten his visit and go straight to his sister's place in Berkshire. He feared he could not be ready before twelve noon— would not Colonel Fitzwilliam delay in starting, and accept of a seat in his curricle? The Colonel regretted it was not in his power, but thought Mr. Yates was doing wisely in going away; and in his own mind added the heartily-expressed wish that that well-meaning gentleman had never come.

Chapter 7

THE DARCYS TRAVELLED SLOWLY, and they had not been at home for long before a letter from their cousin, who had gone direct to London from Bath, was received by Darcy. Colonel Fitzwilliam briefly related what had occurred after their departure, his application to Ferrars and Yates, with its more or less successful result, and his totally unsuccessful visit to Mrs. Grant. He omitted, of course, all reference to the second part of Yates's conversation with Lady Catherine, and stated his few facts with the smallest amount of comment, adding that he was grateful to his cousins for their kindness in the affair, but in the circumstances he thought it would be better not to return to Pemberley for the present, but to try to occupy his mind with some work. He had therefore accepted an offer made to him by one of his brother officers, to collaborate in writing a history of his regiment; and he proposed to remain in London, where he would have access to manuscripts and authorities. Darcy need have no fear that he would not correspond as regularly as usual, and he would call in at the Hursts' while they remained in town, so that he would be in continual touch with, as he said in conclusion, "the best friends a man ever had." Elizabeth sighed over this letter, but consoled herself presently with the thought that Mrs. Grant and Miss Crawford might possibly be in town during the summer. Darcy, on the other hand, was well satisfied with it, deeming that his cousin had acted with perfect uprightness, and he begged Elizabeth to give up the idea of trying to bring them all together at some future time. "Fitzwilliam, my dear, is of an age when he can be trusted to manage his own affairs, as this proves to us," he said to her.

"I do not think it proves much, except that Aunt Catherine is the cruel domineering old woman we always knew her to be," replied Elizabeth. "Poor Robert! to think of his being so abominably treated! Of course a true, honest man, as he is, was powerless among these insufferable people, who have not a word of truth amongst them."

Elizabeth indeed felt acutely disappointed at such a disastrous and unforeseen ending to her hopes. She blamed herself bitterly for her share in the disaster, and again regretted having persuaded Miss Crawford to come to the reception. She had written to Mary, according to promise, at the first opportunity, but not for more than a week after their return home was an answer received, and then it was a disappointment, like all the rest; merely a note, brief and tremulous, acknowledging Mrs. Darcy's kindness and apologies, begging that no more might be said as to the offence, and breaking off with assurance of the writer's good-will, but of her inability to express herself at greater length. The only sign of the real Mary appeared in the postscript, "I will write again by and by, dear Mrs. Darcy, if you will not mind very stupid letters." The lines of the note clearly showed the writer's shaken health, although her pride forbade her to make it her excuse. Elizabeth was grieved, and felt herself, for the time being, repulsed; she resolved to send, after a time, a cheerful letter on different subjects which might re-establish their friendship on new ground, so that the painful memories which Miss Crawford at present associated with the Darcy family might by degrees be eradicated.

These anxieties occupying her thoughts, and her time being taken up with her children and with Georgiana, who had returned to Pemberley in greatly improved health and spirits, she still did not fail to remark the absence of any news of Lady Catherine, for she had fully expected a speedy communication announcing the lady's triumph over Miss Crawford and ignoring all that had followed it. When her husband, therefore, in opening a letter one morning, observed that it was from his aunt, she was prepared for something considerably more disagreeable than its contents proved to be.

The letter began by announcing Lady Catherine's recent return home with her daughter, and the extreme pleasure of Mr. and Mrs. Collins, and of all their neighbours, in seeing them again. The worthy Rector and his wife had come up to Rosings to pay their respects on the very first evening. Mrs. Jenkinson had not yet come back from her vacation; she had in fact written to ask leave to stay for another week, which was excessively inconvenient, as dear Anne depended upon her so much. Anne's sensibility was indeed very great! She might not have inherited her mother's strength of character, but she had such warm affections! They sometimes led her to form attachments to people who proved unworthy of such devotion. There had just been an unfortunate instance of that during their stay at Bath.

Darcy, who had been reading the letter out loud to his wife and sister, hesitated at this point, but Elizabeth urged him to go on, saying that Georgiana knew all about the Ferrars, and was as anxious as herself to learn whether their reign was over.

"You and Elizabeth have probably heard something of the regrettable termination to my reception on your last evening in Bath. The young lady whom Elizabeth was so obstinately anxious for me to patronize must have acted at some former time with extreme imprudence, to say the least of it, though I really do not feel it to be my duty to investigate the rights and wrongs of the matter; still, the information I received was so positive, that I was bound to act upon it, and to point out to her that I regretted having brought her into my immediate circle of friends. I think I may say that she, or, at any rate, her sister, admitted the justice of my remarks. There I hoped the matter would have ended, but immediately afterwards I learned that the very persons from whom I had received this friendly warning about Miss Crawford had been themselves acting towards me in a scandalously hypocritical and underhand manner. You will guess that I refer to the Robert Ferrars and Miss Steele. I cannot enter into particulars of their conduct; suffice it to say that for all the latter part of their stay in Bath it has been a continual course of deception, of nefarious and vulgar schemes for their own aggrandizement. They have traded upon my kindness, and upon the warm regard which my poor innocent-hearted Anne displayed towards Miss Steele, to foster the most impudent designs. Never have I been so mistaken in people whom I regarded as deserving of my interest, never have I met with such vile ingratitude. You may imagine that I lost no time in sending for the whole family and informing them that our acquaintance was at an end, for the reasons I have given, and naturally I declined to listen to any defence; Miss Steele was utterly confounded, but Mrs. Ferrars, seeing that her whole plot was exposed, showed herself in her true colours; she lost control of herself, and used expressions more insolent than anyone has ever dared to do in my presence. Indeed, she was so determined to be heard, that it was only by leaving the room myself and sending my footman to show them out that I was able to rid myself of their presence. The man is a mere weak fool; I could see that by the way he ineffectually tried to control his wife, but even he seemed to have no sense of the impropriety of her conduct and her sister's.

"It is easily conjectured that after such a shock as this all enjoyment in Bath for me was entirely at an end. We should have left immediately, but that Anne was too unwell, on hearing what had happened, to travel for another week. My indignation at the whole affair is still beyond words."

Darcy paused, and Elizabeth asked: "Is that all the letter, Fitzwilliam?"

"Yes," he replied, "that is, she signs her name there, but there is a postscript which is evidently intended for your perusal."

Elizabeth took the letter which he handed to her, and read: "Were it not that out of pure perversity Elizabeth always chooses to act exactly the opposite to my advice, I should suggest that you proceed very cautiously in any further dealings you may have with the young lady I mentioned above." Elizabeth flushed deeply and laid down the letter, but immediately took it up again and re-read Lady Catherine's version of the Ferrars's defeat.

Meanwhile Georgiana was eagerly asking: "What does Aunt Catherine mean, Darcy? She writes strangely, does she not? How can those people have nefarious schemes or designs against her? She does not say how she knew they had."

"I hardly understand it all," said Darcy, "but you know your aunt has often been disappointed in people before, when they have desired more of her favour than she was prepared to give."

"Yes, she takes great fancies, and then forgets about people," returned Georgiana, "but she really seems to be dreadfully angry this time. Elizabeth says that you and she did not like those people, the Ferrars."

"No, we did not, for we considered them undesirable," replied Darcy, "and whatever reason your aunt has for quarreling with them, undoubtedly it is well she should have done so."

Georgiana perceived that she was not to hear more about the Ferrars, and dropped the subject, which, in fact, was what Darcy wished for. It was a distasteful one to him, for they had aroused his dislike more than most of his aunt's protégés, and he was glad to hear they had fallen from favour, without being interested in the reason for it. Elizabeth was quite aware of this, and accordingly refrained from any further discussion of her aunt's letter with her husband. She could not forbear a little private smile over the exposure of the "impudent designs," the nature of which she had quickly surmised; in the circumstances she thought they had hardly merited such severe strictures as those passed on them by Lady Catherine, and but for Mrs. Ferrars's unpardonable conduct towards Miss Crawford,

Elizabeth might have spared her some pity for the manner of her dismissal from Pulteney Street.

Georgiana took an early opportunity of asking Elizabeth about the references to Miss Crawford. "That is your friend of whom you told me, is it not, Elizabeth? I wonder what really happened, and why Aunt Catherine speaks of her so harshly. It seems very unkind."

"It was very unkind, Georgiana. Of course Aunt Catherine was entirely misinformed; she listened to some malicious gossip, and was terribly rude to Miss Crawford at the end of the evening after we left. I heard about it from Robert, who stayed later than we did. And the worst of it is, that in consequence Miss Crawford feels deeply wounded, I fear, as regards the whole family."

"Oh, I am so sorry. What a pity it is. Cannot anything be done? Surely you will be able to put it all right again some time, will you not?"

"I hope so; yes, of course, I shall do whatever is possible: I should be so extremely sorry to lose sight of her now."

"She must be charming, from all you say," commented Georgiana, and then asked rather shyly and with a deep blush: "Did Cousin Robert like her too?"

"Yes, he liked her very much, I think. You know, she played the harp, and he is so fond of anything to do with music."

"Yes, I know," said Georgiana; and added, in a low voice: "I remember he would always much rather have listened to my playing than have talked to me."

"Do not let yourself grieve, Georgiana," said Elizabeth, kissing the young girl's fair brow; "you know that Robert has the greatest possible regard for you, and you will find, next time you meet, that you are the best of friends."

Georgiana smiled rather sadly; she often felt that she must have not only fallen in the estimation of a cousin she revered, but that she must also be possessed of no qualities capable of inspiring affection, and what was even worse, of no heart of her own to give. Elizabeth understood her well, and tried often to give her more self-confidence and to raise her lowly opinion of herself; but though she was growing less reserved, and more disposed little by little to trust her own judgments, the old habits of timidity, of reliance on the guidance of those whom she loved, were still strong in her. Elizabeth would often refuse to decide a thing for her, but when she was helped to weigh it in the balance, to judge it by all the standards available, her choice could always be recommended for discretion and clear-sightedness.

The month of May was now nearly half-way through, and the time was approaching when James Morland was expected to pay a visit to his friends at Pemberley. So much of their stay at Bath had been productive of disappointment, that they looked back upon their acquaintance with this young man as its one circumstance of unalloyed pleasure. Darcy, whose regard for him had grown very warm, had received letters from home which enabled him, prior to leaving Bath, to inform Morland that a living in his gift would shortly be vacant, and that he would have the pleasure in offering it to Morland when the time came. This important communication had been received by the young clergyman with a depth of joy and gratitude which had increased the Darcys' satisfaction in being able to assist him. The living, though not a rich one, would suffice for his needs, as he possessed some capital advanced by his father: and its situation, in a hilly and bracing country district, made it most desirable for a person whose health, like his own, had to be considered. The conversation between himself and Darcy, which had been very short, had taken place only the day before the latter's departure, and Morland, still scarcely realizing his good fortune, had hurried round to the hotel the following morning to repeat his acknowledgments to both his friends and to make his adieux. There was time only for a very few words to be exchanged at the house door, and Morland found it difficult to express himself fluently on a subject which lay so near his heart, but Elizabeth and her husband set him at his ease with a few kind remarks, repeating cordially an invitation already given, that he come and stay with them on the conclusion of his visit to the Portinscales. Since their return home the resignation of the old Rector at Kympton, the living in question, had been made public. He was to leave within a few weeks; so that Morland's visit would afford him, as the rector-designate, an opportunity of getting to know the place and of meeting some of his future parishioners. Pemberley was not in the parish, for Kympton was eighteen miles away, but the link between the two places had always been strong, and the distance was frequently bridged, for Desborough Park, the home of the Bingleys, was the principal house in Kympton Parish, and only a mile and a half from the parsonage house. Morland's pleasure was extreme on hearing that his nearest neighbours would be the brother-in-law and favourite sister of Mrs. Darcy. Next to being within a stone's throw of the Darcys themselves, it was the best thing imaginable.

Morland arrived at Pemberley late one afternoon, just in time to prepare for dinner, and was introduced to Miss Darcy when they all assembled in the drawing-room before the meal.

Georgiana's intense shyness generally caused her to appear at a disadvantage with strangers, but there was something in the young man's open countenance and pleasing, unaffected manners that attracted everyone to him at first sight, and they were soon chatting together completely at their ease. Morland was deeply interested in everything that he could learn of his future home, and asked eager questions of his hosts. Georgiana had been so lately staying at Desborough, and had, while there, so frequently called on old Dr. and Mrs. Taylor, that she was able to give more particulars of the house and garden than her brother and sister were able to recollect. The evening passed quickly away with conversation and music, and Morland learned that on the following morning the whole party were to drive over to Desborough Park to dinner, starting early that they might have time to walk through the village and inspect the church and parsonage as well.

The weather proved propitious, and the drive, through some of the most beautiful vales of Derbyshire, was agreeable to all, but especially delightful to Morland, feeling as he did that he was within reach of the goal he had so long desired—restored health and the power to do the work he loved amid congenial surroundings. It was in vain that Darcy, not wishing to raise his hopes too high, told him that the parish was very scattered and the roads bad, that the climate was exceedingly cold and the distant cottages were almost inaccessible in stormy weather, that some of the farmers were people of a very independent way of thinking, difficult to get on with—he could discover no drawback, only fresh incentives to throw himself into his task. Elizabeth commended him for his enthusiasm, but added a sly reminder that he might be disappointed in the house; large, rambling and picturesque though it may seem when tenanted by the

Taylors and their seven children, it would, she feared, be an inconvenient residence to a bachelor.

"It will be too big, I have no doubt," responded Morland, "but, you know, I need not furnish more than a part of it. Besides, I intend, as soon as I am thoroughly settled to have my sister Sarah to stay with me if she can be spared from home."

Georgiana was interested in hearing of the sister, and James Morland at her request gave an account of his home at Fullerton, and of his brother and sisters, eight besides himself and Catherine, who was now Mrs. Henry Tilney. Catherine was evidently the favourite—there was a smile and a lightening of the eye when he spoke of her—he wished it had been possible for her to come and help him with his settling-in, but they lived such a great distance away—Woodston was forty miles away from Bath, quite at the other end of Somerset.

Mr. Darcy's chaise and four rolled through the village of Kympton not long after twelve o'clock, and paused to put down its owner, his sister and his young guest. There was so much to see, but Georgiana was an untiring walker, and intended staying with the gentlemen until the carriage should be sent back to bring them to Desborough in time for an early dinner. Elizabeth drove on for another two miles, and was presently alighting at the door of a handsome modern house built in the Italian style, and being warmly welcomed by Bingley and Jane, whom she had not seen for some weeks.

Bingley, on hearing what had become of the rest of the party, immediately decided to walk down to meet them; and the sisters strolled into the garden, for the weather was remarkably warm and sunny for that time of year, and they could venture to seat themselves upon a bench that was sheltered by an angle of the house, whence a beautiful view was obtained of the wide-spreading park, with its chestnut trees in full bloom and clumps of pink and white hawthorns. Desborough was not so imposing and extensive a place as Pemberley, but it was pleasant and homelike, and the grounds were particularly delightful, including as they did an orchard, a shrubbery, and lawns and flower-borders laid out in a series of terraces which sloped towards the park. The Bingleys took great pleasure in their garden, and had made many additions and improvements during the two years of their occupancy.

"I am overjoyed that you are come, Lizzie," began Jane, "for I have so much to tell and ask. I have not seen you since we brought Georgiana home, nearly a month ago. You really think she is better?"

Elizabeth warmly assented, and declared that Georgiana seemed in greater spirits than she had been for many months. Jane anxiously inquired after Fitzwilliam, and Elizabeth made out as good an account of him as she could, but as she was naturally not at liberty to mention what had passed at Bath, she could not perfectly satisfy Jane as to his well-being. Choosing a safer subject, she talked of Mr. Morland, praised his modesty, ability and good sense, and repeated her conviction that the Bingleys would find him a thoroughly agreeable neighbour. Jane listened with interest and promised every kind of help and support to the new Rector, who was to come with such strong recommendations; but she was clearly a little preoccupied, and Elizabeth, seeing this, asked what news she had to communicate.

"I am afraid it is not very good news," began Jane hesitatingly; "but—you will have guessed it, I expect—I have had a letter from Lydia. She is going abroad, Elizabeth, fancy, almost immediately! Poor Lydia! Wickham's regiment is ordered to the West Indies, and he insists on her going with him."

"I am not sure why it should be 'poor Lydia,'" returned Elizabeth, smiling; "you have such a terribly compassionate heart, Jane! I should think Lydia would like the West Indies very much, though she probably dreads the voyage."

"Oh, no, she does not think she will like them at all; it is so hot there, and she cannot bear the idea of being waited on by negro servants. She says there is only one consolation, very few of the ladies of the regiment are going; there will not be more than six of them, and no one as young as herself."

"Since so many are staying behind, I should have thought she could have arranged to do the same; though I confess I think it is much better she should be with Wickham."

"Yes, you are right, I believe, Elizabeth; she says she would rather have stayed in England, and that Wickham declares he does not particularly want her, only he cannot afford to keep up an establishment for her at home while he is abroad." Jane sighed. "It is very sad that they talk like that to one another; I only hope they do not mean it."

Elizabeth preferred to waive this question, and continued: "I suppose she goes on to ask you for money?"

Jane admitted that this was so, but said that Lydia would need a suitable outfit for the West Indies, and everything of that kind was very expensive, it appeared. She added that Lydia was anxious to come to Derbyshire before she went away, if a remittance for the journey could be sent, but Jane had not made any response to the suggestion.

"No, I do not think that that is at all necessary," Elizabeth remarked. "Well, Jane, of course I will give you some bank-notes to send with your own, on the usual condition that Lydia does not know from whom they come; but I only wish one could believe that they will be used for paying debts to the Newcastle tradespeople—of which there are sure to be plenty. Could you not persuade her to give you a statement of what she owes? You could then perhaps arrange for some of them to be paid off first."

"I will try; I will ask Bingley about it; but it is very difficult to help Lydia the way one would like. She does expect the most extraordinary things! What do you think of her inviting Kitty to go to the West Indies with her, my father, of course, paying all expenses?"

"I am past feeling any astonishment at Lydia's demands," Elizabeth said; "but I hope Kitty had too much good sense even to think such a thing possible."

"Oh, no, I think she knew it would not be allowed, though perhaps the idea was tempting to her, poor Kitty! But she had her promised visit here to plead as an excuse; she is coming, you know, towards the end of next month."

"It has been arranged, then? I am so glad to hear it; she must come on to Pemberley, and she and Georgiana will enjoy being together again."

"Yes, indeed; but I hope she will stay with me until the autumn. I wanted her to have come a little earlier; but she has received an invitation from some people called Knightley, in London, which she is very desirous of accepting, and my father sees no objection."

"Yes, I know of whom you mean, I think; they are friend of my Uncle and Aunt Gardiner's, and live in Brunswick Square."

"I fancy it is not those Knightleys, but relations of theirs; still, we shall hear all about it very soon, for I am expecting a letter from Kitty at any moment, to give me her direction in London and to tell me when she will be ready to leave, for Bingley is to go to fetch her."

"Is Bingley going to town? Then I wonder if it could possibly be arranged for him to escort Georgiana? Darcy had thought of going, but he would be very glad not to, if Bingley would not find it any inconvenience."

"I am sure Bingley would be delighted. She is going to the Hursts', is she not? I have heard mention of it."

"Yes, Mrs. Hurst and Caroline have both written, begging for a long visit from her. I do not think it can be for more than a month, as Aunt Catherine is sure to want her to go on to Rosings when she hears she is so near. Georgiana does not like being away from home for long, nor do we like to spare her."

"I can quite understand that. She has such a sweet disposition, such sympathy, and brightness and intelligence, that it is a joy to have her companionship. And you have improved her so much, Elizabeth. At one time I thought her very difficult to approach; but her manners have gained so much ease and elegance that everyone must be charmed with her from the first meeting. I often think Fitzwilliam must regret what he has lost."

"My dear Jane, let me assure you for the twentieth time that he does not regret it, nor can he be said to have lost what he never possessed. Their hearts were never united; but now you will see that each will marry happily, and their old friendship will survive unimpaired. If you had seen Fitzwilliam at Bath, you would have wasted no regrets on him. Now, shall we walk about a little? I want to discover if your lilacs are further advanced than ours."

Three o'clock brought back the remainder of the party, and Mr. Morland was introduced to Mrs. Bingley, and found her a most sympathizing listener to his enthusiasm over his new home. He was full of plans, and was interested in everything, from the beautiful little church down to the honeysuckle growing over the Rectory porch. Darcy had promised him to have certain repairs and renovations made as soon as the Taylor family should have quitted the house; and faulty chimneys and new wall-papers formed topics for a kind of discussion which Bingley thoroughly enjoyed, and he would have presented his young guest with the contents of several rooms at Desborough, and the greater part of the stables, if there had been the slightest chance of his accepting them.

There was not time to do more than begin on these important subjects to-day, for by half-past four the visitors had to be in the carriage again; but the proposal that Bingley should take Georgiana on her journey to London was brought forward and approved of by all concerned. Bingley was also going to his sister's house, and it was immaterial to him what day he arrived there, or how long he had to wait in London for Kitty Bennet. He thought he had heard something about a ball for which Kitty wished to stay, but was uncertain about the date.

It was decided that their next letters from their relations in town should determine the time of their departure.

Chapter 8

MORLAND WAS EASILY PERSUADED to prolong his stay at Pemberley until his induction to his new living should take place. This was expected to be not later than the end of June, for Dr. Taylor was anxious to hand over his duties to his successor as soon as possible. Morland was by no means an idler; he spent a considerable part of his time in study, and read and worked with Mr. Ferrars, helping him occasionally in parish duties. The acquaintance of these two men, formed directly after Morland's arrival, promised to ripen into a friendship; there were similarities in their characters that mutually attracted them, and on the tranquil simplicity of the life at the Parsonage Morland hoped to model his own. The Ferrars had so recently arrived at Pemberley, having, as has been said, exchanged livings with the former incumbent, and left Delaford shortly after Colonel Brandon's death, that there had not been time for much intercourse between them and the Darcys, though Elizabeth had been greatly pleased with what she had seen of Mrs. Ferrars. Since the former's return from Bath, and after her experiences there of the other branch of the family, she could appreciate fully the immense superiority of the Edward Ferrars over their relations. Ferrars himself was too quiet, diffident, and reserved a man to recommend himself easily, but in his wife all recognized a woman of a rare and noble nature, distinguished alike by the sweetness of her character and by its strength. The Darcys rejoiced in the increased opportunities of meeting afforded by the presence of their guest, and various walks, drives and out-of-doors excursions were organized, for which the glorious weather of early June afforded every opportunity.

The first diminution their party suffered was in the departure of Georgiana for London, which occurred on the seventeenth of the month. The visit had long been talked of, and Georgiana really looked forward with no little pleasure to seeing her old friends, for Caroline Bingley and Louisa took pains not to show to her, of whom they were exceedingly fond, the cold-hearted and worldly aspect of their dispositions; but when she found herself actually in the travelling carriage with Bingley, with her maid seated opposite; she felt, as she did every year, the sensation of leaving all that she cared for behind her, and of entering scenes alarming because unfamiliar. Bingley good-naturedly endeavoured to divert her in every way, talked of the pleasures awaiting her, and of the friends she would see in London, Kitty Bennet and Mrs. Annesley, besides her hostesses, and casually mentioned the possibility of her coming across Colonel Fitzwilliam. Georgiana had been prepared for this by Elizabeth, and had first shrunk from the idea; but afterwards became reconciled to the view put before her, that the first meeting, which must necessarily be painful, must come some time, and it would be best to get it over in a crowd, with a few ordinary words of greeting, which would put them on a comfortable footing for the future. She, therefore, made an effort to reply cheerfully to all Bingley's suggestions, and had not found the journey tedious when they drew up in Grosvenor Street in time for dinner on the third day.

Caroline and Louisa could not make enough of her, and the evening was spent in talking over the plans they had formed for her amusement, and in detailing the engagements they had entered into. It soon appeared that the ball which Bingley had mentioned was on their list; for they were also acquainted with Mrs. George Knightley, whose entertainment it was, and had secured invitations from her for their brother and their young friend. Bingley inquired of the date of the ball, explaining how it affected his movements; and his sisters endeavoured to conceal their surprise on hearing that Miss Kitty Bennet was staying with the Knightleys.

"I thought, when you spoke of coming to fetch her, Charles, that she was with her uncle and aunt in Gracechurch Street," said Miss Bingley.

"To tell the truth, I was not very clear about it myself," returned Bingley. "Jane told me that she was going to stay over this ball, but whether she was with the Gardiners or the Knightleys I did not make out until just before we came away. It does not make a vast deal of difference, to my thinking."

"There is certainly some difference; the Knightleys live in Portland Square, for one thing," replied Miss Bingley.

"Do they? I am glad of that, for it means I shall not have to drive so far round to pick Kitty up," was Bingley's cheerful answer, and he moved away to speak to Mr. Hurst, leaving his sisters to their speculations as to how Miss Bennet could have come to know the George Knightleys. Georgiana did not know, but conjectured it was through Mr. and Mrs. Gardiner; and the ladies, though they refrained from showing their perplexity, were even more puzzled to account for the uncle who lived in Cheapside being acquainted with such people of fashion.

"Have you seen anything of Fitzwilliam, Louisa?" inquired Bingley of his eldest sister, when he came to have his coffee-cup refilled."

"Really, Charles, what a foolish question to ask," replied Mrs. Hurst, with affected carelessness. "Of course we see him frequently when he is in town."

"Very good; I hope he will come round while I am here, and, if not, I shall get you to give me his direction, for I must certainly look him up before I go back."

Mrs. Hurst made a vague answer, for both she and her sister were sincerely anxious to spare Georgiana any embarrassment, and they would not of their own accord have referred to Fitzwilliam until they knew how she was able to bear the mention of his name in public. Caroline immediately began speaking of another subject, but Georgiana, divining their intentions, felt that she must not indulge in a foolish sensibility which might give her friends a false impression of the state of things; so, summoning all her courage, she said, with a deep blush but a tolerably firm voice: "Yes, I hope my cousin may be in town this month. Elizabeth and my brother gave me many messages for him, if I should see him."

She was conscious that the ladies were looking at her in surprise, but that Bingley noticed nothing but the amount of milk

Louisa was putting in his coffee was a great help, and Caroline, the next moment, said quietly: "Oh, yes, no doubt he will call," which made it unnecessary for Georgiana to say any more. Bingley, having secured his cup, next produced a notebook and proceeded to write down the address of Fitzwilliam's lodgings and the name of his club, and, as an afterthought, the various engagements to which he had been pledged by his sisters. Georgiana found that Mrs. Hurst and Caroline were anxious she should go with them on the following day to call in Portman Square and meet Mrs. George Knightley.

Mrs. Knightley, formerly Emma Woodhouse, had, since her marriage been able to enjoy a larger measure of the social power and influence in the use of which she had always delighted. Since Mr. Woodhouse's death she had persuaded her husband to go into Parliament, and except for short visits to Donwell, they now lived entirely in London—an arrangement which just suited Emma, who had long desired some stir and variety in her life, after having spent so many unbroken years in a country village. Mr. Knightley still took the greatest interest in the farming of his property, and as soon as he was trustee to his sister-in-law, Mrs. John Knightley, for the estate of Hartfield, which he passed to her on her father's death, he found as much to do out of London as in it; while Emma, though fond of Donwell, had grown weary of the neighbourhood, and took a keen pleasure in forming round her in London a large circle of acquaintances, whom she loved to entertain, and in whose characters and careers she took the deepest interest.

Mrs. Knightley's ball had become an annual fixture in the month of June, and this year she had a special incentive for

giving it and for making it as gay as possible. At her sister's
house she had met Mrs. Gardiner, whose husband had long
been a close friend in business of Mr. John Knightley. Mrs.
Gardiner was chaperoning a niece, Miss Catherine Bennet, a
slender, blooming young girl, and pretty without being very
striking; but Mrs. Knightley was impressed with her pleasing
manners, and the enthusiasm with which she received the
prospect of a theatre party which was being discussed on that
occasion. It was the work of a moment for Emma to decide that
she must ask her sister to bring Miss Bennet to the ball; but during the remainder of the evening, while she considered and
observed, an improvement on the first idea suggested itself; Miss
Bennet must be invited to stay in Portman Square for the great
occasion. What better arrangement could there be? Isabella
would not want to stay late, but young girls liked to dance till
the last moment, and she, Emma, would have the benefit of Miss
Bennet's help in the preparations, and would be able to introduce her to her partners beforehand. Yes, Miss Bennet was certainly very pretty, prettier than she had appeared at first—such
a slim, upright figure, such a profusion of hair, such a delicate
fairness of complexion; she would be a great success! It would be
as delightful as when last year, the girl who was at the ball as
Mrs. Knightley's special friend and protégée had finished the
evening triumphantly becoming engaged to the most eligible
man present, Sir William Manvers. Emma felt a thrill at the recollection. The event had justified all her admiration for Sophia
Lennox, and Mr. Knightley, who had been so sceptical, had been
obliged to admit that sometimes people did marry those whom
one had destined for them. There was no Sir William Manvers

this year, it was true; but Miss Bennet was still young, and there was plenty of time for the right man to appear. In fact, it was really only her due that she should be properly taken out in London, in order that she might have every chance, and this her aunt, Mrs. Gardiner, was quite evidently not able to give her.

What wonder that the upshot of these reflections was a courteous note to Mrs. Gardiner, begging for the pleasure of a visit from Miss Bennet as soon as her stay in Gracechurch Street should be concluded. Kitty was in transports of happiness when all was arranged and she found herself actually Mrs. George Knightley's guest, with a ball in prospect, and each day one round of visits and shopping and other delights, with intervals only long enough to admit of changing one elegant gown for another, for her mother and sisters had taken care she should be provided with an ample wardrobe. She soon ceased to regret not having been allowed to accompany Lydia to the West Indies, and before many days were over had discovered a reason to rejoice that she had not gone.

Among Mrs. Knightley's frequent visitors at this time was a young naval lieutenant named William Price, whom she had met a short time previously at the house of the same Mr. Yates who had paid a visit to Bath in the preceding spring. Mr. Yates lived in Cavendish Square, and as his wife was a first cousin of William Price's, they had begged the young man to make their house his home whenever he happened to be in London. Young Price had lately been attached to a ship of the line, the *Andromeda,* which he had been obliged to put into Portsmouth for repairs, and he had been employing some of the period of his enforced leisure in taking up a course of signalling and gunnery, as he was extremely anxious to gain promotion as speedily as possible; but he had found that it was necessary to use other means than those of mere hard work, and at the present time he was living in London, keeping in touch with the Admiralty and endeavouring to recommend himself to every high official and person of influence with whom he could contrive to become acquainted. In the intervals he paid hasty visits to his sisters, who were settled in Northamptonshire, and to his mother at Portsmouth; and being a young man of excellent address, great charm of manner and marked abilities, he had gained a deserved popularity, and could not help enjoying the gaiety of London life, available to him through the hospitality of numerous friends. Mrs. Knightley was extremely pleased with him, and with his next brother, David, who was a clerk in the India Office, and both young men found it a very agreeable house to come to, especially when to the welcome of their hostess was added that of a pretty girl who, warm-hearted and impulsive, did not attempt to conceal her pleasure in their company.

David Price was two or three years her junior, and in him Kitty Bennet found only a merry and boyish companion; but the manliness of the young sailor aroused different feelings, and it was not long before she realized that the visits of William Price were becoming the most important thing in her life. She dreamt of him before he came, she had no eyes for anyone else when he was present, and she treasured his words when he had gone; and although she could not honestly read into those words more than a passing friendliness, yet she allowed herself to cherish hopes that each *next* time there might be something warmer. Poor Kitty had secretly longed to be married ever since she was sixteen; and now at last it seemed as if Destiny itself was working for her, in placing her with so kind a hostess, who was always giving invitations and affording opportunities, and in sending her such a splendid hero of romance to fall in love with, for a hero he was, of a campaign at sea, when he had distinguished himself as much by bravery as he had on shore by industry; a hero with good looks, an assured position, and prize-money saved, and at the present moment with nothing particular to do but fall in love with Miss Kitty Bennet! It was impossible not to feel, under the circumstances, that the course of events was plainly marked out. Mrs. Knightley certainly thought so too, and although she refrained from definite statements, her sympathetic attitude encouraged Kitty to talk herself into hope and self-confidence.

The importance of the ball itself in the great scheme of things was not overlooked, and Emma even dreamt now of a brilliant dénouement like last year's. She had invited a large number of people, and was anxious to have as many dancing couples as possible, so Mrs. Hurst's request for permission to bring her brother and Miss Darcy was warmly acceded to, and it was only a matter of regret that their friend Colonel Fitzwilliam could not be induced to go to any balls this season. Kitty was delighted at the prospect of meeting Georgiana again, and when the call spoken of by Mrs. Hurst was being paid, on the day following Georgiana's arrival, she availed herself of a pause in the conversation, and a nod and a smile from Mrs. Knightley, to ask her friend to come to another room for a few moments, on the plea of showing her some new possessions.

Georgiana duly admired the bonnets and pelisses, and the gold chain which was Mrs. Knightley's present, and the rose-coloured ball dress which was to make its first appearance on the much-talked-of occasion. Kitty's head was evidently full of this event; she dwelt on it constantly, and from her quick nervous manner Georgiana guessed at some kind of special preoccupation with the subject.

"And so you are very happy here, Kitty? Perhaps I need not ask that," she said, as Kitty turned to unfold another new muslin gown.

"Oh, very, very happy, perfectly happy," exclaimed Kitty with eagerness. "Mrs. Knightley is so kind, and such nice people come here, you have no idea, Georgiana. Now, do look; is not that beautiful? A real India muslin, and the colour just suits me. You ought to like it, for I bought it with some money Elizabeth gave me."

"Yes, dear, I do like it, of course," returned Georgiana; "but tell me some more about yourself. How long were you with the Gardiners?"

"I forget just how long, but I came here on the first of June. Oh, I do not know how ever I shall be able to leave! Georgiana, I must tell you! I have been longing to do so, and yet I do not know how I can, after all, for it has not really happened yet.

"Of course you have guessed," she went on, in answer to Georgiana's affectionately inquiring glance; "it can only be one thing: but pray do not mention it to anyone, for no one has any idea of it except Mrs. Knightley. It is so wonderful! Georgiana, do you believe in love at first sight?"

"I have never thought about it," answered Georgiana honestly, "but I should think it might be possible."

"Indeed, indeed, it is possible! It does happen. When you see him, you will know how easily. You will see him on Tuesday night; I do wonder what you will think of him. You must be sure to tell me quite truthfully."

"Dear Kitty, you cannot think how glad I am. You mean you are engaged, or just about to be?"

"Oh, no, no, no!" exclaimed Kitty, "you do not understand. I think—I hope—but I do not even know if he cares. Sometimes I feel sure he does, and then, again, he seems to be perfectly indifferent, and it is so terrible then, more terrible than you can imagine. But you will see—you will judge for yourself; I shall depend so much upon you for comfort and counsel, especially if Bingley asks him to come down and stay at Desborough, as I mean to persuade him to do."

Georgiana was not much enlightened, and her shyness and natural reserve made her hesitate to ask questions on such a subject, which, had she been Kitty, she could not have mentioned to any living creature. But Kitty was evidently longing for sympathy, and poured out her hopes and fears and her reasons for both, mingling with them a description of William Price, painted in the most vivid colours and emphasizing his courage and distinction as an officer, his amiability as a man, his perfection as a ball-room partner, and the high opinion Mr. Knightley and all sensible men had formed of him. Georgiana listened, and was interested almost against her will; she had known Kitty to take fancies several times before for persons who had not returned her regard or thought of doing so; but in this case, from what she could gather, the young man seemed really to deserve Kitty's enthusiasm; they had met under Mrs. Knightley's auspices, he had been very often at the house, and certainly, everything considered, it was much more likely that he should fall in love with Kitty than not. Nevertheless, she hardly knew how to answer her; to encourage her in hopes which might prove false would be the cruellest kindness, so, while, murmuring her wishes for her friend's happiness, she agreed that she must wait for the evening of the ball before she could really tell how far Kitty's dreams were likely to be realized.

They talked so long that eventually she had to propose a return to the drawing-room, fearing to be guilty of discourtesy towards Mrs. Knightley; but she was glad that only a moment was left for Kitty's hurried inquiry about her own affairs, as they hastened down the staircase, and that she could therefore dismiss the subject with a light word. Kitty was scarcely satisfied, but finding that Georgiana could not be induced to speak of Colonel Fitzwilliam, returned to her own all-absorbing topic with the remark, "I do wish you could meet someone just like my dear Mr. Price!"

Chapter 9

THE NEXT FEW DAYS passed rapidly for both girls, and were so full of engagements that they were not able to arrange another meeting, and Georgiana deeply regretted the fact that, except for a glimpse of her at the ball, she should not see Kitty again before Bingley's departure from town. She could only hope that all would go well, and looked forward to a fuller intercourse in Derbyshire in a few weeks' time. Meanwhile, there were many friends to see, and Georgiana would have enjoyed herself thoroughly had she not dreaded the first meeting with Colonel Fitzwilliam, which she felt hanging over her, since Bingley had called on the Colonel and reported him to be in town, but which she did not know when to expect. A slight change in her plans, necessitating a short absence from Mr. Hurst's house, led her to imagine that it would be temporarily averted; but on the very day of the ball, when she and her hostesses had remained at home, and a larger number of visitors than usual happened to be in the room, she experienced a painful shock on hearing his name announced and on seeing him walk into the room. Next moment she was angry with herself for losing her composure, even momentarily, and bracing herself for a possible encounter, she endeavoured to continue to bear her part in a conversation with two or three of Mrs. Hurst's friends, who, she realized gratefully, were strangers to her until that day. It was some minutes afterwards that she was aware of Colonel Fitzwilliam approaching her, guided by Miss Bingley, whose kindly intentions of making the occasion as ordinary as possible only served to intensify its discomfort. Georgiana, however, thought the fault all hers, as, not reassured at all by Caroline's cheerful "Colonel Fitzwilliam was so glad to hear you were staying with us, Georgiana," she found herself only just able to give him her hand with an almost inaudible greeting, while her face, suffused with deepest blushes, must, she felt, have made her noticeable to all around. It was Colonel Fitzwilliam's part to set her at her ease, which he did, to some extent with a few kindly and naturally-expressed sentences, inquiring about her journey, and the health of those she had left behind.

Georgiana presently ventured to let her eyes rest on him, and was startled to see how much older he looked even in the short time since she'd seen him, and how ill and worn. A terror seized her heart that she might be guilty of these altered looks, but it passed in an instant; there was not any doubt that their parting had been for the good of both; but poor Cousin Robert, it was plain to see that he had been suffering, from whatever cause, and her sympathy went out to him unconsciously, even while she could hardly talk to him from embarrassment of knowing that Caroline Bingley was standing by, apparently occupied with other people, but drawing conclusions from every word she could hear.

"I had intended coming to see you, anyhow, Georgiana," said Fitzwilliam, "but I am very busy, you know—I do not go out much; and you live in a perpetual whirl of gaiety, I expect." He smiled as he spoke, and Georgiana tried to answer in the same spirit, telling him that they had a good many plans, and people were very kind, but she was not really in a whirl, in fact, the very next morning she was leaving for Grosvenor Street for a few days, to spend them quietly with her old friend Mrs. Annesley, who lived in Hans Place, quite away from the bustle of London.

"Mrs. Annesley?" repeated Fitzwilliam; "of course I remember her; she will enjoy having you, but how have Mrs. Hurst and Miss Bingley become reconciled to parting with you even for a week?"

Georgiana explained hurriedly that it had been quite a sudden engagement; her old friend had been to see her, and had begged for a short visit from her, if possible, for Mrs. Annesley was on the point of going to India, to live with a married son who had lost his wife, and she might not have the opportunity of seeing her former pupil again for many years. Georgiana had been happy in the opportunity of going to her friend at such a time; her present hostesses had acquiesced, and a week was to be spared to Mrs. Annesley.

"But it will be made up in Grosvenor Street next month, I assume," said Colonel Fitzwilliam.

"I hardly know—I believe Elizabeth and my brother want me at home again soon—but of course I like being here too," said Georgiana, stumbling over her words, and feeling that she was disgracing herself. If only Caroline would not stand there and seem to be observing them so closely! She did not believe it would be so distressing to talk to Cousin Robert if only they could be together somewhere among strangers. This thought impelled her to ask him, quite at random, for she had every reason to know what his reply would be, whether he was going to Mrs. Knightley's ball.

"I am afraid not, Georgiana. I think I am getting too old for balls; but I wish you a great deal of pleasure there."

"Oh, Cousin Robert, you are not too old, but you—" she checked herself in this impetuous speech, and ended rather confusedly, "but you look tired"; which was not what she would have wished to say.

Her cousin glanced kindly at her, but turned her remark off with a laugh; and as he seemed about to move away, Georgiana, in desperation, and astonished at herself, said timidly: "I hope we may meet again, even though you do not go to balls."

"I hope so, too, Georgiana But of course we shall. I must come some morning and take you all to Kensington Gardens."

Georgiana felt that this would not be a great improvement on the present situation, but she could not say any more, and supposed their conversation was at an end, when Fitzwilliam, who had made a step from her, seemed struck with a sudden idea, and turned to her again, saying: "May I come and call on you at Mrs. Annesley's? She will perhaps remember me and—I may not be in town later on."

Georgiana flushed with surprise and pleasure, and her eager assent left Fitzwilliam in no doubt as to his reception. He stayed only to assure himself of the number of Mrs. Annesley's house, then bowed and walked rapidly away, as Miss Bingley approached with the evident intention of breaking up their conclave. Georgiana had to submit to a certain amount of comment from the sisters, who, while condoling with her for having had to pass through a uncomfortable few minutes, appeared surprised that she should have been able to talk to Colonel Fitzwilliam, but she herself felt nothing but happiness in having met her cousin again, and found it possible to think of being on those terms with him that Elizabeth had predicted.

She spent a part of the afternoon in writing a long letter to her sister, telling her what had happened; but she did not like to send an account of her cousin that might alarm them at home, so she contented herself with saying that he was not looking at all well, and that she wished Elizabeth would persuade him to go down to Pemberley, as he must be working too hard in London. She concluded her writing with the words, "I will leave this open till to-morrow, dear Elizabeth, that I may tell you about the ball, and how Kitty looked."

Kitty, indeed, was the chief subject of her thoughts when they dwelt upon the prospect of the evening, and when the time for dressing arrived Kitty's rose-coloured silk occupied her mind far more than her own white satin and pearls. When Mr. and Mrs. Hurst's party entered the ante-room where Mrs. Knightley was receiving her guests, the two girls managed to exchange a few words, and Georgiana gathered that the hero of the evening had not yet appeared, but Kitty was separated from her by the crowd of arrivals, and so it eventually came about that it was their hostess who performed the introduction of Mr. William Price to Miss Darcy.

Georgiana's first thought, when she looked at the noble brow and clear blue eye of the young man, was that Kitty's attachment was easily understood, and each moment that she spent in his company strengthened that assurance. She was desirous of liking him, eager to find everything to praise in the admired—and perhaps the admirer—of her friend, and the opportunity came at once in the infectious gaiety and good spirits of the young man and the unaffected warmth of his manner.

He asked her for the honour of her hand in several dances; but the first two, she noticed, he danced with Kitty, and from the sparkle in Kitty's eye, and her quick movement as he approached to claim them, Georgiana conjectured that the engagement had been made previously.

When Georgiana's turn came, among the excellencies that she discovered in her partner was that of being a perfect dancer; and, moreover, one who moved through the set as if he enjoyed every step. Somewhat shyly she commented on this.

"Yes, indeed, Miss Darcy, I am fond of dancing; I began very early, when I was such a small person that you probably wouldn't have seen me in a room, much less have danced with me. We all used to jump about as children, I believe; and on board ship one somehow managed to learn, so as to be ready for the balls."

"Were there balls so often?" asked Georgiana.

"Yes; wherever we were stationed somebody always seized the opportunity to give a ball, either a private person, or the Governor, or the regiment, or someone. There seems to be a connection established in people's minds between naval men and dancing; anyhow, as soon as there were a few days' quiet, someone would produce musicians and a waxed floor, and we were expected to go and perform. So I decided that I had better like it."

"You are a very fortunate person to be able to be able to like what you have to do," said Georgiana, highly diverted.

"It is not a matter of fortune, is it? Anybody can do it," rejoined William Price. "I am sure you can, Miss Darcy."

"No, indeed; I dislike very much some things I have to do."

"But if you found you positively had to do them, and there was no way out, then you would decide to like them, would you not? It would make them so much easier."

This was a new idea to Georgiana, and she considered it a little before replying, with a smile: "I am sure there are some things I should never like doing, such as sitting on the back seat of a carriage."

"I know that it is disagreeable to some people, but I am sure, if one thought long enough, one could find a way to make it less so," said the young lieutenant, with great earnestness. "For instance"—he considered—"when the window was open the rain and wind would not do so much damage to the feathers in a lady's bonnet as if she were opposite; and at night one could shut one's eyes and imagine one was travelling forwards—it would be difficult to tell the difference." He looked inquiringly at Georgiana, who was so much entertained by his arguments that she said, laughingly: "I was right in calling you fortunate, Mr. Price, for you seemed to have secured a sovereign remedy against all ills. Do tell me how you would console yourself if you slipped down now and broke your leg, so that you could not dance any more for a long time? I should like to know whether your principle always holds good."

"Now, Miss Darcy, you are driving me into a corner. I only said if I positively had to do the distasteful thing and there was no way out. I beg to inform you in the plainest language that there is a way out of your suggestion—that is, not to fall and break my leg, and it is the way I mean to adopt. But if such a thing did happen to me, I should certainly try to console myself—as yet I am not quite sure how—yes, I have thought of a method, but I do not think I had better tell you what it is."

"He means he would have Kitty to sit beside him and talk to him," thought Georgiana. "I wonder what he would be like if he were ill? He would have just the same merry smile, I believe." Aloud she said: "I am not so strong-minded as you, Mr. Price, I'm afraid. I should never be able to think of any way of consoling myself for a broken leg."

"I hope you will never have to endure anything one-twentieth a part disagreeable, Miss Darcy," her partner replied, dropping his gay manner for a moment. "Although it helped me to get through my examinations, even now I cannot think very kindly of it."

"Were you—has it actually happened to you?" exclaimed Georgiana, with a horrified face; and she never felt less pleasure at the arrival of a new partner than at that moment. Most unwillingly she placed her arm in his to be led away, wanting far more to hear the history of William Price's misfortune; while the young man, full of concern at having startled her, walked a few steps beside her to say: "It is all right, Miss Darcy, because, you see, that guarantees that it will not happen again to-night."

Bingley, who was her partner, asked the name of her companion, and Georgiana told what she knew of him, describing him as Kitty's friend. Bingley recollected having heard of him from Kitty, and pleased with his appearance, and always attracted by a new face, expressed a wish to know him, and Georgiana looked forward to making the introduction when her dances with Bingley should be over. This, however, was not to be. Kitty and Mr. Price were dancing together, and occasionally passed them in the set, when Georgiana could observe her friend's flushed cheek and air of radiant happiness; but at its conclusion they were swept away in a crowd, and Bingley and Georgiana, looking round for chairs, were accosted by Mr. Knightley, with the request to present Mr. and Mrs. Yates, who were anxious to know them. The name was unfamiliar to both, and so were the faces of the couple who approached—Mr. Yates with his usual aspect of complete self-satisfaction, and his wife, a woman of fashion, with a considerable share of good looks, but an expression of countenance from which weariness and impatience were never long absent.

The lady fell to Bingley's share, and Georgiana, on her part, learned from Mr. Yates that he had heard her name and wished for the pleasure of her acquaintance, as he had already made that of her brother and sister in Bath. Georgiana replied to inquiries after their health and Colonel Fitzwilliam's, whom, Mr. Yates told her, he knew very well indeed, and he desired to send his compliments to the Colonel, if Miss Darcy should be seeing him. "He is in London, I believe?" Georgiana assented.

"Ah, yes, I understood that; and the lady is in town, too, I fancy." Georgiana's look in reply to this was so blank that Mr. Yates, evidently not caring to trust himself in the deep waters of explanation, continued: "Do present him my cordial regards, and say I hope he has forgiven me. I was so unfortunate as to do him a little disservice, but it was easily put right; I saw to that myself. Lady Catherine de Bourgh, I am sure, had made *amende honorable*. You know Lady Catherine, Miss Darcy? Your aunt? Of course, I beg your pardon; I should have recollected. Do, pray, remember me to her, too. You were not in Bath this year, were you? Well, you did not lose much; I have known pleasanter seasons."

Georgiana only bowed; Mr. Yates's familiar allusion to Colonel Fitzwilliam had not pleased her, and an instinct, which she had not time to analyse, led her to connect it with her cousin's depressed spirits. The next moment her companion introduced a more welcome subject by saying: "I think I saw you dancing with my young cousin, William Price; a smart young fellow, is he not?"

"Is he your cousin?" asked Georgiana, in some surprise.

"Yes, or rather, my wife's, through the mother; but we have all known him for years, he seems quite like one of ourselves, and spends half his time at our house when in town. Though I often tell my wife it is no compliment to us, for he is for ever playing with our children; we cannot get him out of the nursery."

Georgiana felt that this was just as it should be; Mr. Price's being fond of the children accorded him well with the "merry, kind smile" that was so characteristic of him. She ventured upon an inquiry as to his naval career, and Mr. Yates, who liked nothing better than to be talking either of himself or of those belonging to him, immediately entered upon a description of William's notable conduct at the battle of St. Domingo, and the extraordinary courage he had displayed in the taking of a French ship and in defending the colours of his own. Bingley's attention was caught, and Georgiana was grateful to him for asking questions to prolong the story, and for interpolating expressions of admiration which she felt but could not utter. The more she saw and heard of him, the more delighted she was with the young hero, for such he now appeared to be; and the more she commended Kitty's good sense in bestowing her devotion upon such a worthy object. She looked forward to further opportunities of hearing from Mr. Price's own lips the account of some of his adventures; but recollecting that if events took the much-desired course there would be plenty of such opportunities, she decided that it would be best to employ the remainder of the time which she might spend in his company that evening by discoursing of Kitty, in the hope of gaining some assurance of the strength of his inclinations. He knew her to be Kitty's friend, and the subject of Kitty would naturally become the chief bond between them when they came to know each other a little better.

Shortly after supper, William Price claimed her hand for a second time; and at the first interval in the dance long enough for any connected conversation, Georgiana began: "Who is that dancing with Miss Bennet? Do you know, Mr. Price?"

"It is a Mr. Churchill, a great friend of the Knightleys. I believe he is rather agreeable, but Miss Bennet tells me she does not like him," replied William Price, laughing.

"Why should she not like him, I wonder?" asked Georgiana.

"Oh, I hardly know. Just a fancy, I think. He and I had a great set-to here one day—an argument, I mean; and I was fairly worsted—it was about foxhunting, so perhaps I deserved to be; but Miss Bennet very kindly took my side, and was quite vexed with Mr. Churchill when he retired with the honours of war."

"Kitty is so loyal to her friends," said Georgiana.

"Yes, she is a delightful girl, and Mrs. Knightley, too, is the kindest person imaginable. She has been so good to both my brother and myself, and I have never enjoyed my leave so much."

"It must be a very pleasant house to stay in," said Georgiana. "Miss Bennet is very sorry to be going away, I know."

"Yes, is it not a pity she has to go? And down to the depths of the country, too. I must not disparage it, Miss Darcy, for I am reminded that it is your home as well; but when people go so far off one is desperately afraid of not seeing them again. You are not leaving town with Miss Bennet, are you?"

Georgiana was explaining their respective plans when the summons came for them to rejoin the set; but an interruption soon occurred in the shape of a slight accident. A lady dancing next to William Price, in turning sharply, trod upon her dress, with the result that she slipped and fell upon the polished floor with her foot twisted under her. The young lieutenant sprang forward, lifted her with skillful and gentle touch, and carried her, pale and suffering, to an adjoining room, where Mrs. Knightley and several friends hastened to her aid. A servant was sent for a surgeon, and William Price returned to Georgiana with the news that, pending his arrival, the lady was being treated for what appeared to be a severe sprain.

"Poor thing!" said Georgiana, trembling. "I am so sorry for her. It must have caused intense pain. I was afraid she might have broken it."

"No, it is bad enough, but fortunately it is not broken; I could perceive that," replied the young man. "You must not prognosticate such sad things, Miss Darcy; you see they very nearly come true."

Georgiana looked into his face for enlightenment, then broke into a smile. "Oh, Mr. Price, you are unkind to assume that I was responsible for it. I only suggested a broken leg, and it was you who said it had been a reality in your case. How did it happen? Was it in action?"

William led her to a seat, as the incident had unnerved her for more dancing, but could not be persuaded to give a narrative in the style of Mr. Yates; he only laughed and said that it had been about as glorious an affair as falling down in a ball-room. "One of our fellows had foolishly got himself into a very awkward place at the storming of a fort, and I was so stupid as to get in the way of a shower of falling rocks, one of which, when it reached me, decided to stay as close to me as it could; so I was severely reprimanded, and had to spend six weeks in hospital at the very busiest time."

Georgiana listened with interest, certain that there was another version of the story which would show her companion up in a different light, and she inquired: "What did you say about examinations?"

"Only that I had some books, and a good friend who helped me to the utmost of his power, so that while I was lying by I contrived to work up my subject enough to have scraped through."

They talked for some time longer, until William had to go in search of his next partner, while Georgiana was carried off by her hostess, who placed her at a small table to drink coffee with herself and Mr. and Mrs. Gardiner. The Gardiners were, of course, no strangers to Georgiana, and she showed the pleasure she felt in meeting them again.

"Is it not kind of Mrs. Gardiner to have lent Kitty to me for so long, Miss Darcy?" said Mrs. Knightley. "I feel I can ill spare her now; I shall miss her after the happy time we have had together."

Georgiana said what was proper, and Mrs. Gardiner added: "Perhaps she will be able to come to you another year."

"Indeed, I hope so. I should like her to come any time; but another year, you know, she may not be so free; the claims of a house of her own may be paramount."

"Certainly they may be; but it seems early to anticipate that," said Mrs. Gardiner.

"Early? Oh, no, I do not think so. I shall not be at all surprised to be asked to help in buying Kitty's wedding clothes before Christmas," returned Mrs. Knightley, smiling mysteriously.

Mrs. Gardiner expressed inquiring surprise, while Georgiana listened with interest for what Mrs. Knightley would say, regarding her as the chief authority in the affair, as far as it had gone.

Her hostess proceeded: "It is quite between ourselves, you know, Mrs. Gardiner; I know I am perfectly safe in mentioning it, as you are Kitty's aunt and Miss Darcy her greatest friend; and you can imagine whether it is a pleasure to me to find that two young people in whom I am interested are so much interested in each other."

"Undoubtedly," said Mrs. Gardiner; "but pray enlighten me, Mrs. Knightley, as to who the other person is."

"You have met him to-night, Mrs. Gardiner, the young naval officer, Mr. Price, whom I introduced to you."

Mrs. Gardiner was very anxious to learn more particulars, and Mrs. Knightley gave her full information as to William Price's career and prospects, while as to Kitty, she affirmed she had every reason to believe that both were equally attracted, and that an engagement would shortly be formed between them, subject to the approval of their friends.

Mrs. Gardiner agreed that it was very good news if the young man was all Mrs. Knightley believed him, and remarked what a delight it would be to her sister, Mrs. Bennet, who had always wanted Kitty to be settled.

"Mr. Price *is* all we think him, I can assure you; Mr. Knightley will answer for him. But, pray, do not mention a word of this to anyone; let it not go beyond us four; I am most desirous that the affair should pass to its easy and natural conclusion."

"I quite understand that, and of course we shall wait until Kitty tells us," said her aunt. "What do you think of it all, Miss Darcy? Has Kitty mentioned the matter to you?"

Georgiana replied that she had, and on further questioning owned that she felt sure that if what Mrs. Knightley expected came to pass, it would make Kitty very happy. Mrs. Knightley called upon her to join in commendations of the young man, and this she could sincerely do; and she rose from the table feeling as if everything were settled, and it only remained to congratulate the two persons most concerned.

A minute later she met Kitty, flying in search of her. Kitty seized her friend's hand and drew her into a quiet corner of Mrs. Knightley's morning-room, where the two girls could seat themselves on a sofa partly hidden by a screen and be quite secluded.

"I wanted so much to see you before I went, Georgiana," began Kitty in an excited undertone. "I thought I should never get to you, and this is my last chance, as we start so early on Friday. Now do tell me what you think of him. You can judge now, cannot you? Is he not delightful? Is he not handsome, and a noble creature? Is he not all I said?"

"Yes, indeed, dear Kitty, he is," responded Georgiana, with tender sympathy. "I can quite understand your feelings. I am sure anyone would be very proud to have gained the affection of such a man."

"Oh, I am so glad to hear you say so. Do you think I have gained it? Sometimes I think so; sometimes I am not sure. Mrs. Knightley thinks I have."

"I know she does; I have heard her say so, and she would not mislead you, Kitty, I am sure. She cares so much for your welfare."

"Yes, indeed, she has been very kind. I cannot tell you what I should have done without her. She has done everything, she thinks of everything. To-night, when she was arranging the supper partners, I was standing near him, but not very near, and he had not asked me; I suppose he was waiting to see if he might, as we had already danced together a great deal, and she looked up from her list and said: 'And Mr. Price, I do not think I have put anyone down for you: will you take Miss Bennet?' in that kind way, not to make me feel uncomfortable, as if it had been planned. So he came and offered me his arm with such an air! And, after all, we did not talk much at supper; I was too happy, but when I asked him if he liked my dress, he paid me such an elegant compliment on it—something about a rose."

"He is a most agreeable companion," said Georgiana. "I should never tire of hearing him converse. The marvellous adventures he has had! It is like a glimpse of a new world to meet a person who has actually been through those things, and who describes them with such modesty and simplicity. Such a man seldom comes into our quiet lives."

"Oh, but they are so horrible, it quite frightens me to hear about them; if I were married to him I would never let him go to sea again, for fear of his coming back without an arm, or a leg, or an eye."

"But it is his profession, Kitty."

"I know, but it is a horrid profession, the only thing about him that I don't like, except for the uniform, and a man in a black coat looks positively nothing beside him."

"Oh, Kitty, as if the uniform mattered! Do not let me hear you talk so foolishly," said Georgiana, really pained.

"Well, perhaps it is foolish, but it does make a difference, you know. Bingley has been teasing me half the evening about a young man that he says they have got for me down in the country, whom I shall be sure to like, the Rector of Kympton, I believe. As if I could possibly look at a clergyman after knowing William Price."

"Perhaps it is not fair to compare two such different types of men, but Mr. Morland is very nice, Kitty; I am sure you will think so."

"I am sure I shall not; I don't want to see him: how can I think anyone nice when I am away from here? Oh, if I could only see Price once more, just once more, to make sure; but as he says, how can one ever see anybody down in the wilds of Derbyshire?"

"Kitty, here is the music beginning again, and we shall be asked for," said Georgiana, standing up. "Do not be unhappy or over-anxious about this, and do not show too much what you feel, for I am sure it will all come out right if you have the patience."

"Do you really think it is so? That is such a comfort; but I wish he had spoken to-night. Mrs. Knightley thought he would."

"Dear Kitty, whenever it comes, I wish you all the happiness in the world; write to me very fully, and, as I said, have patience and self-command. Now we really ought to go."

Kitty pressed her friend's hand, and Georgiana tried to calm her as they walked back to the ball-room, by talking on indifferent topics, for she feared the girl's burning cheeks and nervous manner would betray her agitation and its cause. Miss Bingley met them as they entered the room, and asked Georgiana if she was ready to go, as Mrs. Hurst seemed inclined for it.

"Yes, I am quite ready," said Georgiana. "I think I am engaged to Mr. Bingley for another dance, but he will not mind missing it."

"Charles is over there, talking to Mr. Price, but I have told him we want to go, so he will be expecting us," said Miss Bingley, and led the way across the room, Kitty not unnaturally following. Mr. Bingley welcomed them warmly, calling out: "Here, Kitty, come and add your entreaties to mine. I want this young gentleman to come down to Desborough and shoot our pheasants in November, but he is not sure if he can manage it; I never heard such nonsense. If anyone is entitled to ask for leave when he wants it, I should think he is."

Kitty was rendered perfectly incapable of speech for the first moment after hearing these words; never had a wish been so suddenly and gloriously placed in the way of accomplishment; but she found an unexpected ally in Miss Bingley, who supported her brother's invitation, having, like him, been attracted by the young lieutenant's agreeable demeanour and high reputation. William Price stood still, looking diffidently from one to another, and expressing in disjointed sentences his gratitude, his uncertainty, and his extreme pleasure should he be able to accept. Mr. Bingley exerted all his powers of persuasion, and Kitty's bright eyes shot glances not less eloquent. Georgiana turned a little away, feeling suddenly very tired and spiritless, and Mr. and Mrs. Hurst, who came up at that moment, remarked on it.

"Georgiana tired?" exclaimed Bingley; "then let us go at once. You are not used to these late hours, and I don't know what Mrs. Darcy will say to me if I take them a poor account of you. We are all neighbours in the country, you know, Mr. Price. Then that is settled? You will come to us if you can possibly get away, and I hope nothing will prevent it. You do not expect to receive the command of the Mediterranean squadron, do you?"

"No, sir," replied William, laughing, "neither that nor any other command this year, I am afraid."

"Well, well, I wish you luck. Shall I see you again before I leave town?"

William was beginning to reply negatively, when Miss Bingley, who was leading the whole party towards the cloak-room, turned and asked Mr. Price if he would not come and see them some time in Grosvenor Street. She called on her sister to ratify the invitation, which Mrs. Hurst did, and it was courteously accepted. There followed a confusion of good-byes and a getting of cloaks, and the three ladies were placed in the coach while the two gentlemen prepared to walk. Georgiana had warmly embraced Kitty at parting, and had intimated that she knew how much the arrangement by Bingley meant to her friend; and her last impression of Mrs. Knightley's ball was of William Price waving farewell in the doorway and then ascending the steps to where Kitty awaited him in the vestibule.

Chapter 10

COLONEL FITZWILLIAM HAD COME to London because he thought it was the place where he would be most likely to meet Miss Crawford again, and he had taken up literary work merely to pass away the time until that longed-for event should occur. Two months had elapsed before he heard of her arrival, with her sister, but it was not many days after that he contrived to be present at the house of a mutual friend, where he knew her to be expected. Her manner of greeting him on this occasion was not free from embarrassment; it was neither cordial nor unfriendly, and so brief was the encounter that he could discover but little from it of the state of her mind towards him. Another casual meeting seemed to promise more hopefully, but hardly had they exchanged a few sentences when the appearance of Sir Walter and Miss Elliot turned the conversation into channels more congenial to the new-comers, and Colonel Fitzwilliam was forced to stand aside and see Miss Crawford taken possession of without any semblance of unwillingness on her part. He then devoted himself to Mrs. Grant, and tried to propose an expedition, a theatre party, but that lady hesitatingly replied that she could arrange nothing without her sister. Colonel Fitzwilliam applied for permission to call, which was readily accorded, but on availing himself of it the following day only learned that the ladies were gone to Richmond with a party. The manservant obliged him, unasked, with the information that it was Mr. Crawford's party, and the Colonel was left to speculate gloomily on the chances of Sir Walter Elliot being one of the number, and what was of greater import whether, if it was so, it was with Miss Crawford's approval.

He had gone to call on the Hursts after leaving Mrs. Grant's house, and had not again seen the object of his thoughts and hopes, when, a few days later, he directed his steps towards Mrs. Annesley's residence in Hans Place. He could scarcely believe it was but three months since the severance of his engagement with Georgiana, it seemed to have retreated so far into the background of events, but he had pondered earnestly over their interview in Grosvenor Street, and from her demeanour had concluded that his presence was not objectionable to her, so that any further meeting might help to re-establish their old cousinly relations, a result which their friends would rejoice in. It was therefore with a tolerably easy mind that was ushered into the presence of the two ladies, and found Georgiana in great good looks and far less shy and confused than on the previous occasion; indeed, in a few moments any awkwardness between them seemed to have quite melted away, and she was readily answering his questions about Mrs. Knightley's ball.

"It certainly seems to have been a great success, for I never knew you so enthusiastic about a ball before, Georgiana," said her cousin, smiling. "It was better than the Bath assemblies, I gather?"

"Oh—Bath!" exclaimed Georgiana, with a note of contempt in her voice which spoke volumes. "You laugh at me, Cousin Robert, but it was a beautiful ball. Even Mr. Bingley said so, and he must have been to a great number."

"Hundreds, if not thousands, I should think," returned her cousin. "Bingley's shoemaker must have made a fortune. But who were the partners who contributed to such enjoyment? for they are usually the really important part. Two Mr. Prices you have mentioned, Captain Carter and Mr. Dixon; who else?"

"Oh, I forget who else; Mr. Hurst and Mr. Bingley, of course, and Mr. Knightley, but he was very grave and terrible , I was almost too frightened to move, and Mr. Gardiner, and then there was Mr. Yates , but I did not dance with him. Do you remember him, Cousin Robert? he said he knew you at Bath."

Georgiana had been so disagreeably struck by Mr. Yates's way of speaking of her relatives whom he had met, that she had not intended to mention it to Colonel Fitzwilliam, but the rest of his talk had eradicated his first impression, and she had unguardedly given utterance to his name. Fruitless regret and vexation overcame her when, glancing up at her cousin, she perceived his countenance darken, and noted the change in his voice as he replied, with an effort: "Yes, we did meet in Bath, but not in the pleasantest of circumstances. Mr. Yates may be a more agreeable man away from the companions he then had."

"I do not think he was particularly agreeable," said Georgiana, falteringly, "but I thought—he appeared to me to be an interesting talker."

"Yes, that is quite his line; if Yates can do nothing else he can certainly use his tongue," replied Colonel Fitzwilliam, not without bitterness. "But do not let us concern ourselves with him, Georgiana; what about the walk in Kensington Gardens that we had thought of? Will Mrs. Annesley very kindly let me escort you both there this delightfully fine morning?"

Mrs. Annesley willingly acceded, and the two ladies having attired themselves, a hackney coach was called, which conveyed them a mile on their way towards Kensington Place. Georgiana was somewhat silent during the drive. She did not wish to speculate on her cousin's private affairs, but having been the innocent cause of recalling painful thoughts to him inevitably produced the wish to atone, to help; and she found herself wondering, while trying not to wonder, what could possibly be the connection between Mr. Yates, Cousin Robert and a lady in Bath now said to be in London. To be sure, it was none of her business, she had no right to wish to know, and yet she did wish she knew whether that had anything to do with Cousin Robert's looking so sad and worn. Stay—that letter of Lady Catherine's which her brother had read aloud—a lady in Bath, a friend of Elizabeth's—a misunderstanding—Georgiana felt for one instant, with a thrill of fear and excitement, as though she had laid hold of the thread; and was almost glad when the stopping of the carriage obliged her to let it go, by scattering her thoughts and her bringing her back to the present moment. She reproached herself for prying into others' secrets, and pressing close to Mrs. Annesley's side, she eagerly responded to that lady's eulogies of the beautiful scene around them. The gardens were indeed looking their best in the glory of their June array, and crowds of well-dressed persons strolling gaily about added to the general sense of brilliancy and festivity.

They had taken a few turns, and Fitzwilliam had greeted several of his acquaintances, while Georgiana was beginning to think that she, too, might see someone she knew, when her attention was arrested by some comments of Mrs. Annesley's, made in a low voice, on the singular beauty of a young lady who was approaching them, escorted by two gentlemen. The lady was dark and extremely animated, and her fine eyes seemed to be glancing in the direction of their party. As the two groups slowly passed each other, Colonel Fitzwilliam's bow was acknowledged by the lady and her friends, and she half paused, as if about to speak, but passed on without doing so. Mrs. Annesley, seeing the recognition, made a laughing apology to her companion. "I beg you pardon, Colonel Fitzwilliam, I did not know you knew that lady, but really, she is such a lovely creature that one cannot help remarking on it."

"I am quite of your opinion Mrs. Annesley," returned the Colonel, and Georgiana saw that though he endeavoured to speak lightly something had happened which necessitated the exercise of a degree of self-command. "It is very obliging of you to voice sentiments which I am always wanting to put into words when I meet Miss Crawford. Although no words can exactly describe her special charm."

"It is her expression, is it not?" said Mrs. Annesley, "so full of changing life and brightness, and that vivid complexion, and graceful carriage of the head. All that one can see at a glance. And I imagine we are not in the minority in admiring her."

"No, indeed," said Fitzwilliam, "she holds quite a little court."

He was interrupted by a gentleman who detained him for a moment, and the ladies walked on, Georgiana's mind full of tumultuous thoughts. She had recollected the name Crawford in a moment as being that of Elizabeth's friend to whom Lady Catherine had behaved so unkindly, but she did not like to admit her knowledge, for fear it might be painful to her cousin to have the whole chain of circumstances discussed. What they were, Georgiana could not help longing to know, but the only one that was quite clear to her was her cousin's deep admiration for this lady. Her heart went out in sympathy to him, both for his attachment and for the difficulties in his way, if difficulties there were. Did Miss Crawford perhaps not care for him? Yet she had looked as if she wanted to speak. Were there friends or relations influencing her? He had alluded to "a little court." But how could anyone separate Miss Crawford from Colonel Fitzwilliam, if she really loved him, he so noble, so kind, so true? Georgiana blushed deeply at her thoughts, perceiving the rapid pace at which they had led her on, and the somewhat inconsistent conclusion that they had reached, but their very sincerity reassured her, in the knowledge that her own love for Colonel Fitzwilliam was the sisterly love that longed to see him happily and suitably united. No idea crossed her mind of helping towards this end; she had too lowly an opinion of her own powers as a force in other person's lives; her only wish was for an opportunity of showing her sympathy towards her cousin in some practical form. In vain she tried to plan how this might be done, for she could not speak of it until he had opened his heart to her, a most unlikely thing to happen, and not at all could it be mentioned before Mrs. Annesley.

Fortune seemed to favour her, for when Colonel Fitzwilliam rejoined them, Mrs. Annesley confessed that she felt a little tired, the heat was so great, and she would like to rest a while. "But do not come with me," she added, as Fitzwilliam instantly proposed moving towards the chairs, "if you are not tired yet, it is much more amusing for you and Georgiana to walk about, and probably you would like to go nearer to the music. I will go and sit by my friend Mrs. Sackville, whom I see over there, until you are ready."

The cousins accordingly found themselves together, and Georgiana, hardly knowing how to begin, but feeling no time was to be lost, broke silence again after a few minutes after a few minutes by saying timidly: "I think I have heard Elizabeth speak of Miss Crawford; you all knew her in Bath, did you not?"

"Have you indeed? That is good," exclaimed Colonel Fitzwilliam. "I had forgotten that you would know her name. Yes, we all met in Bath." He seemed about to say more, but after a pause concluded with: "Ask Elizabeth to tell you about her."

Georgiana was disappointed, but told herself that she could not have expected anything else. How could he make a confidant of her, who had shown herself unworthy of any trust.

They walked on for some little distance, until Fitzwilliam, observing two vacant seats in a group of chairs, placed close to the edge of the grass, asked Georgiana if she would like to sit down for a little before turning back. It was a charming spot, in the shade of a tree and immediately facing a large sheet of artificial water, and Georgiana willingly assented, remarking: "How fortunate that we should be able to get two chairs. They seem to be nearly all occupied."

"It is generally so; people come and sit here the whole morning when it is so fine and warm," returned Fitzwilliam, placing himself at her side, but not resuming their conversation of a few moments before. Georgiana was not content to be silent, and her cousin was wrapped in thoughts of Miss Crawford and did not dream of the anxious solicitude for him in Georgiana's heart.

The other man in Mary's party, he reflected, must be her brother, Henry Crawford; there was a slight resemblance; besides, he answered to the description Mary had given of him. How well he remembered her laughing looks and tones as she uttered it: "Henry is not tall, Colonel Fitzwilliam, no, I allow him every other imaginable beauty, but he is not tall; thin, dark, rather plain; of course, to me, singularly handsome; did I not say so? Do you think you would recognize him if you saw him?" And the Colonel did see him now, for the second time, a few steps away, approaching with his sister, who walked between him and Sir Walter Elliot, as before.

Mary glanced towards Miss Darcy, and in an instant the Colonel was at her side. "How do you do, Miss Crawford? I was sorry to miss you the other morning when I called. Would you allow me to present to you my cousin, Miss Darcy? She has heard of you from her brother and sister."

Mary coloured deeply as she returned his salutation, but immediately complied with his request, pausing only to say to her brother in a low voice: "Henry, please walk on; do not wait for me." To Georgiana it was such a surprise and delight to see Miss Crawford being brought towards her, and to find a wish granted which she had scarcely dared to formulate, that instead of being exceedingly shy, as she would ordinarily have been, she forgot to think of herself, and rising and looking into Miss Crawford's lovely and expressive face, she entered fully into what she believed her cousin to be feeling towards its owner. In reality the shyness was on Mary's side, for she could not help in seeing in Colonel Fitzwilliam's action another proof of the generosity and devotion of the friend whom she had exiled from her.

A few words passed between them all three about the beauty of the day and their surroundings, then Miss Crawford, turning to Georgiana, inquired after Mr. and Mrs. Darcy. This was a subject to unloose Georgiana's tongue and drew forth animated replies, and Mary, still addressing her, made a few civil inquiries about her journey to town and the probable duration of her visit. It was Colonel Fitzwilliam who presently begged Miss Crawford to take his seat, which, after a slight demur, no other chair being within sight, she consented to do. He remained standing near them for a few moments, and then moved a little distance, thinking they might be able to talk more comfortably if left to themselves.

"You are staying with your aunt, Lady Catherine de Bourgh?" asked Miss Crawford, when he was out of earshot.

"No," replied Georgiana, "my aunt is not in town. For the moment I am with my old governess, Mrs. Annesley, but I am really on a visit to some other friends, Mrs. Hurst and Miss Bingley."

"I see; and your cousin is with you there just now?" Mary pursued.

"Oh, no, no, no," said Georgiana, smiling, "no, he has been living in town by himself for some time. You have not happened to meet him since you were in London?"

Mary answered that she had met Colonel Fitzwilliam once or twice, but murmured something about thinking he and the Darcys were all like one family. Georgiana assented to this.

"He is indeed like one of ourselves; my brother and sister are devoted to him, and he is the oldest friend I have," she replied. "After my own brother, he is the kindest and best person I have ever met. People do not know for a long time how good he is, because he is so modest and retiring."

Georgiana was conscious that she was perhaps transgressing the bounds of good taste in this vehement praise; but she did not care what Miss Crawford thought of her, so long as she would think well of her cousin. At all events it appeared that Miss Crawford was not offended, for she smiled faintly and said: "He is fortunate in having you and Mrs. Darcy for his advocates."

"It is just the same," said Georgiana eagerly, "with whoever speaks of him. His friends are all devoted to him, and he is so staunch to them, whatever they do; he never changes, or fails them when they want him."

"I think I know one who would not fail *him*, Miss Darcy," said Miss Crawford, still smiling; "but, indeed," she added, as Georgiana turned away her head, "I am sure you are quite right in all you say. Who should know Colonel Fitzwilliam well, if not his old friends? And I know myself that he is even loyal to them when he is angry with them, which is the great test."

Georgiana could heartily agree, though without understanding Mary's allusion. Their talk drifted to other subjects, in the midst of which the Colonel returned and tried to interest Miss Crawford in some such plan as he had suggested to her sister. Mary said "it was kind of him," "it would be pleasant," without pledging herself to anything; and replied, "Pray do," when he asked if he might call to talk it over; but it appeared that she and her sister were so full of engagements that it was doubtful if they would be at home any morning before the end of that week. By this time she had risen, and appeared anxious to return to her friends. Mr. Crawford, indeed, was seen approaching, so Colonel Fitzwilliam could only bow his adieux, while promising himself the pleasure of calling early in the following week, for though he would have liked to make Henry Crawford's acquaintance for himself, he did not wish to be responsible for introducing him to Georgiana. She, on her part, only perceived that Miss Crawford was taking leave, and she pressed the hand that her new friend extended to her, saying in a low voice: "It has been such a pleasure—I hope I shall see you again."

"Indeed, I hope we may meet; I should like it," responded Mary cordially. "You go about so much that I have no doubt we shall. Pray remember me to your sister and Mr. Darcy."

Georgiana promised, and turned away with Colonel Fitzwilliam, but she ventured to say to her companion nothing more than a few shy words of appreciation of Miss Crawford's beauty and charm.

"I am so glad you like her," he replied. "I thought that you would, though it never occurred to me that we were likely to meet her here. Elizabeth talked of inviting her to Pemberley, and I hope some day she will. If we can get up a water party, Georgiana, you must come to it. Do you think you could persuade Mrs. Annesley to bring you?"

"Indeed I am sure I could, if I am still with her. But I go back to Grosvenor Street on Saturday afternoon, you know."

"Well, we must contrive it somehow; I doubt if Miss Bingley would care much for such simple pleasures."

Georgiana laughed, regarding a river party as a very distinguished and elaborate form of entertainment. Their progress towards Mrs. Annesley was slow, as Colonel Fitzwilliam was frequently accosted by some friend or other, one of whom stopped him to call out: "Do not forget that you are going with us to see Siddons in *Macbeth* on Friday night."

"Are you, Cousin Robert? How I envy you!" said Georgiana, as they passed on. "We have tickets to see her next week in *King John*; but I hear Lady Macbeth is her finest part."

"I am ashamed to say that I have never witnessed any of her performances as yet," replied Fitzwilliam; "I hardly know how I have missed them, but it behooves me to make up for lost time. I shall come round on Saturday morning and harrow your feelings with a description of the play."

"Do, please, and then I can write to Elizabeth about it. How much I shall have to tell her this week; about my coming to this beautiful place and meeting Miss Crawford."

Georgiana thought her cousin looked happier when they were driving home than she had yet seen him look in London, and they discussed the details of a plan to go to Hampton Court and dine there, which seemed to contain all the elements of perfect bliss. Fitzwilliam was indeed experiencing greater peace of mind than he had done since he parted from Mary in Bath, though for what reason he could scarcely explain to himself. Her manner had been merely that of courtesy, and had not contained a hint of the old friendliness; and Sir Walter Elliot had had been, as ever, at her elbow. Yet Fitzwilliam felt that each interview he could obtain opened the way towards her a little more, and he had resolved to press straight onward, letting no such obstacles arise as he had formed an effectual barrier between them in Bath, but, rather, making use of every incident that occurred, such as Georgiana's accidental presence and the ensuing introduction, to bring himself nearer to her.

He was keeping this object ever in view when he joined his friends at the theatre a few evenings later, and in glancing round the house after the first act, observed Miss Crawford with several other persons in a box at some distance from him. He immediately began to consider the possibility of going up to speak to her, although unacquainted with the hostess, for Mrs. Grant was not there, and he conjectured that the party were in the charge of Sir Walter and Miss Elliot, by the manner in which that lady and gentleman rose to welcome a visitor who had just entered the box. Fitzwilliam determined to obtain an introduction through some friend, and for this purpose to go up to the box during the third interval, which was the longest of the evening.

The second interval, however, was destined to produce something of a disconcerting nature. Fitzwilliam was conversing with the wife of his friend, General Stuart, whose guest he was, and learning from her the names and other particulars of many of the persons present, for she had long lived in London and had a wide acquaintance. She was reckoned to be a lively companion, though the information she gave, and her manner of imparting it were, the one so positive and the other so vigorous, that her hearers were tempted frequently to forget, until after they had assimilated it, that she might have spoken without the best authority. She had chanced to notice the people in the Elliots' box, and she drew Colonel Fitzwilliam's rather unwilling attention to them. He did not wish to discuss, or hear discussed, the Crawfords or their friends, and implied at once that several of them were known to him. Mrs. Stuart was all interest, and inquired if it was that charming Miss Crawford that he knew, and, if so, whether he could explain why it was that she was going to marry that insufferable old coxcomb, Sir Walter Elliot, Colonel Fitzwilliam replied, concealing his apprehension as best he could, that he did not know that she was; he had never heard it.

"Then you are the only one in the population of London who has not heard it, my dear Colonel. Why, where have you been, to be out of the way of such a piece of news? At least fifty people have told me, and of course all of them have it straight from the most reliable source. It is hard to believe that such a beautiful creature should throw herself away like that on a foolish, impecunious old fellow who is old enough to be her father, and has nothing in the world but his title and his tailor to recommend him. I cannot comprehend why girls do these things; one can only suppose that she is tired of the single life and wants a suitable settlement."

"I am almost sure there must be some mistake, Mrs. Stuart," interposed Colonel Fitzwilliam. "I saw Miss Crawford the only lately, and she—there was nothing said about her engagement." He stopped, feeling how very lame such a refutation was, unsupported by any testimony.

"Nonsense, my dear sir. You have been living in your books, or you would have heard of it. Do you see that short, stout young man over there? He is a Mr. John Thorpe, and he was speaking of it at our house the other evening, and asserted positively that he had heard it mentioned in Bath months ago."

"I am quite certain that Miss Crawford was not engaged when she was in Bath," was all Colonel Fitzwilliam would permit himself to say.

"Well, you are very uncivil, I must say; you had better obtain someone else's assurance if you will not accept mine. Though anyone can see how it has come about; naturally the Elliots have pushed it forward to the utmost of their power. Sir Walter wants a pretty wife, and as he cannot support one out of that vanished fortune of his, he must choose one who has enough for both. And Miss Elliot would like to establish a connection between the families for the sake of a certain Mr. Henry Crawford, who is still unmarried—he is a rake, of course, but she does not mind that. You know which he is?—the dark young man standing up at the back of the box."

Colonel Fitzwilliam was so excessively disturbed and irritated by this conversation, which he had endeavoured to check by saying: "You must be quite satisfied now, Mrs. Stuart, with the answers you have provided to your own question," that the rising of the curtain was a great relief; he could sit silent, inattentive to the play, wrapped in his own anxious thoughts. Mrs. Stuart's was certainly not the last word on this terribly important matter, for he felt he must hear the facts from some other quarter before he could credit them. The fine scene of Banquo's murder was played, as far as he was concerned, to deaf ears, and his eyes continually sought the box above, where he could just see Mary's white cloak, and Sir Walter's fashionable attire always, it seemed, in proximity to it. The instant the curtain fell again he rose from his seat and made the best of his way towards the exit, but so many gentlemen were leaving their seats at the same time that he found himself in a crowd where it was impossible to progress at any great rate of speed. At this moment he heard his name pronounced behind him, and looking round, he recognized two friends, former brother officers of his own, who had remained seated near the end of one of the rows.

Impatient of the delay, he nevertheless went to them and remained a few minutes in talk, finding that one of his friends,

Captain Ross, was lame and had difficulty moving along the narrow gangways. They were presently joined by a Mr. Palmer, whom Fitzwilliam knew as a man of few words, reserved, and of almost unamiable temper, but thoroughly trustworthy, and too little interested in his neighbours' affairs to be possessed of any superfluous knowledge concerning them.

Fitzwilliam had a slight acquaintance with him, and after a little consideration he asked him, as if casually: "Do you know anything of Sir Walter Elliot, Palmer?"

"As much as I want to," was the reply. "A stupid fellow. If he were framed and glazed he would be a good deal more useful than he now is, I consider."

Captain Ross laughingly agreed with him, claiming some knowledge of Sir Walter Elliot himself, and calling on his hearers to witness the inequality of human justice, when such a man as that could find a young and charming wife.

"Is it true then," asked Fitzwilliam, summoning all his fortitude, "that Sir Walter Elliot is going to be married?"

"Perfectly true," rejoined Captain Ross and his companion, "and you know to whom—that lady in the box with him now."

Colonel Fitzwilliam had no need to look; it was enough to know that the worst he dreaded was about to befall. His friends seemed to notice nothing in his agitated manner of asking "Are you sure?" in such haste were they to pour out their information.

"Yes, it has been talked of for a long time, but is quite settled now. I was in the club last night when Elliot was having supper there, and he told us all to drink to his health to-day, for he would be the happiest man in the world. So that party up there is doubtless celebrating the betrothal."

"Besides, do you not recollect," added Captain Ross, "that when I met Miss Elliot the other night she told me her father would probably have some legal business to arrange, when Mr. Crawford returned from Paris, and then, she hoped, would come the announcement of a happy event? Crawford is there now, you see."

"The legal business in this case may include a settlement to be made on Elliot himself," laughed the other officer. "Can you understand people advertising their affairs so freely beforehand? He must have had reason to feel pretty confident. Well, I shall always think it a great shame. Miss Crawford is much too good for him, but it is not the first time she has played with a man in this way, and now, I suppose she finds herself too much involved to draw back, or Elliot has been sharp enough to make sure of her, unlike that dilatory young Bertram."

"Why, yes, besides being presumably a better bargain than a mere country parson," added Captain Ross. "I imagine they will live at Kellynch. When I last saw Wentworth he told me his sister, the tenant, was just leaving."

Fitzwilliam felt as if he could not bear more of this, but, making a great effort, he turned once more to Mr. Palmer and asked if he thought the rumour to be true. Mr. Palmer looked at him in some surprise.

"Yes, certainly, why not? There is not the slightest reason to doubt it. We have the evidence of our eyes and the word of one of the principal parties. My wife and her mother are going to call to-morrow and offer their congratulations."

Colonel Fitzwilliam hardly knew how he got away, what his three friends thought of him, or what General Stuart, whom he had met outside the lobby, could comprehend of his excuses for his abrupt departure. He only knew that he could not return to his place, watching the woman who possessed his whole heart in the company of the lover to whom she had promised herself. He must be alone, in the darkness and silence, to brace himself to endure the shock of what he had heard and realize all that would follow from it. He hastened through the streets, and shut himself up in his rooms, conscious only that this was a defeat, not a mere repulse such as he had received at Bath, but a defeat the completeness and finality of which admitted no rally on the losing side. Long he paced his room, struggling to fight down the anguish of his mind and to see clearly through his utter wretchedness what had happened and how. Even in the midst of his sufferings it was not difficult for him to piece together all the items of his knowledge into a connected whole. She had wearied of him at Bath; that must have been the beginning of it; he had not been able to gain her affection in a sufficient degree for it to be proof against Lady Catherine's attack. That catastrophe had swept him, equally with his cousins, away from whatever place he had held in Mary Crawford's esteem; and when he met her again in London, and could resume his efforts to recover that place, it was already occupied.

Was that, then, why she had seemed not to wish to be too friendly—because it was too late? He was forced to believe it; he could indeed easily believe anything that was a proof against her consideration, her goodness of heart, that had endeavoured to save him pain. He could and did believe that he had failed to win her, but that she could have accepted Sir Walter Elliot left him for many hours stunned and incredulous. That she, with her many gifts of mind and body, her true elegance, her sensibility, her refinement of breeding, placing her in almost a different world from the vulgar pretentiousness of Sir Walter and his daughter, which in Bath had so often seemed uncongenial to her, should now actually find such a man all-sufficient, and should consent to join her life with his, was an outrage, a madness—all the more so if she had drifted into it in the way the onlookers imagined. She could not know what she was doing. Her friends—what were they about? She must be warned. Fitzwilliam impulsively strode to the door, then stopped and flung himself down with a bitter laugh at his own folly—he to be raging through all the commonplace jealousies of a rejected lover, like any boy of nineteen! What could he or anyone else do? Miss Crawford was perfectly free to choose; she had a brother, with whose knowledge she was probably acting, and there was nothing to be alleged against Sir Walter Elliot's character. Recollecting the comments he had heard that evening, Fitzwilliam was forced to the same conclusions; to acknowledging that Miss Elliot, Mary's own friend, had in all probability promoted the match; that Henry Crawford, weak and unstable where women's persuasions were concerned, had allowed himself to be drawn into the Elliot net, and that his sister, though she could have little real regard for Sir Walter, wished to settle down and, her fortune making her independent of means in her future husband, had chosen where her fancy and a title attracted her.

How mean, how sordid was the whole story! Not the least heartrending of Colonel Fitzwilliam's reflections that night was that it could not be his Mary, the true Mary who had shown herself to him for a short time, who was now taking this step, so unworthy of her best self. For the woman he knew her to be, what happiness could be in store?

Chapter 11

GEORGIANA WAS ALONE IN the drawing-room of Mrs. Annesley's house on the following morning, practising the pianoforte, when the expected rap at the front door was heard, and Colonel Fitzwilliam was presently ushered into the room. She sprang up to welcome him, prepared for a cheerful greeting, but was unspeakably concerned at the sight of his haggard face and worn, exhausted looks, the more so because he made no attempt to account for them, but forced a smile, accepted the chair which she offered him, and endeavoured to speak as usual. Georgiana begged him to partake of some refreshment, and expressed a fear that he was ill, not daring to give utterance to her real conjecture.

"No, no, Georgiana, thank you. I will not have anything; I assure you I am not ill. I have only come to wish you good-bye, as I have changed my plans; I—I am thinking of going to Ireland."

"To Ireland!" repeated Georgiana in consternation.

"Yes, I have friend who owns an estate there, and he has often invited me to come over and fish and shoot with him, so I shall start to-night, and take him by surprise, arriving early next week."

"But—to Ireland!" Georgiana could only repeat, so utterly bewildered was she. "Dear Cousin Robert, I am so sorry; I wish you need not . . . would you not go to Pemberley? Elizabeth and Darcy would so gladly receive you, or do anything—"

"I know they would; there is nothing that goodness and kindness suggest that would not occur to them, but I do not think I could go there just at present. Will you give them my love, Georgiana when you are next writing, and tell them of my movements? I will write to them from Ireland and give them my direction."

"Indeed, indeed, I will, but may I not tell them anything more? Oh, how I wish I could help you in any way," exclaimed Georgiana, anxiety showing itself so acutely in every syllable that Fitzwilliam was forced to get up to avert his face from hers, lest his self-command should be too sorely tried.

"My dear, kind little cousin, I shall always be grateful to you, even though I fear it is not in your power to help me just now. Some day, perhaps, we may speak of it; in the meantime—I have had a great disappointment, and I think I had better go away for awhile, so as to be more fit to meet my friends when I return." He came back to her, raised her up, and spoke with resolution and cheerfulness. "Come, Georgiana, do not be sad, it is not worth while. I shall probably be at Pemberley in the autumn, and we must do something then to make up for the loss of our exploration party now. Do not think of me—at least, only think of me as catching and eating a great many salmon. I hope you will have great deal of pleasure still in London. You return to the Hursts today, do you not? Will you make my excuses to Mrs. Annesley?"

During this speech Georgiana had striven to recover her composure, and she managed at the conclusion of it to look up at him with a tolerably calm face and to promise to deliver his messages. She felt convinced that he had been refused by Miss Crawford, and the situation was to her so dreadful, so far beyond repair, that it was a relief to see her cousin's courage, and to know that he did not wish to hear vain and spiritless words of consolation, words which she hardly could have been able to utter, even had he been able to listen, from the very surcharge of tender feeling that burdened her heart. Nevertheless, her sympathy was reflected in her eyes, and in the gentle voice with which she bid him adieu and wished him well. Fitzwilliam was not insensible to it. It gave him the only comfort he could have received at such a time; and pressing her hand warmly, with a very earnest "God bless you!" he quitted the room.

As his footsteps died away Georgiana sank into a chair and wept bitterly. So brief had been his visit—a few ticks of the clock had seen his arrival and his departure; and in those few moments the aspect of everything had changed. Since their last meeting Georgiana had dwelt incessantly upon his prospects of happiness, and allowed herself to think of them as being in a fair way to become realized. The difficulty which Elizabeth must have referred to, and Mr. Yates had actually hinted at, could surely be cleared away now that he and Miss Crawford had met again; and Georgiana had not been able to read cruelty or harshness in that fair face. Time only—a very short time—would be necessary, and once Miss Crawford knew Fitzwilliam as he was, the rest would follow as a matter of course: for how could any woman whom he really loved be able to resist him? So reasoned Georgiana, and the collapse of her kindly hopes brought back all her old sense of personal guilt; she, too, was partly responsible for her cousin's dire fate, for was she not one of the two women who had failed to make him happy? She who had not been able to inspire him with a real love, and Miss Crawford who could not respond to it now it was fully awakened.

The luxury of grief could not be long indulged in, for tear-stained features must not be shown to her friends, nor was there leisure that day to pour out her heart in a letter to Elizabeth. Georgiana had to keep her sorrowful thoughts to herself, and fortunately it was not necessary to give any explanation of Colonel Fitzwilliam's abrupt departure from town to Mrs. Annesley; the simple statement that he had gone, leaving apologies and suitable compliments, was sufficient. With her hostesses in Grosvenor Street, however, it was a different matter, and Georgiana lacked courage to introduce the subject until a morning or two later, at breakfast, choosing the moment when the letters had just been brought in and everyone had only that remnant of attention to spare which their meal and their correspondence had not absorbed. Mr. Hurst asked a question or two, which, as his wife and sister were speaking at the same time, went so long unanswered that he quite forgot them; Louisa showed surprise and offended dignity that the Colonel had not paid a farewell call on her before leaving; while Caroline, with less pride and a great deal of curiosity, attempted at first to draw Georgiana into some admission beyond the mere mention of the fact, but remembering by happy chance to have heard the name of the friend in Ireland, and even that of his estate, she was able to her own satisfaction to convert the mysterious journey into an engagement of respectably long standing. Georgiana breathed more freely; she had dreaded Miss Bingley's cross-examination, and still so dreaded anyone guessing at her cousin's misfortune that she even deviated so far from her usual truthfulness as to say, "Yes, probably he had been intending to go all the time, as soon as the weather should be suitable."

It was the greatest comfort to feel that with Elizabeth there need be no concealment. Already a description of the meeting with Miss Crawford had travelled to Pemberley, but with none but the simplest and most obvious comment; Georgiana asked, as directed by Fitzwilliam, for more particulars connected with her new acquaintance, but until she had been openly admitted to a share in her elders' knowledge she did not like to speak of what was still mere guesswork. But now, although Elizabeth's answer had not yet been received, she felt she could write more freely; she only had been allowed a glimpse of her cousin's inmost heart, she only had witnessed his grief and had been allowed to surmise its origin; she could be the indirect means of bringing him the quick sympathy of his two best friends, and she was justified in telling her sister of all she knew and all she conjectured. "He had been refused, dear Elizabeth," ran one sentence, "it can be nothing else, and I fear it is irrevocable. Poor Cousin Robert! He feels it so terribly. Can nothing be done for him? You know her, you know them both, he is sure to tell you all. Do help him, dear Elizabeth; you always help people who are in trouble."

Her letter closed and dispatched, she experienced a feeling of relief from strain, having left her cousin's affairs in more capable hands than her own. His sad face long haunted her, but the words she had written reminded her of another person who was now probably calling upon Elizabeth for sympathy and help. Not that Kitty had been by any means forgotten, but in the silence that followed on her departure, and the new interest that had occupied the last few days, the ball and its attendant emotions had been rather pushed to one side. But Georgiana had returned to Grosvenor Street fully expecting to find a letter from Derbyshire, or intelligence of Kitty in some other form.

Her own letter to Elizabeth, concluded the morning after the ball, had contained, in addition to an account of that memorable event, a paragraph to this effect: "Kitty has something extremely interesting to tell you. I shall not spoil her pleasure by anticipating her, but only add that I believe everything is going to turn out just as happily as she would like and as we should like for her. Pray, pray, give me your opinion on this important matter as soon as you can form one. I am longing to have it." A reply to this letter was indeed awaiting her, but did not give the desired information, as Elizabeth, though anxious to hear Kitty's news, had not yet had an opportunity of seeing her, and Kitty herself had not written. She was a wretched correspondent, and the delights of the first few days with Jane and the children doubtless absorbed both head and hands. Bingley's own notes to his sisters during that week were useless. One announced his and Kitty's safe arrival, another requested the forwarding of some stockings he had left behind; was it likely that such communications would have any bearing upon an important matter like the progress of a young lady's love affair? As to Mr. Price, Georgiana knew nothing, and was prepared for anything; it was quite possible that he had been unable to wait for the shooting of Mr. Bingley's pheasants and was at that moment in Derbyshire.

Upon this point, however, elucidation was presently forthcoming. At the dinner-table that afternoon Miss Bingley suddenly inquired: "Did I tell you, Georgiana, that we had a call from Charles's friend, Mr. Price, one day last week?"

"No," replied Georgiana, startled by such an abrupt incursion into the subject. "I had not heard. Were you at home? Did you see him?"

"Yes, we were all at home. He is an agreeable young fellow; manners a little too self-possessed, perhaps, for his age, but they are what these naval men acquire. He asked after you, rather as if he expected to find you here."

Georgiana said to herself that he wanted the latest news of Kitty, or, at all events, any he could not obtain from Mrs. Knightley, and was glad to be saved the necessity of replying aloud by Mrs. Hurst's beginning to speak. Yes, they had quite liked him; she thought of inviting him to fill a vacant place at a dinner she was giving the following week, for these young men who had travelled could always talk entertainingly enough to be worth while; but she would like to be assured of his character; she fancied he had been a good deal run after and spoilt, and certainly he was a great flirt.

Georgiana's heart swelled, and her pulse beat quick at such an accusation, while she uttered a mild but steady protest against it. Mrs. Hurst maintained her ground, but her young guest was supported by Miss Bingley, who said: "Nonsense, Louisa, you know I have told you there is really nothing in that. All these young officers, especially those who have seen service, are bound to be run after, whether they will or not. And as to his being a great flirt, we have seen him once or twice going about with a very good-looking woman, and that is all the reason we have for thinking so."

"How can you say such a thing, Caroline? Mr. Price is perfectly at liberty to go about with as many handsome women as he likes, even if their brothers are notoriously vicious, but if he is engaged to one of them—and from all we heard and saw at Emma Knightley's the other night he certainly ought to be—one has a right to expect a little more discretion."

"It is not at all certain that he is engaged to Kitty Bennet, I believe," said Caroline; "you know Emma Knightley's great schemes do not always come to anything." Georgiana was thereupon appealed to by both sisters to give a denial or confirmation of the fact alleged, and she could only say that she believed that at present he and Kitty were not engaged.

"That rather supports my opinion of him," said Mrs. Hurst. "But I shall be glad to be proved wrong. Georgiana, if you are behind the scenes, you must let us know as soon as there is anything to be told."

"And in the meantime, unless you think Mr. Price likely to injure our morals, you had better invite him to dinner," added her sister.

Georgiana felt unaccountably disturbed by this conversation. She could not bear hearing a person ill spoken of whom she had every wish and reason to like and esteem, and though she felt sure her own impressions of Mr. Price, which differed so widely from Mrs. Hurst's, were far more likely to be the correct ones, her timidity in trusting her own judgments caused her to pause and wonder whether she had been too hasty in being so impulsively delighted with him; ought she not, as Kitty's friend, to be more cautious until she had been sure that he was not going to disappoint the hopes of that friend? That he *had* raised high hopes, Georgiana knew, but even supposing Kitty's imagination had been her strong ally, his attentions, and Kitty's willing acceptance of them, had clearly been such as to expose her to remark. Georgiana sighed over the difficulties of the whole problem. She could not bring herself to believe that William Price was a flirt, though the picture of him in constant attendance upon a handsome woman who had doubtful relations, when he should have thought only of Kitty, was an unwelcome one. No one with that countenance, that frank smile and clear honest eye could surely be other than he seemed, and yet— Georgiana had not to look far into the past to find a disappointment, as unexpected, as severe, as Mr. Price's defection could be. The persons who were apparently most attractive could often fail one most disastrously. With Miss Crawford's image on one side of her, and William Price's on the other, Georgiana felt that anything was possible, but she resolved to keep an open mind; she recollected that Kitty and Mrs. Knightley must know him more intimately than Mrs. Hurst did, and in trying to obliterate the latter's words from her mind she fell into a reverie, wherein she lived again through every joyous moment of Mrs. Knightley's ball.

During the ensuing week the long-wished-for letters arrived, but, as is usual in such cases, they fell far short of expectation. Which of us has not looked forward, some time or another, to receiving a letter which we are convinced will have an important effect upon our minds? It will clear up a mystery, give specific information, console us in affliction, or furnish the exact counsels which we need; we depend upon it for one or all of these things, and we continue to do so, even though the letter which arrives after so much anticipation is almost always inadequate. It tells us half instead of all we expected our correspondent to know, its advice has overlooked our difficulties and does not meet the case, its words of comfort are few and arid. Yet hope leads us ever on, and the envelope bearing our friend's handwriting is torn open with as much eagerness at the fiftieth crisis as at the first. Georgiana put down Elizabeth's letter with a feeling of disappointment, yet telling herself that she could not have expected anything else. Elizabeth wrote that various matters had prevented her from seeing Kitty up to that time, but that she had heard from Jane all particulars of Kitty's acquaintanceship with Mr. Price, with additional interest from having heard his name already from the Wentworths, and was inclined to entertain the most favourable hopes regarding it; it was difficult to say more without seeing the young people together, and they could only look forward to the visit in November, and trust to it to bring about the happiest results. This was the ordinary, sensible view, and Georgiana took up Kitty's letter wondering whether she was now calm enough in mind to be induced to take the same.

"Desborough Park,

"July.

"My Dear Georgiana,

"I make no apology for not writing, for you know what it is like here the first few days, so much to see, and Jane wanting me all the time, besides, you have all the news, now that I have left London there is nothing for me to relate. I received your letter from Mrs. Annesley's, but pray write again as soon as you possibly can and tell me if you have seen anything of Mr. P——. I was so enchanted to hear Miss Bingley ask him to call, as it meant I should hear of him from you. He stayed on quite a long time at the ball, and Mrs. Knightley told me he thanked her in such a *particular* and *unmistakable* way when he said good-night! I forgot to ask you, do you not think he dances exquisitely? I have never worn that rose-coloured gown since. How I long for November! What shall I do if he is prevented? I cannot describe how thankful I am that I did not go with Lydia to the West Indies. I have seen Mr. Morland, whom you told me of, a great many times; indeed, he spends half his time here, as Jane and Bingley are very fond of him. He is very pleasant, considering he is a clergyman. He is laying out his garden at the Rectory afresh, and Jane is giving him a quantity of plants, so we go down there frequently to help him to put them in. Now I must conclude, as Mr. Morland is coming to take me out in a boat on the lake. It will be very amusing, as I have never been able to get near enough to the water-lilies to gather them, but as I say to Mr. Morland, we can neither of us swim, and what will happen then? Jane sends you many messages.

"Your affectionate friend."

A postscript on another page added: "Mrs. K. says that Mr. P. is likely to be made commander very soon. I hope he will not be, for he would have to join the ship immediately, but would not *Captain Price* sound well?"

Captain Price sounded very well; even Georgiana could not help thinking so, as she smiled over Kitty's artless question, which resented the promotion while it welcomed the title. This letter, too, was just what might have been expected; Kitty was nursing her attachment in the country just as she had nursed it in town, and Georgiana was called upon to supply it with nourishment. She would have to wait until after she had seen Mr. Price to know whether any was forthcoming.

Mrs. Hurst's dinner-party took place, and closely resembled every other function of the same kind in fashionable houses, being very long, very correct and very sumptuous. Georgiana wished that Louisa would place her next to Mr. Price, but this was not done, and accordingly, though he walked straight towards her after having spoken to his host and hostesses, he had scarcely inquired after her health before he was drawn away to be introduced to his dinner partner, while Georgiana was accosted by hers, a certain Captain Wentworth whom, with his wife, she had met in Bath the year before. The Wentworths went there regularly, and the friendship which existed between them and the Darcy family had been renewed there in the previous April. On one occasion, when they had all happened to be in town together, Elizabeth had introduced the Wentworths to Mrs. Hurst, and the result had been a liking on the part of that lady stronger than with her cold and narrow disposition she was usually inclined to form. The liking was not, perhaps, quite so heartily returned, but Captain Wentworth was sociable and enjoyed mixing with the world, and Anne's tender solicitude for him caused her to accept willingly any invitations likely to procure him amusement, both at Winchester, where they lived, and in the course of their frequent visits to town.

Captain Wentworth well remembered Mr. and Mrs. Darcy's shy, handsome sister, and prepared for a pleasant evening when he found in her less of the former quality, and even more than she had used to possess of the latter. On her other side was seated the alarming Mr. Knightley, and Georgiana was glad to find she had at all events one companion so conversable as Captain Wentworth, who belonged to the profession she was most interested in, even though he was not the representative of it which she would have chosen.

Their talk was lively, for Captain Wentworth had the art of treating subjects amusingly, and of drawing from his companion professions of opinion which she had not till then known herself to hold. Somehow or other they had drifted on to the topic of inconsistency in sailors, and Captain Wentworth gravely undertook their defence against this charge.

"I assure you, Miss Darcy, it is a great mistake, made only because people are unacquainted with our true character. It is of long standing, but a fallacy just as much as many other accepted fallacies—for instance, that parrots always talk bad language, that ladies cannot keep accounts, that the King can do no wrong, etc."

"Oh, stop, please, Captain Wentworth," interposed Georgiana. "You are opening up too many vexed questions. I was going to say," she added more seriously, "that no doubt you are quite right, but I should think if they are inconstant it would not be so very strange, for they must have so many temptations."

"Not at all; I protest they have no more excuse on that head than any other class of man. If a man is inconstant by nature, he will be so, whether he is a sailor or a butcher's assistant. I speak from experience, for I know I tried very hard to be inconstant, and could not succeed, though I had as many temptations as mist."

"Knowing Mrs. Wentworth," said Georgiana, with a smile at that lady, "I cannot help being aware of how strong a temptation you had to be the reverse."

"Exactly; and so would it be with anyone who had once given whatever affection he had to bestow. How have you got the idea, Miss Darcy, that we poor men of the sea are so fickle?"

"Indeed, no, I have not got it," replied Georgiana, trying to speak lightly. "I was merely speculating, for I know too little about it to form any judgments. It was put into my mind through hearing someone say that young officers were so much sought after everywhere; and I thought, if that were so, it was only natural that the amiable ones might find, eventually, that they had formed many more friendships than they could possibly keep up."

"Very considerably put, Miss Darcy; but, in effect, what you mean is that they continually 'love and ride away.' Sailors may have more opportunity for that kind of living, but, upon my word, I do not believe they have more inclination. But granting that it is so, I gather that you are prepared to forgive them this little weakness?"

"That is asking rather too much, Captain Wentworth," replied Georgiana, in the same spirit of gaiety. Had she spoken the whole truth, she would have said: "Certainly not, if any friend of mine were involved," but not wishing her companion to think that their chat had any personal application, she continued: "I shall be able to tell better when I have met with such a case," and turned the subject off with a smile.

Soon after the ladies returned to the drawing-room Georgiana seated herself beside Mrs. Wentworth, whose gentle manners, combined with serenity of temper and the power she had of entering, unobtrusively, but none the less sincerely, into the feelings of others, had for Georgiana a strong attraction. They had not met for so long that there was much to be talked over between them. Mrs. Wentworth presently asked after Colonel Fitzwilliam, and explained that she happened to know he was in town through seeing him a few nights previously at the theatre, where she had been with a party invited by her father and sister. Georgiana replied that he was well, but had gone away since then; and so as not to dwell on the subject, asked for a description of the play, which led them on to other topics of interest, when they were interrupted by Mrs. Knightley's joining them. Her errand was merely to ask for news of Kitty, and Georgiana, rather than resenting the smile of mutual understanding with which the question was put, answered as briefly as she could without discourtesy.

Mrs. Knightley then began talking of other things, and re-settled herself in her chair, so that Georgiana despaired of having Mrs. Wentworth to herself any more that evening; but perceiving she was not wanted elsewhere, she continued to retain her place until the gentlemen entered the room, simultaneously with the tea and coffee, which the servants began to dispense. Mr. Price obtained cups immediately, and brought them across the room to the group of ladies, at once warmly greeting Mrs. Wentworth. Mrs. Knightley remained beside them, and Georgiana indulged in a little private regret, partly on her own account and partly on his, for she knew he must be wanting to talk to her about Kitty, and since there was music during the evening, the present might be the only opportunity they would have. She began to think of moving away, for Mr. Price seemed quite monopolized by Mrs. Knightley, who was endeavouring to show him off by asking him questions and calling Mrs. Wentworth's attention to the answers; and though Georgiana was grateful to his efforts to draw her in, by an occasional smiling glance at her and a "Don't you think so, Miss Darcy?" there did not seem to be any place for a fourth in their conversation.

Presently, however, an interruption arrived in the person of Captain Wentworth, who came, with coffee-cup in hand, to join their group, and as Mr. Price stood aside to give him room, he exclaimed cheerfully: "Well, Price, have you and my wife undertaken the conversion of Miss Darcy yet? Here has someone been deluding her with most horrible picture of us sailors—'one foot on sea, and one on shore, to one thing constant never'—you know the rest of it. I have been trying to persuade her that it is all wrong."

Georgiana, blushing and smiling, began to protest, and Mrs. Wentworth, to spare her, also treated it as a joke, but Mrs. Knightley, when she had comprehended Captain Wentworth's meaning, gave her a look of no great goodwill, and said: "Surely Miss Darcy does not take seriously what is merely a vulgar tradition. 'Men were deceivers ever' was not written with special reference to sailors, I imagine, but to men in general."

"Of course not," said Captain Wentworth, with mock gravity; "but Miss Darcy does not base her suspicions on those lines only, but on far more serious premises."

"Frederick, I will not have you tease Miss Darcy so unmercifully," said Mrs. Wentworth. "It is really too bad. I am sure you have placed words in her mouth which she never uttered, has he not, Miss Darcy?"

Georgiana, struggling with embarrassment, amusement and not a little real vexation, as she was conscious of Mr. Price's eyes being turned silently upon her, could not protest as intelligibly as she would have wished. "Yes, Mrs. Wentworth, it is quite untrue—I never said anything of the kind. Captain Wentworth, you are unfair—not that it really matters—but I said I had no opinion on the subject—I only thought I could quite understand their being changeable, if they were."

Whether her hearers could extract any meaning from these words, she did not know, but it was certain that her confusion stood her in good stead, for Captain Wentworth immediately apologized with just as much seriousness as was needful. "I am very sorry, Miss Darcy; pray excuse my stupidity. I was so distressed to feel that we, as a class, should merit your disapproval in even one particular, that I wanted to clear our characters—and, after all, you are so kind as to imply that they needed no clearing."

"I do not think Miss Darcy implied that," said Mrs. Knightley, "and I confess myself curious to learn why she thinks naval men are likely to be changeable; it would be interesting to compare notes, for my experience of them has led me to the opposite conclusion."

Georgiana felt the double edge in Mrs. Knightley's words, and it was painful to her to be so completely misunderstood, even in such a trifling matter; but she had hardly recovered her composure enough to defend herself when Captain Wentworth took the matter out of her hands.

"Miss Darcy's experience of inconstancy in sailors has been a sad one, Mrs. Knightley," he said solemnly. "It is drawn entirely from books and plays, and we know how persistently they look on the dark side of human nature. She only needs to become acquainted better with real life, as personified in myself, Mr. Price" (with a bow to William) "and many other admirable specimens of naval men, to form the soundest of opinions of us. Pardon me, Miss Darcy, for assuming the rôle of spokesman, but I fancied the fear of offending my modesty might have prevented you from expressing such sentiments as you would wish."

"I hope you will always interpret me as correctly as you have done, Captain Wentworth," returned Georgiana, smiling; and seeing that Mrs. Knightley was beginning to speak in a low tone to Mr. Price, and not wishing to hear any of her comments, she turned to Mrs. Wentworth and proposed that they should move to chairs nearer the pianoforte. They therefore turned in that direction, but Mr. Price could hardly have any time to reply to Mrs. Knightley, for an instant later he was at Georgiana's side, asking if he might find her a seat; and Mrs. Wentworth being just then drawn away by Miss Bingley, she not unwillingly allowed him to lead her to a sofa on the opposite side of the room, to procure her another cup of coffee, her own having been removed, and to sit beside her, talking quietly and agreeably in a manner that soothed her nerves, irritated as they were by Captain Wentworth's ill-timed raillery. She listened absently, without saying much, grateful to him for not renewing the subject which had just been dropped and hoping he had not attached any importance to it; but her attention was all alert when after a pause he inquired: "Have you good accounts of Miss Bennet since she left town?"

She tried to collect her scattered ideas, to remember what Kitty expected of her. Yes, she had had good accounts; she thought her friend was very well and, she believed, enjoying the country, though it probably seemed very quiet to her after such a long visit to London.

William Price assented, and said that Miss Bennet had so much freshness and enthusiasm, she could enjoy many things, and enter keenly into them all.

Georgiana fully endorsed this, but thought that Kitty had had a particularly delightful visit to town this year and really regretted leaving.

William Price said that Miss Bennet's friends were very sorry to lose her.

"This is all very well," thought Georgiana, "but we do not get any farther. Am I shy of him, or is he shy of me? Oh, I wonder what Kitty would like me to say? If I were Mrs. Knightley I could probably bring in the inconstancy of sailors with good effect. I suppose she thinks that I mean to throw a doubt on Mr. Price; how unlucky that it should have had that appearance!"

She was assisted in her meditations by Mr. Price's remarking that he had never been in Derbyshire, and imagined it to be a beautiful county, and this afforded her the opportunity of descanting on the loveliness of its scenery and the particular attractions of the country round Desborough Park. She added that she hoped there would be nothing to prevent him from seeing it for himself that autumn, and he replied warmly, agreeing and saying that if he were still his own master at that time nothing should prevent it.

A question or two about Pemberley followed, and the relative positions of the two houses; he had heard of it as being a show place from his sister, Mrs. Bertram, who had made a tour through the midland counties to visit all the cathedrals and old churches, but, he declared, had actually been so worldly as to look at one or two of the grand mansions as well. Georgiana questioned its worldliness, and was told that his brother and sister were the dearest people, but dreadfully good; they thought everything wrong.

This description, of which Georgiana would have liked to have heard more, was interrupted by a song, and at its conclusion Mr. Price was waiting with the inquiry: "Do you return to Pemberley soon, Miss Darcy?"

"In about a month, I think; but I leave town in a fortnight's time to stay with my aunt at Hunsford."

"I am leaving London almost immediately, I am sorry to say," said William Price. "I have to go down to Portsmouth, where my mother is changing houses, and as she has that and a quantity of lawyers' business on her hands, since my father died, she wishes me to help her."

Georgiana could not but approve of this decision, but she thought it partly accounted for the young man's being in far less good spirits this evening than on the previous occasion; he evidently did not like to quit London. She was endeavouring to think of a way of conveying to him that she would see Kitty almost as soon as she reached home, when the opening of a solo on the harp caused her to forget everything but the sound of the instrument, in which she had always taken extreme delight. Mr. Price, too, listened with close attention, and when it was over, and they were commending the performance, he exclaimed: "The harp always reminds me of one of the most charming women I ever knew, who used to play it—still does, I daresay, at all events it is associated inseparably with her."

Curiosity as well as politeness impelled Georgiana to ask for more particulars, for she privately wished very much to know what her companion's idea of a charming woman might be, and he answered readily enough: "She was a lady I first met some years ago at Mansfield before my sister's marriage; she was a friend of the whole Bertram family, and, in a way, of my sister's also; but circumstances divided them, Miss Crawford's people left the neighbourhood, and now I only see her occasionally in town."

Miss Darcy's start and heightening of colour did not escape him; he looked inquiringly at her, and question and answer broke from them both simultaneously. "Yes, I have met Miss Crawford," said Georgiana, "what a very strange thing! I was introduced to her in the gardens the other day by—by a mutual friend, and I had heard of her before from my brother and sister."

"That is indeed strange! I wish I had known when I was with her last. I have been seeing a good deal of Mrs. Grant, her sister, and Miss Crawford lately, being myself that abomination, an idle man about town, but it has just this once had its agreeable side."

Georgiana murmured that she had supposed he was seldom in London for so long, and he continued, with perfect ease and frankness: "Quite true; indeed, I have never before had time to see the sights; and Miss Crawford, who is a regular Londoner, takes me about to them, in order, she says, to waste my time as usefully as possible. To-day we were at a picture gallery, and last week we went to see an exhibition of silver, models of ships, most interesting and unusual it was; I would not have missed it for the world. The curious design and rigging of them! I should like to have shown them to you, Miss Darcy."

Georgiana echoed his wish, but was so much interested in pursuing her theory that Miss Crawford was the handsome young woman Mrs. Hurst had spoken of, that she ventured one more question: "You said you had known Miss Crawford for some time, Mr. Price?"

"Oh, yes, for years; looking back on it, I must have been quite a small boy when we first met; at all events, I regarded her as being one of my elders. That is a very ungallant thing to say, is it not? I do not know why I said it. But I always had a great regard for her, and when the families were alienated I always tried to keep in touch with her and Mrs. Grant, for the severance was through no fault of hers, only her brother's—though I know the blame for it has often been laid at her door."

How easy it is to believe in people, if only we wish to do so! This speech fully accounted for all that had been heard of Mr. Price, and acquitted him of any lightness of conduct; he had merely been faithful to an old friend; and Miss Crawford was only proved more worthy than before of Colonel Fitzwilliam's esteem. Georgiana longed to inquire further, to see if Mr. Price could throw more light on the recent perplexing event, but felt it would be presumption to do so, and he sat musing for a few moments, unaware of the sentiments he had aroused in his companion, until, in response to a remark from her, he exclaimed warmly: "Yes, she is indeed a beautiful woman, and as charming as beautiful. You would like her, Miss Darcy, if you knew her. I heard this evening that she was engaged; I do not know if it is true, but I am inclined to hope not if I heard the name aright; still, one must presume it will be all for the best."

He spoke the last words somewhat hurriedly, as if not wishing to dwell on them, but could not overlook the anxiety in

Georgiana's face and voice. "Is she engaged, Mr. Price? I thought perhaps that might be the case. Do you know to whom it is?"

"I heard a name mentioned, Miss Darcy, but I do not like— I am uncertain whether it is correct—I should like to verify it first," said William Price, in some embarrassment.

"Of course, I quite understand. It would not be fair to say anything until you are sure. But no doubt it is true." And Georgiana, with a sigh, fell into a reverie, which her companion, observing her with solicitude, did not venture to interrupt.

They were divided a few minutes later, Georgiana being called upon to contribute a solo upon the pianoforte, and she could not help feeling gratified to see that William Price listened attentively to her playing, for the love of music was in her eyes, an additionally attractive feature in anyone's character. These were the pleasantest impressions she derived from the evening, for on the whole they had been sad ones; she had inadvertently exposed herself to being misunderstood by Mrs. Knightley, and perhaps by Mrs. Wentworth, for whose esteem she cared far more; she had not been able to say one word to help Kitty, and would have no news to give of the kind that Kitty was longing for; and, worst of all, her fears for her cousin were confirmed; instead of anyone being able to help him, he could only be told that the disappointment he had experienced was a final and permanent one. Georgiana's thoughts were all for him; they hardly even strayed to speculate upon Miss Crawford's choice, except for a touch of wondering pity for one who had possessed his regard and thrown it away for another's. No; the world was determinedly awry, and Georgiana went to bed longing for the comfort of Elizabeth and Pemberley, and dreading the days to be spent under the judicial and unsympathetic eye of her Aunt Catherine.

Chapter 12

ELIZABETH AND HER HUSBAND desired Georgiana's return as much as she did herself, but Lady Catherine had been very urgent that her niece should visit her, and they judged it right that she should take the opportunity of going, while comparatively near Rosings. Georgiana had never before stayed there without the protection of her brother's or sister's presence; but she found it to be less alarming than she feared, for her aunt was probably disposed to be more complaisant and less dictatorial to her than to any other living creature; and while not comprehending her niece's character in the least, wished to make her happy, if it were possible to be happy, in the best Rosings manner. So Georgiana obediently played the piano, joined in games of quadrille, drove out with her cousin in the pony chaise, endured her aunt's admonishments, and listened politely to Lady Catherine's long stories about her own youth; and the time did at length pass away, though not until she had many times decided that London, even with the agitations that it had afforded this year, was far less wearing to the temper and spirits.

The date of her homecoming was fixed for the fifth of August, and an escort was unexpectedly found in the person of Mr. Bennet, who had made one of his sudden resolves to go and stay with his two daughters, Mrs. Bennet having the prospect of her sister, Mrs. Phillips's companionship throughout that month. Georgiana was enchanted when this decision was conveyed to her, as it ensured that no postponement of the journey would be made upon any pretext. Mr. Bennet had proposed visiting his daughters and bringing back Kitty, and the first part of this suggestion was warmly welcomed; the second they could not promise to accede to, but Mr. Bennet would be conferring a signal service if he would meet Miss Darcy in London and bring her home. Mr. Bennet declared himself quite agreeable; let Miss Darcy name her own day for starting, and it should be his; but once named, it must be considered fixed, for Mr. Bennet, it must be noted, had a wife and five daughters, and knew something of the variability of the female mind. He had, however, never been in less danger of a change of plans than on this occasion.

Elizabeth had received the first intimation of her father's intended visit shortly after dispatching to Georgiana the letter which has been mentioned, and having now so many matters to talk over with Jane, she determined on going to Desborough without delay. An hour or two's chat would not be sufficient, and she therefore arranged to stay for a night and return the following afternoon, and pressed Darcy to accompany her; but this he declined to do, telling her that he should only be in the way when she, Jane and Kitty were putting their heads together for a feminine conclave, and Bingley was as bad as the rest.

It happened that Jane was alone when she arrived, Bingley being out riding with Kitty and Mr. Morland; but he was not long in returning, and when Kitty had greeted her sister, and retired to change her dress, he joined the conference, as Darcy had foretold.

"Well, Elizabeth," he began, "and how do you find Kitty? I never saw her in better looks. And has Jane told you about my young friend in London, who, it appears, is an admirer of hers? I declare I had not an idea of it when I asked him to come down, but it turns out very well as it happens."

Elizabeth admitted herself informed, and asked Bingley for particulars of Mr. Price's character, appearance and manners, of which it was to be presumed he could give a more reasonable account than Kitty. He spoke warmly in the young man's praise, and mentioned what he had heard of his family and connections from Mr. Yates.

"It seems most satisfactory," said Elizabeth, "and his being a friend of the Wentworths is a further recommendation. I am quite looking forward to meeting him, though time alone will show if there is anything in it."

"Kitty has set her heart on it to such an extent, that I feel extremely anxious that she may have no disappointment," said Jane with tenderness. "It would be enough to make her ill, her sensibilities are so acute! One can see how she watches for the letters from Mrs. Knightley, and the eagerness with which she reads them."

"Whatever Mrs. Knightley may do," said Elizabeth, "in my opinion we should not be acting wisely by Kitty in encouraging her to talk and think much about it. On the young man's side it has not gone beyond a promising inclination, I infer, and it may never be more."

"You are a prudent creature, Elizabeth," exclaimed her brother-in-law; "but as regards Kitty, your precautions are too late, as I know to my cost. There was I was thinking I was bringing down the very girl for Morland to fall in love with—indeed, I had almost told him so—and now it appears she is more than half engaged to someone else, and what good is that to a man who wants a wife to establish in that big house of his?"

"Well," said Elizabeth, laughing, "you need not reproach yourself, Charles. A house and living were promised to Mr. Morland; but a wife, I believe, was not in the bond."

"It would have been very pleasant to have provided him with one, nevertheless," returned Bingley. "As it is, they see a great deal of each other, and are such excellent friends, that if it were not all such a profound secret it would be incumbent on me to give him a hint of the state of things."

Elizabeth looked at her sister for confirmation of this, and Jane replied: "Yes, they are good friends. Kitty seems to enjoy his companionship, and he has evidently a strong liking for her, so that I sometimes feel afraid lest it should develop into anything likely to cause him pain hereafter. But, of course, as I have repeatedly told Bingley, even in view of such a contingency we have no right to betray our knowledge of Kitty's private hopes."

As Mr. Morland dined at Desborough, Elizabeth had an opportunity of observing the young people, and she thought she had seldom seen Kitty to greater advantage; her particularly delicate beauty was heightened partly by excitement and partly by the healthful country life. She was at perfect ease, happy with her sisters and Mr. Bingley, and treating Mr. Morland much as she would have treated an elderly friend of the family, not as a man to be captivated. The feeling of frank goodfellowship which he seemed to inspire was a simple and wholesome one, and Elizabeth tried to rest assured that Mr. Morland was aware of Kitty's attitude towards him and wished for nothing more. That, indeed, was the impression he gave; but the longer she was with him, the more clearly she perceived that now his circumstances were more settled a quiet contentment, an evenness of temper, had become habitual to him, without taking away the earnestness, the steadfastness of purpose, which underlay the whole. She felt that she did not yet thoroughly know Mr. Morland; and the following morning, in the course of a brief talk with Kitty, she suggested to her in the gentlest possible way of the desirability of not allowing so excellent a young man, who was also a solitary one, to entertain thoughts of her which might be so much more easily admitted to his mind than expelled from it. Kitty had just been giving wings to her imagination in a description of Mr. Price, which Elizabeth had felt herself hard-hearted to be obliged to check, and the young girl with difficulty came down to earth again to Mr. Morland, to assure Elizabeth, with all haste of indifference, that she was positive that Morland did not think of her in that way; he only cared for his parish and his house, and as for his being solitary—why, his sister Sarah was coming to live with him.

Elizabeth was compelled to be content, and, in addition, she secured a promise from Jane that Kitty should come to Pemberley about the middle of September. Kitty was delighted with the arrangement, so long as there was one which secured her return to Desborough for the shooting-party early in November. Her eldest sister exhibited an almost equal amount of eagerness on her behalf to settle this important matter; and

Kitty, who had been living in terror lest some cruel fate should intervene to send her back to Longbourn before that time, breathed more freely when her sisters undertook to obtain her father's consent to such a long absence.

Mr. Bennet and Georgiana duly arrived at Pemberley, and were welcomed with all the warmth that affection could show. They had been a curiously assorted pair of travelling companions, and their relations had speculated with amusement upon their chances of congeniality. Neither being talkers, they had at least had that in common, though after their arrival Georgiana smilingly reproached Mr. Bennet with having intently studied a book of Latin poetry throughout the whole journey, and Mr. Bennet gravely apologized for not having selected a volume more suitable for reading aloud; he was sorry he had not been at more pains to while away the time for a young lady who was exceedingly punctual, and always ready when the carriage came round. For his own part, he declared that he felt himself becoming more conversational with every mile of the way, in proof of which he twice voluntarily told Elizabeth during the first hour that he was glad to see her again, and announced that, after his own library, there was no place he would sooner be in than Mr. Darcy's.

The first evening was a cheerful one, there was so much to say, so many friends to inquire after, adventures to relate, and plans to detail. The children were brought in, and, according to the time-honoured custom everywhere, were pronounced to have grown, though it is to be feared that Mr. Bennet was not an ideal grandparent, for he so far miscalculated as to bring them toys which they could not properly appreciate for some years at least; and Elizabeth wanted to hear of little William and

Elizabeth Collins, with whom Georgiana had often played at Hunsford Parsonage, and who were described as being striking like their father and mother respectively.

It was not until the following day, when the sisters were alone together, that any words passed between them concerning Colonel Fitzwilliam. Elizabeth showed Georgiana a few brief lines she had received from him, stating little more than the bare facts of his departure and its cause. "She is engaged, and it is all over for me now. At all events, I know the worst," he wrote. "Do not be too compassionate for me, Elizabeth. I have been a fool, to think that anything so bright and lovely should become mine. Yet I did not think she would bestow herself where she has. I was a laggard, I suppose, and I threw my chance away in Bath; and how could she wait until I had reinstated myself? No, my dream is over. You will hear of her engagement, no doubt, and I beg you to tell her that I join with you in wishes for her happiness. I shall be with you at Pemberley before long. Georgiana is an angel. I did not deserve from her one quarter of the kindness she showed me."

In a postscript he added: "Will Darcy trust me to choose him a horse? I have seen a beautiful pair of bays, that would suit your large carriage, besides a perfect chestnut hunter."

Georgiana sighed and smiled over the letter, and Elizabeth said: "Yes, he evidently does not wish us to think he is over-whelmed by it, though from what he does *not* say I can realize the depth of his feeling. It is incredible; for, of course, it must be Sir Walter Elliot."

Sir Walter's was only a name to Georgiana, a vague recollection from the last year at Bath, and she replied that she had heard of the engagement from another source, without particulars.

Elizabeth gave a vigorous description of him and ended by saying that she should wait and see if the necessity for writing to Miss Crawford arose, for she did not feel much disposed to congratulate her.

Kitty's affairs were, of course, passed under review, and Elizabeth was somewhat surprised to find that Georgiana was a staunch upholder of the notion that William Price was likely to make her an offer, as she had fancied that the accounts might have been exaggerated, and that Georgiana would be the one to take a sober and dispassionate view. But her asseverations of her belief that Mr. Price's truth and steadiness, and in Kitty's being unlikely to have deceived herself in this case, went farther to convince Elizabeth than anything she had heard before.

The next few weeks passed in tranquil enjoyment for all the persons in the Pemberley circle, in which must be comprised the party from Desborough, as no plan of any importance could be carried through without the joining of forces, and the inclusion of Mr. Morland on the one side and the Ferrars from Pemberley Rectory on the other. The Bingleys, with the two young people, frequently drove over to spend a day or two days, and when Mr. Bennet removed to Desborough towards the end of August, it was not felt to be so much of a break-up as a changing of the scene of their activities. Boating expeditions, rides over the moors, blackberry gatherings, or evenings spent quietly at home in games or music, something could always be found to suit the tastes of a party of people who were bent on finding pleasure in each other's company; even Kitty felt that only one thing was wanting to fill her cup of happiness to the brim, for her father had sanctioned her staying on until November, the month, she hoped, which would see its overflow.

For one person, however, this peaceful time was about to end in pain and disappointment. Mrs. Bingley and her sister were sitting indoors together one morning in the middle of September, when Mr. Morland was observed approaching the house. He was such a frequent caller that it had become a habit with him to walk straight in, and the ladies, after waiting for some time, wondered at his non-appearance, and still more at the intelligence brought by a servant, in answer to Jane's summons, that Mr. Morland had asked only for Mr. Bennet, and had been shown into the library.

"What can he want with my father?" said Jane, a suspicion of the truth shooting across her mind and checking her utterance, as she glanced anxiously at her sister; but no such idea seemed to have occurred to Kitty, who innocently conjectured their interview to be a literary conference, or a discussion that had arisen out of Mr. Morland's sermon-making.

Mr. Bennet, on perceiving his visitor, might have anticipated something of the kind, but Mr. Morland's first words corrected him. The young man's errand was indeed nothing more or less than to make a formal proposal for the hand of Mr. Bennet's daughter and to request permission to address her. He was nervous, as men in his situation are apt to be, but genuine feeling and sound sense enabled him to state his case well, if not very fluently, as he represented the strength of his attachment and described his worldly position and prospects.

Mr. Bennet had long ceased to be surprised at receiving applications of the kind, however unexpected they might be, and certainly this one found him quite unprepared. What little thought he had given to the subject had certainly not led him to the supposition of Mr. Morland's becoming his son-in-law, and he endeavoured to make his answer a discouraging one.

"My daughter will be much honoured by your high opinion of her, Mr. Morland, and I have no reason to think ill of your pretensions; but I must admit that I have not remarked on her part any strong prepossession in your favour."

"It is one of the things I have found most charming in Miss Bennet's character, sir," replied Morland, "that she would not easily give her heart away, or readily suppose a man to be enslaved by her. No one else could have failed to perceive the depth of my admiration, but she has seemed quite unconscious of it, though at the same time I am fully aware that there is no brilliancy or distinction about me, nothing to attract anyone who herself possesses a full measure of those qualities."

He looked so downcast that Mr. Bennet remarked: "If that were the question, Mr. Morland, you might set your mind at rest, for my daughter, though a very good girl, is not brilliant, nor would she be comfortable with a husband of that description."

This observation inspired Mr. Morland to a fairly long speech, in which he extolled Kitty's amiable qualities and dwelt on his own demerits, but notwithstanding the contrast thereby presented, he was able to deduce a number of excellent reasons for his being allowed to propose to Miss Bennet without delay. Mr. Bennet heard him in silence, and at the end replied that, though flattered by Mr. Morland's first referring to him, who was merely the father of the young lady, he could not answer for his daughter's sentiments; he had found that in these matters his girls had always made up their own minds, and no doubt would continue to do so.

"Indeed, yes, it is with Miss Bennet that I must plead my own cause; but you will not refuse me your sanction?" said the young man, eagerly. "You think so far favourably of my suit that you will place no bar in the way of my—I trust I may in time say *our* perfect happiness?"

"No, Mr. Morland, the way to your perfect happiness is open as far as I am concerned," replied Mr. Bennet, taking up a book.

Morland's satisfaction at having the father even passively on his side was very great, and he spoke his gratitude very warmly, mingling with it such praises of Kitty, and such rosy prognostications of the future, as caused Mr. Bennet to reply, in characteristic fashion: "Let me know when the time comes to wish you joy, Mr. Morland, and I will do it, but life is so uncertain that I think for the present I had better refrain. Have you ascertained whether Kitty can cook, make her own gowns, and trim hats? I understand it is a great promoter of married happiness when the wife can do so, and I am not sure whether all my girls have turned their education to such good account."

Mr. Morland only replied by asking if he might be allowed to see Miss Bennet at once, and her father left the room, foreseeing that, whatever happened, he should not have one more quiet hour during that day. His anticipations were soon in the way to be fulfilled, for on finding his daughters, and sending Kitty to the library, he had to give Jane and outline of what had just passed, then repeat it to Bingley, who joined them, and listened to their exclamations of surprise, and regret at the probable downfall of Mr. Morland's hopes. Jane and Bingley were both too convinced of Kitty's prior attachment to have the slightest expectation of his success, and Mr. Bennet was put in full possession of the facts relating to it, while they anxiously awaited the termination of the interview.

SYBIL G. BRINTON

It came, after some minutes, in a glimpse of Kitty emerging from the library and hurrying upstairs with streaming eyes, and while they all debated as to their next move, Mr. Morland was seen to cross the hall rapidly, looking nowhere but in front of him, and leave the house with precipitation. Jane herself, almost equally distressed, longed to go to Kitty, and Bingley questioned whether he ought not to hasten after the young man, while Mr. Bennet was disposed to think they would be better left to them-selves for a time, and wished heartily that there were only just enough lovers in the world to go round, one to each young lady, and none over.

In spite of this, Jane was not long in finding her way to her agitated sister and in showing her the tenderest consideration. Kitty's distress was very great, and also very sincere, for she had in truth been far from guessing that Mr. Morland took a more than common interest in her, and as is usual in such cases, the declaration of the young man's love woke in her feelings which she had not known to exist, of reciprocal kindness and even affection, which only did not share the nature and strength of his. Kitty could never have been hard-hearted to any lover, least of all to one whom she liked as much as she did James Morland, and his devotion touched her as deeply as the knowledge that she could not accept it wounded her. Between regrets for what had happened, pity for him and for herself, and the excited thoughts of William Price which the incident itself was bound to evoke, she was in a sad state, and Jane easily prevailed upon her to have her dinner upstairs and go early to bed. Not so eas-ily could she check the tears which flowed continuously, and Jane, to occupy her mind and body, proposed that she should go to-morrow to Pemberley, instead of in three days' time, as arranged; she could very well be sent over, and the change would be beneficial; besides, she was not really leaving them, for there was the November visit to look forward to. Kitty caught at the suggestion, and declining the offices of the maid, began to busy herself about her packing, as Jane hoped she would do, while the latter descended to consult with her husband and father.

Mr. Bennet and Bingley both approved, and Jane hastily wrote a few lines to Elizabeth to apprise her of what had happened, that she might be prepared for Kitty's arrival. The two gentlemen walked to the nearest post town to convey the letter; and after dinner the indefatigable Bingley again set out, this time to the Rectory, to perform the same kind office by James Morland as his wife had been doing by Kitty. The young man, though calmer, proved far more unreceptive of consolation. He had felt his rebuff acutely, for Kitty had been too much taken by surprise, too sure of herself, to make it otherwise than decisive, and even the modest hopes he had ventured to entertain, of being able to make more progress with her once the subject was opened between them, had been most thoroughly dispelled. Miss Bennet would not hear another word of it—begged him never to speak of it again—with tears reproached him for having spoilt everything, so that in addition to his own disappointment he had the pain of feeling that she thought less well of him than before. Bingley could deny this, but could not affirm anything else likely to give him comfort. It remained for Morland himself to declare, which he did in a firm though melancholy tone, that he regretted having distressed Miss Bennet, and would endeavour so to meet her in the future that she would not suffer through being reminded of it by any act of word of his. Bingley commended his courage, told him of Kitty's departure, and begged him to continue coming to Desborough just the same; and walked home with a full report of what had just passed.

Jane shook her head over it, for, while sympathizing with both, she was more truly sorry for Mr. Morland, since for him she could see no immediate prospect of compensation, in spite of he father's assurances that a young clergyman was seldom allowed to remain inconsolable for more than six months, and if Kitty's other young man only did what was expected of him, her fate would be a certainty in half that time.

Chapter 13

NEEDLESS TO SAY, KITTY was heartily welcomed by Georgiana and Elizabeth, and given every opportunity to relieve her mind by descriptions of the tragical affair in all its aspects. Both regretted it deeply for Mr. Morland's sake, and Elizabeth privately did so for Kitty's sake, having such a good opinion of him as to make her wish that Kitty could have been persuaded out of her fancy for a young man, who, however excellent, was comparatively a stranger to them all, and whose intentions, at present, were extremely uncertain. She would have rejoiced if Kitty and Morland could have made each other happy, and had entertained a slight hope that her hint to Kitty might perhaps have helped matters, in directing her thoughts into another channel, but it seemed to be of no avail, and Georgiana gave her friend her warmest support, implying entire agreement with her point of view. "I could not help it, now, could I, Georgiana? You know yourself, Lizzie, that I never dreamt it. How could I do anything else but refuse him outright? I was amazingly grieved to do so, but you know very well, Georgiana, that if I could think of one man more than another, *he* is not that one." She paused for assent, which Georgiana gave by a silent caress, and then continued: "It is all so unfortunate. It will never be as pleasant at Desborough now. Poor Mr. Morland! I wish I had not had to hurt him. He does want someone so badly in the Rectory."

"Well, my dear, do not make yourself ill with these vain regrets," said Elizabeth. "It is, as you say, very unfortunate, but no one blames you. If you could not care for him, you could not do it, and someone else will have to inhabit that nice Rectory."

Kitty looked as if this prospect were not very pleasing either, but Georgiana, seeing what Elizabeth wished, began to talk cheerfully of something else, and Kitty gradually joined in, though whenever the two girls were alone together she found it difficult to abstain long from referring to some branch of the subject.

Georgiana's loyalty and patience never failed, but she wished for November almost as earnestly as Kitty herself, so that matters might reach some definite conclusion, for Kitty's restlessness had considerably increased since she had received James Morland's offer, and she was constantly nervous and excitable and not mistress of herself. On the day when the Bingleys and Mr. Bennet came over for the latter to take leave before returning to Longbourn, this was specially noticeable in her state of anxious flutter when drawing Jane aside to inquire after Mr. Morland. Mr. Bennet bade her farewell gravely and more affectionately than was his wont, telling her that he left her in good hands, and would only give her one piece of advice, namely, that second thoughts were sometimes best. Kitty blushed deeply and could not pretend to misunderstand him, but told Georgiana afterwards that it was impossible to have better second thoughts when Price was the first.

With his elder daughter Mr. Bennet was rather more explicit, telling Elizabeth that he considered it was a great pity that so unobjectionable a young man should have been sent about his business. Elizabeth entirely agreed with him, and thought it would not be going too far to express Mr. Morland's praise in even warmer terms.

"He will never set the Thames on fire, but there seems good stuff in him," was Mr. Bennet's reply. "When he proposed for her I had not taken much notice of him, except to think him a tolerably sensible fellow, and of course I had to readjust my ideas; but I soon began to see that he must not be judged by that alone. I have really liked him better, too, for his way of taking his refusal."

"My dear father, it does not always indicate a want of sense to wish to be married," interposed Elizabeth.

"Perhaps not, but Morland is much better off as he is than in marrying a girl he knows so little about. Kitty is flighty and expensive; she ought to stay longer with you and Jane, and not think of being married for the next ten years."

Elizabeth smiled and said she thought that it was unnecessary, but that it would certainly be better for Kitty to marry a clergyman than an officer in the navy, who would be compelled to spend long periods away from home.

"As to that, of course it is a complete absurdity, and I cannot think why you women, who are so fond of making matches, did not originate something less ridiculously unsuitable among yourselves."

Elizabeth thought it wiser not to explain who actually had originated the idea, and said after a pause: "You were saying that you have liked Mr. Morland better of late?"

"Yes, he has positively shown some sort of self-command and dignity. He turned up at the house a day or two afterwards, apparently *not* bent on making us all uncomfortable by the sight of his misery, as most rejected lovers do. Besides, Bingley had had the foresight to produce some excellent port."

"I hear from Jane," said Elizabeth, "that he does not avoid or seek the mention of Kitty, and she thinks he is trying to give up all hope of her."

"Her absence for a few weeks will no doubt materially assist him," said Mr. Bennet.

Kitty seized the opportunity offered by this visit to speak a private word to her brother-in-law with reference to the hero, as Bingley persisted in calling him. She herself had no news, for Mrs. Knightley's frequent letters reported him still at Portsmouth, and Bingley had heard nothing, but promised to write and renew his invitation as soon as October was fairly in.

The same silence prevailed at Pemberley with regard to Miss Crawford. No announcement of her marriage had reached any of them, and Elizabeth had a half inclination to make some inquiries, but was dissuaded by Darcy, who said: "Whatever precisely has happened, Elizabeth, we can be sure of one thing, that Miss Crawford has allowed Fitzwilliam to understand that she does not wish him to approach her again. Under these circumstances it is better that you should have no news to give him."

Elizabeth sighed as she agreed to the wisdom of this decision, but when shortly after her father's departure a letter was received from Colonel Fitzwilliam to say he would be returning at the end of the month, she could not help wishing that she was more fully informed of the present state of affairs. It would be a relief, even though a sad one, to Fitzwilliam's mind to know that Miss Crawford was actually married and he would be unselfish enough to wish to hear that she was happy. Nothing occurred, however, to enlighten them, and Fitzwilliam arrived on the appointed day, looking much as usual except for a few more lines about the eyes and an increased number of grey hairs.

It was the first time he and Georgiana had been together at Pemberley since the rupture of their engagement, and both must have felt conscious of it, Georgiana in particular being prepared to be miserable for a time, from the belief that her cousin, instead of being cheered and invigorated as formerly by his return home, must be reminded at every turn of the failure of their experiment, the failure caused by her wretched weakness and incapacity. Worse still, her brother must be reminded of it, and there might be a repetition of his stern looks, his cold manner. She trembled at the thought, unaware that Darcy had long been persuaded of the wisdom of their parting, ever since events in Bath had shown him where his cousin's real affections were likely to be bestowed, and the only difference which Georgiana perceived after Fitzwilliam's arrival was in the particular kindness he showed her, and the complete renewal of the old comfortable relations amongst them all.

When inquiries after the Hursts and Mrs. Annesley had been made, and Georgiana had mentioned the dinner-party and the persons who had been present, little more was said with reference to London; indeed, there was little more for either to say, for Georgiana dared not refer to the person who had chiefly occupied his mind there. Fitzwilliam talked of his book and of Ireland, inquired about the prospects of the shooting, showed interest in the minutest details of life in the neighbourhood, and in every way endeavoured to prove that he was exactly his old self; and only when walking with Elizabeth in the Park one morning did he betray how far that was from being the case.

There was no doubt that his disappointment had coloured his whole life. He had allowed himself to think of Miss Crawford, and to build high upon his hopes, and to find himself again mistaken had been a blow which cut at the foundations of all his happiness. His gaiety was feigned, his pursuits had lost their zest, his friends no longer sufficed him: and as he said to Elizabeth, he had felt he had better adopt some country occupation and settle down to it, and there grow old as quietly and quickly as might be.

Elizabeth's heart was wrung; the spectacle of her cousin's fine nature locked away, as it were, in a closed room, as a thing no one had any need for, was inexpressively painful to her, and nothing else would have caused her to venture upon a reopening of the subject which he himself had not approached. With the utmost gentleness she spoke a few words of commiseration, and then, still proceeding with extreme caution, she told him of the absence of news and her assumption that Miss Crawford's marriage with Sir Walter Elliot had been delayed.

"I daresay it has," returned Colonel Fitzwilliam, with a kind of listlessness, striking with his stick at the head of some tall grasses which bordered their path.

"There can be no doubt of it, I suppose?" pursued Elizabeth.

"None at all, I should imagine," replied the Colonel. "Miss Crawford is not the kind of woman who would break her word, once the engagement had been announced."

"No, of course not," said Elizabeth; "but I had expected that she or Mrs. Grant would have written to me, or even Mrs. Wentworth, as they must know I should be interested."

Colonel Fitzwilliam could not immediately recall anything of Mrs. Wentworth beyond her name, and on being reminded

OLD FRIENDS AND NEW FANCIES

that she was Sir Walter Elliot's daughter, presently replied: "I do not think it altogether surprising she should not have written to you. She probably cares little for the marriage, and still less for the one which it was anticipated would follow it—I mean Miss Elliot's to Mr. Crawford."

This was a new idea to Elizabeth, and while she was pondering over it, and the inferences to be drawn from it, Colonel Fitzwilliam broke the silence by saying: "Perhaps we had better not speak of this anymore, Elizabeth. I know your great kindness of heart, but I feel it does no good, rather harm, to be reviving thoughts which I must in honour suppress as much as possible. I was anxious to know whether you had heard anything, and to ask you again, when you have the chance, to tell her that I wish her well; but now we have mentioned it, it would, I think, be best for my contemptibly weak character to put it as far away as possible."

With tears in her eyes, Elizabeth assured him that through the tenderest regard for him, not through any fear of overtaxing his fortitude, she would respect his wishes, but could not help begging him to remain with them at Pemberley as heretofore, so as to give them an opportunity of showing him how completely their happiness was bound up with his, and of making use of any opportunity which might arise for them to be of service to him. Fitzwilliam gratefully promised to stay for the present, and said that his only engagement was to go to some friends in Leicestershire in November, for the hunting.

Elizabeth was, nevertheless, not perfectly satisfied, and took occasion to ask Georgiana shortly afterwards whether it was from Mrs. Wentworth that she had heard confirmation of the fact that Sir Walter Elliot was engaged to Miss Crawford.

"No," said Georgiana, in surprise, "it was from Mr. Price. Mrs. Wentworth never mentioned it. Mrs. Wentworth! Of course, I recollect now, she is Sir Walter Elliot's daughter; but at the time I never thought of it, for, you see, I did not know Sir Walter was the man."

"Very true; I had also forgotten that you did not know," said Elizabeth, "and would never connect her with Miss Crawford. I have been thinking that I should like, for our own satisfaction, to know when the wedding is going to take place, and the simplest way will be to write and ask Mrs. Wentworth. I wish I had done so before, but I did not wish to be in haste, and I felt so convinced we should hear from others."

Georgiana agreed that this was the best course to pursue, and Elizabeth, having told Darcy of her intention, to which, on account of her promise to Fitzwilliam, he could no longer object, wrote and dispatched her letter.

The season was now drawing on, and with the shortening days the family at Pemberley found themselves thrown more upon the resources of their own immediate circle for amusement. The weather was consistently bad, and though this did not prevent the gentlemen from covering great distances for the purpose of slaughtering their game, the ladies were of necessity restricted to a smaller area, and their walks seldom extended beyond the park, except when their inclinations led them along a tolerably clean road towards the Rectory. This happened pretty frequently, for both Elizabeth and Georgiana were extremely attached to Elinor Ferrars. Their friendship was of a particularly sincere and well-balanced kind, and was not marred by their constant intercourse, as each knew how to maintain that degree of reserve which prevents indiscriminate confidences and so greatly strengthens mutual respect. Kitty was the one who perhaps found the society of the Rectory the least congenial; but it is to be feared that she was extremely difficult to please that autumn, and in the impatience with which she waited for one young man she might have sometimes regretted the solace which the company of the other would have afforded.

In such a small neighbourhood everyone was of some value, and they all heard with interest of the approaching visit to Mr. and Mrs. Edward Ferrars of an old friend, Mrs. Jennings, who was coming early in October to spend six or seven weeks with them. Mrs. Ferrars was in delicate health, and Mrs. Jennings, besides having an almost maternal affection for her, was well qualified to be of service as sick nurse and enlivening companion, so that Elinor's warning to Mrs. Darcy that her friend, although the kindest of women, had not always the most refined manner of expressing herself, did not prevent them from being anxious to make her acquaintance.

Mrs. Jennings performed in safety the long journey from her son-in-law's house in Devonshire, and arrived in her customary high spirits. It was her first visit to the Ferrars's since their removal from Delaford, and she had to examine the house, to criticize minutely the arrangement of their furniture, and to compare their surroundings, social and material, with what they had been in their old home. Mrs. Darcy paid an early call on the new arrival, and the morning after her visit Georgiana and Kitty also found their way to the Rectory.

Mrs. Jennings's exuberance, her loud laugh and general noisy cheerfulness did not recommend her strongly to either of the girls in the first few minutes, and Georgiana was glad to move to a chair by Mrs. Ferrars, to enter into a quieter conversation with her; but before long, judging by the sounds which reached them, Mrs. Jennings and Kitty had found some subjects in common. This perhaps was not so surprising, as Mrs. Jennings was exceedingly fond of the society of all young girls, and cared not at all whether they returned her partiality or no. In this case she had begun, with the utmost frankness, to discourse on the subject nearest her heart at the moment, namely, her dear Mrs. Ferrars, and was relating all the circumstances under which their friendship had been formed, the Dashwood girls' visit to London, the disagreeable conduct of Mrs. Ferrars's mother and sister, and the absurd misunderstanding as to Colonel Brandon's attentions, the whole being punctuated by frequent bursts of laughter; and she would doubtless have gone on to describe in detail the events attending the engagement of her two young friends, had not Elinor mildly but decisively interposed.

"Dear madam," she said, breaking off in the midst of a remark to Georgiana, "I am sure Miss Bennet does not wish to hear the history of such a very dull old couple as ourselves. You are so kind as to be more interested in it than most people could be."

"Lord, my dear," cried Mrs. Jennings, "why did you not stop me? I declare I am very sorry if I said a word I ought not. I know my tongue does run on, and Miss Bennet must excuse me, for it was only for the pleasure of talking to you and Mr. Edward. And as for its being dull, I don't believe there is anybody who does not like to hear of other people's love-affairs; it makes one think of one's own, now, does it not, Miss Bennet?"

Kitty blushed and looked embarrassed, and Mrs. Jennings laughed heartily, saying: "It is just as I thought; Miss Bennet could tell us a pretty tale too, I'll be bound, if only she would."

"Miss Bennet can tell us some wonderful tales of the West

Indies," said Elinor, endeavouring to turn Mrs. Jennings's mind from her favourite topic; "she has a sister there, who writes to her constantly, does she not, Miss Bennet? Those tropical places must be very beautiful. Do you remember how Colonel Brandon used to talk to us of his travels in the East, ma'am?"

"That I do, my dear," replied Mrs. Jennings emphatically, "and I never want to hear again of such fearful things as he had seen—swamps, and great things like alligators . . . and insects that did everything insects ought not. I hope you will tell your sister not to get amongst them, Miss Bennet."

Kitty replied that her sister had written chiefly of the beautiful balls and illuminations which they frequently had, and lately of some shocks of earthquake which had frightened them terribly. Mrs. Jennings exclaimed at this, and declared that the finest ball in the world would not compensate her if there was the fear that the ground would open under her feet while she was dancing. "But I know young people do not care what risks they run," said she. "There was Sir John Middleton three weeks ago wanted to have a moonlight picnic; my daughter Middleton was all against it, for the weather was so threatening, but have it he would, and the consequence was that they all ate their supper, or as much of it as they could, in a roaring thunderstorm. I can tell you they were in a pretty pickle when they got back! All the girls so cross, and the young men not a dry thread among them through trying to protect the ladies. But Sir John, he made no bones about it at all, but said they would go again another night, when for sure it would be fine."

Her hearers could not help laughing at such a picture of undaunted pleasure-seeking, and Elinor inquired if the second party had taken place.

"Oh, Lord, yes; they all came, but their fathers and mothers made them promise not to stir beyond the grounds. I heard, at any rate, they turned it into a dance instead. But, as I say, young people don't care for a drop of rain. I am sure, when I was young, I would as lief have had it as not, for there was no hardship in sheltering under a hedge, with the right young man to hold an umbrella over you, do you think so, Miss Bennet?"

"Still, I fancy that most people, old or young, prefer outdoor expeditions to be in dry weather," said Elinor. "That reminds me that I must show you what terrible havoc last night's rain and wind worked in my flower borders. When I looked out first, I was quite in despair, thinking I should not have another nosegay all the autumn. There is a gleam of sunshine now, so shall we take a turn in the garden?"

Georgiana gladly walked out with her, and Mrs. Jennings and Kitty followed at a distance, the former questioning her young companion about her sister abroad and hearing laments over the gaieties which that sister had been able to offer her, but which she had never been able to accept. Mrs. Jennings's hearty comments of "Well, there now, that is a shame!" and "A regiment too! You would have broken all their hearts, I vow!" and other such remarks pleased Kitty, while she knew in her heart they ought not to do so.

The two girls shortly after took their leave, and while walking homeward naturally compared notes upon the stranger whom they had just met. Georgiana expressed herself guardedly, not wishing to condemn any friend of Mrs. Ferrars's, although feeling as if that friend could not be in any way an accession to their party; but Kitty's first unfavorable impression seemed to have been obliterated, and she declared frankly that she liked Mrs. Jennings and thought she was very merry and good-natured. Georgiana could not quite agree with this, for she found Mrs. Jennings's style of raillery not at all to her mind, but admitted that she might be pleasanter when one got to know her well.

At dinner these opinions were canvassed, and Georgiana found, as she expected, that her own were largely shared by Elizabeth, who, however, was amused at her severity, and told her that she would often meet people who, with more refined manners, were yet at heart far more vulgar than Mrs. Jennings and had not a tenth part of her redeeming qualities.

"I do not think I want to meet them, then," said Georgiana. "But I am sure you are right, Elizabeth, and I daresay she will be a great comfort to Mrs. Ferrars."

When the ladies were together after dinner, Kitty, whose gravity and preoccupation had been noticeable for the last half-hour, after wandering several times round the room, stationed herself near to her sister and began, in a solemn tone: "Lizzie, I want to ask you something very important."

Elizabeth, smiling, professed herself all attention, and Kitty continued: "You know you have never kept your promise, that you made before you were married, of having a ball here, for each winter something has happened to prevent it."

"Quite true, Kitty; so a ball is in your mind; and what made you think of it just now?"

"I never come here without thinking of it, but I had somehow not expected to be staying long enough this year, as I imagined I should go home directly after the shooting party. But Mrs. Jennings said to-day she supposed you sometimes had balls in this lovely house, and she was sure Georgiana and I were fond of dancing."

"And Mrs. Jennings is quite right about the latter statement, is she not?"

Georgiana looked up with a smile, to assent to her share of the question, and Kitty clasped her hands rapturously, exclaiming: "Oh, Lizzie, you know how much I love a ball! It would be so kind of you and Darcy! Everyone would enjoy it!"

"I am very fond of balls myself," said Elizabeth. "Darcy, as you know, is not, but I think even he might admit that it is sometimes a duty to give one. The idea had crossed my own mind, I confess, but I had not considered whether our party or our numbers would be suitable."

Kitty's joy at the favourable reception of her proposal was excessive; she could not refrain from beginning to practise her steps about the room, and singing the while from sheer delight, and the gentlemen, entering at that moment, paused in astonishment on the threshold.

"What is this, Kitty?" inquired Darcy, approaching; "something Mrs. Jennings has taught you?"

Extreme merriment at the idea of Mrs. Jennings as an instructress of dancing prevented Kitty from immediately replying, but the whole matter was presently explained and laid before Darcy for approval. Seeing that her brother-in-law did not instantly dismiss the whole scheme, Kitty poured out a flood of reasons to commend it; it was just the right time of year, not too cold and snowy; Jane and Bingley would have a party they could bring over; no ball had been given at Pemberley since Georgiana was grown up; the house was so conveniently built, as if on purpose for balls; and finally, it would be a most delightful thing for everybody.

"I know you want time to think it over," said Elizabeth to her husband, "and there is no hurry at all; but I think it is quite feasible, and we really owe the neighbourhood some entertainment of the kind."

Darcy declared that he did not see why his house should be required to furnish his neighbours with the so-called amusement of watching each other promenading about a polished floor, and though no doubt it was a great compliment to the original architect, he did not believe that Pemberley had really been primarily designed for giving balls in; but his family could perceive that his opposition was not intended to be very serious, and the discussion terminated with his promising to talk it over with Elizabeth, and even to consider the middle of November as being a date likely to suit the convenience of both households.

Kitty regarded the matter as settled, and carried her news to the Rectory the following morning in the highest spirits, assuring Mrs. Jennings that it was owing to her suggestion that the subject had been brought forward at the right moment. The sincerity of that lady's delight, and the warmth of her congratulations, were most gratifying, and she immediately began to ask Kitty who her partners would be, and what variety the young men of the neighbourhood could afford.

Kitty confessed that there were not many living very near them, with the exception of the officers of a regiment stationed at Ashbourne, with some of whom her brother was acquainted, but that her sister, Mrs. Bingley, would bring over one, or even two, who she knew for certain danced extremely well.

"Aha!" cried Mrs. Jennings, "very pretty! And they are single men, too, I warrant you."

Kitty's look of consciousness gave Mrs. Jennings far too fine an opportunity to resist, and it did not take her long to ascertain enough particulars about a certain young naval officer to convince her that this ball was going to be the occasion for two young people to be made happy and all their friends regaled with some interesting news. There was no need for her to hear very minute descriptions of Mr. Price's conduct and the impressions it had left on the beholders; the mere mention of his existence, and a hint of Kitty's partiality, were sufficient material upon which to build up a whole romance. Miss Bennet might depend upon it, he was only waiting to come down here and make the acquaintance of the rest of her family, and then not a moment would be lost.

Although these assurances gave her pleasure and revived sensations which Elizabeth and Georgiana had not wished to encourage, Kitty could not help feeling a certain absurdity in accepting them from someone whose convictions were based solely on a good-natured interest in the affair, and she was tempted into giving a longer version of all that had happened in London, in order that Mrs. Jennings might be more fully informed. It was a decided relief to talk to a friend whose opinions coincided with those of Mrs. Knightley, and as Mrs. Ferrars was not in the room there was nothing to put a check on their confidences. She had, however, an instinctive feeling of delicacy which made her stop short of divulging a more recent experience, and the unconscious Mr. Morland was saved, had he but known it, many witty sallies on his deserted condition.

Elizabeth and Georgiana were amused to notice how willing Kitty henceforward became to go to the Rectory, for whereas she had formerly rather endured than enjoyed her visits there, she now volunteered to join the others whenever they went. She was generally to be found, during some part of the time, chatting with Mrs. Jennings; and when the good lady called at Pemberley it was Kitty's office to escort her home again. Mrs. Jennings had early discovered that Miss Darcy was grave and quiet, and could on no account be induced to join in any joking references to lovers, while Mrs. Darcy's general style and manner were not such as to warrant the intimacy implied by such a conversation.

There were many other topics, for Mrs. Jennings was thoroughly kind and friendly, and took the deepest interest in all her neighbours' concerns besides the sentimental ones: their children, their gardens, their poultry, their houses and their clothes. The ball, too, afforded unending subjects for discussion. There was to be no disappointment; Mr. Darcy had allowed himself to be talked into it, and the fifteenth of November was fixed for the momentous occasion. Cards were sent out; the officers accepted in a body; Colonel Fitzwilliam promised to stay for it; new dresses were ordered from London; and not least among the minor excitements was reckoned the arrival of a letter from Jane, expressing the pleasure of herself and Bingley at the prospect, and engaging to bring with them at that time, namely, Miss Bingley, Mr. Price and a Tom Bertram. This last name was accounted for by Jane's explanation that Bingley had asked Mr. Price to bring his brother with him, or some other man who could shoot, and the brother not being available, Mr. Price had secured instead his cousin, the elder son of Sir Thomas Bertram of Mansfield Park.

Perhaps not one of the party at the breakfast-table, to whom this letter was read aloud, could hear it altogether unmoved.

Elizabeth and her husband were naturally deeply interested in all that concerned Kitty, and were glad to know there was a certainty of seeing at last young man of whom they had heard so much; while Georgiana rejoiced in this clear proof of his anxiety to meet Kitty again, and built upon it hopes of the progress of the affair speedily and uninterruptedly to its desired ending. There need not, surely, be anything to delay it; on the contrary, no young lovers had ever more favourable circumstances, his own brief stay on shore an excuse for apparent haste, and Kitty's being surrounded by her friends, whose approval would be equivalent to that of her parents, making everything easy. Indeed, it was impossible to see what obstacles could arise; he could not be diffident enough to entertain doubts as to whether his feelings, or what were supposed to be his feelings, were returned. Georgiana could not help a little smile at this thought, though at the same time regretting that Kitty should allow her heart to be read so clearly. To Kitty, the announcement of his intended arrival at Desborough was scarcely less tremendous than if he had walked into the room himself at that moment, demanding her hand as he approached. The latter incident could hardly have caused her a greater tremor than the former did, and as soon as she could get Georgiana alone she poured out afresh the old hopes, fears and anxieties, desiring Georgiana to confirm all her own surmises with positive assertions; to reply: "I am *sure* he will," when Kitty said "I *hope* he will"; and to say, "Of course, most certainly," when Kitty speculated upon the various ways in which Mr. Price might be expected to commit himself. Although feeling tolerably confident, Georgiana tried to confine herself to assurances of warm sympathy, and pointed out to Kitty that it was not prudent or delicate to assume so much when no actual declaration had been made, but with Mr. Price's coming so nearly in view, this idea detracted from Kitty's perfect satisfaction; she privately found Mrs. Jennings, and her arrangement of the coming events, far more encouraging.

Colonel Fitzwilliam's attention was caught by the names of Mrs. Bingley's guests in rather a different manner. Mr. Price he recollected as Georgiana's acquaintance, but the name of Bertram awoke associations of a kind which he was trying to subdue. It was the name he had more than once heard coupled with Miss Crawford's; it belonged to the people who were fatally connected with her past life. Had he only the right to protect her, the meeting with this representative of the family might have afforded him an opportunity of refuting for ever the vague scandals which were doing her so much harm; but he had no right; that privilege belonged to Sir Walter Elliot, and the truest kindness he could do her was to remain silent. In the new life she had chosen all the past should be forgotten. He strove resolutely to put away these saddening reflections, and to throw himself into the general interest of the subject by making a few inquiries about the two young men. Georgiana was the only person who could supply any information about Mr. Bertram, for Mr. Price had told her his sister was married to his cousin, a Mr. Edmund Bertram, also of Mansfield. It was evident that this must be the older brother.

Fresh excitement was caused shortly afterwards by a second letter from Mrs. Bingley. Jane wrote that Mr. Price and Mr. Bertram were to arrive at Desborough on the sixth of November, and begged that the two girls would come over on the previous day to spend a week there Mr. Morland, she took care to inform them, was intending to pass the greater part of the month with his friends the Portinscales, and so, as Elizabeth had no doubt already heard, would be unable to be present at the Pemberley ball. In Kitty, this intelligence aroused the most fleeting of regrets, but the others had leisure to feel sorry, while commending his prudence, that circumstances should prevent his taking part in the general gaiety. Jane had special reason for feeling kindly towards him, for she had wished to ask Kitty to join the party, but had not liked to do so in view of Mr. Morland's being at home, but he, suspecting that it would be an occasion for inviting some of the relatives from Pemberley, had quietly made his arrangements without allowing anyone to perceive the hardship it was to him to deny himself a glimpse of Miss Catherine Bennet.

The invitation was rapturously accepted on the part of Kitty, and very willingly by Georgiana, for she liked being with Jane, and was pleased at the prospect of seeing William again for his own sake. Elizabeth felt it most important that the girls should be together, for Georgiana to watch over Kitty and be a check on her impulsiveness; and Darcy gave a sign of his confidence in his sister, very precious to her, by saying: "It is a good thing you are asked, Georgiana, for there is no one else who can be trusted to keep Kitty in order and bring us a sensible account of this young man and his intentions."

To Desborough, then, they were to go, and to bear with them Mr. and Mrs. Darcy's invitations to Mrs. Bingley's guests for the Pemberley ball.

Chapter 14

OCTOBER WAS RAPIDLY PASSING; and Elizabeth had received no acknowledgment of her letter to Mrs. Wentworth. This occasioned her to some surprise, for Anne was a punctilious correspondent, and certainly would not have allowed such an important question as had been put to her to remain long unanswered. At last, when Elizabeth had begun to fear that either letter or reply must have miscarried, the wished-for packet was discerned among the morning's post; and she carried it to her own private room before perusing it.

"My dear Mrs. Darcy,

"I do not like to imagine what you must be thinking of me, for my long and inexplicable silence. Your letter bears the date October the second, almost a month ago. Will you forgive me when you hear that I only just received it? We have been travelling abroad, as Frederick wished to take advantage of this period of comparative peace to visit some of the old Dutch cities, and we returned only this week, after a delightful but extremely fatiguing tour. Our letters have followed us about to our continually changing addresses, and it is little short of a miracle that so many of them have reached us. Yours has now reappeared at Winchester after its wanderings! This must be my excuse for not writing instantly to correct a misconception under which I grieve to think you have been labouring. My father is not engaged to Miss Crawford, and there is no probability of a marriage between them either now or at some future time. I know that some months ago a rumour to that effect was in existence, for, indeed, it must be confessed that my father's attentions to Miss Crawford were very marked, and my sister was among those who were confident that an engagement would ultimately result; but before we went abroad Elizabeth wrote to me from Brighton, where she and my father had removed, to say that the affair was at an end, Miss Crawford having given my father a definite refusal. I think they were a great deal vexed and disappointed, which was perhaps natural, for my father had counted upon succeeding, and it would have been a very advantageous match for him; but I cannot help thinking that there would not have been any great happiness in it for either of them. It was not altogether suitable—but, dear Mrs. Darcy, I should not weary you with my comments. In such a case as this everyone can supply their own. I do not know where Mrs. Grant and Miss Crawford are now, but I conclude in Bath. The only news of them that has reached me, besides what I have stated, was, I am sorry to say, that Miss Crawford had been ill, but I heard no particulars. All this seems bald and unsatisfactory; I wish I could have given you better and earlier information. Pray give our warm regards to Mr. Darcy and his sister. It was a great delight to me to renew my acquaintance with the latter, and to see her looking so lovely and blooming. Her countenance expresses so much sensibility, that one is convinced she must have a tender heart, and one hopes that life may always be kind to her. I had a great wish to invite her to pay us a visit when we returned to Winchester from London, and was disappointed to learn she had already travelled north. Will you mention it to her, and say how glad we should be if ever she was disposed to come in this direction? We would try to give her a pleasant time. Your children must be reaching a delightful age. Alas! with what a pang do I view our empty nursery! Accept my very cordial remembrances, and believe me," etc.

It was well that Elizabeth had taken the precaution of being alone to read this letter, for the agitation it caused could not easily have been concealed. A thousand confusing thoughts surged through her mind. Action, of some sort, she felt she must take, being the only person of their circle in possession of this knowledge; but what action would be safe, prudent and productive of results? While believing that Fitzwilliam had been refused, she had always found it hard to credit that he should have been refused for Sir Walter Elliot, and the denial of the statement found willing acceptance. It was so unnatural, so horrible, almost, to think of Miss Crawford as Lady Elliot! Before Elizabeth had even time to think of Fitzwilliam she had rejoiced over Miss Crawford's not having committed an act so unworthy of her. She next tried to recollect exactly what she had heard with reference to Fitzwilliam's dismissal. He had been confident that she was lost to him, through her engagement, he assumed; but since she had never been engaged, clearly there had been indications which, as Darcy had said, had forced him to believe that she was ill-disposed towards him. What, then, could anyone do for him now? It was not by any means certain that because she had rejected Sir Walter Elliot she could be induced to accept Colonel Fitzwilliam. And yet the knowledge that she was free, free still to be won, was a reason for not withdrawing utterly until he knew what would be the fate of his own pretensions, taken on their own merit. Elizabeth could not feel satisfied, remembering what had happened at Bath, that he had ever had a fair opportunity of pleading his cause. He might, indeed, have had a refusal as definite as Sir Walter's, and in that case there would be no kindness in reopening the subject; it would profit him little to know that another suitor had fared no better than himself, even though that suitor might be one who should never have aspired. But what if it had all arisen through a misunderstanding?

After long and earnest consideration Elizabeth determined that whatever steps she now took towards her cousin and the chances of a reconciliation, he must know nothing of them; if she had finally decided against him, there was no reason why he should be put to the pain of hearing it a second time. This at least seemed clear, and it paved the way for her next resolution, namely to write to Mrs. Grant, without mentioning anything she had heard, beyond the intimation of Miss Crawford's illness, and ask for news of them both.

Darcy entered while she was preparing to write, and she immediately handed him Mrs. Wentworth's letter. Having read it, he handed it back to her, saying gravely: "What are you going to do now, Elizabeth? for I suppose you are going to do something."

Elizabeth described her plan and its motives, and Darcy listened without giving her much encouragement. At length he said: "Have you realized what a great responsibility you are taking upon yourself in endeavouring to bring these two people together again?"

"Yes," said Elizabeth, "and, dear Darcy, do you not think we should be prepared to take it? I shall do nothing which could possibly give Fitzwilliam a moment's uneasiness; he has already suffered too much, and is a changed man, as you were agreeing the other day; but if there is the slightest chance of making him happy, I think we ought not to let it slip. No one but ourselves can possibly make any attempt to reunite him and Miss Crawford."

"I know you are prepared to undertake herculean tasks in the interests of your friends, my dear, but when a man has been so decidedly repulsed, it is a delicate manner to heal the breach. I imagine your scheme would be straightaway to invite Miss Crawford here, and send them both off for a walk, with instructions to return in half an hour an engaged couple?"

This was spoken without the ghost of a smile, but the idea it suggested to Elizabeth was so brilliant that she forgot to remonstrate her husband for not being sufficiently serious. "I never thought of it, but I will do it!" she exclaimed. "Not send them off for a walk, of course, but invite Miss Crawford and her sister to come and stay here. They shall come, if they will, as soon as the ball is over, for Robert is leaving the next day, and in the course of a quite fortnight it will be strange if I cannot discover whether she cares in the least for him."

"And after that time Fitzwilliam is to be summoned home with all speed, I suppose?"

"Oh, I cannot look so far ahead; if my endeavours prove unavailing, of course we must not let him know that they have been here at all."

"Well, Elizabeth, I am glad you are providing for all contingencies; and do not forget the most probable one, namely, that they will not be persuaded to accept your invitation. Miss

Crawford may not want to lend a helping hand, or Mrs. Grant to play Fitzwilliam's game for him."

"Naturally, I shall tell them distinctly that he will not be here and we shall be quite to ourselves. If she has been ill, she may like to have a change. I decline to be discouraged, Darcy, by whatever you may suggest, for I am convinced that this plan can do no harm, and may do a great deal of good."

"Perhaps you are right, my dear; it seems to me to be a considerable risk, and we cannot emphasize too strongly the need for absolute secrecy; but you know I cannot wish Fitzwilliam anything better than a thoroughly happy marriage, when I think of what mine has done for me."

"Darcy! for you to be paying me compliments! The world must be coming to an end. And now here is nurse bringing the children, so I shall have to postpone my writing for the present."

The letter was posted, and Elizabeth had to wait longer than she would have wished for an answer to this one also, but after about ten days she had a note in a hand she did not know was brought to her. It proved to be from Mrs. Grant, who dated it from Everingham, Norfolk, and said that she was writing in place of her sister, who was still so far from well that it was necessary to spare her all trouble and fatigue. She had been extremely ill during August and September, and had seemed to make so little progress towards recovery that they had come to stay with their brother a few weeks ago, in the hope of obtaining some benefit from the more bracing air. Unfortunately, she had not gained all the good they had hoped for, and they were still anxious about her. On first receiving Mrs. Darcy's kind invitation she had felt it was impossible to accept it, as her state of health and spirits made her languid and disinclined for exertion, but Mrs. Grant and Mr.

Crawford had at length, using all their powers of persuasion, induced her to reconsider her decision, for they both felt that to mix with her friends once more, and to be in the midst of such agreeable and stimulating surroundings as a visit to Mrs. Darcy would afford, would be the best possible remedy for the nervous complaint from which she had suffered. In any case, they would shortly have to leave Everingham, as it was too cold and exposed a spot, but her sister was scarcely equal to the journey to Bath yet, so that Mrs. Darcy's letter had come at a most fortunate time.

Miss Crawford was very desirous that Mrs. Grant should explain that she was still an invalid to a great extent—"and she insists on my saying a tiresome and exacting one, though I cannot endorse that," added Mrs. Grant. "But she is afraid of giving trouble, and of being, on account of her want of health, an unacceptable visitor; and she says that if she is going to trespass upon your kindness, she cannot do so on false pretenses, and so wishes you to know just how you will find her, in case you would rather postpone having her until some future time, when she is more of a rational being."

Elizabeth perceived something of Miss Crawford's old spirit peeping out in this message, the spirit of independence, which would laugh at her own weakness rather than appeal for pity, and made her reluctant to accept a kindness which might wear the aspect of an indulgence. Had it not been for her recent illness, and the consequent pressure put upon her by her brother and sister, it was clear she would not have come to Pemberley; Elizabeth was conscious, in the wording of the letter, of a shrinking from it, and the earnest way in which Mrs. Grant, on her sister's behalf, begged to be assured that they would find Mr. and

Mrs. Darcy *quite alone* at home, emphasized something more than an invalid's wish for seclusion.

In her reply Elizabeth endeavoured to convey a complete assurance of the quietness of Pemberley and its suitability for anyone in Miss Crawford's delicate condition. There would be no one at home but themselves, she said, excepting, of course, Mr. Darcy's sister, whom Miss Crawford had met, and who was one of the household; the patient should have every care, and could lead whatever kind of life she preferred; she should not be troubled in any way, or even be asked to join the rest of the party, until she felt stronger, as Elizabeth hoped and believed she soon would. The letter was expressive of the writer's goodwill, and she trusted that it might do away with any remaining unwillingness that Miss Crawford might have felt in renewing an acquaintance which had indirectly caused her so much pain. Elizabeth rejoiced in having accomplished the first step. Miss Crawford's acceptance might have been wrung from her, but it was unlikely she would withdraw it, and once she were safely established at Pemberley, whether Colonel Fitzwilliam were to be made happy or not, at least there would be no more misunderstandings.

Elizabeth proposed a date to Mrs. Grant for the arrival of the two ladies, but decided to maintain her reserve on the subject towards everyone, except her husband, until the ball should be over and her cousin should have left the house, for she was particularly anxious that no hint of it should reach his ears. Georgiana's discretion could have been depended upon, but Elizabeth felt it would be better to postpone telling even her of Mrs. Wentworth's reply until matters should be further advanced.

Chapter 15

GEORGIANA FOUND THAT HER presence as a check on Kitty, and an outlet for her excitement, was very necessary, for Kitty had come to regard herself as the central figure in the little drama that was to be played during the next few days. Her manner of speaking of Mr. Price during the first evening would certainly have betrayed to Miss Bingley the state of her feelings towards him, if that lady had not been already possessed of the information. Georgiana felt both sorry and vexed, for she could read clearly the expression on Miss Bingley's face, and knew that Kitty was exposing herself to a not altogether friendly criticism. Miss Bingley had never learnt to do more than tolerate the rest of the Bennet family, in spite of her openly professed affection for Jane, and when, as in this case, she happened to have taken a liking to the admirer of one member of it, she evidently found their inferiority greater than ever. That Mr. Price was a great deal too good for Kitty Bennet she managed to convey by looks and tones which were not intended for anyone but Kitty, but which

Georgiana could not help but notice and resent. To Georgiana herself, Miss Bingley said with a great air of frankness that now this affair had been so much talked of, and was expected on all sides, she trusted it would soon become an accomplished fact; of course it was all Emma Knightley's doing, but as Kitty was evidently so much in love, she *hoped* (with a good deal of emphasis) that Mr. Price felt the same.

The great day arrived, and Mr. Tom Bertram's curricle drove up to the door late in the afternoon, laden with its two passengers and a manservant, and all the necessary complement of bags, gun-cases and a spaniel on a chain. William Price had been staying at Mansfield, and consequently the journey for both was a comparatively easy one. There were many greetings to be made, and introductions to be performed, in the short half-hour before everyone retired to dress for dinner. Bingley, in the warmth of his welcome, could not make enough of his guests, and wanted to be talking to them both at once; but the look of delighted surprise on William Price's face when he caught sight of the two young girls did not escape observation, any more than the remarkable fact of Kitty's being suddenly struck almost dumb with shyness, and being unable to reply except in monosyllables, and with deep blushes, to his inquiries after her health. Georgiana, with greater self-possession, shook hands in her own grave manner, looked him straight in the face, answered him simply, and bowed with quiet courtesy in acknowledgment of the pleasure he expressed in meeting them again.

At dinner, Kitty was placed between Georgiana and Mr. Price, the latter being on Mrs. Bingley's right hand; and as Jane considerately talked for most of the time to Mr. Tom Bertram, who sat on her other side, Kitty was able to enjoy Mr. Price's conversation almost uninterruptedly. He had much to tell, and she to ask, of London and their mutual friends there, of his stay in Portsmouth and the King's visit to review the ships, of the shooting parties at Mansfield and the astonishing sagacity of his cousin's new dog. Georgiana heard scraps of it, and noticed with satisfaction the good understanding that seemed to exist. "It is much the wisest beginning," she thought. "Far better to have a basis of common interests on which to found a friendship before love comes, than to rush blindly into a violent attachment, which may as rapidly subside. Mr. Price will gradually bring out the best that is in Kitty. He will care for the same things she does, but more moderately; and he will develop her finer taste. She will have so much to make her happy that her charm of nature will not fade."

Mr. Price was evidently too sensible to expect to have the exclusive enjoyment of Kitty's company in such a small party. He was ready to reply to anyone who might address him, seemed to wish to get acquainted with Mrs. Bingley, and always had a lively word or glance for his cousin opposite. Tom Bertram would put up with a greater amount of good-natured teasing and joking from his cousin than he had ever done from anyone in his life; but his illness had sobered him, and though not much less careless and selfish than formerly, he entertained a secret admiration for the younger man, who had already done so much with his own life, and he had shown himself strongly amenable to influence from that quarter. To exercise an influence was the last thing William Price would have thought of doing; and yet it was entirely through his half-laughing, half-serious representations that Tom had been induced to settle down at home, to interest himself in the work of managing the estate, and to show more consideration for his parents. At the moment, he had allowed himself to be carried off from home, knowing that it was part of a general scheme to distract his mind from a matrimonial entanglement in which he was on the verge of becoming involved, and which his family cordially disliked; but there was reason to fear that Miss Isabella Thorpe had played her cards too well, and that in spite of the efforts of friends she would eventually reign at Mansfield Park as the next Lady Bertram.

When the gentlemen rejoined the ladies after dinner, William Price immediately approached Georgiana, and made a few remarks upon indifferent subjects, until the attention of the others being directed to a story narrated by Mr. Bertram, he inquired if she had heard anything more of Miss Crawford since their last meeting.

Owing to Elizabeth's reticence on the subject, Georgiana was able to answer, with truth, that she had heard nothing. When she had spoken, her reply seemed to her so curt that she added: "My sister, Mrs. Darcy, has written to a friend—to Mrs. Wentworth, in fact, to make inquiries, but I do not know with what result."

"To Mrs. Wentworth?" repeated William Price. "Then, of course, that means you know what I was so churlish as to refuse to tell you, that evening at Mrs. Hurst's—Sir Walter Elliot's name. I hope you have forgiven me, Miss Darcy, and will understand why I did not feel at liberty to repeat it at that time."

"I am sure you were right, Mr. Price, and indeed we have never heard the rumour confirmed yet," said Georgiana. "I wish I had seen Miss Crawford again, but there was no opportunity."

"I did not see her again, either," said William. "I had to leave town directly after, and when I returned they were gone. I wish I could learn something! I so trust it may not be true; for Miss Crawford to marry that man would be not one, but a thousand pities. It is difficult to understand why anyone should make a so-called marriage of convenience; but one feels that she of all people is worthy of a better fate."

"One must hope, if it really is decided upon, that it is not altogether a mere convenience; that that there is some mutual regard also," said Georgiana.

"Oh, no doubt, there is a great deal of regard on *his* side, but he is not the sort of man to appreciate her properly," rejoined Mr. Price. "If you knew him, Miss Darcy, even your kindness of heart would fail to find suitable excuses."

"I know Miss Crawford's friends are dissatisfied about it," said Georgiana; "but I cannot help feeling that there is no need for her to make any marriage at all unless she is confident it will conduce to her happiness, so that, whatever she is doing, one must assume that she is using her judgment."

"You put the case so admirably, Miss Darcy, that I declare you have nearly consoled me. It is just what I have tried to remind myself of, that she can afford to marry where she chooses, and as there is no compulsion except her own good nature, I can hardly believe she will make such an unwise choice. That absolutely settles it; I believe you have got private information, which you have conveyed to me from your own mind without speaking a word, and which has reassured me."

"No, indeed, I have no private information," replied Georgiana with a faint smile, "and I think you have reassured your-self by your own close knowledge of Miss Crawford's character."

"I may know Miss Crawford better, but in matters of this kind women are far better judges of one another than are men of them. You read each other as you would yourselves, and deduce each other's motives from your knowledge of your own; consequently, you bring a far keener insight to bear than we can."

"I think that perhaps women understand each other better, and it is natural that they should," said Georgiana, after a moment's reflection. "But then you must remember that they are expected to acquire the habit of entering into the feelings of others. Their position as onlookers in the active world enables them to find their pleasure in studying the characters of those around them, and their happiness is in proportion to the amount of sympathy and comprehension which is excited in themselves."

"That is too modest an estimation of the qualities of your sex, Miss Darcy. I should go further, and say that some persons do not need to acquire the habit you mention, for they have naturally such quick and generous sympathies, such a power of reading with true kindliness the dispositions of others, and drawing out the best that is in them, that I think it is impossible for them to receive more happiness than they give. You must have met some such; and that is what I mean by a woman's power of insight."

He looked at her earnestly as he said this, and Georgiana had never seen him so grave. That he meant Kitty, she had not a moment's doubt; and they seemed to be within half a sentence of her name. She fully expected his next words to be: "There is someone we both know, I think, Miss Darcy," or something similar, and in her confusion, she did not stop to reflect how unlikely it was that he would speak so openly when Kitty was standing a few yards away. But as he continued to look at her without saying anything further, she strove to interrupt a pause which threatened to become embarrassing, and murmured, not very collectedly: "Yes, indeed it is so. My brother's wife, Mrs. Darcy," she added, not daring to show her thoughts were following the same direction as his, "is one of those you were describing. She understands everyone so well; she knows what one would say even when one has the greatest difficulty in expressing it. I think she is the cleverest person I have ever met."

She thought he looked a little disappointed at her change of theme, but he bowed, and said courteously that he had a great wish to meet Mrs. Darcy. Georgiana caught at this remark as a means of extricating himself from a conversation which was almost too interesting to be pursued just then. "I hope very much that you will meet her," she said. "I do not know if Mr. Bingley has mentioned it, but there is to be a ball at Pemberley next week, and my sister hoped Mr. and Mrs. Bingley would bring you all over with them."

William's face displayed the pleasure he felt, before he could give utterance to it, and Georgiana, recollecting that she had not intended to give the invitation, but to leave to Kitty the gratification of doing so, turned round impulsively and called to her friend, who was standing close by Jane's chair on the opposite side of the fireplace, but casting many wistful glances towards Georgiana and her companion.

"Kitty, I have been telling Mr. Price about the ball," said Georgiana, as Kitty darted towards them; "that is, that we hope he is coming to it; but you must tell him what an achievement it is to have persuaded Elizabeth and my brother. We owe it entirely to your suggestion that there is going to be any ball."

"Oh, Georgiana, why did you tell Mr. Price? I was keeping it for a great surprise" exclaimed Kitty reproachfully; and turning to William, she demanded his approval for the scheme, the details of which were quickly expounded. William gave a proper meed of praise and admiration, and Georgiana presently slipped away to join the others, who were preparing to sit down to a round game; but William and Kitty remained talking together until tea was brought in.

Chapter 16

THE FOLLOWING DAY THE sportsmen went out early and returned late, and as some friends from the neighbourhood were dining at Desborough, there was no opportunity for much conversation between the young ladies and Mr. Bingley's guests. Kitty passed their chief of the day in writing a long letter to Mrs. Knightley, and Georgiana was taken possession of by Miss Bingley, who wished to practice vocal and instrumental duets. Miss Bingley had a good deal to say, during the intervals of their performance, about Mr. Price, whom she acknowledged she liked very much, and she endeavoured to prove to Georgiana, by a number of arguments, the improbability of his having any matrimonial intentions in general, and towards Kitty in particular. Georgiana would not discuss the point with her. Her won esteem for Mr. Price depended on his not disappointing Kitty, and she would admit no suspicion which might imperil it.

On the third afternoon, the shooting party having returned earlier on account of bad weather, they were all assembled in the library. Bingley was showing Mr. Bertram some hunting prints that hung on the walls, and the rest were gathered round the fire, the ladies sitting, and William Price leaning on the overmantel glancing at the pieces of porcelain and the miniatures arranged upon it.

"What beautiful little Chinese figures these are, Mrs. Bingley," he suddenly exclaimed. "They are genuinely old, are they not? A man I know brought back just such a pair from Hong Kong, and I know he regarded them as priceless. I do not think they can be imitated in Europe."

"Yes, I believe they are really old," replied Mrs. Bingley. "I do not know the history of them, but they have been in Mr. Bingley's family for a long time, and they are special favourites of his; perhaps you can tell us, Caroline?"

Miss Bingley was beginning to speak when she was interrupted by a cry of dismay from Mr. Price. He had taken the little figure in his hand to examine it more closely, and the head had immediately fallen off and rolled on the hearth. Fortunately a thick rug had received it, and after a search it was discovered intact; but Mr. Price was overwhelmed with self-reproach for his carelessness, until stopped by Mrs. Bingley saying: "You need not mind, Mr. Price, for it was not in the least your fault. The head was broken off already. Look, it has been slung between the shoulders by a piece of wire. I should have mended it, but could not manage to attach a new length of wire."

"I am relieved to find I am not the guilty party," said Mr. Price; "that is, if you are quite sure, Mrs. Bingley."

"Indeed I am; and Kitty," she added, turning toward her sister, "perhaps you can help me to clear Mr. Price's character. Do you happen to know anything about the breaking of this little mandarin? We found it so a few days after you left, and no one in the house could account for it. I have always meant to ask you about it, but had forgotten until now."

Owing to the comparative dimness of the firelight, Jane was unable to perceive her sister's growing confusion; but it became evident in the embarrassed pause which followed her question. Kitty began to speak, broke off, and began again, stumbling over her words: "I had thought it had been broken—that is, I knew it had—but something put it out of my head—I forgot it too till now."

"What a pity you did not mention it," said Miss Bingley severely; "it might have been worse injured next time it was touched by anyone not knowing the head was loose."

"Oh, well, never mind, dear Kitty," said Jane kindly; "it does not matter; it can easily be repaired, no doubt."

Kitty, on the verge of tears, looked distressfully from one to the other, torn between her dislike to recalling the occasion, and her desire to exonerate herself in the eyes of William Price. The latter consideration prevailed, and addressing Jane, she murmured with deepest blushes; "It was not I who broke it, it was Mr. Morland."

"Mr. Morland!" repeated Jane, perplexed. "Yes, it was that last morning he was here. We—he was in the library, you know. He had the Chinese figure in his hand, and I recollect noticing it was in two pieces. I never thought of it again until now, and I suppose he forgot it too."

Kitty's self-consciousness, increased as it was by the knowledge that Jane and Georgiana would now perfectly understand the reason for the disaster which had befallen the porcelain ornament, quite mystified her other two hearers, to whom the explanation taken by itself would have been sufficiently simple. All they could plainly perceive was that the association of Mr.

Morland with the incident made Kitty extremely uncomfortable, and they were left to draw what conclusions they might by her hasty departure from the room. William Price, with a delicacy of feeling for which Georgiana's heart went out to him, immediately filled up the moment of awkwardness by reverting to the original subject of their discussion, which he still held in his hand. "At any rate," he said, smiling, "I have helped to decapitate this poor mandarin, so it seems only fair that I should try to mend him. Have I your permission, Mrs. Bingley? I believe, with a fresh bit of wire and some sealing-wax, I could make him nod as benevolently as ever."

Bingley was called upon to produce the necessary articles, and being warned by a glance from his wife not to pursue his inquiry as to whether they had discovered who had damaged the old fellow, the incident seemed likely to arouse no further remark. Georgiana evaded Miss Bingley's eyes, and went away as soon as she could to Kitty's room, finding her friend lying upon the bed and weeping bitterly.

"Georgiana, what must he have thought?" she began instantly, throwing herself into her friend's arms. "Why did Jane ask me that unfortunate question, just at that time? It could not have happened worse. I was thinking about it a little, because, you know, I had not been in that room since Mr. Morland and I were there together. We were standing in just the same place as we were all in to-night, and it made me quite miserable to remember it. And now Mr. Price will not know what to think, hearing Mr. Morland's name like that. He will suspect something, and perhaps it will prevent him from speaking. I wish we were back at Pemberley; I knew things would never go so well here again."

Georgiana comforted her, assured her that what had happened would never make the slightest difference to Mr. Price, laughingly reproached her with having run away, saying that no one would have perceived anything out of the ordinary but for that, and counselled her to behave just as usual when she met the others again, and everything would be forgotten. Nevertheless, Kitty was far from comfortable during the rest of their stay, and was in continual expectation of some occurrence which might affect Mr. Price's attitude towards her, although the cheerful friendliness of his manner never varied.

This apprehension rendered her particularly uneasy the following day, which was Sunday. They all went to church, where the service was read by a stranger, and Kitty's sensibility was sorely tried by having to listen to various questions asked by their visitors during the walk back. Was that the regular clergyman? He was absent; ah, indeed! Was he a pleasant neighbour? a good preacher? And so that was the Rectory; what a commodious, attractive-looking house! No doubt the parson was a married man, and he was certainly a lucky fellow to be so circumstanced, commented Mr. Bertram. Bingley made brief answers out of compassion for Kitty, and Jane began a conversation with the two girls about something different; but she could not attend. It was so distressing to think of Mr. Morland, whom Bingley praised so highly and whom the others thought so enviable, having been driven away from home on her account; that a man so charming and so desirable should have fallen in love with her when she was not able to care for him. There seemed something particularly unfortunate, particularly wasteful, about the whole affair! If he had been a Mr. Collins, that nobody, not even Maria Lucas, would have minded refusing! Poor Kitty walked home silently, and as far from Mr. Price as possible, with her muff held up to conceal a countenance which she knew was unfit to be seen.

On Monday, Bingley and Mr. Bertram went out hunting, and the ladies, escorted by Mr. Price, drove to the spot where the fox-hounds were to meet, in the hope of seeing a little sport. Bingley had offered to mount Mr. Price also, but the latter had declined, laughingly declaring that, like all sailors, he was not much of a horseman, and though he had once hunted from Mansfield Park when he was a careless youngster, he thought it would be wiser not to venture over the Derbyshire country, with its rough moors and high stone walls, on a borrowed horse. "It is most kind of you, Mr. Bingley," he said; "and for my cousin, it is all right, for he has hunted here before. But I am sure you would not be pleased, if you saw me come crashing down at the first big fence, with your hundred-guinea hunter doubled up in the further ditch."

The ladies held up hands of horror, but Bingley, much amused, said he would not believe a word of it, and that he felt sure Mr. Price could ride as well as he could shoot. William shook his head.

"I have ridden all sorts of horses at different times, when occasion has required it, and have even managed to adhere to the animal as a rule; but my good luck might desert me to-day. Perhaps you will let me go for a jogging ride along the lanes before I go, on your least valuable horse."

"Seeing that I am in charge of you just now, William, I highly applaud your decision," said his cousin, "as I don't want to have to send you back to Portsmouth with a broken neck, which is certainly what could happen."

"You in charge of me! I like that," exclaimed William. "Say much more, and I will borrow a gypsy's donkey and come to meet you on it, announcing to everybody that I am bringing along your second mount."

Mrs. Bingley was a little afraid of the cold wind, and decided not to go, so Mr. Price took his seat in the barouche with the other three, and greatly enhanced the gaiety of their party. They drove about for more than two hours, and when at last, the hunt having gone away among the hills, they decided to turn homewards, Mr. Price created consternation among his fair companions by asking permission to get out and walk.

"Walk, Mr. Price?" exclaimed Miss Bingley, who, placed on the front seat, had assumed the direction of the party. "Why should you want to walk? And in this desolate wilderness! Why, we must be six or seven miles from home."

"Yes, I thought it was about that," said William "I rather wanted a walk, and do you know, I like this desolate wilderness, as you call it. I should enjoy exploring my way homewards, and I have noted all the landmarks. It is so cold, too; a splendid day for a walk."

"Oh, Mr. Price, do not go; we are all so snugly tucked in here," said Kitty imploringly.

"Oh, if you prefer walking, pray do not let us detain you," said Miss Bingley, speaking at the same moment, and in rather an offended voice.

William looked in surprise from one to the other; it had evidently not occurred to him for one moment that he would be missed by any of them. Unconsciously, his eye sought Georgiana's, and she said quickly: "Mr. Price must be cold with sitting still so long; I expect he would enjoy a walk. It really is not so far; from the top of the hill one can see Kympton Church, I know, and on foot one can take an almost straight route."

The carriage had stopped and the servants awaited their orders. William remained irresolute; he had one lady's leave to go, another was doing her best to appear indifferent, and the third plied him with entreaties not to break up their comfortable little party. Georgiana was amused, but also a little ashamed to see Caroline and Kitty, for once united in the object of their wishes, showing those wishes so plainly. It was clear that William Price felt the awkwardness thus created, for his hesitation only lasted a second or two, and he said lightly: "Why, of course, I will not get out, if it would be disturbing anybody. Probably the negotiation of those short cuts would make me very late for dinner. Shall they drive on?"

Miss Bingley gave the order in a dignified tone, and assured him that he had done wisely to desist, for he certainly would have been late. Georgiana could not help remarking that it was a pity he should have missed his walk, for the others would not be in before five; but he gave her a glance and a half smile, which showed her that he was not allowing it to trouble him. Kitty, delighted that Mr. Price had given this proof of a wish to please him, talked all the way home, and described with great animation several *dreadful* walks that Bingley had taken her on the moors, when, according to her account, they had narrowly escaped death on many occasions—wild cattle, dangerous bogs, rushing torrents and venomous snakes being among the risks to be encountered on such expeditions.

Mr. Price listened with interest, but his courage did not appear to be shaken, for as soon as they descended from the carriage, he paused only to glance at the clock, and to divest himself of his heavy coat, before asking Miss Darcy if she would accompany him on a walk. "It will be as short as, or as long, as brisk or as leisurely, as you are disposed for," he said, and Georgiana declined with real regret.

"I should have enjoyed it very much, Mr. Price, but I think I had better not; it is rather late, and the others may be wanting me before dinner. Besides," she added, as she saw his disappointed look, "I know you want a good walk, and you can go further if you have not to adapt yourself to the slow paces of a lady."

"I should esteem it an honour to have to adapt myself to yours," replied William Price, with the quick, bright smile which was so noticeable in him.

"We must all go together to-morrow morning," said Georgiana, as she turned away. "Mr. Bingley can show us what is the best direction. I hope it will keep fine, but it looks very like snow."

Mr. Price did not move from where he stood for some minutes, and Georgiana, as she ascended the stairs, felt strongly to return and accede to his suggestion, but the fear that Kitty would not like it withheld her. She wished that he had asked Kitty instead, or as well, for although anyone might well have assumed—after the descriptions she had given—that a country walk, for its own sake, was to her the most uncongenial form of amusement, yet Georgiana knew well that it would be viewed in a very different light were a particular companion available.

The promised walk did not take place, for the snow, which had been threatening, fell the following day, not thickly, but with enough of fog and dampness in the atmosphere to make the fireside seem by far the most agreeable place. The gentlemen shot in the first part of the morning, but returned home soon after one, ready for any entertainment that they might be expected to provide or be provided with; and Tom Bertram's inclinations, as usual, were in favour of the former. Not being a card-player, or enthusiast for music, and having found Mr. Bingley to be at billiards an adversary unworthy of his skill, he was obliged to seek some other method of spending a winter's afternoon, and without hesitation he broached to the assembled party his idea that they should act some charades.

Mrs. Bingley looked doubtful, and William Price gave his cousin no support; but the notion was warmly taken up by Bingley, his sister and sister-in-law, and Mr. Bertram set himself to persuade Mrs. Bingley that, next to a real play, charades were the most delightful things imaginable, and that they had a party collected about them remarkably well qualified to undertake any and every kind of character.

His hostess proved not difficult to persuade when she perceived what pleasurable anticipations were aroused by the suggestion; and only needed to be assured by her husband that it was a capital notion, and the young people would thoroughly enjoy it, to promise help of whatever kind was needed. William Price was ready to enter into it, when it became evident that it was the general wish; and even Georgiana began to be interested, and concealed her nervousness at the idea of taking part.

"You need not be frightened, Georgiana," said Miss Bingley; "all you will be required to do is to stand perfectly still and assume a particular expression. Louisa and I have often taken part in them; there is no acting, it is all the pose."

"Excuse me, Miss Bingley," interposed Mr. Bertram, "the kind of charades I propose we should do involves a certain amount of movement—acting, in short; and others require impromptu speeches. I recollect once, at the house of my friend—"

"I am sure you are mistaken, Mr. Bertram; the correct charade is not acting at all; it is simply a series of pictures, or tableaux, to represent the various syllables."

The discussion threatened to become keen, especially when the two younger girls joined in protesting that they could not possibly recite any impromptu speeches; but Bingley finally settled the point by agreeing with Mr. Bertram's vehement assertion that it would be much more amusing if they acted their parts, and that he could show them how to do it in such a way that no speaking would be necessary, though Miss Bingley doubted if *all* the company would be equal to such a demand upon their capabilities.

The next point was to choose the words, a matter of prodigious importance, for which many books were brought out and consulted, and the merits and possibilities of each word exhaustively debated. It was not until they renewed the consideration of the subject at the dinner-table that they made the discovery that if all of them were to appear in different scenes of the same charade, there would be no one left to guess the meaning.

"This becomes really serious," said Bingley. "If it was a play, we could act to ourselves, and the chairs and tables, and be perfectly happy; but the very existence of a charade is threatened if no one is ignorant of it. And from what I hear of intended costumes, it will take the rest of the evening for our preparations, so that we shall be ready to begin the performance just as our ladies have to leave us to-morrow."

"But who is leaving to-morrow? Not Miss Bennet and Miss Darcy?" exclaimed Tom Bertram in real alarm. "This cannot be allowed. Pray, Mr. Bingley, use your authority. I am sure they could remain another day."

"Oh, yes, I am sure we could," cried Kitty; "they could not wish us to miss the charades—it would spoil everything if we could not be here."

Bingley looked at Georgiana and asked her, smiling, if she thought it could be managed, but she had already given an imploring, though unheeded, glance towards Kitty, and now replied, in a low voice: "It is very kind of you, but we ought not to stay, I am sure. The carriage will be coming for us, and we ought not to detain it for a whole day."

"What does it matter, Georgiana," Kitty exclaimed, "only for one day! Elizabeth will not mind. Don't you care about the charades, and about putting a stop to the whole thing? We can easily be spared, if that is what you are thinking; the ball is not until Friday."

Georgiana, blushing, and distressed by finding herself the object of attack, was endeavouring to maintain her ground without giving offence, when Jane came to her assistance.

"Georgiana is perfectly in the right," she said, "and sorry though I am to lose them both, there is no doubt that they will be expected back to-morrow without fail. But that is no reason why the charades need be given up, for as we shall all be coming over to Pemberley on the following day, we can give them there that evening, if my sister and Mr. Darcy will consent to be audience, and our performance to-night will serve as a kind of rehearsal."

This suggestion was enthusiastically received, as it met all difficulties, and Kitty forgot to reprove Georgiana for hurrying her away, in the contemplation of the news with which they would return home, and the delightful bustle of preparation that would ensue. Jane and Bingley had not quite the same views, and they spoke privately to Georgiana before she left, asking her to take a message begging Elizabeth and Darcy not to put themselves to any trouble about the arrangements for the stage, which need only be of the very simplest nature, a sufficiency screen and lamps being all that would be asked for.

The rehearsal proceeded in admirable style. Mr. Bertram had constituted himself stage-manager, and gave everyone minute instructions as to their movements and attitudes, shouted directions from the midst of an imaginary audience, and hastened at the last moment to take his place in the scenes where he was required to be actor as well. With some assistance from Mr. Bingley, he had allotted the various parts, and as he was so fortunate as to be able to regard all four ladies from an absolutely impartial standpoint, his judgments were, on the whole, tolerably good; although the usual difficulties of such an occasion arose, and had to be smoothed away, as, for instance, when Mrs. Bingley positively declined to play a part which required any acting, although she was the only person who looked the Queen to perfection; or when Miss Darcy wanted to give up an important part to Miss Bennet, whom it did not suit at all, simply because the latter was anxious to wear the dress that went with it; or when Miss Bingley desired to represent both Lady Macbeth and Joan of Arc, and could not be made to understand that she could take only one, on account of the necessity for passing quickly from one scene to another. All, however, was amicably arranged before the evening ended, and when the others went to bed, Tom Bertram sat up, desperately writing lists of the properties and accessories which he deemed necessary to the performance.

Chapter 17

KITTY WAS PARTLY CONSOLED for the agony of quitting
Desborough Park by the prospect of a reunion of the family under
such enticing circumstances, and Georgiana was sensible of the
advantage of having two or more evenings of excitement to prepare for and look forward to, to sustain Kitty's spirits, which
might otherwise have suffered some diminution of liveliness in
consequence of Mr. Price's not having made his offer before they
left. Kitty talked of it, and of him, and of the charades, incessantly and inextricably all the way home; and it was fortunate
that Elizabeth was alone when they arrived, for it was hardly possible for Kitty to disentangle the three subjects in giving a
description of their visit. Elizabeth made her happy by a kindly
reception of the plan for the following evening, and a promise to
invite the Ferrars and Mrs. Jennings to witness the charades; and
when she had darted away to the nursery with some presents sent
by Jane to the little Darcys, Elizabeth smilingly asked Georgiana
if, from her own observation, she could confirm Kitty's eager
anticipations. Georgiana could only reply that she believed all

was going well; that Mr. Price was more charming than ever, and the only difficulty in the way of forming a judgment was that he was equally charming to everyone.

"I suppose Kitty's preference for him was very clearly marked?" said Elizabeth

"Yes," replied Georgiana, "I am rather afraid it was; but he appeared to accept it without any embarrassment, and the understanding between them seemed so good that I do not think there *can* be any fear of his disappointing her; we were almost always all together at Desborough, and I used to think he was only awaiting an opportunity of seeing her alone."

"Or she used to think so, perhaps?" said Elizabeth. "Well, I trust it is going to end satisfactorily; meantime, I am most anxious to see this paragon, with whom Jane, for her letter, seems to be nearly as much delighted as you and Kitty are."

Kitty was allowed to be the bearer of the note, conveying the invitation, to the Rectory party the next morning; and while Mrs. Ferrars was writing a reply in another room, the enthusiastic young lady was able to pour out her heart to the equally enthusiastic old lady. Mrs. Jennings received her with much warmth, and immediately began a series of questions which she usually answered herself at the same time that Kitty was giving a reply, so that the real and the imaginary descriptions were inseparably mingled together.

"And how was the young officer, my dear? Ay, ay, you need not tell me: as handsome and as attentive as ever, I can see by your eyes."

"Yes, just as handsome as ever, dear Mrs. Jennings, and attentive—yes—but you see we were a small party, so he could not devote himself entirely—"

"Ah, but I fancy he *did*—did he not now? You need not be so modest about it; these small parties are the very thing for the right people always to pair off together. Lord! how well I remember when Mr. Palmer was courting Charlotte, and there was a young man, too, coming after my niece, and my sister used to say: 'It won't be a match this time, Sarah,' and I'd say, 'You wait and see Henrietta; each of the girls has got her beau, and there's a room for each to sit in; and the weather's very bad;' and sure enough, the very next Monday—did you not say you had bad weather, too, my dear?"

"I did not say so, Mrs. Jennings, but we did have some rain and snow."

"I thought as much; well, well, you are a lucky girl, to have it all your own way, and your friends liking him so much, too; I suppose he will speak to Mr. Darcy when he comes over here, as your father is not just at hand."

"Dear Mrs. Jennings, you are making too much of it; he has not spoken to me yet, you know: it is only that we are good friends, and he seems to enjoy talking to me, and Jane was so kind, and let us sit together."

"That is quite right, my dear, just as it should be; I'll warrant your sister Jane is a very sensible woman; and these charades, too, just the thing. There, I am downright pleased to think I shall see the finish of it. This acting, I suppose was the young man's idea? he is a clever one, I know."

"No, it was not his; though, of course, he does it better than anyone else. It was Mr. Bertram's idea—his cousin, who came with him."

"His cousin! Ah, yes, the other young man, I recollect. He was invited for Miss Darcy, wasn't he? Come, come, now, Miss

Bennet, no secrets among friends."

"There is no secret, ma'am," returned Kitty, laughing, "I do not think he was invited for Miss Darcy, or anyone; my sister did not know him before."

"You may be sure that was in her mind. Is he not heir to some great property? It seems to me I have heard so."

"He is heir to his father, Sir Thomas Bertram, in Northamptonshire; I do not know if it is a great property."

"You may make up your mind that it is, and that something will come of it, my dear Miss Bennet. A baronet! the very thing for Miss Darcy. Her brother and your sister would be sure to look high. Was he not a fine young man, and did they not make a nice couple?"

"I do not know—I did not think of it; but, Mrs. Jennings—"

"No, no, indeed, of course not. We all know what your thoughts were full of" (laughing heartily), "and very naturally, too. Never mind, my dear, we shall hear all about it before long, and you shall see if I ain't right. Lord! what a thing this will be to Elinor! She thinks no one is good enough for Miss Darcy. Well, well, it will be an evening to look forward to. Only come and tell me when I am to make my congratulations, for they will be on the tip of my tongue, and monstrous glad I shall be to get them off. Will it be to-night, I wonder, or to-morrow night? These young sailors can't afford to let the grass grow under their feet. And your dress, my dear, what did you say it was going to be?"

In such pleasant anticipants the time passed quickly until the re-entrance of Mrs. Ferrars with her note, when Kitty felt obliged to return to Pemberley, as their visitors were to arrive early, and there were still many preparations to be completed. As she walked homewards, she was in a glow of delight over the visions which their talk had evoked, and Mrs. Jennings's prophecy with regard to Georgiana and Mr. Bertram fitted into its place in the same cheerful picture. Undoubtedly Mrs. Jennings was quite right; she so seldom erred in her judgments! Kitty could not recollect that those two had ever seemed specially pleased with each other, but in all probability they were, for, now that she came to think of it, there was no one else for Georgiana, and Mr. Bertram matched her as naturally as Mr. Price did Kitty herself. Yes, it was most likely that they would soon be engaged, perhaps married, before another, and to Kitty, a more interesting couple! No, that would certainly not do. If the wedding at Longbourn must be a less magnificent affair than the one at Pemberley, if Kitty could not aspire to a wedding-dress trimmed with such lace as Miss Darcy had inherited from her mother, at all events she would have the honour and importance of being married first. With smiles of satisfaction, she pictured the sending out of the invitations, and had decided on the form of them, and the number of recipients, by the time she re-entered the house.

The same subject absorbed the attention of the two ladies she had just left. Mrs. Jennings could not refrain from recounting to her hostess the conjecture she had instantly founded upon her knowledge of Mr. Bertram's existence; and though Mrs. Ferrars was well acquainted with her friend's flights of imagination, she had no positive arguments to array against this one, and was obliged to content herself with urging Mrs. Jennings to let no hint drop of her suspicions until something should occur to confirm them, as it would be so painful for both the young people. Mrs. Jennings promised caution, at the same time being evidently unwilling to relinquish an idea that pleased her so much, and Mrs. Ferrars perceived that it would be necessary to repeat the warnings very often before the following evening, when her friend and her husband would go to the Pemberley ball without her, as she dreaded over-fatigue; on the first evening, the occasion of the charades, she intended to be present, and hoped to be able to control and check Mrs. Jennings's remarks, should they threaten to become embarrassing. Knowing her intense and freely-expressed interest in her fellow-creatures, Mrs. Jennings's friends would have been glad to bargain for not more than *one* love affair to be in progress at one time under her eyes!

The arrival of the party from Desborough could not fail to bring, even to dignified Pemberley, a pleasant sense of bustle and excitement; and in the first flood of greetings, introductions, and inquiries, Elizabeth and her husband were only aware of a generally agreeable impression of Mr. Bingley's two young guests; of Tom Bertram, good-looking, fashionable, easy and talkative, and of William Price, with his shorter, sturdier figure, fine open countenance, and manners which, with no want of animation, yet attracted by their quiet simplicity. Even in the short time since the two sets of friends had been parted, a great deal seemed to have happened which must be talked over. Bingley wished to narrate, to anyone who would listen to him, the wonderful achievements of his shooting-party yesterday, who had accounted for an incredible number of pheasants; Mr. Bertram had taken possession of Georgiana, in order to propound to her at great length a scheme for altering and improving several of the charade scenes; and William Price, who was somehow established on a settee by Kitty, was telling her how far he had succeeded in the task she had bequeathed to him, of endeavouring to teach Mrs. Bingley's parrot to talk. The whole party were comfortably disposed round the drawing-room fire, and looked like remaining there until it was time to dress for dinner; but Tom Bertram, not satisfied with explaining, wished to demonstrate, and presently asked if he might see the acting-room, after which he was not long in requesting the presence of his whole company there, to see if they understood their movements and positions on the new stage. Kitty had undertaken to show him all their preparations, and had carried off William Price with her, and Bingley followed, with many good-humoured grumblings, summoning his sister, who was not anxious to break off conversation with Colonel Fitzwilliam, in the course of which she was examining him closely as to his reasons for quitting London so abruptly in the summer. It was necessary, however, to assert her position as leading lady, so she joined the others, Georgiana slipping in with her, and watching for opportunities to make herself useful, while in the intervals she put the final stitches in a head-dress for Kitty. Mrs. Bingley was allowed to excuse herself, pleading fatigue, and the presence of a sufficiently large number of persons at this informal rehearsal, a reason fully justified by the bursts of laughter and sounds of prolonged argument which occasionally penetrated through the folding doors.

When, after a hasty toilet, the actors returned to the saloon, the dinner guests had already arrived. Kitty was so distressingly conscious of the confidences she had so freely given, that she kept in the background while the two young men were being introduced to Mrs. Jennings, and avoided meeting her eye. Mrs. Jennings shook hands with them both warmly, and congratulated them upon having discovered such a delightful form of amusement for themselves and the young ladies as acting charades, these long evenings.

"Madam," returned Tom Bertram, with a bow, "let us hope that the amusement will not be entirely on the side of the performers, since the hard work is not the exclusive share of the spectators."

"Oh, law, Mr. Bertram, you quite mistake me; as to amusement, I can assure you it will be the greatest treat to me and Mrs. Ferrars; but you must admit that the hard work is not just the sort a young fellow gets soon tired of, is it, now?"

"You think so, because you cannot see behind the scenes, Mrs. Jennings," interposed William Price, assuming an air of solemnity; "I do not imagine my cousin would care to have command of a troupe of actors, such as we are, for long together; you have no conception of what amount of trouble we give him, I mean, the unruly ones."

Mrs. Jennings highly appreciated the allusion which she supposed these words to contain, and tapping William on the arm with her fan, she exclaimed: "Ay, ay, Mr. Price, I understand you, but you and Mr. Bertram will have the whip-hand by and by, and then you can get some of your own back."

"I am sure Mr. Bertram is an excellent stage-manager," said Mrs. Ferrars, who had not heard all that passed, but judged by Mr. Price's puzzled look, and Mrs. Jennings's laughter, that it was time to intervene; "I cannot think how you have been able to work up your charades and be ready for an audience within so short a time."

"It can only be proved that the charades are sufficiently worked up, when we see whether the audience are sufficiently perplexed by them," said Bingley. "If you guess the words at once, we shall feel that we have utterly failed."

"Do not overestimate our intellects, my dear Bingley," said his host. "As Mrs. Jennings says, these charades are sport to you, and as a natural consequence they are presumably death to us."

"Nonsense, Darcy," exclaimed Bingley, in the midst of the storm of laughing protests evoked by this remark, "think of the acting, and the splendid *mise en scène*, if your hearts fails within you. Besides, you can always applaud. Nowadays it is the fashion to admire loudest what one understands least."

Darcy led the way to the dining-room with Mrs. Jennings, and as the ladies of the party out-numbered the gentlemen, William Price found that it fell to his lot to escort both Miss Darcy and Miss Bennet. The former, seeing this, stepped on for a pace or two in advance, and Kitty, as she took his arm, murmured: "How *discouraging* Darcy is! He always manages to make one feel that he despises the things we are doing."

William glanced to see if Mr. Darcy's sister had heard, and rejoined, "I should hardly have thought so. He is only teasing, I fancy, and you know he was speaking to Mr. Bingley, and they probably understand each other particularly well."

"Still," said Kitty, "I must say I do not like that sort of teasing; it is very provoking to be continually laughed at, and for one's best friend to do it makes it all the worse."

"No, no, Miss Bennet, I am afraid I can't agree with you there; one can put up with anything from one's best friend, or at all events with things which one would not stand for a moment from anyone else. I wonder if Miss Darcy feels that too?" he added, as they settled themselves into their places at the table.

"I am not quite sure," replied Georgiana, when the question had been explained to her. "I think that ridicule may be harder to bear from our friends than from an uninterested person, merely because one feels they ought to know best what is painful to one—if it is of a painful kind; but on the other hand, one may always feel sure that a real friend had no intention of saying any-thing of the sort."

"That would not be much good to *me!*" cried Kitty. "I find it is too late, when I have already been very much vexed with any-one, to remember that they really did not mean to vex me."

"Of course, it is not much consolation, when the blow has been already dealt," said Georgiana musingly; "I meant that when one has reason to believe no unkind motive exists behind anything one's friend says, then one is not expecting to be hurt."

Kitty did not want to seem inclined to pursue the subject, and William Price, after a moment's pause, said: "I imagine that you mean, by a motive, the general feeling of goodwill in your friend's mind towards you. I should doubt if people really have a distinct motive for every little thing they do and say—at all events, they would have some difficulty in defining one. But per-haps you yourself, Miss Darcy, are a student of motives—perhaps your own actions are determined by a clear purpose?"

"Mine? Oh, dear, no," said Georgiana, looking up at him, and down again with a bright blush. "I think it is rather interest-ing to speculate upon other people's motives and to wonder what hidden impulses make them do certain things which seem hard to account for; but as to myself—oh, no, I never understand my own motives—I do not always know what they are. Do you understand yours?"

"Well, yes, I think so; not that I have ever troubled much about it, but on general principals, I think I always do things, or try to do them, either because I want to very much, or because it is a matter of professional duty."

"Then you are decidedly to be congratulated, Mr. Price," said Georgiana, smiling. "I should—I mean, most people would think themselves fortunate if they had two such burning lights to guide them. I suppose the way is so clear that you do not need to seek any further motives, as to why you want to do the thing so much, for instance?"

"Of course not," promptly replied William, "that would be looking back. How would one ever steer a ship, unless one kept one's eyes fixed on the course ahead? If you suspect there are rocks, you must avoid them, but it would be a waste of time wondering how you came to be where you are. You see that, too, do you not?"

"Yes, I see what you mean," replied Georgiana, "but I am afraid I have not learnt to steer my ship quite so well, or perhaps I have too many lights, and they are confusing."

William began to reply, but was interrupted by Kitty, tired of a conversation in which she had no share. "Mr. Price, do you know what you have done? refused the lobster sauce! What can you be thinking of? your turbot will not be half so nice without it!"

William made proper apologies to the bearer of the lobster sauce, who returned it at Kitty's summons, and she was pacified by Mr. Price's applying himself to his dinner, and entering heartily into a reminiscence of hers at a dinner-party at Mrs. Knightley's, when they had met for the first time, and when there had also—strange coincidence—been turbot for dinner.

Georgiana was glad to sit for a while in silent thought. Mr. Price's suggestion, that her life was governed by a distinct purpose, appeared sadly wide of the mark. Did not the mistakes she had made in the past show that she was merely drifting, lamentably weak, and having no sound judgment of her own? Whereas people like Kitty, who had given themselves up to the guidance of a definite aspiration, and Mr. Price, too, who had owned what lights he was steering by, would they not soon be in safe harbour? It seemed so, and Georgiana almost envied them of that delightful security, for of late she had allowed herself to wonder if such heights of happiness would ever be attainable by herself, and a longing had sometimes crept over her, since she had known and liked Mr. Price, that she might meet someone who could be to her what he was to Kitty.

Throughout the remainder of dinner she did not have any further conversation with William Price, though occasionally appealed to by one or other of them to give an opinion upon some point at issue, generally connected with the charades. With Mrs. Ferrars, who sat on her other side, she enjoyed a quiet little talk, and before they left the table Elinor inquired casually whether Mr. Bertram was nice—whether they had found him pleasant.

"Yes, I think so—I think we all like him very much," replied Georgiana, who until that moment had not formed any estimate of him. "He is very lively—and he has taken an immense deal of trouble about the charades—and Mr. Bingley, I know, considers him an excellent shot."

"That is quite an adequate description of him in a few words," said Elinor. "I wondered what you all thought of him, as I know you had not met before. He is not much like his cousin, is he?"

"No, indeed," responded Georgiana, speaking with more animation. "Could you imagine a greater contrast? One can see at a glance how different their lives and professions have been, and how different their characters must be."

"I should be interested to hear," said Elinor in a low tone, and with a smile, "what you take to be the chief points of unlikeness in their characters, if you were not sitting too near to one of them to tell me."

Georgiana smiled and shook her head. "I could not very well, and I am sure you can read faces as well as anybody."

"I understand," said Elinor, "that the one we mentioned first is heir to a title and a large estate."

"I believe so," replied Georgiana, "but the other is fortunate in needing neither titles nor large estates to recommend him."

Elinor needed nothing further to convince her that Mrs. Jennings's suspicions, as far as Georgiana was concerned, were perfectly groundless; what the Bingleys might be desiring of her, or Mr. Bertram aiming at, was another matter. Certainly an onlooker could hardly help thinking of the probabilities of the match, with a handsome and wealthy young man on the one side, and a girl of Georgiana's beauty, accomplishments and high birth on the other.

Chapter 18

ALL WENT WELL; THE dinner came to an end; the actors retired to dress, and the six members of the audience disposed themselves in armchairs in front of the curtain, and prepared to be mystified. The performance commenced after no longer delay than is usual on occasions of this kind, and opened with a duel scene, in which Bingley and Tom Bertram aimed pistols at one another in a most realistic manner, but failed to kill each other, owing to one weapon missing fire, and the ball of the other not penetrating a vital part. Two of the ladies rushed in and made demonstrations of relief at finding the wounded hero able to walk off the field. The next scene represented a card-room, with a party of players, and Bingley as the inveterate gambler staking higher and higher, until all was lost on turning up of a fatal four of hearts. Next was seen William Price as Richard I, in prison, aroused from despair at the sound of Blondel's harp, and the vision at the barred window of the minstrel, impersonated by Miss Bingley, cloaked and hooded and playing on a zither. The whole

word gave a fine opportunity to Tom Bertram to exhibit his com-
edy powers in the part of a gentleman whose pocket is picked of a
purse of money, his lamentations to his family, his efforts to recover
it, and the final restoration of the purse, by then totally empty.

Much laughter and applause followed this conclusion, and
though the word "misfortune" was presently discovered by the
audience without any further help, they were delighted with the
spirited and vigorous quality of the acting, which had conveyed
so much to them in dumb show, not a word being spoken on the
stage. Darcy's only adverse criticism was that so far there had not
been enough for the ladies to do; but this defect was remedied in
the next word, which consisted of only three scenes. In the first,
Miss Bingley made a very tolerable Lady Macbeth, striving to
cleanse her hands of blood while she walks in her sleep, and is
observed by her gentlewoman and doctor; the second showed Joan
of Arc, in the person of Kitty, led to the stake, while the others
grouped themselves round and endeavoured to look as numerous
as possible, in the parts of the judges, soldiers and executioners.
Poor Kitty's slight figure, and insignificant presence, made it difficult for the character to be well realized in her; and Mr. Bertram's
frown as he looked at her was not an assumed one, for he had originally cast Miss Darcy for the part, and had expostulated vehemently when she had insisted on yielding to the broadly-hinted-at
wishes of her friend. Finally, Mrs. Bingley, as Cleopatra, looked
exceedingly handsome in a robe as Egyptian as it could be made
on short notice, and received the asp from a basket held by
Georgiana, while Miss Bingley represented her other "handmaid."

This word was not so easily guessed as the other, and Darcy
and Fitzwilliam were the first to arrive at it, while Elizabeth had

to attend to the panegyrics of Mrs. Jennings and the more quietly expressed admiration of Mr. and Mrs. Ferrars. The former had indeed forgotten that there was anything to guess, so enchanted was she with the whole proceeding, so convinced that Miss Bennet and Miss Darcy were two of the most beautiful and gifted beings who had ever appeared on any stage, and it was only by making really meritorious effort at self-control, that she refrained from descanting on the good fortune of the two young men whom she supposed to be their respective admirers. She was still talking eagerly about the dresses, and the snake, and the pile of wood that looked so terribly real, and Mr. Bertram's being so clever and funny when he pretended to be angry, when the curtain rose on a new scene, and the spectators found themselves in another period of the past. Miss Bingley, an unmistakable Queen Elizabeth, graciously received a folio from Shakespeare, handed a ring to Essex, and on departing, stepped on a cloak laid down for her by Raleigh. In spite of this astonishing disregard for chronology, the scene was greatly enjoyed, as was also the next, which with the aid of a great deal of imagination, represented the deck of a ship. Here William Price had the leading part; he received a party of ladies on board, showed them all round the vessel, in such a lively manner that the deficiencies in the setting of the stage were hardly observed, gave orders to his sailors, and finally took an affectionate farewell of his friends, with much waving of handkerchiefs as the ship was supposed to sail away, and Kitty wept real tears of nervousness and excitement. The audience had had time to put the first and second syllables together while the ship was being cleared away, and they were in a measure prepared for the subject of the last scene, which reflected great credit on the stage-manager. It was a very pretty adaptation of *The Taming of the Shrew*, and showed the young girls in the characters of Bianca and Katharina, Kitty, of course, taking that of her namesake, in an episode of her stormy wooing by Petruchio, while Georgiana, as Bianca, submitted to a gentler form of love-making over a music lesson. The curtain was lowered for a moment before the sequel was given, wherein the two husbands, enacted by Tom Bertram and William Price, wager of their wives' obedience, and the conduct of the sisters proved how far marriage had altered them. To Mrs. Jennings's extreme delight, the part of Petruchio was taken by William Price, and this seemed to her to settle the whole manner finally, a view which was confirmed when she heard the word "courtship" passed from one to another of her companions.

"What do you think of that now, my dear?" she whispered loudly into the ear of Mrs. Ferrars. "What have I been telling you all along? Nothing could be clearer. A very pretty way of showing their friends, I say. 'Courtship,' you see, my dear. Ha ha! very pretty indeed. No, no, trust me. I shall not say a word until I am told. I know better than that. And the other one, too. It all points the same way, does it not? Well, I declare, I have not seen anything to please me so much this long time."

The actors presently reappeared, when they had resumed ordinary dress, all a good deal fatigued, but in high spirits and much gratified by the unstinted congratulations of their friends. Mrs. Bingley and Miss Darcy, indeed, shrank from praise, for to Georgiana it had all been rather an ordeal when the time came, and she had been conscious of doing her part stiffly and without natural ease, and Jane declared she had not acted at all, for she would not have known how to do it; she had simply stood about, under Mr. Bertram's directions, and worn the clothes that had been contrived for her. But the others were not so diffident, for Bingley and William Price had enjoyed the whole thing heartily, and appreciated the joke of throwing themselves into an imaginary character. Kitty had enjoyed the acting and the applause, the pleasure of being with William Price had been quite intoxicating, and not being altogether without aptitude, she had really acquitted herself with some spirit, particularly in the scenes from *The Taming of the Shrew.* But it was to Miss Bingley and Mr. Bertram, in their own estimation, that the honours of the evening belonged. They received all compliments with the utmost complacency, and Caroline was heard explaining to Mr. Ferrars and Colonel Fitzwilliam, as they all moved towards the dining-room for supper, that she had modelled her conception of Lady Macbeth on that of Mrs. Siddons, which she had seen so frequently and studied so closely as to be quite at home in the portrayal of it. The lady might perhaps have selected other listeners had she known the associations which one of them had with that play.

"It does you great credit, Miss Bingley," said Darcy, who had been listening to her. "It has been an evening of surprises, has it not, Elizabeth? I could not have believed that there was so much hidden talent among us, which would never have been unburied but for the happy idea of these charades."

"It is always so, I can assure you, Mr. Darcy," said Tom Bertram. "Once you decide to act, you can always discover talent in any collection of people, ample for your needs. Of course, one or two will always stand out, by reason of greater ability; but you must know how to select your players, so that everyone has a part worthy of him."

"I am afraid some of us had parts we were not worthy of, to-night," cried William. "I never felt such a fool as when I was playing Petruchio, and nothing but the kindness of Miss Bennet could have pulled me through. It needs a fellow about six feet high; I always said you ought to have done it yourself, Tom."

"My dear William, we have been through all this before. You know, I should have liked nothing better, but I decided, after due consideration, that I could not do justice to the principal part, when I had to be directing the full company, all on stage at once. You hardly realize my responsibility. But, rest assured, you did not do it so badly."

"I think you managed most wonderfully, Mr. Bertram," said Mrs. Ferrars. "To have to arrange the scenes, drill the other performers, and appear in every scene yourself! It was a task few people could have undertaken." Mr. Bertram bowed, as if there were a foregone conclusion.

"Mr. Bertram has had a good deal of experience in private theatricals," said Georgiana.

"I have, indeed," said that gentlemen. "Few men in England have had more, I should say, and anyone who is known to be fairly well up in these things, is naturally in request whenever they are going forward. And I have been lucky, too, in my companies. I do not think I have ever known a real failure, except perhaps once—"

Mrs. Ferrars's attention was just then called off, and he turned to Georgiana. "Did I ever tell you, Miss Darcy, about that one time when we attempted to do a little acting at my father's house—at Mansfield Park?"

"No, I do not think you did."

"Well, it is a long story; it might not wholly interest you—thank you, yes, some cold chicken—but the substance of it was that we had decided to act a play, amongst ourselves, you know; a pleasant party—divided among the two households, as this might be; just the very people for acting; free to rehearse—it is true my brother had made some difficulties; but all was going smoothly and our friends seemed to be then all one could wish. I am not sure that Miss Crawford had much idea of acting; but still, she might have improved."

"Miss Crawford!" exclaimed Georgiana, and involuntarily glanced round to make sure that Colonel Fitzwilliam had not overheard her. Seeing him occupied in talking to William Price, she continued in a lower tone: "I did not know that you knew Miss Crawford, and I am so much interested. Have you heard anything of her lately?"

Mr. Bertram could hardly believe his ears. He looked at Miss Darcy in the greatest astonishment. "Certainly I know, or used to know, Miss Crawford, but, naturally, I have not heard anything of her for several years."

Georgiana was puzzled by his manner, and felt that in some strange way she had made a mistake; so after a moment's pause she said: "It was stupid of me not to recollect that you must be acquainted with Miss Crawford too, as I was already aware that Mr. Price was. I suppose it was at the same time you were speaking of—at your father's house—that he met her."

Mr. Bertram had by this time partly recovered from the shock of finding there was anyone who did not know of the Rushworth-Crawford case, and said: "I beg your pardon, Miss Darcy, but your question was a surprise to me. No, I have quite lost sight of Miss Crawford, and I daresay you know more of her now than I do. You are a friend of hers, I assume."

"No," returned Georgiana, beginning to regret having pursued the subject, "I have only met her once, for a few minutes, but my brother and sister knew her fairly well in Bath."

"In Bath? Ah, yes, I heard that they had settled there."

Georgiana now wished nothing better than to find a new topic or a new companion without delay; but Mr. Bertram, having rapidly disposed of his cold chicken, began again: "You must not mistake me, Miss Darcy. I should be very glad to hear good news of Miss Crawford once more. It is a long time since our families held any intercourse, for—without going into details, her brother behaved like—indeed, is—an intolerable scoundrel; but as to his sister, she had nothing to do with that. She enjoyed amusing herself, I fancy, as much as most people do, but there was really no harm in it, as events proved. We all thought her a very bright, pretty, accomplished girl. But one thing followed another, and, of course, people are bound to hold by their relations, are they not?"

"Yes, indeed," assented Georgiana warmly, who had listened with the deepest interest to this recital, which, fragmentary though it was, seemed to agree with that strange rumour which Lady Catherine had written about from Bath. She pondered over it, and though reluctant to be indebted to Mr. Bertram for further information, she could not help wanting to have her own opinion once more confirmed.

"I am glad to hear you say that, Mr. Bertram. I thought Miss Crawford charming, and I heard the same from everyone who met her; but I think she may have been misjudged—blamed, perhaps, some time or other, for the faults of those who belonged to her."

"Quite true, Miss Darcy; I have no doubt you have hit upon the secret. Indeed, my brother-in-law, Yates, used to say much the same. She was certainly a very handsome girl, and it was a thousand pities she never had the chance to play Amelia. I did not finish telling you about our play: the parts were all cast, the stage was prepared, the rehearsals in full progress. Yates was, after myself, the leading spirit—I think you said you had met my friend Yates, Miss Darcy—"

He was fairly started, and Georgiana had time to grow weary of the history of *Lovers' Vows* and its ultimate conclusion, before the announcement was made of "Mr. and Mrs. Ferrars's carriage," which broke up the party. Everyone moved towards the hall, and cloaks were fetched while Mrs. Jennings loudly uttered her good-nights interspersed with many complimentary remarks to the actors. William Price had had hurried back to the room they had called the green room, to search for a cherished ornament of Kitty's which she had mislaid, so he escaped from congratulations to which, in his case, Mrs. Jennings would have given a double edge, and Kitty contrived to avert her share by murmuring as she embraced her guest: "I shall come and see you to-morrow." Nevertheless, Mrs. Jennings was not to be entirely baulked of her intention, and the long conversation between Mr. Bertram and Miss Darcy had attracted her notice; so in wishing Tom Bertram good-night, she managed to add a few words, felicitating him upon his success in another field besides that of the drama. Laughing heartily at his look of blank astonishment, she passed on, and as she never felt quite as well able to approach Miss Darcy on these subjects as other people, she contented herself with a sly glance, remarking: "Well, Miss Darcy, and what a delightful evening it has been! We have not heard the last of these charades yet, for many a long day, have we? Why, all the pleasantest part of them is still to come, I fancy."

Georgiana succeeded in avoiding a reply; she supposed the allusion was to Kitty, but she always preferred *not* to understand Mrs. Jennings whenever possible. The visitors directly afterwards went away, and the ladies retired, the gentlemen sitting up for some time longer.

Chapter 19

IT WAS IMPOSSIBLE FOR either Kitty or Georgiana to think of anything else when they first awoke the next morning, than that it was the concluding day of William Price's visit. Twenty-four hours more, and he would be on the point of departure. Twenty-four short hours were all that was left for an event of such prodigious importance. Georgiana knew of her friend's half-formed hopes that the acting in the last scene of the charades might have afforded an opening for the reality, and Kitty had not been a little chagrined at William's pronouncement that he wished Mr. Bertram had taken the part, but a night's rest had dispersed these clouds, and in the happiest frame of mind, Miss Bennet went down early, ready to make the most of every instant of this precious day. A disappointment awaited her shortly after breakfast, for Mr. Darcy was so barbarous as to propose taking the gentlemen to see the farm and the horses, and to this they actually agreed, Bingley only stipulating that they should return in good time, as he had made an arrangement to ride with

Georgiana. The damp and muddy state of the ground would not permit of the ladies accompanying them, even the most venturesome, and when they had all set out, Kitty found that there was nothing for her to do until their return but to hurry to the Rectory in search of the consolation which Mrs. Jennings was always ready to offer.

Mrs. Darcy found an opportunity during the morning for a little quiet talk with her sister. Jane so thoroughly liked and respected Mr. Price that she was delighted to find Elizabeth in agreement with her and related many instances of his sterling common sense, good taste, and amiable disposition, which she had had time, during her longer acquaintance, to meet with. Elizabeth hazarded the suggestion as to his presumed intentions towards Kitty, that however earnest they may be, it was possible that he did not mean to make her an offer at present, for his circumstances might not permit of it; he was still young, and his prospects might not be assured enough to warrant him in taking a wife. Jane was not inclined to think that any such obstacles stood in his way. His cousin had told her that he had saved a considerable sum of money, and that his brothers now being all out in the world, his family were no longer dependent on his help. Besides which, he knew he would be made a commander by the end of the year, and after that, it was only a matter of short time, to an officer of his experience, especially if a little interest could be exercised, before he obtained a ship of his own. Bingley had heard of him from several persons in London, and all agreed that there was not a more promising young lieutenant in the service. These were the days of quick promotion, and his career so far gave rise to no expectation that he would be left behind.

Elizabeth heard it all with pleasure, and would not give utterance to her solitary regret, that Kitty should have been fated to fall in love with a man who, in the event of their marriage, would be obliged to spend the greater part of the year away from her.

The gentlemen had returned from their walk by twelve o'clock, and Fitzwilliam and the two cousins waited near the front door to watch Bingley and Miss Darcy starting for their ride. Hardly had the horses moved off, and Colonel Fitzwilliam was considering what the guests might like to do next, when Tom Bertram seized William by the arm, and with a word of apology to the Colonel, carried him off to a distant patch.

"I want to speak to you, William," he began, with some abruptness, "and Miss Bennet will be popping out on us if I do not take this chance. I want to know—did you happen hear what that gossiping old woman, Mrs. Jenkins, or what ever she is called, said to me last night, just as she was leaving?"

"I certainly did not hear anything particular, but I'm afraid one never does pay much attention to Mrs. Jennings," returned William.

"Then let me tell you, she had the impertinence to give me the broadest hint I ever had in my life—to give *me*, if you please!—that I was paying court to Miss Darcy. I never was more astounded. I forget exactly what she said, but she made it quite clear, and—yes, one remark I do recollect, something about the 'charming future Lady Bertram.'"

"Good heavens!" exclaimed William, "what unpardonable insolence! I have never heard anything more outrageously offensive. Was she—I hope, I hope, Tom, that Miss Darcy did not hear any of this?"

"No, she was nowhere near at the time, but imagine my feelings, William, never having dreamed of such a thing, and then having it suddenly brandished in my face, as it were, by that odiously vulgar woman."

"It was disagreeable, certainly, but I am thinking more of Miss Darcy's feelings, as from what I know of her, I can conceive nothing which would be more repugnant to her, than to have such a subject bandied about in jest."

"Well, you may make your mind easy, for she was certainly not listening. But that was not what I wanted to say. Of course, it was a complete surprise to me, but once it had been put into my head, I could not help thinking of it, and, indeed, I have been pondering over it ever since, and have come to the conclusion that it would not be bad at all a bad thing."

"What is this?" exclaimed William. "Do you expect me to listen to you with patience, Tom, when not three weeks ago you were sighing over Miss Thorpe, and regretted your parents' objection to her, and declaring there was not such another girl in the world?"

"You need not be so hasty, William. You talk as if I were already on my knees to Miss Darcy, when I have no intentions whatever towards her; the idea has simply been put into my head by the circumstances, and naturally I must think it out."

"The idea has been put into your head by a foolish, chattering old woman, if you call her a circumstance, and, coming from that quarter, is not worth taking seriously for an instant."

"I do not know so much about that: it is true, she had no business to say it, but there was a reason in what she said; Miss Darcy would make an admirable Lady Bertram. Imagine my father's and mother's satisfaction, if I could present such a girl to them as their daughter."

"Good God, Tom!" exclaimed William, tearing his arm away, "the cold-blooded way in which you talk is more than one can bear. Weighing one girl against another, as if it were a question of relative merit, which you would throw the handkerchief to. It is not much of a compliment to Miss Darcy, to admit that you never thought whether she had attractions or not, until Mrs. Jennings suggested it to you."

"I am not considering paying compliments to Miss Darcy, and I do not see why you should get so hot," rejoined his cousin. "I merely wanted to talk it out with you quietly, and ask your opinion; but it is perfectly useless if you will fly into a passion at a word."

"Well, what do you want my opinion about?" demanded William, trying to speak in his ordinary tones.

Tom was easily placated, and really wanted to be talking, so he resumed: "My difficulty is that I am more or less involved with Isabella. Of course, we are both perfectly free; nothing has passed between us that she could construe into an engagement; I had to promise my parents that: but at the same time I practically promised myself that I wouldn't do anything until I had seen her again, which I expect to do in January. Now, for the sake of this connection, would it be better for me to break off entirely with the Thorpes by degrees? You know, I like Isabella very much, it is her family that one sticks at, while these Darcys are unexceptionable in every way; but she herself is a devilishly fine girl, with far more style about her than Miss Darcy, you must admit that."

"I think that the two ladies are not to be mentioned in the same breath with each other," said William, with difficulty restraining his indignation.

"You think not? that was what I wanted to arrive at; well, perhaps you are right, though I always thought you needlessly prejudiced against poor Isabella. I certainly feel more and more the advantages of such an alliance as this, on the worldly side, that is; for their dispositions, I fancy that of my old friend would suit me best."

"Tom," said William, turning to face his cousin fully, "I cannot think what possesses you to talk in this detestable way. Can you not feel how horrible it is? If you care for Miss Thorpe, you cannot think of marrying a girl you meet directly after leaving her, and have only known for a week. Whereas, if you think for one moment of Miss Darcy with the feelings a man ought to have, if marriage is in his mind, how can you possibly go on making comparisons between her and Miss Thorpe? Either way, it is abominable treatment of one of them."

"My dear William, you are going to the other extreme. Just now, you told me not to take anything Mrs. Jennings said seriously, yet you are assuming me to be in the most sober earnest all round, when all I want is to give the matter the consideration it deserves. Miss Darcy is very charming, but I am quite heart-whole where she is concerned at present, and so, no doubt, is she as regards me. But everything must have a beginning, and if such difficulties are to be put in way of my marrying Isabella, I could hardly do better than this; at any rate, it is worth thinking of. I shall go home and see how things develop in the course of the weeks. I can always come over again, you know; it is not the ends of the earth."

William broke from his cousin with an impatient gesture, and hurried away to another of the grounds. Mr. Bertram looked after him in surprise, shrugged his shoulders, and returned to the house, to establish himself by the fireside with a newspaper. Many inquiries were made for Mr. Price throughout the afternoon, to which Mr. Bertram could only say that he had seen him last in the garden, and it was not until nearly dinner-time that he reappeared, with a heated, wearied look, and confessed to having walked too far and missed his way in the park.

Kitty had been on the verge of tears, as the hours of his absence went on, and even Georgiana had begun to look grave, but this explanation revived their drooping spirits to a great extent. Anyone might lose their way in such a large park— nearly ten miles round! And on a dark, foggy afternoon the paths looked all alike, and the stream had so many windings! It was quite evident that this unlucky circumstance alone had caused the delay. These considerations, and a most satisfactory glance at her mirror when she was dressed for the ball, renewed Kitty's bright hopes for the evening. She wished Lydia could see her now. How could regimental balls, however smart and gay, compare with the splendour, the importance, of this occasion at Pemberley. The house, as she had always foreseen, was exactly right for a ball; the arrangements, the space, and all details were superior to those at Mrs. Knightley's house: her dress had been given to her by Elizabeth, and was even prettier than the one she had worn in London, and there seemed to be numbers of pleasant partners, including several officers, though these gentlemen were not persons of such consideration to Kitty as formerly, she having now decided that the naval uniform was far handsomer than the military.

It only remained for Mr. Price to ask for her hand in the first two dances, and the gentlemen of the house were so long in appearing that she was in the utmost terror lest she should be obliged to give them away before he arrived, but at last, among a crowd of other men entering the room, she discerned him. He approached, passing close to Georgiana, who was just being led into the ball-room by a neighbour and old friend, and came straight to where Kitty stood by Mrs. Bingley's side. How delightful to hear the words, spoken in his own friendly way, and with his own charming smile: "Well, Miss Bennet, I hope I may have the honour of these two dances, if I am not too late?"

Kitty very joyously accompanied him to a place next to Georgiana and her partner in the set, and with equal joy made an engagement for other dances later in the evening.

Chapter 20

THE ROOMS FILLED AND the ball proceeded, and many present who were frequent visitors to Pemberley nevertheless felt that those noble rooms had never before been the setting for a more brilliant scene. Mr. Darcy received innumerable congratulations upon having at last delighted the neighbourhood by permitting his house to be seen to such advantage, and not having altogether looked forward to the evening, he surprised himself by discovering how much, with Elizabeth at his side, he could enjoy both his own pleasure in entertaining guests, which he had not previously done on so large a scale, and also the pleasure of others who were important to him, Elizabeth, Georgiana, and the Bingleys. Georgiana in particular he watched with affectionate appreciation as she moved through the crowds, handsome and stately, generally grave, but occasionally lighting up into shy animation, and far more admired than she knew or cared about.

William Price had been dancing for a second time with Kitty, and they were sitting in a corridor, on some chairs placed below a cluster of candles in a sconce projecting from the wall, when one of the candles guttered, and a few drops of hot wax fell on the edge of Kitty's chair, narrowly escaping her gown. With an exclamation of annoyance, she sprang up, withdrawing quickly from the post of danger, and looking above them, both perceived that the mischief was caused by a candle having loos-ened in its socket, and fallen a little to one side.

William immediately proposed that they should move to other seats, and should summon a servant to replace the candle, but Kitty was in a wild and excitable mood, and would pay no heed. Laughing and calling out that she would put it right herself in a moment, she sprang upon the chair, reaching as high as she could, and to the dismay of the onlookers, thrust her hand into the midst of the candles in order to grasp the offending one.

"Do, pray, Miss Bennet, come down!" exclaimed William, and several other persons joined their entreaties to his. "Do not try to do it; you will set your dress on fire—your sleeve is so dangerously near. Do let me help you down, lest you fall and hurt yourself."

Mrs. Jennings, who had been observing the couple during the dance, and had followed them at a little distance, now arrived in time to hear Kitty say: "Thank you, Mr. Price, but I have already done it; and all is well; I and my gown are quite safe, you see." And looking down at him with a gay, triumphant smile, she gave him both her hands, and with this assistance jumped to the ground, adding: "Now, was that not skilful of me? and if we had waited to discuss it, you would never have let me attend to it, though it was by far the best."

"I would have tried to prevent your running such risks, cer-tainly," replied William, but his quieter tones were lost in the noisy interposition of Mrs. Jennings. "Oh, my dear Miss Bennet, now how very naughty of you! You have given poor Mr. Price quite a fright. Ah, Mr. Price, she is a sad girl, I fear, but I am glad to see Petruchio is beginning early to learn to keep her in better order. All your rehearsing in the charades will come in useful now, won't it? but I'll warrant this Katherine will be just as apt a pupil as the other." The old lady laughed heartily at Kitty's blushes, and at William's blank, uncomfortable look. "There, my dears, I won't disturb you any longer; only I hope you will both come and talk to me whenever you feel inclined."

Kitty, who had resumed her seat, was the first to break the awkward silence which followed this speech. "Mrs. Jennings is a great talker, is she not?" she said, with a laugh. "She seems able to think of nothing but those charades, and would like to make one believe that the acting was something wonderful."

"Yes," said William, after a pause. He had not sat down, but remained standing with a disconcerted air, twisting Kitty's fan about in his hands. "It is very complimentary. I wonder if— whether all the spectators were equally impressed."

"Oh, I think they were," said Kitty eagerly. "Even Darcy said some words in favour of it, and, you know, it is very hard to get any sort of praise out of him. And Mr. and Mrs. Ferrars were quite delighted. And my sister, too, Mrs. Darcy, said several times how much she liked it; she thought it so clever of Mr. Bertram to have arranged that scene."

She looked anxiously at William, and his face cleared some-what, but he did not sit down again, and replied so absentmind-edly to a few more remarks made by Kitty that when sounds of music reached them, she was quite ready to go, and walked beside him to the ball-room, thinking petulantly that Mrs. Jennings had spoilt everything by coming just then, and saying what she had; that no one liked to be hurried, or could be expected to declare himself in a crowd, and that perhaps he was vexed at having the words taken out of his mouth, as it were; altogether, the incident was thoroughly annoying.

For the next dance, she saw him invite Georgiana, but she was already engaged to Mr. Bertram, and he did not ask anyone else, but stood about watching various people, and occasionally exchanging a few words with Colonel Fitzwilliam and Mrs. Bingley, who were sitting down together during the set. Kitty could see from where she was that they were trying to induce him to find another partner, but he laughingly resisted their persuasions, and continued to walk about the rooms until the dance was over, after which he stationed himself within a short distance of Miss Darcy's chair, and when a suitable interval had elapsed, he went up to her and again made his request.

Miss Darcy acceded readily, and Mr. Bertram left them with by no means as much readiness. He had scarcely moved away when William began: "Miss Darcy, should you mind not standing up for this one? I was wondering whether you would be so kind as to show me some of the pictures in the gallery upstairs, which Mr. Darcy was speaking of at dinner. You know my time is getting very short, and I should be sorry to go away without having seen them."

"With the greatest pleasure," returned Georgiana, "and indeed I shall be glad not to dance any more at present. But you should have made my brother show you the pictures, as he is a far better judge than I am. We may find him up there, as he sometimes takes his friends round on these occasions."

The picture gallery, however, proved to be empty of visitors, and they strolled through, Georgiana pointing out which were considered to be the best paintings. William passed by them rather hurriedly, looking chiefly at the family portraits, and

Georgiana, observing this, conducted him to the end of the gallery, where her brother's likeness hung. William studied it for an instant, glancing at his companion as if trying to trace a resemblance, while Georgiana told him the date of the picture, and repeated that she wished they had come up before, as he would have seen it and all the others so much better in daylight.

She noticed that William hardly seemed to take in what she said, and was not altogether surprised when he turned suddenly to her and said, with scarcely concealed agitation: "Miss Darcy, you are very kind, but at this moment I cannot think of these pictures. Will you let me speak to you for a moment? I have something important to say."

"He is going to tell me he has proposed to Kitty!" flashed through Georgiana's mind, and for one instant a rush of feeling almost overwhelmed her, but controlling herself as well as she could, she said aloud: "Certainly, Mr. Price. Do say anything you wish. Will you not sit down? and I will do the same." She indicated two chairs opposite the portrait, and seated herself in one, but William remained standing, looking at her with such a deep, earnest gaze, while he tightly clasped his hands together, that he did not seem to have heard her words.

"Miss Darcy, you must forgive my presumption. It is a bad beginning to ask for forgiveness, but I know—no one better—that it is not for me to speak to you at present as I must speak. I would have waited, till my position—till I was justified—but circumstances have made it impossible to go away and wait in utter uncertainty, for an unknown future. I do not ask anything as yet, only a hearing—only that you will let me tell you how truly and devotedly I love you, and have loved you from the first moment of my seeing you."

A dreadful misgiving had passed over Georgiana at the beginning of this speech, and only consternation kept her silent till its close. She sprang up, in a horror and dismay that would scarcely find expression, and exclaimed: "Mr. Price! You to say such words to me! What *can* you mean? What can anything mean? *You*—no, no, it is all some horrible mistake."

"No, Miss Darcy, indeed, it is no mistake," broke in William eagerly and earnestly. "Do not be so distressed, I beg you. I do not ask you to give me any definite reply, though you can guess what perfect joy it would be to have one word of hope, however slight, from your lips—but I will wait and try to earn the right to ask for more. Next year my position will have improved, and your brother will not perhaps think it quite out of the question. Nay, I implore you, dearest Miss Darcy, to hear me only this once. I did not mean to trouble you so soon, but I could not bear to go, so far away, with no prospect of seeing you again, and knowing that others might be near you, others far more eligible and desirable than myself—you would understand, I am sure, if you only knew the tithe of what I felt."

"Mr. Price," said Georgiana, signing to him with her hand to stop, and standing erect before him, "I insist that you shall cease. I will hear no more of this. You cannot be in your right mind; at all events, you will not find me so destitute of sense of honour as you think." She paused, choked with emotion at the thought of Kitty.

"Destitute of honour! when you know, Miss Darcy, that I think you the purest, loveliest, best of creatures. Forgive me if I have offended you, only tell me how I may correct it. Do I wrong in speaking to you first? I will do whatever you wish; I would not grieve you for the world."

With great effort, Georgiana collected herself sufficiently to reply: "These professions of yours amaze and horrify me. I cannot tell you whether they are more painful to me if I have to regard them as true, than if, as at present, they seem hypocritical. In any case, it is absolutely inexplicable that you should use such language to me, you who for months past have been recognized by all her friends as the admirer of my friend Miss Bennet."

The words were out, and Georgiana felt hot with shame as she uttered them, conscious that even with the need for openness on this terrible occasion, the betraying of her friend's hopes to the object of them was a shocking thing. She was so overcome as to be unable to look at William Price's horror-struck face.

"Miss Bennet! It is possible that you thought I was paying attentions to Miss Bennet? Miss Darcy, you cannot be serious. This is too frightful. I never thought of doing so, never dreamed of her expecting them, if she did expect them. Miss Bennet was always gay and cheerful—she is a charming girl, as we were excellent companions; but as for anything more—surely you could not have been deceived, whoever else was, when you alone were the subject of all my desires and hopes?"

Georgiana shrank from the task of answering such an appeal, and took hold of another part of his sentence to reply to. "She did expect them, Mr. Price, and she received enough, at all events, to mislead her most cruelly. She has thought of no one but yourself, and of meeting again here, for months past, and everything that has happened in the last week had strengthened her in her belief in your attachment. You cannot deny," continued Georgiana, her indignation rising, "that your constant association, her delight in your society, have given rise to expectation in the minds of her friends, if you dispute its existence in her own."

"No," said William, "I cannot deny that, for I had a proof of it this evening in some remarks dropped by Mrs. Jennings; but though they disturbed me momentarily, I dismissed them from my mind, as I knew she was the kind of person whose chief delight lies in teasing young people about each other, and I thought Miss Bennet, and her other friends, were too sensible to be continually entertaining such fancies."

"Fancies!" repeated Georgiana warmly. "My poor friend is completely wrapped up, heart and soul, in what you designate as a fancy."

"Indeed, I am very sorry," said William, looking utterly downcast, "very grieved and ashamed, if I have caused Miss Bennet a moment's uneasiness, though I can hardly think that others, Mrs. Bingley and Mrs. Darcy, in particular, have so completely failed to perceive—but it is useless to enter into the exact degrees of misunderstanding. I, at least, have been as thoroughly blind as a man could wish to be. What can I do, Miss Darcy, to prove to you my innocence? If I have occasioned this unfortunate error, it has been through ignorance, thoughtlessness, nothing more. Is there any one thing, any incident, you could tell me of, by which you may have been inadvertently misled?"

Georgiana's ideas were so confused, and she was altogether so agitated that at the moment she felt as if she would never be able to collect herself sufficiently to marshal her evidence, now it was required; but, luckily, as she tried to think, one episode darted into her memory, which had frequently been discussed between herself and Kitty, and had seemed to bear naturally but one interpretation. Painful though it was to bring such matters into dispute, she forced herself for Kitty's sake to say: "Did you not tell Mrs. Knightley, after the ball which took place at her house, that you had never enjoyed an evening more, and that there was one person whose presence there had been everything to you? Did you not give her to understand that you meant Miss Bennet?"

Distress and surprise were clearly shown on William's countenance. He began to speak, hesitated, and broke off, and then resumed: "I know what you mean, but it is all too bewildering. Surely Mrs. Knightley did not tell you that? I never spoke or thought of Miss Bennet in that connection. Except that I had some pleasant dances with her, she might not have existed for me that evening. I recollect telling Mrs. Knightley what a delightful evening I had had, and it was she who suggested that one person's presence had contributed more to it than any other. I could do nothing but agree with her, as I thought she had noticed my instant and intense admiration of you. It was so evident to me, that I supposed it was to others. I thought of no one else but you. When Mr. Bingley invited me to stay with him, I was doubtful if I could accept, but directly he said that you lived in the same neighbourhood, I determined that nothing should prevent my coming. Do you recollect anything else, Miss Darcy, our meeting at the Hursts,' and Captain Wentworth saying that you believed sailors to be fickle, which made me so uneasy until I persuaded myself that you did not mean it? Oh, do not shake your head, continue to misbelieve it, I entreat you. And in these last few days, if events have happened to throw me more with Miss Bennet than with yourself, it has not been my doing, or my wish. I implore you to be convinced of this, and to accept my assurances of my unswerving loyalty and devotion towards you."

It was impossible for Georgiana not to be moved by these words, though she had tried to check their passionate flow, and had remained where she was, leaning on a chair, solely because her trembling limbs would hardly support her. Now, however, summoning all her courage, and strengthening herself with thoughts of Kitty, she spoke in a tolerably firm voice. "Mr. Price, I must believe that this unhappy mistake has been made unintentionally, since you say so, but the wretchedness it has caused will not be so easily cleared away. The assurances of your loyalty should not be made to me, you owe them to Miss Bennet and her only."

She could get no further, for she was interrupted by William with a vehemence exceeding any that he had shown before. "Miss Bennet! Except as your friend, and as a lady for whom I have a great liking and respect, Miss Bennet is nothing to me, and never could be. Oh, Miss Darcy, you do not yet understand me. Can you forget Miss Bennet for one moment, and tell me if, apart from all that, there would be the slightest hope for me at some future time? the least chance of your having some faith in me, to enable me to strive to win you as I long to do?"

He had made an error, and saw it before he had finished his sentence. "Forget Miss Bennet?" repeated Georgiana, with a flash of angry pride, as she walked away from him. "I do not think you understand *me*, Mr. Price. When I have desired a friend's happiness so long, I cannot lightly see it thrown away, and never, never would I seek it for my own if it was to be at the expense of hers."

William, on hearing this, made a quick pace forward to intercept her, and, turning, so that they stood face to face, he asked in quieter, but not less ardent tones: "Only one word more, Miss Darcy. Forgive me for what I said, but tell me this. You spoke of happiness. Did you mean that it might be happiness to you, if all this were cleared up? Did you mean that I might be able to make you happy, and that there was any possibility of your ever coming to feel for me even the smallest part of what I feel for you?"

Georgiana, trembling, almost weeping, her anger not subsided, but other sensations surging strongly up, brought herself to look for one moment into the eyes of glowing entreaty bent upon hers. With almost a sob, she broke away from him, exclaiming: "No, no; it is of no use to ask me. Do not talk to me in such a way—I must not—I will not listen—I cannot bear it," and fairly ran out of the gallery.

William stood stunned and motionless for some minutes. At last he roused himself, with a deep sigh, from the contemplation of his ruined hopes, and strove to think of what he ought to do next. While desiring nothing so much as solitude and quiet, he remembered that Georgiana would not have gone straight back to the ball-room, and for the two of them to be absent would give rise to remark. To protect Georgiana was an instinct, and it gave him a ray of satisfaction in the midst of his perplexity and misery to remind himself that though she had refused his love, she now knew of its existence, and whatever misapprehension there might be as to the past, she would perceive what influence guided his actions in the future. He slowly descended the stairs, so bewildered still as scarcely to be conscious of what was going on around him; rehearsing their conversation and thinking too late of things he might have said, which would perhaps have been of some service to his cause. A crowd of persons were streaming into the hall from the ball-room, the second dance since he and Georgiana went upstairs having just ended, and supper being now talked of. He mingled with rest, and presently manœuvered himself into a place near Mrs. Bingley, who was now sitting with Mr. Ferrars, and greeted him with a pleasant smile.

Beyond a causal inquiry as to whether he had seen Kitty, she asked him no questions, and before long he found himself intro-duced to a young lady, and directed to find a place for her at one of the supper tables. What he talked of he did not know, and the rest of the evening passed in the same dreamlike manner. In his desire to attract no special attention, he chatted and laughed and danced, and was persuaded that he did so as gaily as before, but he could not keep his thoughts from wandering to Georgiana, whom he had seen returning, looking very pale, about a quarter of an hour after they had parted, or to Kitty, whose eyes contin-ually and anxiously sought his. It was far more painful for him to see her than Georgiana, whom of course he held blameless, even for her hard words; Kitty he vaguely felt to be in part responsible for the whole trouble, and though bitterly reproaching himself for folly and blindness, he could not bring himself to go near her, to speak to her, or dance with her again, when such a construction had been put upon all their previous intercourse.

Angry at the pain he was giving her, and driven to despair at the sight of Georgiana's pale cheeks, he found the length of the evening almost unendurable, and the only relief he obtained was in going to Mr. Bingley, and asking him to fix as early as possi-ble an hour for their start on the following morning, for it would be necessary for him and his cousin to be well on their long jour-ney towards Mansfield by the afternoon. It had been already arranged that the three gentlemen should return to Desborough independently of Mrs. and Miss Bingley, who were to remain at Pemberley for another day or two to recover from the fatigues of the ball. Mr. Bingley good-naturedly agreed, judging that the young people had decided that it would be better to make their adieux the night before, rather than come down early to a painful scene of parting at the prosaic breakfast-table, so he went away to consult Darcy, and send out orders to the stables. This done, William felt more comfortable; inaction was intolerable to him, and he would have removed himself from the house at once if he could have done so, since to relieve her of a presence which had become embarrassing and distasteful to her was the only thing he could now do for Georgiana.

She had, as he anticipated, sought the refuge of her own room when she fled from the gallery; but even there the old habits of self-command and consideration for others prevailed over the longing to give way to her grief and distress of the mind. She knew she must not allow herself the luxury of a burst of tears, nor even a little quiet thought, in order to realize what had occurred, and decide what, if anything, she should say to Kitty. No, there was no time for that, there would be plenty of opportunity soon, to readjust their view of recent events, and all that they meant to Kitty and herself. Shaken and unnerved by the shock of William Price's declaration, Georgiana shrank from immediately facing its consequences. She could only take a few moments in which to compose herself and endeavour to smooth away the traces of emotion. That she must see him again was a dreadful thought, but it would be a far worse ordeal to have to encounter Kitty's inquiries and lamentations on the following day, and the surprise of Elizabeth and Jane. Georgiana dared not let herself think of all this, when this horrible evening was not yet over. She hastily bathed her face, and opening the windows wide, leaned out for a few minutes, for the night air to cool her throbbing temples, and went down at last, feeling as if her countenance must betray to every observer the secret of what had happened.

She took refuge at once by the side of Elizabeth, who made room for her with a smile, and did not fail to notice her aspect. As soon as she was at liberty, she asked Georgiana if she was very tired, and took care that she was provided with some refreshment. Georgiana owned to a good deal of fatigue, but declared that she should sleep it off, and Elizabeth, who thought her lassitude partly attributable to some worry about Kitty, told her that she might slip away to bed as soon as she chose, and that Kitty must not come into her room for one of their long conversations; they must wait till to-morrow to talk over the ball. Poor Georgiana assented with a grateful glance, but had difficulty in restraining her tears, as she thought how little Elizabeth dreamt that interview with Kitty could be a thing to be dreaded, not welcomed.

After supper, she could not, for fear of making herself conspicuous, avoid one or two invitations to dance; but she was truly glad when Colonel Fitzwilliam, on a hint from Elizabeth, approached her, and said: "Let me take you to a seat in the library, Georgiana. I fear you are tired, and you will be able to rest quietly there, and not say one word to me unless you please—we are old enough friends for that, I should think."

There were but few persons in the large library, at one end of which a table had been set out, where servants dispensed tea and coffee during the evening, and the cousins placed themselves on a leather-covered couch near the fire at the opposite end. True to his undertaking, Colonel Fitzwilliam remained silent after he had established his cousin in comfort, and screened the blaze from her face; but after a few minutes, Georgiana roused herself, thinking anything better than being left to her own reflections, and suddenly recollecting a thing that she had intended to tell Elizabeth, had she been able to see her alone during the day, and deciding that there could be no harm in communicating it to Colonel Fitzwilliam herself, she mentioned having learnt the fact of Mr. Bertram's acquaintance with Miss Crawford, and asked if her cousin happened to know it.

He admitted himself informed, but expressed interest, as he himself had not discussed it with Mr. Bertram.

Georgiana therefore ventured to give him Mr. Bertram's description of her, and pointed out rather timidly that it seemed to agree entirely with what they already knew and had heard.

"Yes," said Colonel Fitzwilliam thoughtfully; and after a pause, he added: "I am glad he spoke so well of her—glad she had an advocate in him, for, as you may have gathered from what he dropped with regard to her brother, it would not be surprising if the Bertram family were a little prejudiced against all the Crawfords. I am glad that he, at least, has the manliness to award blame only where blame is due."

Georgiana listened attentively, half expecting that her cousin would go on to explain the nature of the prejudice against the Crawfords, which had clearly done Miss Crawford so much harm; but he did not, so after a little she hazarded the remark: "He did not seem to know anything about her of late years, so I thought it useless to ask about her marriage."

"You were right; it would have been useless," said the Colonel. "Elizabeth, I know, troubles herself a good deal about not having heard any particulars, but doubtless the world will be informed all in good time, and when there is any news, one may expect it will penetrate even to Derbyshire." He smiled as he spoke, but it was not a cheerful smile, and his voice had the ring of something very like bitterness. Georgiana's heart ached for him; she felt that never before had she known what a disappointment could be.

Colonel Fitzwilliam talked of other things, until they were interrupted by Tom Bertram, who came hurrying in search of them to ask Miss Darcy to dance with him again. "Miss Darcy— so sorry you are tired, but you positively must allow me just these two. People are beginning to go, actually! and, you know, when that happens, a ball always begins to lose some of its spirit. Besides, who knows when we shall have another such a delightful evening as this again? I have been telling Mr. and Mrs. Bingley I can never sufficiently thank them for having brought me here." Georgiana suffered him to lead her to the dance, and to go on talking, for she was quite unequal to arguing with him. At the conclusion of the two dances, Elizabeth, who had been watching her, came up and asked her if she would not like to retire at once, and fortified by this permission, Georgiana turned to say goodnight to her partner, whose protests against her disappearance were as strong as the polite Tom Bertram could make them.

"Why, Miss Darcy, if you remove yourself, the ball may as well break up; and it is really cruel to make me say good-night, when it is good-bye as well."

"Is it? Do you start so early to-morrow? I am very sorry," said Georgiana, with an effort at the cordiality which seemed expected of her.

"We do, indeed; some wild idea of my cousin's, I fancy, that it will take us all day to get to Mansfield, even going round Desborough to meet the curricle. It will not; but Mr. Bingley has just informed me that William wishes to start not a moment later than eight, and you ladies, I fear, are not likely to be on the scene at such an unearthly hour?"

"No, indeed," said Elizabeth, "after such dissipations as charades and a ball, it will be remarkable if any of us are able to leave our rooms for a week. You do not realize what quiet people we are here ordinarily, Mr. Bertram." She chatted on, and under cover of it, Georgiana managed to say a brief adieu and glide away. Could she avoid seeing Mr. Price again? No! he was standing by the foot of the stairs; he seemed to be watching for her; there was no escape. Her head was averted, and her foot placed on the lowest step, when he started forward, and not offering to shake hands, but in a low voice and a look of intense earnestness, he said: "May I say good-bye to you, Miss Darcy?"

Georgiana hardly knew if her "Good-bye, Mr. Price," was audible; but he bowed, and stepped back, his eyes following her as she went up the stairs.

Chapter 21

IN THE GLOOM OF the following morning, at an hour which seemed exceptionally cheerless by reason of the mist and fine rain which prevailed, Mr. Bingley's chaise drove round to the front entrance of Pemberley. Kitty, who, after a night of weeping and wretchedness, had fallen into a doze, was aroused by the sound of movements and voices, but when she peeped through her curtains, she was too late for anything but a heartrending glimpse of the skirts of William Price's great-coat, as he stepped into the carriage. The door was shut, Darcy and Fitzwilliam waved their farewells, and the horses moved off at a brisk trot. Kitty watched and listened to them as long as she could, and then flung herself on her bed in a paroxysm of grief. Though William's avoidance of her during the latter part of the previous evening, his strange altered looks, and his embarrassed way of saying good-night, had undermined her hopes to such an extent that she had been all night facing the terrible desolation caused by the thought, "If he does not care for me after all," yet she had not actually given all up in despair until the moment of hearing him leave the house. Some note, some message, might have arrived—might still arrive; but since parting from him, Kitty had not been able to quell the horrible fear that all was over. The indications, which had been so favourable, had completely changed since Mrs. Jennings had uttered her foolish remark; in vain had she tried to reinstate her old relations with William Price. What could it all mean? Each time she put this question to herself she gave way afresh to unrestrained tears, and, weakened by fatigue and emotion, was totally incapable of following out any train of thought or conjecture. She had longed to hasten to Georgiana the night before, to pour out her heart in an appeal for the support which Georgiana had never failed to give; but Elizabeth had checked her in this intention; and, poor Kitty, unable to bear pain alone with any degree of courage, had worked herself into a deplorable condition by the time her sister arrived at her door in the morning.

Elizabeth and Jane had naturally both surmised something of the state of things as regarded Kitty. It was not difficult for anyone acquainted with the previous development of the affair, to perceive that William Price had not fulfilled the expectations which had been formed of him, and Elizabeth accounted for Georgiana's evident unhappiness by concluding that she had become aware that this would be the case. William Price had looked much as usual, up to the last, but Elizabeth suspected that there had been some elucidation either between him and Georgiana, or through Mrs. Jennings, and she hardly knew how much to blame him. There was no time to talk matters over with Jane, for she felt, as soon as she was up, that her immediate visit must be to the chief sufferer, to comfort and sustain her and, if possible, to shield her from the consequences of her own error.

Kitty would not admit her at first, and when at length Elizabeth persuaded her to do so, she was distressed to see what ravages the shock of disappointment and the hours of weeping had wrought. Kitty's tears broke out anew, but the sense of Elizabeth's affection and companionship somewhat soothed her, and when she could speak more coherently, she begged to see Georgiana, who could perhaps tell her things—who would be able to explain. This Elizabeth could not permit, for she saw that Kitty was in no fit state to talk over her troubles, but she promised her an early opportunity of doing so, and having induced her to swallow some food and a cordial, she soon had the satisfaction of seeing her fall asleep. These precautionary measures were fully justified in the course of the next forty-eight hours, during which time Kitty remained really ill, attacks of strong hysteria alternating with weakness of extreme exhaustion. Every care was lavished on her by her two sisters, by Georgiana, and by Elizabeth's maid; but naturally anything like rational discussion of the cause of her illness was out of the question, and, indeed, Kitty herself, after once asking if Mr. Price had left any message for her, or spoken of returning at some future time, and receiving a negative answer, seemed, after giving way to a torrent of tears, unable or unwilling to puzzle matters out any further.

Georgiana did not escape the inquiries and speculations of Elizabeth and Jane. When she descended from her room the morning after the ball, at an hour little later than her usual one, to take her place in the family circle, she had regained complete control of herself, and declared herself entirely refreshed, and beyond a little heaviness of the eyes and paleness of cheeks, naturally attributable to the fatigues of the last two days, there was nothing in her aspect to cause remark. No one guessed at the sense of guilt which filled her heart when she saw what grief and disappointment had done for Kitty, or at the deep compunction and almost unendurable self-reproach which assailed her when the others discussed his strange defection, and professed themselves unable to account for the curious change in his attitude towards Kitty—a change which several people had noticed the last hour of the ball. Elizabeth and Jane asked her if she was at all prepared for it, whether anything had occurred to make her suspect that Mr. Price would not propose marriage to Kitty after all. These questions were a hard trial to Georgiana, for she could not bear to be other than straightforward, and for a multitude of reasons she could not divulge the true explanation; she could only say in a low, troubled voice, and with as few words as possible, that she had learnt, in the course of the evening, that their expectations were mistaken ones, and that she feared Kitty would take it very much to heart.

Seeing her unhappiness on her friend's behalf, the two ladies forbore to tease her with further inquiries, though Jane still felt that Georgiana could have thrown more light on the mystery had she cared, and in her hearing continually lamented the failure of everything for poor Kitty, who had fallen, as it were, between two stools, the regrettable ending to all this pleasant time, and the fickleness of young men, or, rather, the unfortunate complications that arose through their not knowing their own minds. Georgiana had to listen to this in silence, though conscious that the last was not an accusation that could fairly be brought against William Price, and Elizabeth's more rational way of accounting for things was not much better, when she said that she did not think Mr. Price guilty of more than thoughtlessness, but it was certainly a pity that he had not been able to perceive earlier the extent of Kitty's feeling for him, as no doubt, when he had at last become aware of it, he realized what Elizabeth had already surmised to be in his mind, namely, that his roving life did not warrant him in thinking about matrimony at present. Georgiana thought she might venture to say here that William Price had indeed expressed great sorrow to her on finding that he had been the cause of disappointment to Kitty, and she even went so far into the dangerous fields of explanation as to add that he had had no suspicion of it until surprised by a chance word of raillery from Mrs. Jennings. She was pleased to see that this news partly rehabilitated him in the mind of Elizabeth, if not of Jane; and for fear of betraying more than she ought, she went away, wondering why she should be glad for him not to be misjudged, when she really ought to be only thinking of how wrongly he had behaved.

The hour of enlightenment for Kitty could not be long postponed. By the third day she was well enough to sit up in a large chair in her own room, and on being visited by Georgiana, begged her to stay for a time, and to fasten the door. When assured of their freedom from interruption, she seized her friend's hand, made her sit close beside her, and implored her to relate everything she could that would throw light on Mr. Price's changed conduct and hasty departure. Georgiana nerved herself to reply, but for the first few minutes, Kitty was talking and crying incessantly, pouring out the pent-up grief of the last few days, so that Georgiana had great difficulty in calming her, and dreaded the effect of the revelation about to be made.

"Dear Kitty," remonstrated Georgiana, "you must not cry; you must be more composed, or Elizabeth will not let me stay with you. Do try to be brave; think whether it is right to give way so much; you will make yourself ill again, you know."

"Anyone would be ill after what I have been through," lamented Kitty; "I shall never be happy again. Why does he not care for me? Did he tell you why not, Georgiana? What have I done, or what has Mrs. Jennings done? Something must have happened to offend him, for he changed all in one minute."

"I do not believe anything happened to offend him, Kitty," returned Georgiana. "As he has gone away now and did not do what he all thought he would do, is it not best to assume that he does not care in the way we hoped for, and try to forget about it, and not mind too much? Dear Kitty, I am deeply grieved for you: it has been my fault, more than anyone's, and you are right to reproach me; I can never forgive myself for having led you into the mistake."

"But you are not answering me, Georgiana," cried Kitty, with the petulance of an invalid; "of course, I know he does not care, and has gone away, but I want to know why he has gone. If it is not for anything I have done, he might come back."

Georgiana was silent, and held her down; she shrank still from telling Kitty that he would not come back. Kitty began again impatiently. "It is foolish of you to talk about reproaching yourself. It is not more your fault than anyone else's; not so much as Mrs. Jennings's, but if he spoke to you about it at all, he must have said something, have given some hint. Did he talk to you, Georgiana? You have not told me that yet."

Georgiana gave up what hopes she had had of concealing from Kitty what would make the disappointment far more thorough, and crushing, and as gently as possible managed to convey the fact of William's confession of attachment to herself. She was obliged to say it several times, and in language of unmistakable clearness, before Kitty could grasp her meaning; and even then, as she sat crouched on the ground, her face averted and her cheeks burning with shame, Kitty, who had drawn her hand away, gazed at her in mingled horror and incredulity. In the course of these three days, the notion that Miss Kitty Bennet was *not* the object of William Price's preference had at length penetrated the mind of that young lady, but that her friend should be the chosen one was a thing altogether past comprehension, and the first idea that occurred to her was that there must have been treachery to herself somewhere. Kitty's changes of mood lately had been punctuated by bursts of tears, and this was no exception to the rule, though they were now tears of mortification. Her first angry impulse was to pour out words of blame, accusing Georgiana of not being satisfied with the attentions of Mr. Bertram, but requiring those of his cousin too. Georgiana disdained to reply to such a taunt, but it needed all her patience, all her tenderness, to persuade Kitty out of her bitter frame of mind, and to endeavour to heal the wound to the poor girl's vanity, which had indeed all through been more deeply involved than her affections, little though she realized it. Combined with a love of importance, and the encouragement given by her friends, it had carried her on a wave of excitement through the past months, and had helped to fix her hopes more firmly on William Price than any knowledge of his character, any real congeniality in their natures could have done. But she could not be aware of all this, and there was no immediate comprehension to make the disappointment less acute.

It certainly was consoling to feel that everyone else must have been to blame, that everybody had been equally deceived; that even Georgiana herself had been taken by surprise, and was now heaping upon herself the severest reproaches, while she implored Kitty's forgiveness—not, Kitty discerned in a puzzled way, for having received Mr. Price's proposals, but for having helped to foster the deception which had reacted so cruelly upon her friend. Above all, it would have been a relief, having discovered that Mr. Price must have acted atrociously, to say so, and the more Kitty thought of it, the more she resented his conduct. But Georgiana would not admit this; she would only allow that it was all utterly inexplicable, but that they could not judge fairly of Mr. Price, not being able to see his point of view, and that if that was clear to them, she was sure that he would be found to have acted honestly all the way through.

Kitty immediately suspected that Georgiana had been won round to the said point of view, and began to question her closely as to what had passed between them; but Georgiana indignantly repudiated the suggestion, and assured Kitty, in a manner that forbade further discussion, that she had decidedly refused Mr. Price, refused even to listen to him, and had not the slightest expectation of ever seeing or hearing from him again. She added, that she had refrained from telling Elizabeth, or any of the others, about Mr. Price's offer, and thought it would be best if Kitty decided to do the same, to which, as she had expected, Kitty willingly agreed.

Nothing, in fact, could have suited Kitty better, in the circumstances, than a compact of silence. At the end of their long conversation, when Georgiana left her, by far the more exhausted in spirits of the two, she had begun to have some of the sensations of an injured heroine, and it was much more satisfactory to consider herself badly treated—to have been jilted, to all intents and purposes, than if it came to be known that she had been all the time in love with the wrong man, in which case her position would be shorn of much of its dignity. Her sisters' sympathy was very acceptable to her, and when Jane invited her to return with her to Desborough for a time, she gladly promised to do so, knowing that it would not at first be at all comfortable to remain with Georgiana, the one person who knew the whole story. It was therefore arranged that Jane and Miss Bingley should defer their journey for two days more, when it was hoped she would be quite equal to travelling with them.

The only drawback to the plan, as far as she was concerned, was Miss Bingley's presence for another fortnight at Desborough. That lady had not troubled herself to make any conjectures with regard to William Price's departure, but frankly told Jane and Georgiana that it was exactly what she had expected. She at least had never been misled; she had never supposed Mr. Price to be in love with Miss Bennet or anyone else. She could not imagine why they had all persuaded themselves of it. Nothing was clearer than that he was a young man quite heart-whole. Jane protested, but Georgiana made no comment, only begging her friend privately not to refer to the subject in Kitty's hearing.

The day arrived, Mr. Bingley's carriage again drove to the door, and the three ladies took their seats in it, Kitty's farewell glance being given towards the spot where she had last seen William Price. With their going, the whole episode seemed to be finally closed, and Georgiana turned to re-enter the house, and to take up the duties of a life which, in one short week, seemed to have been robbed of almost all its brightness. She had been making an unsuccessful struggle against low spirits, ever since the ill-omened day of the ball, and being unable to dismiss, had tried hard to account for, the strange sense of depression, of loneliness, and loss, which assailed her continually. It was not only sorrow for Kitty's disappointment, or regret for her own share in it, nor was it the estrangement that had arisen between them; no, it was not a vision of Kitty that so constantly obtruded itself upon her thoughts, but of a very different person, one whose ardent looks and words insisted on being remembered, whose voice she seemed to hear again pleading for what she dared not give. Every detail of their conversation in the gallery crowded upon Georgiana's memory, once she had made her confession to Kitty, and would admit these thoughts; they would not be denied, as she had denied him a hearing, but came back to her with a vivid clearness and an irresistible appeal.

She remembered how he had described the beginnings and the growth of his attachment to her, and looking back over the course of their acquaintance, countless incidents stood out, to verify all he had said. When no longer viewed through Kitty's illusions, every one of their meetings and conversations was seen in its true light, consolidating their friendship, giving each an insight into the other's character. Why was it such a joy, though an indescribably painful one, to recall these things, to live again through the moments spent in the gallery? Georgiana's heart answered her, and she felt that the answer must always have been there, though she had only just awakened to it. It was a joy because everything connected with William Price must be a joy to her, himself, his nobleness, his true worth, and the knowledge that he cared for her, but it was pain, because, sweet though it was to hear what he had to tell her, it was a disloyalty to her friend to listen, the friend whose life had perhaps been spoilt by their mistake. How could she ever think of being happy as long as that friend suffered? For despite her grief at the thought that she had lost him for ever, that she had refused his love and he would never know now that she loved him in return, yet

Georgiana felt that she could not have acted differently. Even had she known at the moment he spoke, what he was to her, she could not have been so traitorous as to take what Kitty longed for, from under her very eyes; and she was glad that Kitty did not guess at the extent of the sacrifice.

Chapter 22

THE DEPARTURE OF THE ladies for Desborough left a small party at Pemberley, for several days previously Colonel Fitzwilliam had gone with his horses to Leicestershire, and good accounts of the hunting prospects had been received from him. The Darcys were not, however, to remain for long alone, for the arrival of Mrs. Garret and Miss Crawford had been fixed for a date early in the following week. Elizabeth delayed no further in preparing Georgiana for their visit, and at same time communicated to her the fact which she had learnt from Mrs. Wentworth, of Miss Crawford's not being engaged to Sir Walter Elliot. Georgiana listened with the greatest interest, and joined warmly in the expression of Elizabeth's hopes that Colonel Fitzwilliam might yet be made happy, although for the present there was nothing to be done but to try to make Miss Crawford feel at home and comfortable among them all.

"I shall confine my efforts solely to that," said Elizabeth laughingly. "It would be useless as well as dangerous to attempt any further matchmaking until we know the extent of feeling on *both* sides, for that want of that knowledge has made us singularly unsuccessful lately, has it not, Georgiana?"

Georgiana assented but could not smile; for just then only the tragical side of unrequited love was turned towards her. A brief letter of thanks had been received by his hostess from William Price, saying all that was necessary in a matter simple and sincere, and closing with a message of "greetings and remembrance to all your family." Georgiana's cheeks burned as she handed it back, and she was glad to turn away, and take her little niece upon her lap, while Darcy, glancing over the letter, said: "He seems an agreeable, manly young fellow, from what I saw of him; I should be sorry to think he would treat a girl ill."

"A girl's fancy does not always keep pace with common-sense, in such a case as the one you speak of," said his wife. "And as I told you, I do not think Kitty was very wisely counselled from the first."

"Probably not," said Darcy, "a young man at his age and in his profession is likely to flutter the dovecotes quite uncon-sciously. But there was something so frank and pleasing about him that one would wish to believe him thoroughly estimable."

Georgiana, through the little one's chatter, heard these words with delight; that William Price should have gained her brother's good opinion was a source of rejoicing, even though that advantage might now avail him nothing.

Miss Crawford looked very thin and ill when she arrived, and the first part of her visit passed very quietly. She spent the chief of her time in her own rooms, descending only to join the family at dinner and during the evening, and when not talking to Elizabeth, seemed to find her greatest pleasure in listening to Georgiana's music. Mrs. Grant watched over her with unremitting solicitude, but by no means treated her as a sick person, evidently desiring that she should rouse herself, take an interest in things around her, and make whatever exertion she felt equal to. The tranquility of the life exactly suited her, and before many days an improvement in her health and spirits became noticeable. She was able to take drives in the mildest part of the day, or go for short walks through the pleasure grounds when the frosts of December came in, and the mornings were bright and invigorating. The beauty of the country around, the healthiness of the air, and the quiet kindness of her host and hostess, gradually had their effect upon a troubled mind and a weakened body; and Colonel Fitzwilliam's name was barely mentioned, Lady Catherine de Bourgh's never.

One morning, when Georgiana and Mrs. Grant had walked down to the Rectory, Elizabeth was sitting with her guest, and with the view of entertaining her, gave her a description of the charades, not omitting the energetic part played by Mr. Bertram in organizing them. Mary's colour changed a little on first hearing his name, but she gave all her attention to the recital, and it was not until some minutes later, when silence had fallen between them, that she said suddenly: "I wonder if Mr. Bertram or Mr. Price spoke of me to you Mrs. Darcy. Were you aware that I knew them both?"

Elizabeth replied that she had heard from Georgiana of Mr. Price's acquaintance with Miss Crawford, but of Mr. Bertram's she had not known, the subject never having been approached while the young men were there.

"I thought not," said Miss Crawford, and after a moment's pause she added, colouring slightly: "I have had too much experience of your kindness to think that you would treat me differently if you did know the whole circumstances; nevertheless, I felt sure that you did not, and I made up my mind before I came here, that I would not be any further indebted to you while you remained in ignorance. Each day I have been expecting you to ask me some question about the reason for Lady Catherine's hostility to us, for you were fully entitled to an explanation after the kind and generous way in which you wrote to me, and which I fear I acknowledged so inadequately." She stopped, emotion and weakness depriving her momentarily of speech, and Elizabeth, who had been endeavouring to check her, took hold of her hand, and with the utmost gentleness begged her not to continue and not to agitate herself.

"Dear Miss Crawford, I am entitled to no explanation, and I do not wish for one. It is you who ought to receive the fullest apologies of the whole family for my aunt's conduct to you. My cousin told us all that happened that evening after we left, and, as I told you in my letter, I can never be sufficiently ashamed and grieved on account of what you were subjected to. If you can forgive us, do not let us revive the subject; it is painful to us both."

Miss Crawford indicated that she wished to be allowed to speak, and after a few moments spent in recovering herself, she went on in a low voice, and looking away from Elizabeth: "I did not mean to refer to that part of it, and least of all with you, whose goodness has almost obliterated it from my mind. I mean the reason for Lady Catherine's attack. You must have surmised that there was some cause for it; she must have told you that she had heard something to my detriment, or, at all events, you have gathered that something of the kind exists? It is that that I wish to make clear; I feel that I owe it to you to tell you exactly, as far as they concern myself, what things are said about me, in order that when you hear them from others, you may be able to separate the true from the false. For some of them are true, you know; that is the unfortunate part of it." As she concluded, she glanced at Elizabeth with an attempt at a smile, though her hands were trembling.

Elizabeth attempted to calm and reassure her. "There is no need for you to tell me anything if you do not feel equal to the effort," she said. "I think I do already know the greater part of the story, and I can assure you that we have never believed the smallest thing disadvantageous to yourself. I had heard enough of it before Mr. Yates appeared to be convinced that you were the person injured and misjudged, and that a maliciously dis-torted version of events was poured down my aunt's ears. I shall be very happy if some day you will give me your confidence, but I fear it might do you harm to talk of it just now, and recall things in which persons you cared for were involved?"

Elizabeth's manner was so kind, that Mary was glad to allow herself to be persuaded, and lay back on her sofa murmuring: "Yes, you are right," looking at the same time tired and relieved. She presently added, with a little more brightness: "I am glad you know, and that you do not think me such a monster as Lady Catherine described."

"I never thought you were a monster, my dear Miss Crawford," assured Elizabeth, smiling and studying her guest's countenance while her own mind was busy. Miss Crawford defi-nitely, if laughingly expressed desire to be reinstated in the good opinion of Mrs. Darcy, probably included in its object the rest of the family; and, if so, then in spite of their abrupt separation at Bath, in spite of all that had happened since in London, Colonel Fitzwilliam must be among the number. Elizabeth felt as if she were groping in the dark, for she had no clue to Miss Crawford's present feelings towards him; but though she had not intended to speak of him yet, this was at least an opportunity of discovering whether they were feelings of goodwill. She accordingly said, as if continuing the same train of thought: "My cousin was so glad that he had happened to remain behind us, and could therefore attempt to do something, even though it was but little, to remedy the evil caused by those objectionable Ferrars."

Mary started and changed her position, and Elizabeth, though not looking directly at her, could perceive a variety of expressions pass across her face. She did not answer immediately, and her reply, when uttered: "It was very kind of Colonel Fitzwilliam," sounded cold and reserved.

"I do not regard it as kindness," said Elizabeth; "his regard for you and his indignation on your behalf made him anxious to do far more. He told me that he bitterly regretted having left you that evening, after we had gone away. If he had stayed near you, he could have prevented much that followed."

Again Mary took some time to reply, and when she did, to Elizabeth's surprise, it was with more than a touch of scornfulness. "Colonel Fitzwilliam has a great power of self-effacement, has he not? He must have practiced the art of disappearing unexpectedly, with as little warning as the magician in the fairy stories."

"But does he so?" asked Elizabeth, whose astonishment increased. "I had not noticed it. We think him generally a staid and sober person, who does things with even more than the usual amount of consideration. Did he not return—did you not see him that evening at my aunt's?"

"Oh, yes, that evening," said Mary. "I believe he did see us to the carriage; I was not thinking so much of that occasion. But in London—I saw him once or twice, and he talked as if he were going to remain, and then he vanished as if the earth had swallowed him. Of course, it did not matter; he had only himself to please; but I heard several people remark on it."

Elizabeth pondered, and to gain time inquired: "Did he speak as though he hoped to see you again while he was there?"

"Yes—at least we thought so; my sister and I may have misunderstood, or he may have meant nothing; people can hardly be expected to account for all their sudden freaks, can they?" replied Mary, speaking with an indifference so marked that her companion could not help fancying it was assumed. Elizabeth hesitated no longer, and was about to speak, with the intention of telling Miss Crawford why Colonel Fitzwilliam had left town so suddenly, when the door opened to admit Mrs. Grant and Georgiana, so that she was obliged to postpone the communication till some future time, and to leave matters in a state which more than ever seemed to need elucidation.

The opportunity, however, was long in coming. After their half-finished talk, Mary Crawford appeared to avoid being alone with her hostess. She came downstairs more, and gradually began to live almost entirely with the rest of the family, but constantly kept close to her sister and Georgiana on various pretexts. The latter did not venture to speak to her of Colonel Fitzwilliam, but Mary was not in discovering that the name of

William Price was a welcome one to her young friend, and seeing that Georgiana wished to *hear*, without having to *ask*, Mary told all she knew of his youth, his family and his past career, descanting on his charm and his fine qualities of character, while Georgiana sat in silence, her downcast eyes and glowing cheeks alone betraying the interest which the subject had for her. Mary guessed at the meaning of it all, but considerately said no word to arouse Georgiana's self-consciousness, and their friendship grew almost unawares, neither knowing how much each thought of, and would have liked to help, the other.

It was not until nearly a week after the subject had first been broached that Elizabeth found it possible to renew it, and then only by deliberately engaging the attention of Miss Crawford, in inviting her to walk with her one morning along the high road. Darcy had driven with Mrs. Grant and Georgiana to a distant part of the estate, and it had been proposed that the other two ladies should come to meet them on their return, so that Miss Crawford could take a seat in the barouche should she feel tired. It was such a beautiful morning, crisp, cold and bright, that Mrs. Grant over-ruled the objections which her sister was beginning to make, and assured her that a brisk walk in such weather could do her nothing but good. Elizabeth half suspected that she would still find some way of avoiding the expedition, but when twelve o'clock arrived, Miss Crawford descended into the hall, saying smilingly: "All ready, you see, Mrs. Darcy. Don't you think I am the most obedient patient you ever saw? At this rate, you will soon be able to send me away a complete cure."

"I hardly think of you as a patient now, and still less do I think of sending you away," returned Elizabeth, as they emerged from the house. "Mr. Darcy and I should be sadly disappointed if you left us directly you were well enough to do so."

"You are always so kind," said Miss Crawford. "But I fear our visit must come to an end soon, as it is less than a fortnight to Christmas, and you will probably be having a large family party for the occasion."

Such a remark could only be interpreted in one way, and Elizabeth, after reiterating her hope that Miss Crawford and Mrs. Grant would make a long stay, and assuring her guest that their numbers at Christmas would be the same as at present, went on almost immediately: "The other day we were speaking of Colonel Fitzwilliam's sudden departure from London, and I wanted to tell you, if it is not tiresome to you to hear, what I believe to have been the reason for it. I am so anxious he should not be misunderstood, or thought capricious."

"Oh, Mrs. Darcy, I did not seem to imply he was. I am sure he has the best of reasons for what he does, and anyhow, they are no business of mine."

Elizabeth would not let the subject be dismissed, and continued very gently: "He had good reasons in this case, and I hope very much you will not dislike my mentioning them, as they concern you. He left London because he cared for you, and had just heard, on what he believed to be unimpeachable authority, that you were engaged to another man. The news was such a blow to him that he could not endure to stay where he might possibly meet you again."

There was a short pause; Mary grew crimson, uttered an exclamation, and then, controlling herself with an effort, said in tones of suppressed anger: "If Colonel Fitzwilliam told you that,

Mrs. Darcy, he is deceiving you and himself. It would be much better to admit candidly that when he saw me again in London he did not care for me as much as he had thought, instead of making my supposed engagement an excuse for his disappearance."

Elizabeth stood still for a moment, completely taken aback by this version of affairs, and could only exclaim: "Miss Crawford!"

"Oh, I beg your pardon; I know I ought not to speak to you, who are his relative," said Mary, walking on with quick impetuous steps. "Pray forgive me, Mrs. Darcy; I know *you* are true, who ever else is not. But you cannot guess how hard it is to be accused of sending a person away before they have even approached one; to be blamed for causing trouble when one has never known to be a free agent, and when the trouble has all reacted upon one's self."

"I would not blame you for the world," said Elizabeth. "You must remember I know but little of the facts, and nothing at all of how they appear from the other side. My principal object, as I have said, is to prevent my cousin from being misjudged, not to make any accusations against anyone; will you not tell me a little more, so that between us we may clear the whole matter up?"

Elizabeth was obliged to proceed with the utmost caution, and to speak less openly than she would have wished, for instinct warned her that Miss Crawford was not yet ready to be guided, or even sympathized with. It was far too soon to assume any special interest on her part in Colonel Fitzwilliam, though her last speech had admitted the existence of a trouble not unconnected to him.

"There is really nothing to tell you, Mrs. Darcy," said Miss Crawford. "What happened is simply a succession of negatives.

Colonel Fitzwilliam reappeared in London, and showed every sign of wishing to renew his friendship with my sister and me, but he departed without doing so. I was not engaged to anyone at that time, nor have I been since, as he might have easily found out if he had asked the right people."

"Miss Crawford!" cried Elizabeth earnestly; "he *had* reason to believe it. Perhaps he did not ask your nearest relatives, but you are surely aware—it involves no reproach to yourself—but it was talked of, and assumed to be a fact, among your friends generally?"

Mary evidently found it difficult to reply, but at length said: "Yes, I know it was talked of, but there was never any truth in it. I know I was foolish. I went about a great deal with those people—with the Elliots; I let myself be drawn into their circle, and I suppose it was pleasant to be fêted and made much of; Mrs. Darcy, I daresay you hardly know what it is to drift into an intimacy that amuses you, and occupies your time, while your heart is never in it the smallest degree."

"I think I understand," said Elizabeth gently. "You had been with them at Bath, and it was difficult to free yourself from the association when you met again?"

"Yes, and my brother liked them—or they liked him—and it is always natural for me to be where he is. But I was not bound to them, and it was not all enjoyment. How often I wished that something would happen to take me out of it! How gladly would I not have gone!"

"My cousin hoped, I think, to have made some arrangements with you and your sister, but he was not sure if they would be acceptable."

"Colonel Fitzwilliam did not put himself to much trouble

about it," returned Mary. "The extent of his plans was, that he asked permission to come and call, and then did not do so."

"Because he had heard in the meantime of your engagement," said Elizabeth. "Dear Miss Crawford, you must, you must, indeed, let me convince you of his sincerity. He cared for you in Bath; you know he did for he told your sister so." She looked anxiously at Mary, and received a glance of reluctant assent. "No one more deeply lamented the misfortune which separated you after that; and can you wonder that, when you meet again, the remembrance of what happened made him diffident as to his reception, and uncertain of the place he still might hold in your esteem? But he was as devoted to you as ever, and only longed for a chance of showing it. Oh!"—Elizabeth broke off impatiently, but smiling at herself—"I ought not to be saying this to you in these cold, bald words; I cannot plead his case as eloquently as he could; but at least I can implore you to believe in him. Grant that he acted with over-caution, and did not consult his own best interests: he was afraid of precipitating matters by speaking before he could divine what you felt for him. But that his affection was there, I know positively. A man who had cared less would have stayed, would have pretended indifference, and would have congratulated you on your engagement."

"I wish he had," said Miss Crawford, trying to smile, though the tears filled her eyes, "for then I could have told him of his mistake, and asked him why he was in such a hurry to credit it."

"I do not think he was in a hurry," said Elizabeth sadly; "he would not have believed it if he could have helped it, and if you could see him now, you would know what real grief can do for a man of his nature."

"I am sorry," said Miss Crawford, without much warmth, but a moment later she exclaimed: "Yes, it is bad for a man to bring unhappiness on himself through an error, but I suppose it never occurred to him that by going off in that way, without a word, he might be leaving the same thing for someone else. If I were a man, I would never accept my dismissal except from the woman herself; I would at least have the courage to put my fate to the touch."

Elizabeth weighed these words for an instant, and then turning to look in her companion's face, she said: "I want to ask you one thing, but you need not reply if you do not wish. If my cousin had put his fate to the touch while he was in London, would he have had the answer, or any hope of answer, that he desired?"

Mary coloured deeply, but did not turn her eyes away from Mrs. Darcy's. "It is hardly fair, is it, to ask me a question which he has never asked?" she said, with a slight smile. "But it is useless to try to keep secrets from such a friend as yourself, and I suppose you are answered by now."

They stopped with one accord beside a gate, and stood looking over the long furrows of brown earth in the field, but neither seeing them. Miss Crawford's blush remained, and her lips were set rather defiantly, when Elizabeth turned to her and said with great earnestness: "I said that Colonel Fitzwilliam was not coming back before Christmas, and that is quite true, but may I not tell him to come? I will do nothing without your permission; will not even say that you are here; but will you not give him leave to come, and speak for himself, and try to atone for the mistakes and unhappiness of the past? Indeed, though at this moment he has no hope of it, I know that he would ask no greater privilege."

Mary laid her hand on her friend's, and replied affection-ately, but without any hesitation: "No, no, Mrs. Darcy, do not tell him to come. I thought you would suggest something of the kind, but I would much rather not. It would be no kindness to either of us." Then, as Elizabeth still looked questioningly at her, she continued: "I really mean it. Since we are to be quite frank, I did feel very much what I thought to be Colonel Fitzwilliam's defection, and Frances would tell you that that accounts for my stupid ill-health this autumn; I do not quite agree, but none the less, I am confident that we had better not meet again. It is too late, when people are getting on towards respectable middle life as we are. You smile, but do you know I am near my thirtieth birthday? No, we have both recovered from the wounds of last summer, and we should be wiser not to risk reopening them."

"It would be a healing, I think, not a reopening," said Elizabeth.

"Do you think so? But one cannot tell. Colonel Fitzwilliam must have been in love with some ideal person, a Mary Crawford who never really existed, or he would not have been frightened away so easily from the actual one. If he were to see me again, there might be a fresh disappointment in store. Does he still think I am to marry Sir Walter Elliot?"

"I do not know. Darcy and I have never told him otherwise."

"Ah, well, do not let him be undeceived; and some day, per-haps in London, we shall be sent in to dinner together, and imagine his surprise and dismay at finding it is plain Miss Crawford, and not Lady Elliot! It will give us something to talk about through the first three courses. Dear Mrs. Darcy, you look disapprovingly at me, but seriously, I do think, if we ever are to meet, it will be best to do so by accident. I could hardly bear a premeditated encounter as it would be here, each of us knowing that we were expected to play a certain part."

"It is better he should not come, of course, if you are not sure whether you could accept him," said Elizabeth.

"That it is; I suppose I am not sure; because, you see, circumstances have combined to make Colonel Fitzwilliam appear in light of a half-hearted admirer, and though I know from you he is not, yet I have no experience of his own powers of recommending himself. Do not be angry with me, or let this spoil our friendship; I am so glad now that you know all, and you will let me come and stay with you sometimes when he is away, will you not?"

A time-honoured custom has ordained that only one reply shall be made to an appeal of this kind, and Elizabeth duly assured her friend that it should make no difference; feeling, indeed, that as she had asked for an explanation, she could not resent Miss Crawford's frankness, nor could she like the high-spirited girl less for the glimpse she had given of her heart. There was no denying, however, that the end of their conversation had been a good deal of a disappointment. Mary's confession had been so much more than Elizabeth had ventured to hope for, that it was melancholy to realize that it came, as she herself had said, too late; too late for Colonel Fitzwilliam to be in any way the gainer by it. Many times during the day and the succeeding ones did Elizabeth turn over in her mind a series of plans to bring her two friends together again, in some way entirely unforeseen by both; but all had to be discarded, for Miss Crawford had been so decisive, and it was not certain that the Colonel would make any better use of his chances, unless he could be warned of how he had failed previously. The more Elizabeth pondered over the events of last year, in the new light now thrown upon them, the better she was able to understand Mary's point of view, and to comprehend that it was not solely Lady Catherine's insulting behaviour, or her cousin's want of self-confidence, or Mary's own pride and recklessness, but something of all three, that had ruined their prospects of happiness; and she mourned sincerely over the wreck and the impossibility of restoring it, while they were so obstinately resolved to remain strangers to one another. If only Fitzwilliam had known, when in London, that the prize lay so near his hand! that he had gained Mary's love, almost without trying to do so, merely by watching and waiting, and not submitting to the rebuff she had given him at the end of their stay in Bath! But the opportunity had passed, and he had lost more ground now than he might ever recover, for Elizabeth knew well that Mary's resentment was the real obstacle: *his* feelings were unaltered, but hers she had striven, perhaps with some measure of success, to harden into indifference.

Chapter 23

COLONEL FITZWILLIAM WROTE THAT he intended stay-
ing in Leicestershire for Christmas, and going to London for the
first fortnight of January. Elizabeth did not fail to make this information public, and accordingly, when the question of their two
guests' departure was again broached, Miss Crawford was more
easily persuaded to prolong their visit, and her sister approved of
whatever she chose to do. Elizabeth had not thought it right to
speak to Mrs. Grant about her conversation with Mary, but that
lady had opened the subject herself, by expressing to Mrs. Darcy
her great relief that the affair with Colonel Fitzwilliam had gone
off, and attributing Mary's illness to fretting and disappointment.
Mrs. Grant blamed no one except the Elliots, who, she asserted,
had persistently stood between Mary and her other friends, but
she lamented the whole series of mishaps, for it was evident that
no one else had ever gained such a large measure of her sister's
regard, and now her whole endeavour seemed to be to banish him
from her thoughts.

Mary meantime was recovering health and vigour, and the colour came back to her cheeks, and the light to her eyes in a manner very gratifying to her friends to observe. Had Elizabeth not been so much occupied with plans for her visitors, and preparations for Christmas, she could not have failed to note the contrast between Miss Crawford and Georgiana, for the younger girl grew paler and graver, and seemed more and more spiritless in comparison with Mary's gay moods. Georgiana made great efforts to throw herself into what was going on, and was per-suaded that she smiled and talked as much as ever, while she took part in the hospitalities of Pemberley, but in reality the weight on her mind, her preoccupation with the thought of two people who were suffering through her fault, prevented her from always knowing when she was silent. She constantly pictured Kitty, grieving in solitude over the downfall of the hopes of many months, and wearied her mind with fruitless speculations as to how they could have acted differently, in order to have averted the blow. No one could possibly have foreseen that Mr. Price would care for her and not for Kitty! else the latter's friends might have persuaded her to try and like Mr. Morland, whose courtship had been under equally auspicious circumstances. But then, Georgiana reflected with a thrill, who could think of a Morland when they had been better attracted by a Price! She was glad to be able to pay that tribute to her friend's good taste. And if the affair had not been checked in its early stages, it must have gone on in the way it had until the gentleman spoke, and poor Kitty's fate was sealed.

Tears rose to Georgiana's eyes as she recalled her interview with William Price, and the feeling of anger and despair that had come over her at the prospect of everything being so utterly wrong, and then thrown into such confusion. And since then, the indignation on Kitty's behalf, which had overwhelmed her at first, had softened into pity, and shared a place in her heart equally with regret for Mr. Price, for *his* disappointment, as sudden and as complete as Kitty's, and far more bewildering. He would never, perhaps, fully understand how it came about, nor fully allow for its causes, and for the obstacle which had necessitated his being refused. Chilled and repulsed, he would think her insensible, unkind; he would believe that she did not care for him, and did not want to care. What a wonder if his feelings towards her underwent a change! What more probable than that now, when she had learnt that his esteem was the only thing necessary to her happiness, and earnestly wished he could know that she no longer blamed him, he had resolved to think of her no more?

* * * * * * * * * * *

Owning to a slight indisposition of Mrs. Bingley's, the Desborough party had not come over to Pemberley at Christmas, as was their custom, but they arrived on New Year's Eve to spend two or three days. Georgiana looked forward rather nervously to the meeting with Kitty, for the latter had only written occasional notes to her and Elizabeth, in a constrained style, since the departure in November, and Georgiana dreaded equally any reopening of the subject in words, or any coldness between them, combined with the unforgiving reproaches which Kitty knew so well how to convey by look and manner. It seemed, however, when they arrived, that Kitty was not going to adopt either attitude precisely. She looked very thin, and Jane told her sister that she had not been eating or sleeping well, but she chatted as vigorously as ever, and was in restless, excitable spirits.

She could not sit long to anything, and when not flying about the house, or playing with the children, was constantly running down to the Rectory, on the plea of wanting to see Mrs. Ferrars's new baby, who had made its appearance in the world a few days before. Georgiana found that any private talk was out of the question, and did not seem to be desired by Kitty, whose principal topic of conversation was, after the loveliness of the baby, the charms of her newest friend, a certain Mrs. Henry Tilney, sister of Mr. Morland, who had been staying with him for some weeks. This young lady was about Kitty's age, but had been married for several years, and had brought one of her children with her, a little girl about the age of the Bingleys' second boy, and there had evidently been a great deal of intercourse between the Park and the Rectory. Mrs. Tilney was reported by Jane and her husband to be a very pleasing, gentle and amiable woman, and Kitty's enthusiasm over her knew no bounds.

Elizabeth had met Mrs. Tilney, and was pleased to hear of her again, as she would have been to hear of anyone connected with Mr. Morland and Lady Portinscale; and the subject offered material for frequent conversation among the whole party, as Mrs. Grant and Miss Crawford had an interest in it also, through their acquaintanceship with the young clergyman in Bath.

Georgiana could not help glancing at Kitty occasionally when his name was mentioned, and noticed that the slight embarrassment Kitty displayed at first soon wore off. There had evidently been a good many visitors at Desborough during the past month; Bingley had had another shooting party, and there had been evenings of music, and even a small dance at the house of a neighbour. Kitty spoke of these things as if the retrospect were one of great enjoyment, and Morland was so often referred to, as to lead to the supposition that their constant meetings were fraught with no discomfort on either side.

"But you have not told all our gaieties, Kitty," said Bingley, as they stood round the drawing-room fire one morning after breakfast. "Did you know, Elizabeth, that we went to see the amateur theatricals at Ashbourne? The officers got them up among themselves and invited everybody; it was quite a spectacle, and they gave us supper afterwards in that fine great messroom. I never saw anything better done."

"Yes, we had an invitation; I was not to go to it, but it is too far," said Elizabeth. "I heard the performance was very good."

"Of course, you would have been asked; you ought to have gone, for it was well worth seeing; our little charades were quite put in the shade. Kitty can give you all information about it, for she had a splendid young officer sitting by her to tell her who everybody was."

"It was only Mr. Cathcart; he knew Colonel Forster once, and wanted to hear about Lydia," said Kitty, colouring and becoming deeply interested in the pattern of her lace handkerchief.

"And the one who escorted you to supper was not Mr. Cathcart; he was somebody even more gorgeous and equally delightful—a field-marshal, at least, I should think," continued her brother-in-law in bantering tones; "altogether, Kitty did very well that evening. I expected Jane would have had half the regiment coming up to her before it was over, to ask leave to call."

"Nonsense, Bingley," said Kitty, in some confusion, getting up and going to help Mary Crawford, who was sorting her music; "you are making too much of it; there was no reason why Mr. Macdonald should not call, if he wished to."

Bingley laughed, and proceeded to give so lively a description of the theatricals, that Kitty could not help coming back and joining in, with sparkling eyes and every sign of pleasure in the reminiscence. Georgiana watched her in some surprise, for nothing could be more unlike the broken-hearted Kitty who had gone away six weeks before. Bingley forbore to tease her any longer; but finding himself alone with Elizabeth and Georgiana later in the morning, he began at once: "I think neither of you need be under any more apprehension about Kitty. She was certainly very low-spirited when she came to us, and I was afraid that young sailor's departure had had a devastating effect; but she has brightened up wonderfully and managed to enjoy herself again, just as a girl ought."

"I am very glad," said Elizabeth. "I knew she had taken it a good deal to heart at the time, but fresh interests will put fresh life into her."

"Exactly; there is no use in a pretty young woman like that moping about a fellow who does not care for her; the best way to forget him is to amuse herself with others, and I feel myself partly responsible for encouraging that young Price, so Jane and I have done our best to distract her thoughts. Those officers are as pleasant a set of fellows as ever stepped, and Kitty by no means disliked them; but unfortunately the regiment is just moving on, and the next one does not come till March. I have asked Bertram down again at the end of the month for some hunting; Kitty and he seemed to get on well, and we thought him a capital fellow, did you not?"

"Very agreeable indeed," said Elizabeth, in a tone of calmer praise, adding: "and I have no doubt he is an excellent young man, though in spite of all, I should be inclined to adhere to Kitty's first preference to his cousin; Mr. Price's manners had more to recommend them, I thought."

Georgiana's heart bounded, and she turned away her face to hide her rising colour, as Bingley responded: "Ah, yes, Elizabeth, you are right. In spite of all, as you say, Price is the man we should have liked for her. There is a sterling character, I do believe. It would have done most of us good to have to begin early, and make our own fortunes, as that youth has done, and we should not be all so frank and modest at his age, I'll wager. Yes, I should be only too glad to get him back, but it is out of the question. I had a letter from him last week from Copenhagen; they expect to be cruising about in the North Sea for another month or two; then he will probably have to go to some distant station."

Georgiana had turned now to look at Bingley, her complexion changing from red to pale. She was grateful to Elizabeth for keeping the conversation going by some slight remark, for she could not have spoken.

"Yes," continued Bingley, "*we* think it a great drawback to a sailor's life, that he should have to be abroad so much, and away from his friends; but cruises now are not as long as they used to be, and when a man has as much spirit as Price, he is glad to be on the move, to show authorities the stuff he is made of. Price is commander on his present ship, you know; the first since his promotion."

The entrance of Jane caused Bingley to break off, and Georgiana waited a little, in the hope that he had more to say on a subject of such an absorbing nature; but, unfortunately, it was Mr. Bertram, not Mr. Price, to whom he reverted, calling upon Jane to confirm his expectations of the former's visit, and Georgiana slipped out of the room as Jane began to tell Elizabeth how she had succeeded in obtaining Mr. Bennet's permission to keep Kitty until Easter. Georgiana needed to think over what she had heard, even though the pain to herself became more intense, in proportion as she gloried in the approval expressed of William Price by her friends. To hear him praised, to know him appreciated, was sweet to her; but how bitter by contrast was the knowledge that she had sacrificed his happiness and her own, in vain, that Kitty had so soon forgotten him as to be able to flirt with officers, and was ready to accept as a compensation for the loss of William Price, the attentions of any young men Bingley could collect around her! Georgiana could scarcely believe that the devotion of half a year could have died a natural death in so short a time. She might almost have thought that Kitty was feigning indifference, in order to conceal her chagrin, but from experience of Kitty's nature she knew that her friend was incapable of acting a sustained part, and that if she appeared to enjoy balls and flirtations, it was because they had for her as much zest as ever.

Georgiana might wonder, but she had no inclination to blame Kitty for any sign of inconsistency. It was undoubtedly much better for Kitty to get over her infatuation for William Price, if she could succeed in doing so; but the consequences to Georgiana were far more grave, and she suffered the more for realizing that Kitty had not, after all, so greatly valued the thing she had sought after, the object which had become more and more precious to Georgiana than anything in the world. Her effort to defend Kitty to William, her refusal to accept his devotion for herself—all had been wasted, fruitless, unnecessary! Not that she would for one moment desire to withdraw the act of loyalty towards her friend; but with heart-breaking regrets did she review the whole sequence of events, which had so cruelly and inevitably separated William Price and herself. Was it, she thought, a just punishment for one who had made two such grievous mistakes previously that she should now be accorded, too late, a glimpse of a happiness that would have transformed her whole life? Bingley's casual mention of his movements had reminded her forcibly how improbable it was that they should ever meet again.

She had borne up bravely until then, but that night, when alone, she could not help giving way to an access of grief severer than any she had known before, and only a dread of arousing comment enabled her to assume an air of tolerable serenity when she appeared in the morning.

It happened that Jane, while admiring a new dress which Georgiana was wearing, was struck with the want of animation in the young girl's face, and her usual kindness prompted her to inquire solicitously how she did. Georgiana would confess to no ailment but a slight cold, which she had had for a week and been unable to throw off, and tried to make light of it when Jane appealed to Elizabeth to suggest what might be done to re-establish her health. Elizabeth felt a real concern as she looked closely at her young sister, and reproached herself for having neglected to give her proper care.

"No, no, indeed, Elizabeth, it is not so," protested Georgiana. "I am perfectly well. A cold always makes one feel stupid, and this mild damp weather is disagreeable, coming after those early frosts."

"Come and stay with us for two or three weeks," said Jane affectionately. "The change will do you good, and Bingley and I shall be happy to have you; your last visit was an unreasonably short one."

Georgiana gratefully but decidedly declined the offer, pleading various excuses, but privately feeling that she would rather not be with Kitty again just yet, amid scenes connected insepa-rably with William Price's presence.

"I think she ought to have a change, nevertheless," said Elizabeth, "and it is too long to wait till we go to Bath in April. Would you not really care to go to Desborough for a little, Georgiana, and see if it does you good?"

Georgiana faltered out something of reluctance, and Jane, smiling kindly at her, went away to leave the sisters to discuss it together. Elizabeth drew the young girl to her, and tenderly asked if there was anything the matter, in which her help or advice would be acceptable, and Georgiana, after a few moments' silent struggle, recovered the self-command which the proffer of sympathy had threatened to disturb, and replied that she was sure she would be quite well directly, and would rather not go away from home until she went with the others.

"You are sure there is nowhere you would like to go, if not Desborough?" asked Elizabeth, pondering. "The Hursts would be delighted, I know, but you have been there lately; what a pity Mrs. Annesley has gone abroad."

Georgiana only shook her head at these suggestions, and suddenly Elizabeth exclaimed: "I have thought of something— Mrs. Wentworth's invitation! You remember that she asked you, in the letter I had from her with reference to her father and Miss

Crawford. You thought at the time that you might like to accept it some day."

The idea seemed to interest Georgiana more than the others. She raised her head from Elizabeth's shoulder, and said: "I remember; it was a very kind message. The Wentworths live at Winchester, do they not?"

"Yes, and Anne Wentworth is so good-hearted, so thoroughly sincere, that I know she would like to be taken at her word, and to have you propose yourself as a visitor. What do you think of it, Georgiana? I think you might be very happy with such kind people, and the change of air and surroundings would be complete. It seems a very long way off, I know, but you could be taken to London in the carriage, with the two servants, as last year; and Captain Wentworth would doubtless be able to meet you there, for he makes that journey constantly. Your brother and I would come and fetch you any time, after Miss Crawford goes, as soon as you wish to come away."

Elizabeth rose and went to her writing-table, to find Mrs. Wentworth's letter, and to show Georgiana the message once more. The cordiality which it expressed could not be doubted, and Georgiana began to feel that if she could ever find pleasure in anything again, it might be in the quiet companionship of such friends as Captain and Mrs. Wentworth. She had been greatly attracted by Mrs. Wentworth, and she had sufficient good sense to know that it would be advantageous to her to have an entire change of environment, to be away for a time from Pemberley, and its associations. It would revive her courage, and help her to appreciate the many blessings that life still held for her. Georgiana was not too young not to believe that her troubles were past mending, but she was also too reasonable deliberately to nurse her unhappiness. She accordingly allowed Elizabeth to write and propose the scheme, and had grown so much accustomed to the idea as to be pleased when an answer arrived in the form of a joint letter from the Wentworths, warmly welcoming her to join their house, with every intimation of the delight it would afford them, and suggesting the last week in January as the date for her journey to London, where her host would meet her, and convey her straight to Winchester, a distance of sixty-five miles.

The arrangement was generally approved. Darcy and Elizabeth regretted losing their sister, even for a time; but they hoped it would be beneficial to her, and they could perceive that it fell in with her inclinations. There was no lack of escort, for Mrs. Grant and Miss Crawford, who were now talking of going in earnest, were anxious to alter their plans and travel to Bath round by London, for the pleasure of her company; but Darcy would not permit this, as he had resolved on taking his sister himself, and Elizabeth induced them to remain with her until his return.

Chapter 24

JANUARY WAS PASSING. THE weather was remarkably mild and open for the time of year, and the hunting men were rejoicing in their opportunities. The ladies were able to take their daily walks and drives, in which Mrs. Ferrars's sister, Mrs. Brandon, a very lovely and amiable woman, who had come to watch over her sister's convalescence, was often invited to join them. Mrs. Jennings had returned to London earlier in the month, sorely disappointed, after such a promising beginning, at not having seen the successful termination of even one love-affair during her stay. None of the family at Pemberley had ever understood what part she played in the catastrophe of November, except that she had shared in the general error made by Kitty's friends, nor were they aware of the destiny she had marked out for Georgiana; but Elinor, when she realized that something had gone seriously wrong in consequence of the ball, had no difficulty in persuading the really good-natured old lady to confine her lamentations, conjectures, and comments to the ears of the Rectory inhabitants only. This end was the more easily attained since, after Kitty's departure, there was no one to keep her supplied with information. When, however, that young lady returned in apparently good spirits, Mrs. Jennings was immeasurably delighted, and quite entered into her willingness to talk of Cathcart and Macdonald, and, indeed, anyone and anything but William Price, and Mrs. Jennings had only to hear that Mr. Bertram was coming to stay at Desborough again, and not at Pemberley, to be ready to console Kitty with a number of entirely new and revised prognostications as to the object of his visit.

The party at Pemberley were sitting together one evening after dinner. It was about eight o'clock, and they had all settled to their customary occupations; Darcy and his wife were reading, Mrs. Grant working and Georgiana was at the instrument, playing short snatches of music while Mary Crawford sat close beside her, and asked for one and another of her favourite pieces. Peace and tranquility reigned, and seemed as little likely to be interrupted as on many previous evenings that had been similarly spent. The sudden sound of carriage wheels, therefore, and the rapid trot of horses, startled everyone, and alarmed one at least, for Elizabeth's first apprehension was that Colonel Fitzwilliam had returned unexpectedly. Georgiana ceased playing, and all listened anxiously, but the suspense lasted for the shortest possible time required by a visitor to get into the house, and on the door being flung open, Darcy had scarcely risen from his chair, before Tom Bertram followed his name into the room with quick steps.

Tom Bertram had acted on many stages, but in none of the parts he had ever played had he made so sensational an entrance. The amazement of the inmates of the room on beholding him, the dismay of Mrs. Grant and her sister, his own disconcerted surprise at seeing who were Mrs. Darcy's guests, all tended to make the first minute one of extreme embarrassment, and it was only the knowledge of his urgency of his errand that enabled him to recover himself sooner than any of the others. Advancing to Mr. and Mrs. Darcy, he greeted them both, bowed to Mrs. Grant, and to the corner of the room where Mary was shrinking out of sight behind Georgiana, and at once began speaking very quickly to the master of the house.

"Mr. Darcy, I fear I have startled, I hope not frightened, you all by intruding at this late hour; but when you know how pressing is the need, you will dispense with apologies. I grieve very much to say to say I am the bearer of bad news, but believing that you ought to know, I constituted myself the messenger. Your cousin, Colonel Fitzwilliam, has met with an accident whilst out hunting to-day. I regret exceedingly to tell you, but his state is considered serious, and his friends thought it would be advisable for you to come."

"Fitzwilliam? Fitzwilliam hurt! Good God, what is this?" exclaimed Darcy, completely roused out of his usual calm. "How did it happen? Tell us all about it. I will go to him instantly" (ringing the bell). "In God's name, Bertram, say he is still living? Where is he? How long will it take to get to him?"

Elizabeth, though dreadfully shocked and distressed, had the wisdom to send another servant for refreshments for Mr. Bertram, while Darcy ordered his own things to be packed and his travelling carriage be brought round, and in the slight bustle caused by these arrangements, Mrs. Grant and Georgiana were able, almost unobserved, to attend to Mary, who had not actually fainted, but had sunk down on a low couch, scarcely

knowing what she did. Her sister and Georgiana supported her
in between them, placed her in a more easy position, rubbed her
hands and shielded her from the light; and Mary, with a very
great effort, collected herself sufficiently to listen to the details
which Mr. Bertram was hurriedly giving in answer to Mr. and
Mrs. Darcy's inquiries. It appeared that Colonel Fitzwilliam had
only just returned from London, and this was his first day out for
some time. The fox had got well away, and the hunt were in the
midst of a fine run, when the Colonel's horse came down with
him at a blind fence. Bertram paused here to give more particulars than his impatient hearers desired, about the height and
width of the fence, and the exact manner in which the horse had
approached it, for it seemed that he himself had been riding near
at the time, and had witnessed the accident. The Colonel was
pinned under the animal, and was taken out unconscious, with
a broken leg, and, it was feared, some grave injury to the spine.
Fortunately, the house of the friend with whom he was staying
was not far off, and he was borne thither, and the services of the
apothecary were promptly obtained; but the only opinion he
could form was very grave, and pending the arrival of a more
experienced surgeon, who had been sent for from Leicester, no
one could tell what an hour might bring forth.

The ladies were sick with horror: Mrs. Grant was weeping
silently, and Georgiana, as she held Mary's cold hand, felt that this
was indeed the last and crowning sorrow, for poor Cousin Robert
to die without knowing the happiness that ought to have been his.

"The pulse is so very weak; I think they fear a collapse of the
whole system, even if he does recover consciousness," said
Bertram, in too low a tone to be heard by those at the other end

of the room. "They were trying stimulants of various kinds when I came away."

Elizabeth's face was hidden. Darcy was too much overwhelmed to speak for some moments, till with a sudden start of recollection he exclaimed: "And you, Bertram? how came you to be there? and how come you are here now?"

Bertram, with a return to something of his nonchalant manner, explained that he, too, had been staying in the same neighbourhood, with a friend, who was, in fact, the master of that pack of hounds, and with whom he often spent a few days in the hunting season, as it was little over twenty miles from his own house, Mansfield Park. "I had been talking to Colonel Fitzwilliam during the morning," he continued, "and helped to carry him back to Ashley's place, and when Ashley said his relations ought to know, I decided at once to come with the news. I only delayed to change my clothes and have the chaise got ready, for I knew time was an object, and I could get over the ground quicker than anyone else they could send."

"I am sure we are deeply indebted to you, Bertram," said Darcy, grasping him warmly by the hand, while Elizabeth joined him in expressing the sincerest gratitude. "You could not have done us a greater service, and it is one we shall never forget. It was an impulse of true goodness and unselfishness that prompted you to ride straight to us, disregarding your own fatigue and inconvenience; few men would have done as much."

Bertram disclaimed, and as Georgiana came forward to add her thanks to those of the others, he bowed to her with gallantry, assuring her that fatigue was nothing, if he could be of use to friends whom he so greatly esteemed, and he only wished that he could have brought news to relieve anxiety, instead of creating it.

By this time word was brought that the more substantial meal which had been ordered for Mr. Bertram was ready in the dining-room, and Darcy escorted him thither, to attend to his wants and to obtain the particulars as to his journey from Leicestershire. The distance was forty-five miles, and Darcy proposed to start within half an hour, and reach his destination some time during the night, but he pressed his visitor to stay at least until the next day, and if he would, to rest himself and his horses.

Their peaceful evening had been turned into confusion and wretchedness. The quiet circle in the drawing-room was broken up, and Mrs. Grant, fearing greatly for her sister, was thankful to lead her to her own room, there to recover as best she might from the frightful shock of Tom Bertram's news. Darcy soon went upstairs to prepare for his journey, and his wife busied herself with helping him, and with placing in his luggage any article she could think of that might conduce to the sick man's comfort, while a maze of thoughts occupied her mind, chilling fear, apprehension, and dread of what might be happening to the loved friend at such a distance, and anxiety on account of Miss Crawford, whose trembling and distressed condition had not escaped her.

A few minutes later Georgiana came to her door, showing traces of tears, but quite calm, and begging to be made useful. Elizabeth was just then giving some directions to the maid, so Georgiana waited until they were done, and then, coming close to her sister, she said: "Elizabeth, do you think we could do anything for Miss Crawford? I went to wish her good-night, and she tried to smile and say something sympathizing, but could hardly utter the words. I am sure she is terribly concerned about all this. She almost looks like a different person, so pale and stricken. Do you think she can possibly be caring for Cousin Robert all the time, and not know it till now? Oh, dear Elizabeth, is it not dreadful to think it may be too late?"

Elizabeth gazed at her sister, listening intently, and pondering all Georgiana said. True, indeed, that it would be a dreadful thing to contemplate, if Mary really loved Fitzwilliam, and the knowledge came too late to do good to either. And even if Mary knew her own heart at last, was it not too late, when pride sealed her lips, and Fitzwilliam was lying near to death, forty miles away, perhaps never more able to see her or hear her? Elizabeth experienced a momentary feeling of despair; the powers ranged against her seemed almost too strong to be attacked; but rallying her forces, and putting in the front of her mind the one hopeful thought that Fitzwilliam might live till Darcy reached him, or longer, she said to Georgiana: "I think I shall try; I will ask her to send him a message, if it is as we think; it will be better than nothing, even if he is only just able to understand it."

"Oh, yes, yes," exclaimed Georgiana, clasping her hands in intense eagerness, "do ask her, dear Elizabeth; she will surely tell you, and my brother will tell him. Whatever happens, she will be glad to think she has done it. Do ask her; do not lose a minute; there is so little time."

Voices were heard in the corridor; Darcy was speaking to the servants, who were carrying out his luggage. Elizabeth hesitated no longer, pausing only to say: "Dear Georgiana, would you mind going to sit with Mr. Bertram? I am afraid it may be tiresome for you to entertain a stranger just now, but he is alone, and it would be only a kind attention, after what he has done for us," and to receive Georgiana's assent, before going swiftly to Miss Crawford's room.

She found that Georgiana's description had been all too accurate. Miss Crawford had not wept, but her expression of hopeless misery sent a pang through Elizabeth's heart. She had sent her sister away, and had been sitting on her bed, too stunned for action, almost for thought, and she made no resistance when Elizabeth placed her on the couch, sat beside her, and taking both her hands, began to plead with her, quickly and simply, without premeditation.

"Dear Miss Crawford, I have come to ask you to do something for my poor cousin, something which only you can do. You heard what Mr. Bertram said, of his dangerous state, and it distressed you as much as us, I know. I would not for a moment seek to pry into your inmost feelings, but we are come to matters of life and death, and it is on *his* account that I do venture to ask you, if you feel that you could listen to him if he were here, then will you send him a word, a message, something to show that you are thinking of him?"

Mary replied after a minute or two, in a stifled voice: "I would send him such a message, but do you think he would care to have it?"

"I do, indeed, most truly. I understand your hesitation; you think you cannot speak of love to him, when he has not spoken to you; but I would stake my life on his devotion and faithfulness. The words you send him will bring comfort and peace of mind, whatever the issue."

Mary shuddered, and withdrew her trembling hands. "Mr. Bertram seems to think he will die."

"We cannot tell; he is a strong man and had not had the best advice when Mr. Bertram was there. We can only hope, and my husband is starting almost immediately, and will carry any message you feel able to send, trusting that he will be in time to deliver it."

"Oh, yes, yes," exclaimed Mary, raising and walking restlessly about the room; "he is so good and generous that if he still cares, he would overlook all, he would pardon the errors and foolishness that have led to this misunderstanding—but the past, Mrs. Darcy, does he know and forgive that? I wish I could tell. Seeing Mr. Bertram brings it all back again—my brother, his sister—the divorce—what Lady Catherine heard, the world believes, you know—and just when one repents it all most, it comes back just like a spectre to haunt one."

Elizabeth replied very earnestly: "At such a time as this, it would be cruel to mislead you, and I only say what I sincerely believe, that Colonel Fitzwilliam knows everything to which you refer, and it makes not the smallest difference to him. It would not, you should be aware, to any man whose love was worthy of the name. That should not weigh with you for a moment. The only thing that signifies in the least is whether you can return that love: the only barrier between you is being unable to return it. I would not urge you against your will, or take advantage of a moment of strong emotion; you alone know whether it would make you happier to send a word of hope to him."

"Happier? Ah, I do not know," said Mary sorrowfully. "I do not seem able to think of happiness. And yet, I should be glad for him to know, since you think he still cares to know, and it is all I can now do for him. You need not be afraid of my not trusting my feelings, Mrs. Darcy. This has shown me all too late what they really are, though my folly and obstinacy have blinded me all these months."

"We will not say too late, dear Miss Crawford," said Elizabeth, going up to where Miss Crawford was standing by the mantelshelf, leaning her head on her arm. "We do not know that it is too late, and I believe that it will be an immense comfort to you to take this one step. Explanations can come after. I am not afraid of Colonel Fitzwilliam being unable to clear away all doubts and fears when he is able to speak for himself again."

There was a moment's pause, and Elizabeth continued: "I must not stay now. Mr. Darcy is so impatient to be off, but I will be back to you. Will you tell me what I may say? so little will suffice; or would you rather write it?"

Mary shook her head, still keeping her face hidden, and said in a barely audible voice: "Ask Mr. Darcy, if he will be so kind—explain things to him how you like—but say I send Colonel Fitzwilliam my—my love; that I beg his forgiveness; and that I hope—he will soon—be able to come home—to me."

Elizabeth just caught the last words, waited to assure herself there was no more, and pressing Mary's hand, went quietly out of the room. Though much moved by their interview, the exigencies of the moment demanded that she should quickly recover her composure, and brace herself for the parting with her husband. There would be time—all too much time—for thought when the moment of action was over; there would be hours of suspense to be borne and another sufferer to console. As she came out upon the gallery, she heard persons talking and moving in the hall below, and distinguished her husband's voice saying: "I ought to be with him soon after one o'clock," words which revived her courage, and she descended to find Darcy, Georgiana and Mr. Bertram standing by the hearth, Darcy completely equipped for his journey, and the servants waiting by the front door.

Georgiana, who had been enduring keen anxiety during Elizabeth's absence, and had been exerting herself to keep the gentlemen occupied in eating and talking, so that Elizabeth might not be interrupted too soon by Darcy's haste to depart, gave her a nervous glance, which was tempered by relief when she saw her sister draw Darcy into the library for a few parting words. She could scarcely attend to Mr. Bertram's amiable chatter, or reply to his inquiries for Mr. and Mrs. Bingley, and the other friends he had met on his previous visit, for picturing in her mind what was going on in the library and trying to decide whether Elizabeth had been successful in her mission.

At last the door opened; they reappeared; Darcy was grave, but Georgiana thought his brow had somewhat lightened since he went in, and Elizabeth gave her a bright and reassuring look. There was no time for more, and the carriage was already waiting; the farewells were quickly spoken, and in another moment Darcy had passed out and was gone.

Chapter 25

TO ELIZABETH AND GEORGIANA, the events of the evening seemed like a dreadful dream. Less than an hour ago they had been sitting at their occupations, as tranquil and secure as if disaster did not exist; and now the bolt had fallen, scattering them and bringing to each its message of terror and dismay. Georgiana felt as if it would be the hardest matter in the world to settle to any pretence of the ordinary life again, until news reached them from her brother; she longed to be able to be alone, to think it all over quietly, or to go to Elizabeth, to hear the result of her appeal to Miss Crawford, and instead she was obliged to establish herself in the drawing-room with Mr. Bertram, who showed no sign of wishing to go to bed, but was evidently prepared to sit up talking and drinking tea until midnight.

Georgiana took out her embroidery frame, and prepared to be as agreeable a listener as she could, for she expected Elizabeth, who had gone to Miss Crawford, would come back at any minute, and she really felt more than a common measure of gratitude to Mr. Bertram for the service he had rendered them. This gratitude she again endeavoured to express, when Mr. Bertram began discussing the heavy state of the roads, and the consequent delays to which Darcy might be subjected.

"Pray do not name it, Miss Darcy; as I said, I am only too glad to have been of the slightest assistance. It was a mere chance that I was there, for I should have returned home this week, but the open weather tempted me to stay on for a day or two longer."

"It was indeed fortunate for us, for we should have had no information until to-morrow, if we had had to wait for a letter."

Tom Bertram repeated that he "was very glad," looking into the fire in an absent-minded way that Georgiana scarcely noticed, so absorbed was she in her thoughts. She paid but little more attention when he suddenly rose, stationed himself with his back to the fire, and a little nearer her, and began to speak, apparently on the same topic, for in the first few minutes she could only gather an impression of his sharing in the events following the accident; his telling Mr. Ashley that he was a friend of Colonel Fitzwilliam's, and knew all his relatives, and would be the fittest person to bear the news to them; of Mr. Ashley's heartily agreeing, and of his haste to get home and order his carriage and start. The narrative went on, Georgiana hearing very little after Leicestershire was left behind, for her thoughts had lingered with the poor sufferer there, when, with a start, she became aware that all this was directed at *her*, that Mr. Bertram was trying to explain that he had welcomed the opportunity of hurrying to Pemberley, because it would doing her and her family a service, than which he could have no greater satisfaction, and because it would afford him the privilege of being in her

presence once more. Georgiana, amazed and horrified, endeavoured to stop him; but Tom was not to be prevented from making a speech which he had been rehearsing for at least four
hours on his journey. Some words which fell from her lips, an
appeal to have some respect for this sad occasion, which she
had snatched at as the argument most likely to move him, were
of no avail. That he could address her at such a time he immediately pointed out to be a proof of his ardour, which merited
pardon by reason of its unquenchable nature, for he had
intended, he explained, to wait until he came to Desborough at
the end of the month, and then to have sought an interview,
but his impatience to throw himself at her feet and declare his
passion would brook no delay.

Nothing could have been more distasteful to Georgiana
than such sentiments. To hear the words "admiration" and
"devotion" uttered by Mr. Bertram was not only an outrage upon
the present hour, occupied as it was with the gravest solicitude
for the life of a friend, but also upon the past, when similar words
had been spoken to her by William Price. From no one else
could she bear to hear them; coming from his cousin, she could
almost have called them an insult. Of course, he could not know
that, but it almost seemed like trading upon having placed them
under an obligation to him, that he should presume to speak in
a manner so repugnant to her. Too vexed to choose her words,
when Mr. Bertram stopped for breath, having brought his per-
oration to a close by an offer in correct form of his hand and
heart, she replied coldly that she was much honoured by his proposals, but it was entirely out of her power to accept them.
Bertram had not expected a favourable reply on the instant, but

he had hardly expected so decisive an unfavorable one. He stepped forward with outstretched hands, and an eager, "But, Miss Darcy—" to which her only response was to move haughtily away, and at that moment, to the relief of the lady and the chagrin of the gentleman, Elizabeth entered the room. Only the good manners habitual to both could have helped them to carry off the situation. Tom Bertram, checked in one of his flights of eloquence, descended to earth again with an observation on the weather, and for the next few minutes the temperature and the prospects of rain were debated with great earnestness.

Elizabeth could hardly have failed to guess what kind of interview she had interrupted, and out of compassion to Georgiana she soon recommended she to go to bed. The young girl needed no second bidding; Bertram opened the door to her with great ceremony, which was acknowledged by the slightest of bows, and she gladly sought the shelter of her room, astonished to find that it was not more than half-past nine o'clock. Could it be possible that it was barely two hours since Mr. Bertram's arrival? Would this interminable evening, with its shocks, surprises and disturbances, and yet more surprises, ever draw to a close? Georgiana was so unnerved that she sat down and shed a few tears, but a few only, for with such a real grief ever present, she could not spare much consideration for Mr. Bertram's unwelcome attack. It had been bewildering and annoying, but she was not going to worry about it. He had acted on some silly impulse, and could not possibly be serious. He scarcely knew her—a week's acquaintance, and he talked of heartfelt devotion, and expected her to be ready to listen to such nonsense! She could not conceive what had actuated him, and resented greatly that merely because he was heir to a title and fortune, and had ridden forty-five miles in a great hurry, he should suppose himself to be an acceptable suitor. Some expressions he had used, showing that he was confident of having the approval of her family, roused her special indignation. If only she had not so unluckily been alone with him—if Mrs. Grant had not gone upstairs!

Mrs. Grant! Georgiana started violently, for until that moment she had completely forgotten the association of Mr. Bertram with their two guests. She had supposed Mary's agitation to be caused merely by the news of Colonel Fitzwilliam, and now perceived that the sight of the messenger must have been painful enough apart from all else. What miserable complications had resulted from the fact that it should have been Tom Bertram, of all their acquaintance, who had happened to be hunting with the Belvoir hounds that day! But she could not wish his deed of kindness undone, nor she believed could Miss Crawford, or anyone else, whatever the present inconvenience to themselves, for everything was unimportant compared with what his coming had effected; and now, it would not matter if only he would go away again immediately. Georgiana sat meditating schemes by which she, Mary and Mrs. Grant might all avoid seeing him again, when a knock at her door was followed by the entrance of Elizabeth.

"Yes, Georgiana," Elizabeth said, smiling in response to the girl's shy glance, "Mr. Bertram has made me his confidante. I am sorry if you were upset, my dear; he seems to be afraid it was something of a surprise to you, but he hopes you will take time, and do him the honour of thinking it over."

"Oh, no, no, Elizabeth," Georgiana burst out, her cheeks crimsoning, "I do not want time—I shall not think it over. I do not care for Mr. Bertram in the least, and I never shall. Please tell him to go away and forget all about it."

"Why, my dear, this is very determined. He began in the wrong way, I think, and certainly at the wrong time, but he is very anxious to be allowed to come back, and set about his wooing more gradually. I told him I thought you were quite unaware of his feelings."

"So I was, but I do not want to hear about them," said Georgiana, more quietly, for she was beginning to be a little ashamed of her anger. "I am very much obliged to Mr. Bertram—I know it is very kind of him, and everything, but I cannot possibly marry him."

"Are you sure it is entirely out of the question?" asked Elizabeth. "You were a little startled, perhaps. It is true, we have not seen much of him, but he is very agreeable, and his position is unexceptionable. Above all, he bears a high character as far as we know, and has a good heart, as his action of to-day proves. His cousin, Mr. Price, spoke very warmly of him. Unless you are quite certain, I think your brother would like you to give the matter due consideration, as at any other time than this you might feel more in a mood for such subjects."

"Pray, pray, Elizabeth," exclaimed Georgiana, nervously, "do not ask me. Even if we were not in trouble to-day, as we are, it would make no difference. I am sure Mr. Bertram is excellent and amiable, but I do not—I cannot—I hope Fitzwilliam will not be angry, but I dislike the idea so very much."

"If that is so, my dear Georgiana, you shall not be tormented about it any more. I do not know if I am glad or sorry, it has all happened so quickly, but it is right that you should judge for yourself. Mr. Bertram will be greatly disappointed, still, that cannot be helped. I suppose I am to be deputed to get rid of the poor man."

"If you would be so very kind, Elizabeth"

"Well, I must break it to him early to-morrow morning, since I really think we have had agitations enough for one evening. In any case, I should have had to ask him to cut his visit short, for from what I have heard, I do not think that Miss Crawford would care to see him again."

"No, no, indeed, that must be prevented if possible. And now, do tell me, for I have been longing for an opportunity to ask you, what was the result of your conversation, if I may be allowed to hear it?"

Elizabeth related briefly what had passed between them, and told how her husband could scarcely believe at first that Miss Crawford had yielded, and had voluntarily sent the message that he was asked to deliver, but on being convinced of her sincerity, he willingly promised that if his cousin's state permitted it, he would convey to him the words of hope and comfort, and would endeavour to make anything clear that Fitzwilliam might not be able to understand.

"Of course, we had so few minutes together," said Elizabeth, "and your brother had not thought of it all for so long. He quite believed that all was over between them; he did not even know that she had owned to caring for him once. It was difficult for him to realize that she always had cared, though he did not need me to tell him what happiness it would be to poor Robert to know it, if he reached him in time."

"I am so glad, so very glad," cried Georgiana, the tears of joy standing in her eyes. "It is as it should be. My brother will see it all plainly, when he thinks it over. Poor Miss Crawford! How she must have suffered! She did not realize it herself, I suppose, and that was why she would not meet him again. I do not quite understand how it all happened, but it does not signify now. If he lives, nothing need keep them apart, and at all events, he will have her message. Nothing will make me believe that it is too late for that."

This naturally led them back to a discussion of the accident, the condition of the victim, and all the chances and possibilities of the case, which could not be gone over often enough. Elizabeth at last prepared to leave the room, as the hour was late, but struck by a passing recollection, she looked back from the door to say, with a smile: "I must tell you, Georgiana, that *your* attitude has surprised me more than Mr. Bertram's. Lately, when you have been looking so pale and unlike yourself, it has occurred to me that there must be some person of whom you were thinking a great deal, with a disturbing effect; and I confess that when I interrupted you and Mr. Bertram this evening, it crossed my mind that he might be that person."

"Elizabeth! how could you think such a thing?" exclaimed Georgiana, turning away, blushing and confused, and thankful that Elizabeth had not directly asked her whether any such person was in existence.

Chapter 26

THE DISCONSOLATE MR. BERTRAM duly took his leave the following morning, having seen no one besides Mrs. Darcy and Mrs. Grant, but a brief interview with the former had convinced him of the futility of any second application to her sister-in-law. He was quite unable to account for his rebuff, and his vexation, combined with the awkwardness that he felt in Mrs. Grant's presence, made their party round the breakfast-table an exceedingly uncomfortable one. Tom Bertram was possessed of a great deal more conscience than Mr. Yates, and could never have used Miss Crawford's name as freely as that gentleman had done; moreover, he was quite conscious that his own family deserved a share of the blame for the *esclandre*, which was usually borne by the two chief culprits; consequently a meeting with any of the Crawfords was quite as unwelcome to him as to them, and he was greatly relieved when, after an exchange of formal civilities, he could betake himself to his carriage and give directions to be conveyed to Desborough Park. To be sure, he was antedating his visit there by ten or twelve days; but he knew that he would be welcomed by the hospitable Bingleys, and they would all be eager to hear the shocking news.

The ladies at Pemberley passed the next few hours in the deepest anxiety and suspense. They tried to talk of other things, but they could think of little but the one subject. Georgiana would have forgotten Mr. Bertram as soon as he was out of the house, for she could not believe his regard for her to be very genuine, or his wound very deep, but that she so dreaded the disapprobation of her brother, when he should come to hear of what had happened. Even Elizabeth would not have been surprised if she had wished to accept him! It was mortifying in a way, though a relief in another, that no one ever supposed it was possible that Mr. Price could have cared for *her*!

Darcy had promised to send off an express letter as early as he could, and a servant had gone to the neighbouring town to meet it, and so avoid delay. Dinner was just over, a meal which they could only make a pretence of eating, when the butler entered, and they saw that he had brought the longed-for dispatch. It was taken to Mrs. Darcy, and she lost not a moment in communicating its contents. The news was not what they had dreaded; indeed, the account was as good as could be expected; Darcy found his cousin's condition to be grave, but not hopeless, for Colonel Fitzwilliam had recovered consciousness before his arrival. He was not permitted to talk, but was able to understand what was said to him. The surgeon had enjoined perfect quiet, and though at present he could scarcely diagnose all the injuries, he believed that the head had escaped. The danger was not over, but the patient's good constitution would help him materially, and the fact that he was enduring severe pain was not considered to be an altogether unfavorable symptom.

The report was, in general, an intense relief, though anxiety still prevailed, and deep compassion and concern must still possess those who listened. Still it was much to be thankful for; on reflection, it seemed to be the best they could have hoped. Georgiana remained with Mrs. Grant, talking it over, while Elizabeth drew Miss Crawford into her boudoir, and said: "I know you will like to hear the rest of my husband's letter. It is meant for you only. He writes: 'As soon as I was allowed to speak to Fitzwilliam, and had ascertained that he was comfortable as he could be made, I told him what you desired me to say respecting Miss Crawford's presence in our house, and the confidence she made to you. It seemed to be a great surprise to him, and I feared would excite him too much; but when I repeated her message, in the exact words which you gave me, I could perceive an immediate effect on him for good. He seemed slow to believe it, and murmured a few syllables about its being too great a happiness; but, after about half an hour, he signed that he wished to speak to me again, and whispered: "Send her my love: tell her that she has given me something to live for." He was not able to say more and soon after fell asleep; you must recollect that there is a great deal of fever, and consequent weakness. Still, he is decidedly not worse, and I am more than half inclined to think that the stimulus his mind has received may help towards his recovery. You know I am not given to conjecture, but he is surprisingly ready to do everything he is told, and anxious to think himself better. If I am right, the responsibility will be Miss Crawford's, and it is one which I think she will not be unwilling to bear. Pray give her my warmest regards, and tell her I hope the time is not far distant when we shall be happily reunited at Pemberley.'"

Such a letter could not all at once be realized, or recovered from. Mary Crawford tried to utter some words of thanks, but tears impeded her speech. Only when the joy burst upon her was she fully conscious of all the misery of the last few months; the light served to make the darkness more visible. Looking back upon the mists of pride, of resentfulness, and misunderstanding, from which she had emerged, it seemed almost incredible for a time that she had reached the clearer air, the sunshine of love and mutual comprehension. She longed to turn to her kind friend, to talk freely with her, over all that had seemed puzzling, and when, after a very few anxious days, better accounts from Leicestershire began to come in, and the gloom lifted, they could venture to let their minds dwell on hopeful possibilities once more. It was satisfactory that the whole situation was already known to the other members of their little party, and that Georgiana, as well as Mrs. Grant, could freely offer the affection and sympathy of a sister.

"Mrs. Darcy," said Mary one day, "I am possessed with a curiosity to know which you think worst of me for—my keeping Colonel Fitzwilliam at arm's length while in London, or my confession of weakness the other day, after the bold assertions I made when you spoke to me during our walk?"

"Indeed, I do not think ill of you for any of those things," returned Elizabeth; "they seem to me to have been most natural; but what do I think was a little bit foolish, was your allowing Sir Walter Elliot to be so attentive that the world concluded you were engaged. Your friends ought to have warned you that it might deter persons you really esteemed from approaching you."

"I was afraid you were going to say something about that!" exclaimed Miss Crawford, holding her hands to her ears in mock dismay. "I quite expect that Colonel Fitzwilliam and I shall spend some hours in violent mutual recrimination when he arrives, and that will be one of our subjects. But, seriously, Mrs. Darcy, although I know now it was unpardonably foolish, I was not conscious then of the comments that were being made. Our friendship with the Elliots had quite another aspect for me, other possibilities connected with my brother—but that will not interest you. I tolerated Sir Walter Elliot, but I never liked him, and I never thought of him as having any serious intentions, until a good-natured friend, Mrs. Palmer, called to congratulate me on my supposed engagement. By the way, she told me that her mother, Mrs. Jennings, had meant to come by with her, but had been prevented; I did not know the worthy Mrs. Jennings then, but since I have met her I have felt thankful she was not present on that occasion; it would have been rather overwhelming."

"She must have been sorry to miss such an opportunity," said Elizabeth, with a smile.

"Yes, poor Mrs. Jennings! But congratulations on a thing that has *not* happened are rather difficult to receive at any time, are they not? From that moment, I do assure you, I got a horrid fright, and determined to change my attitude towards Sir Walter Elliot completely. I must have been partly successful, for it precipitated things to such an extent—at all events, the result was not agreeable. It really was a wretched time! and Colonel Fitzwilliam disappeared and no one knew where or why."

Elizabeth had long realized that her cousin had not been the only sufferer in the past year, and she knew that Miss Crawford's lively manner of talking was often assumed to hide deeper emotions. She truly rejoiced that whatever fears and anxieties might have to be endured before the lovers met again, nothing could shake the foundations of their happiness.

After about ten days, Darcy's letters made it clear that the danger was past, and steady, if slow, progress might be looked for. He was, of course, quite unable to visit, and Georgiana, who had written to Mrs. Wentworth to postpone her visit, consulted Elizabeth as to whether it would be better to abandon it altogether, but Elizabeth thought that it would be unnecessary to do so, and also a pity, for Georgiana's sake, and Darcy, on being applied to give his consent to her journeying to London with the escort of two servants, as had been originally proposed.

The plan, therefore, was to stand. A date was arranged with Captain Wentworth, and on a cold windy evening of the second week in February, Mr. Darcy's carriage with Mr. Darcy's sister, drove up to the hotel in St. James's Street where her host was to meet her. The said carriage was to return through Leicestershire, for it was hoped, that, in the course of the next few days, Colonel Fitzwilliam might be well enough to be brought back in it to Pemberley.

The inclement weather, solitude, and fatigue had sent Georgiana's spirits down to a low ebb as she looked out at the wet streets, and recalled her last visit to London, under such very different circumstances. It was impossible for her not to be thinking of William Price, and the occasion when they had been together there, and wondering if he was in town at that minute. She would have liked to know that he was, even though it was so utterly improbable that they should meet, since neither of them could know what the other's movements were. Such thoughts were bad companions for Georgiana, but the arrival of Captain Wentworth, kind and cheerful as ever, and with the heartiest of welcomes, did much to disperse the gloom, and he proved such an enlivening companion on the following day that when they reached Winchester in time for a late dinner, she did not feel as bad as if she had been travelling for so many hours.

To see Mrs. Wentworth again was a keen pleasure. The letters they had exchanged formed the groundwork of a more intimate friendship, for despite Anne's seniority in years, their natures were thoroughly congenial, and within a few hours Georgiana felt completely at home in the charming little house not far from the Cathedral, which Captain Wentworth had purchased soon after his marriage.

She and her hostess were sitting together, the first day of her visit, exchanging inquiries after their mutual friends, and Georgiana was half hoping to hear some mention of William Price's name, as from what she had seen at Mrs. Hurst's dinner-party, she judged that the Wentworths knew him tolerably well. Yes—Mrs. Wentworth referred to that evening—said that she had seen Mrs. Hurst when last she was in town—Miss Darcy had heard more lately, probably—did she remember the young officer, Captain Price now, who had been present on that occasion?

Georgiana could reply in quite her ordinary manner that she had frequently seen Mr. Price since, and told of his visits to Desborough and Pemberley.

Mrs. Wentworth listened with interest. "I am very glad you have seen something in him, for I am sure you must all have liked him, do you not?" she said. "But, now, what an odd creature he is, never to have mentioned it. To be sure, I have not seen him since, or he would probably have done so, but hearing from a friend that he was in England again, and knowing you had met, I wrote to ask him to come and spend a few days here during your visit. It was a great liberty, I know, dear Miss Darcy, but he is a first favourite with Captain Wentworth and me, and we thought it would have been pleasant for him to have come just now; young people always amuse each other. He has so little time on shore, and up to last week I believed he was still abroad."

Georgiana's heart beat as if it would suffocate her, but she managed to return her friend's look, and say in a steady voice: "Yes, it would have been very nice. Is Captain Price not able to come?"

"No, most unfortunately not. I am very sorry, more so than ever now I know he has been to your part of the world. But he writes to say he fears he ought not to come—all sorts of regrets, and to tell Miss Darcy he is very sorry not to see her again. It is not at all clear why he cannot come, for he only repeats that he is sailing again some time next month, and thinks he had better stay in London, or go down to see his sister, until he goes."

Georgiana sat perfectly silent, gazing into the fire. Even from Mrs. Wentworth's first words she had not expected that William Price was coming, but to feel that the opportunity had been within his reach, and he could not—her heart told her that it was *would* not—avail himself of it, was very hard to bear. He was right not to come, if he believed that the reason for his rejection still existed; Georgiana honoured him for that; but was there anything else? Had he changed his mind? Was he ceasing to care? Georgiana hardly knew, until that bitter moment, how much she had been pinning her hopes upon seeing him again some day; and she thought, with something like bitterness, that it had not been much use to picture him in London, and consequently somewhat nearer to her, when, as things stood, he was immeasurably far away, whether in London or in Derbyshire or on the North Sea.

Her want of response passed unnoticed as Captain Wentworth entered the room, proposing to take the ladies out. His wife observed that she had been telling Miss Darcy of Captain Price's refusal of their invitation, and of their puzzle to account for it.

"Yes, it is a very ungallant thing, is it not, Miss Darcy? particularly when he has been told what an attraction we had for him. I thought he would have come, as he is so often up and down this road, between Southampton and London, but I suppose he has got some other irons in the fire."

Georgiana was glad to be able to leave the room, passing off the subject with a smile and a vague expression of regret, but the tumult of her mind was so painfully great that it was some days before she could find anything like the quiet enjoyment in her surroundings which she had promised herself. All those feelings which she had striven to repress were rising up again with renewed force. She struggled with herself alone, for she could not bear to tell Mrs. Wentworth the whole story; it was different for Miss Crawford with Elizabeth, but in this case the best-intentioned friend could not disentangle the skein.

Not long after her arrival she had the delight of hearing from Elizabeth that the engagement of Fitzwilliam and Mary was an accomplished fact. He was at home again, none the worse for the journey, and gaining strength rapidly under so many efficient nurses, "which of course means *one!*" wrote Elizabeth. Her pleasure was enhanced, a few days later, by receiving a letter from her cousin himself, the first he had been allowed to write, in which he spoke with gratitude of the happiness he had so nearly missed, and thanked Georgiana affectionately for her share in bringing it about. "Indeed," he said, "we owe to the kindness and patience of our friends a debt we can never repay. How cantankerous and troublesome you must have thought me when we were in London! and yet you bore with me, then and always, with unfailing sweetness. I can wish you nothing better, my dearest cousin, than to be as happy as I am, though I do not know who is fit, by fortune and merit, to deserve you."

Mary wrote in much the same strain, and Georgiana could read their letters without a pang of selfish envy, with no feeling but that of rejoicing on her friends' behalf. This was heartily shared in by Mrs. Wentworth, who proved the most sympathetic of listeners, having seen the early stages of the affair at Bath, and knowing, from her own observation and by what she had collected from Mrs. Darcy's letter, more than Georgiana of the obstacles which had hindered its progress up to now; but both preferred to talk only of its happy conclusion, and of the strange and unexpected means by which it had been brought about.

Chapter 27

ABOUT FIVE WEEKS AFTER he had posted his letter to Mrs.
Wentworth, William Price was walking along Wigmore Street,
on his way to the Yates's house in Cavendish Square. It was a
cold, foggy evening in March, and the murky gloom of the wet
streets, which the oil lamps at intervals rather emphasized than
relieved, seemed to William to be a fit surrounding for anyone in
his dreary frame of mind. He could not wish the letter unwritten;
it was better not to see Georgiana as long as there was the barrier
between them raised by what she had told him in November, that
she had never thought of caring for him, believing that he
returned Kitty's affection. And yet it was too hard a task not to
wish to see her again, since he was leaving England the following
day on a voyage which would last for many months. He had no
longer any fear of his cousin's rivalry, for during his last visit to
Mansfield Tom Bertram had replied, with great coolness, when
anxiously interrogated, that on the occasion of his going to
Pemberley with the news of Colonel Fitzwilliam's accident, he

had come to the conclusion that he and Miss Darcy would not suit. But even if by some dispensation of Providence she had not married anyone else in the course of a year, how could the situation be sufficiently elucidated to set William free ever to address her again?

During the three months that had elapsed since the Pemberley ball his simple and straightforward nature had wrestled with the most difficult problem he had ever been called upon to face. The great events of his life—the various steps in his career, his sister's marriage, his father's death, and the providing for the family, had all come in the natural order of things, and for him the right line of conduct, as of feeling, had been at the same time the obvious one. And so he had supposed it would be when it came to affairs of the heart. If a man fell in love, he would try to win the affection of the woman he had chosen, and ask her to marry him; and if she did not care for him enough, he must either give it up, or wait awhile before making another effort. But to be refused, because another woman happened to have fallen in love with him! William had accepted his dismissal at the time in sheer bewilderment; but the more he thought it over, the more inadequate the reason seemed for separating him and Georgiana. She had not absolutely said that it was impossible to care for him; she had only refused to listen to him or talk of it, which was only natural if she thought him in honour bound to Kitty; but William's conscience was perfectly clear towards Kitty, and he tormented himself incessantly with the thought of all that he might have done towards gaining Georgiana's affection, during the weeks that they were together, had it not been for this wretched misunderstanding. She had taken it all as intended for Kitty; why had they not seen the truth? Kitty might have seen, everyone might have seen, everyone was deserving of blame, except Georgiana. One moment William was marvelling that anyone could have misunderstood what to him was the simplest, most natural thing in the world, and the next had dropped back with despair into the thought: "She might have cared, if she had only known. And now she will not even have forgiven me for making Miss Kitty unhappy, and I have no chance of setting that right."

"It is just like a ship that has run aground on a sandbank in the fog," mused William. "You can't do anything until it has cleared—at least, I can't. If she had refused me out and out, I would have gone down to Winchester and had another good try—a fellow who has only three months on shore to every nine at sea deserves that, I think—but I can't face her again as long as I can imagine her saying to herself, 'What about my poor Kitty?' Oh, what a blind fool I was, and how I wasted those ten days!"

He was so deep in thought that in crossing a side street he almost ran into a gentleman who was going towards Portman Square. Recognition followed on the mutual apologies, and Mr. Knightley exclaimed: "Why, William! I am glad to see you again—if it can be called seeing in this atmosphere; I thought you were gone."

"No, sir, but I sail to-morrow from Portsmouth: the *Medusa*, you know. They altered our destination at the last minute."

"And what is it to be?"

"Nova Scotia first, sir; we are taking out a draft to increase the garrison there."

"Lucky fellow that you are; you will have seen the whole world in a year or two. I'm afraid it sounds like a long absence this time, but you never mind that, do you?"

"Well, sir—" William hesitated, then looked up with a frank smile—"it won't be any good, but for once in a way I wish I could get to a home station for a bit."

Mr. Knightley waited, but perceiving that he was not to hear any more, said kindly: "Unless you are in a great hurry, come in and say good-bye to Mrs. Knightley; she would be sorry to miss you, especially as you are so near."

William readily turned back, for apart from the kindness of the Knightleys, their house had a special attraction for him; and when a few minutes later they entered the drawing-room, his thoughts flew back to the moment when he had first seen Georgiana: she had been standing by that very chair, that velvet screen had been the background to the lovely figure in the white ball-dress. It was necessary to put such thoughts as these resolutely away, and give his attention to Mrs. Knightley, whom they found alone, reading some letters which had just arrived by the country post. She greeted William cordially, without any surprise at seeing him still in England; it was always a little difficult for Emma to realize that people had important affairs of their own; and that they should have had any existence apart from that which she had chosen to imagine for them constituted the surprise. Therefore she looked earnestly and inquiringly at William as he sat down, and made so long a pause that he began to wonder what he was expected to say, until Mr. Knightley came in from the hall, where he had been ordering the servant to bring in lamps, and explained the circumstances of William's call. It was then Emma's turn to be astonished: "Going to sea, again Captain Price? That is indeed a sad thing; I thought you were going to settle in England for a time; your friends have seen nothing of you."

"There's no such thing as settling in England for a sailor, Mrs. Knightley," returned William, trying to speak cheerily; "at least, not at twenty-four. And I have been home for a long time now; the North Sea cruise this winter counts for nothing, you know."

"The North Sea!" repeated Emma, still more overwhelmed. "I thought you were with your mother, or in Derbyshire."

"Oh, no," replied William, in as indifferent a tone as he could. "I have not been to Derbyshire since the middle of November. We were at Copenhagen for three weeks, the rest of the time moving about, and I have just come from spending a week at Mansfield."

Emma was then almost speechless with disappointment. Mr. Knightley, regretful, but amused, drew his chair up to the fire and began asking about William's plans, which were to leave London on the following morning by the twelve o'clock coach, thus allowing ample time to reach Portsmouth and bestow himself and his baggage on board before the ship sailed at seven in the evening. Mr. Knightley inquired what would happen if he arrived too late, but William could hardly picture the consequences of such a breach of discipline. He had never known it to happen; he supposed the culprit would be court-martialled, and probably degraded three years; he imagined that no circumstances could possibly be allowed to extenuate so grievous a crime. Mr. Knightley suggested that a breakdown of the coach or other conveyance might cause inevitable delay, and William's answer to this was that one took the risk of these things in putting off one's return to the very last day of one's leave; some accident, of course, might occur, but in general, those officers who were not obliged to be on board earlier spent every moment of their leave of absence on shore.

"I probably should have gone back yesterday, however," he added, "but the mother of a friend of mine, Cooper, who is on board the *Queen Charlotte* at Southampton, is very ill in London, and he cannot come to see her, so he asked me to call at the house and bring him the latest reports. I was returning from there when I met you this evening. I intended going earlier in the day, but I am glad now that I was prevented from doing so."

"Emma, my dear," said Mr. Knightley, "you are not appreciating our friend's pretty speeches." Emma started, smiled, then tried to rouse herself and say something to William in the nature of cordial good wishes for his voyage, and in moving her chair, the letters she had been reading fell from her knee to the floor. William, as he picked them up, reflected that probably something in their contents was occupying Mrs. Knightley's mind; and he was beginning to think about making his adieux, when Mr. Knightley continued, speaking to his wife: "Have you any interesting news there, as a parting gift for a traveler?"

"No, I think not," replied Emma. "This is from Mrs. Weston, but there is nothing but Highbury gossip in it, which Captain Price would not—and this other one I have not read; I thought it was Harriet's writing. No!" holding it up to a candle, "it is not, after all. It is—well—I can hardly—it looks like—in fact, I believe it is from Kitty Bennet."

"Indeed!" said Mr. Knightley, and added, after a momentary pause: "We have not heard anything of her for a great while."

Emma could not help glancing towards William Price, but her glance told her nothing, for he sat perfectly passive, looking at no one, with perhaps a trifle deeper tinge of colour in his cheeks. The pause threatened to grow embarrassing, so she began to open the letter, hurriedly saying: "Miss Bennet seems still to be in Derbyshire. I should have thought she would have returned home before this."

"You stayed at Pemberley, did you not, William, as well as at Mr. Bingley's?" inquired Mr. Knightley.

"Yes," said William. "Mr. and Mrs. Darcy were so kind as to invite me there with the rest, for their ball. What a beautiful place it is! Even at that time of year one was struck with it."

"And you have not seen any of them since, I conclude, as you have been abroad," proceeded Mr. Knightley.

William was replying in the negative, when stopped by an exclamation from Mrs. Knightley, who was reading the letter with every sign of astonishment. "George!" she cried, "what do you think has happened? You will never guess! It is perfectly amazing! I can hardly believe it myself. Well—!" as she turned over a page, "if she had not told me herself, I could never—was there ever anything so unexpected?"

"We shall know better when you have told us what this astounding news is, my dear," said her husband. "Has Miss Bennett become engaged to be married, by any chance?"

"How could you have guessed it?" exclaimed Mrs. Knightley, dropping the letter to gaze at him. "It is the very last thing I should have thought of. Oh, Captain Price!" remembering her visitor in some confusion. "But I am sure you might know it, as she does not say it is private."

"The reason I guessed it," said Mr. Knightley, smiling, "is because no other intelligence causes quite the same amount of excitement, as you must admit, Emma. May we hear some more particulars, now that we have got over the first shock?" Mr.

Knightley was talking partly in order to spare his young friend, thinking it just possible that the news of Kitty's engagement might not be very welcome to the young man.

William, however, was leaning forward with an expression of eager interest, and Mrs. Knightley, looking at her letter, went on: "She is engaged to a Mr. James Morland, the rector of the parish in which Mr. and Mrs. Bingley live. He is quite young—only appointed last year—she met him first when she went down there in June—perfectly charming—the most agreeable man she has ever met—does not disapprove of dancing—Mr. Bingley and her sister so delighted—a lovely old house—so near to dear Jane—exquisitely happy—she is going home directly, and hopes to come to town and see me."

William could contain himself no longer. He sprang up, looked at the clock, took a few quick steps through the room, then, coming back, he abruptly asked: "Is this really true, Mrs. Knightley?"

"Quite true, Captain Price, I am afraid—at least, I mean there can be no doubt of it; in fact, they are going to be married in June, she says. I assure you, I had not the slightest suspicion. I have only heard the gentleman's name once or twice, no more. It is so odd, so inexplicable—"

Mr. Knightley could not forbear smiling at his wife's perplexity, for he perceived that for some reason or other William was in no need of commiseration, and, indeed, could hardly wait for Mrs. Knightley to finish. Holding out his hand, he said: "Pray give Miss Bennet my congratulations, and a thousand good wishes for her happiness. I fear I must not stay longer now, so will say good-bye, Mrs. Knightley, with many thanks for all your kindness—I am indeed grateful for all you have done for me."

"But Captain Price, you are not going already?" exclaimed Emma, now completely bewildered. "Do not, I beg, let me drive you away, we will not talk about anything disagreeable. We were just going to have dinner; it is late to-night on account of Mr. Knightley's having had to go out, and I hoped you would have stayed to dine with us."

Mr. Knightley seconded the invitation, but William unhesitatingly declined. "You are very good, but I must not delay so long. It is only six, and I think I can catch the eight o'clock coach, if I hurry, as my things are nearly packed."

"The eight o'clock coach?" repeated Mr. Knightley, helping his guest into his coat when it became evident that he was determined to go. "I thought you said you were not returning until to-morrow morning."

"Yes, I did, but I find now that I shall have to go to Winchester; I shall just have time; it is the most fortunate thing that could have happened."

"It is not very fortunate for us," said Emma. "But you surely will not attempt to get to Winchester to-night?"

"No, but I shall get as far as Guilford, in all probability. I beg your pardon, Mrs. Knightley, I am shockingly ill-mannered; what must you be thinking of me? Do overlook it just this once; nothing but the most urgent affairs would carry me away from here so much sooner than I had intended."

His smile and winning manner were irresistible, and Emma was obliged to let him go, saying she would expect to hear all about the urgent affairs some day. William seemed to get to the front door in two strides, and was fumbling with the lock before his host could reach him, with offers of refreshment, which he would not stay to accept. Mr. Knightley shook hands with him, saying kindly: "Well, William, I am sorry you had to run away, especially as we shall not see you for so long. Besides, it is really too cruel, after having whetted our curiosity by this mysterious change of plan."

"Oh, sir, I know it is too bad—if I only had a little more time—but it is the sailing to-morrow that is the very mischief—if you knew, you would understand that my only chance is to go now, as quickly as I can. I will write and tell you how I get on. Please make my apologies to Mrs. Knightley."

"The only thing Mrs. Knightley will not forgive is your having no dinner to-night. Yes, indeed, we shall look forward to hearing. Good-bye, and good luck be with you."

The good luck had begun already, William thought, as he plunged into the streets, which no longer appeared dark and foggy, since the aspect of the whole world had changed to him in the last few minutes. Was it not the most extraordinary stroke of good fortune which had led him to meet Mr. Knightley that evening? He had not intended to call, for he had believed them to be at their house in the country, and he would have heard nothing, and would have passed through Winchester the next day, within a mile of Georgiana, without knowing that he was free! A day later—the horror of it was almost too great to contemplate—would have been too late, too late to speak or write, even if anyone had troubled to send him the information. Mrs. Knightley herself had not suspected that Miss Bennet's engagement was a matter of such stupendous importance to him. William did not trouble to think of what she had suspected, his only idea being to make his way to Georgiana with all speed. He must see her before he sailed—that was the pressing necessity; everything else would right itself. What if he did not find her? If she were ill, or out of the house, or gone home again? Every kind of apprehension sprang up in his mind, to be reasoned away or fought down by vigorous action. His impatience was so great that he hardly knew how he got through the journey, beginning with the hasty drive to the coach office, the finding there was a seat still vacant, booking it, and tramping about till the time of starting; the innumerable frets and delays along the road; the arrival at Guilford, the bespeaking of a post-chaise, and descending before daylight the next morning to claim it; the hurried breakfast at Farnham, and the last interminable twenty miles, until the moment when he drove down the long hill into Winchester and heard the Cathedral clock striking eleven.

Leaving his portmanteaux at the "George," he walked straight to the Wentworths's house, which he knew well from previous visits, and was shown into a room where Captain and Mrs. Wentworth sat together. His early appearance created some surprise and excessive pleasure; they were totally unsuspicious of its real cause, and concluded only that he had reconsidered his refusal. His eager inquiry as to whether Miss Darcy were still with them, and whether he could see her, aroused a momentary fear that he had brought bad news for her, but it speedily became evident that he was on quite a different errand.

"Oho, William, you sly fellow, so it is Miss Darcy you are come to see?" exclaimed Captain Wentworth. "Well, we congratulate you upon your good sense, do we not, Anne? But why in the world did you not come down weeks ago, when you had the chance?"

William avoided answering this, and as his friends still did not understand the urgency of the case, he was obliged again to go through the particulars of the *Medusa*, and Portsmouth, and seven o'clock. Now, indeed, were the precious moments not to be wasted; Anne left the room, but returned directly, saying: "Captain Price, I am very sorry, but I find Miss Darcy has gone out. She talked of wishing to do some errands in the town, but I did not know she had already started. What is to be done?"

William was quite clear that there was only one thing to be done, namely, to go in search of Miss Darcy, and asked which shops she was likely to have visited. Mrs. Wentworth named one or two, and called after him as he was hurrying away, to suggest that if he was not successful in finding her in either, it was possible she might, as the day was so fine, have gone to finish her walk in the grounds of Wolvesey Palace, a favourite spot of hers for a stroll. Armed with information William was gone on the instant.

It was fortunate that he had obtained it, for his inquiries in the High Street were fruitless, and he thereupon retraced his steps under the archway and past the Cathedral, turned along College Street, and finally found himself in the old Palace gardens, where, seated with a book among a quiet part of the ruins, he presently came upon Georgiana. She did not see him until he was close at hand, when she sprang up, scarce able to believe her eyes, and the colour deepening in her cheeks; and William forgetting all the lengthy explanations he had intended to make, darted towards her, impulsively exclaiming: "Oh, how glad I am to see you again! I came back—I could not help it—everything is all right—you will let me speak now—am I too late? Have I the least chance–any chance at all?"

Georgiana unconsciously yielded her hand to his, but shrank back a little as she faltered: "But—but Kitty?"

Breathless from haste, and full of anxiety as to his reception, William hardly knew whether he had been intelligible, but there was something in Georgiana's look which showed him, even while she hesitated, that he was understood—even more—welcomed. Her very question was an answer to him, and that he quickly disposed of it, and yet in a manner entirely satisfactory to her, could not be doubted, making thereby the glorious discovery that his cause was won, when he had been almost ready to despair of achieving anything in the short time at his command.

It seemed at first impossible that it could be true, but the surprise of receiving a good fortune beyond one's desserts is one to which it is easy to grow accustomed. The fact of Kitty's engagement, once realized, could be put aside as something delightful to be thought over at leisure; but for the present moment there were only two people in the world, and those two could give themselves up, unchecked by any sense of guilt or responsibility, to the exquisite happiness of love acknowledged and returned. Perfect confidence might now exist between them; William might repeat, and far more eloquently, all that he had said in the picture gallery at Pemberley; and Georgiana might now venture to confess the feelings which in that interview had awakened to life. To her, indeed, it was easier to listen than to talk, for after her long self-repression, the relief, the wonderful change, were almost overwhelming; her heart had been too deeply stirred, and her habitual shyness was not soon to be overcome. But William's joy in the fruition of his hopes, so infinitely more complete than any he had dared to hope for, and his gratitude to herself, had to be put into words in his own frank and eager way, touched now with the earnest gravity befitting so great an occasion.

It was one of those beautiful mornings which sometimes occur in the ungenial early months of the year, as a reminder that spring is actually on its way. By noon, the pale sunshine had some warmth, and the lovers paced to and fro, or sat in the sheltered corner which had seen their meeting, while a soft breeze rustled in the ivy and the murmuring of the stream could be heard just beyond the old wall. Georgiana lifted a face of delight to the blue sky, and watched the rooks busy in the elm trees near, while occasionally other sounds came to them, unnoticed at the time, but being woven into the picture which their memories would always hold of that hour, voices, gay with youth and spirits, of the college boys as they passed in and out of their gateway, and the slow sweet chimes from the tower of the Cathedral.

Georgiana knew something of William's plans, but to learn that their parting must take place almost immediately was indeed a blow, until consoling reflections came, and they reminded each other of what a trial of faith and patience his departure in other circumstances would have meant. Of course, it would have made no real difference; neither would admit the possibility of its having caused any change in their feelings, but there was comfort in knowing that now theirs was an attachment which separations could only strengthen, and in the light of which misunderstandings could no longer exist. Both lamented William's being unable to see Mr. and Mrs. Darcy before he sailed, but Georgiana anticipated no opposition on their part, and this thought gave perhaps the crowning touch to a felicity so intense that she could hardly believe it to be hers.

Captain and Mrs. Wentworth's warmth of kindness was to be expected, in view of their affection for both the young people. William stayed with them until four o'clock, which gave time for many plans to be made, and the more important letters to be written, and when at last he said his farewells he buoyed himself and Georgiana up with the promise that it should be no more than six months before he returned to claim her.

When he had actually gone, she went to her room, feeling in need of solitude to compose her mind after a day of such wonders. It was impossible that she should not let fall a few tears at the thought of William's going every moment farther and farther from her when they had only just begun to realize the delight, the security of their new relation to each other, but they were not the bitter tears of hopelessness that she had so often shed in the last few months.

Whatever the period of his absence, it would be long, and the lot of the one left behind, inactive, would be the hardest; but Georgiana was willing to wait in thankfulness and quiet trust for whatever the future might bring. That there might be anxieties and alarms, she knew, but the heart which had once and for all been given to William Price was strong in courage as in tenderness, and the remembrance of the vows they had exchanged had glorified her life.

Elizabeth and Mr. Darcy came to Winchester shortly afterwards, to take her home. Her news, while explaining many things, had been a considerable surprise to them, and Darcy deemed it necessary to make further inquiries about the young man, who, it appeared, now desired to be even more closely connected with his family than had at first been thought. Though regretting, for his sister's sake, the profession of the man she had chosen, he could not withhold his approval when she had convinced him how completely her happiness was bound up in the affair; and, indeed, he could hear nothing on any side but what was in Captain Price's favour, so while Lady Catherine, who had made a show of objection, was appeased by the substantial fortune and the relationship with the Bertrams, Darcy and Elizabeth found contentment in their knowledge of his character and position.

All went as delightfully as Georgiana could have wished. Darcy, who had been inclined to regret Mr. Bertram's dismissal when he first heard of it, became so entirely reconciled to the idea of his cousin as a substitute, that Georgiana never heard a word of the dreaded scolding; and Captain Wentworth promised that all his own, and his brother-in-law, Admiral Croft's, interest should be used towards hastening William's promotion and shortening his absence, for he declared it would be impossible to do too much for a lady who, in spite of early prejudices, was venturing to trust so far in the fidelity of sailors as actually to be going to marry one of them.

Georgiana had many questions to ask about Kitty's engagement, and from what Elizabeth told her of the particulars given by Jane, she was able to piece the story together for herself. Morland had sincerely tried to forget Kitty, but her return to Desborough, more bewitching than ever, had shown him how vain had been his efforts. And when the intimacy between the Rectory and the Park had been renewed under his sister's auspices, what wonder if Kitty's feelings towards him changed somewhat with the changed circumstances? If, touched by his continued devotion, and a little piqued by the want of appreciation in another quarter, she had allowed him to see that a second attempt would not be treated like the first? Georgiana rejoiced to think that Kitty had the power of consoling herself, and that she was at that moment adoring Mr. Morland as wholeheartedly as she had ever adored Mr. Price.

The two girls exchanged letters of congratulations, but it was no longer possible to write with quite the same openness as of old, though Georgiana's good wishes lacked nothing of affectionate sincerity. Kitty declared herself too busy with the preparation of her wedding clothes to send a long letter, and perhaps also a small feeling of resentment lingered in her mind, and prompted the remark: "I thought you must have been in love with him all the time, though you would not admit it."

She had, however, nothing to envy Georgiana, for had she not achieved the distinction of being the first of the three brides? The ceremony at the parish church near Longbourn was fixed for Midsummer, and was attended by a number of relatives and friends; while the Darcys soon after had the pleasure of witnessing the marriage of Mary Crawford and Colonel Fitzwilliam, which took place in London in the following month. The latter couple settled in town, but also possessed themselves of a small hunting lodge in Leicestershire, whence the road to Pemberley and back was frequently traversed, though it is to be hoped with less haste and agitation than by two persons who made the journey on a certain melancholy day in January.

It was long before William learned the true history of his cousin's second visit to Pemberley, but Georgiana could afford to smile at the recollection of it, when, some three months after the announcement of her engagement, the families of Darcy and Bingley received the wedding cards of Mr. Thomas Bertram and Miss Isabella Thorpe.

THE END